THE RELUCTANT MARTYR

Rick Elliott

Rick Elliott

ISBN: 9780984600403

LCCN: 2010 917017

Printed in the United States of America

~~~~~~R~~~~~R~~~~~P~~~~~~
Rising River Press
Springfield, Missouri

www.risingriverpress.com

CHAPTER ONE

"*As-salaamu `alaykum,*" Captain Farroque offered, nodding slowly in acknowledgement toward one of his illicit passengers. The young man had stepped out of the swirling fog to stand beside him, here on the dimly lit aft deck of the aging freighter. He was one of four the captain had secreted aboard while docked in Lagos, Nigeria.

"*Wa `alaykum `as-salaam,*" the passenger replied, reciprocating the traditional greeting. His dark beard and coarse, ivory-colored robe billowed in the strengthening breeze.

It was a ritual of Captain Farroque's to have a smoke in the late evening at the stern of the ship as he contemplated the day's events. Hypnotized and calmed by the foamy wake from the ship and its churning propeller, he would retire to his cabin for the night, wishing for sleep.

Captain Farroque's middle-aged girth strained at the buttons of his black wool coat as he lit his pipe, cupping the match in his hand to shield it from the wind. Stalling for time, he searched his memory, trying in vain to remember this one's name. A recurring drizzle caused ringlets of moisture to collect in his own beard and more gathered on the brim of his cap before coalescing into large drops poised to obey gravity.

The four young men boarded the *Empress of Sayda* in the dead of the night, five days earlier at the port of Lagos. Captain Farroque met them only once as a group after boarding, exchanging guarded greetings with each. It was during their first full day at sea. After that introduction, they'd kept to themselves for the most part, avoiding the rest of the ship's crew. Twice since then, the captain saw them on the main forward deck prostrated on their prayer rugs.

The first time he watched as an argument ensued amongst them concerning the direction of Mecca. This was their first experience at sea. With no land in sight, plus an overcast sky, one could understand their confusion. Their leader, Jamal, came to the captain for an answer. And Captain Farroque knew the answer, but as a seasoned navigator, not as a devout Muslim.

This one standing beside him now was the hothead of the quartet's argument on that first day. The captain reflected upon his own youth; about the quick temper he had possessed, a miserable vice, one he admittedly still owned, but the intervening years had made his threshold of provocation higher.

"Ahh, Captain Farroque, the fog wraps around us like a…, a thick quilt. Is that the correct term?"

He spoke English rather well, the captain thought, though his familiarity with some colloquialisms of the language appeared to be lacking.

"Blanket is what most Americans would say," the captain offered with a forced smile, correcting him politely in his own slight, middle-eastern accent. It was hardly noticeable compared to the thick sounds of his younger counterpart standing beside him now.

The smoke from Captain Farroque's pipe disappeared instantly into the white vapor that engulfed them. The fog, if you stared into it long enough, as if searching for a distant object, would hypnotize you as it raced by. If not for the ever-present vibration from the overtaxed diesel engine, one could easily be convinced they were floating in a cloud with nothing above or below.

"Have you been there, Captain?"

"To America you mean?"

"Yes."

"A few times, but it's been nearly two years since my last port of call there," he explained more cautiously than intended.

"Which port was that if I might ask?"

"New Orleans," Captain Farroque answered, taking another draw on his pipe. He shifted the ornate scrimshaw bowl to the palm of his large, weathered hand as he continued. "We off loaded pallets stacked with crates of clothing and then filled the hold with wheat for the return voyage."

"Did you enjoy it there?"

On the outside, Captain Farroque shrugged his shoulders with indifference. Inside, he felt his heart quicken with each question from this devout pup standing here beside him on the *Empress*. But why should he be nervous, he wondered, reminding himself to keep his voice even and devoid of inflection. This passenger knew nothing of him and his family; or so he hoped. Besides, if all had gone as planned, his wife and their only living child, a daughter he doted on when home from the sea, were already on their way to America.

The money he had saved quietly over the years, in addition to the handsome payoff gained by transporting these four to Buenos Aires, would be enough for them to start a new life, a good life, in the United States. Still, he *was* nervous. He had hauled clandestine passengers before, but never a lot of this many or this pious and young. Some he transported in the past had been quite entertaining with their conversation, making the long trips away from his family bearable.

Best to avoid this group though, he thought, this hot-tempered one in particular. With his type, the talk would lead in only one direction.

"How much further until we reach our destination?"

"We're six hundred miles from Buenos Aires. We should be there in another day and a half if all goes well."

"*Inshaa `allah*, you mean, Captain Farroque."

"Certainly…, god willing, of course."

The captain had hesitated, unsure of the suitable response. Perhaps, he considered, the Arabic version, *inshaa `allah*, would have been more appropriate to appease this one.

Captain Farroque moved along the cable railing, pretending to inspect parts of the ship over the edge of the deck, dismayed to find his younger shadow following him. His piercing stare provoked an uneasy feeling in the captain. Still, it would be rude to ignore his questions, he decided, and, perhaps cause unintended suspicions.

"How far down to the water is it?" His persistent passenger asked.

"We're about thirty feet above the waterline," Captain Farroque answered, staring down into the roiling sea.

"And how far up to the flag?"

The captain turned to see him pointing up toward the Panamanian flag. It strained at its grommets in the building westerlies, barely visible through the drizzle if not for the faint glow coming from the pilothouse directly below it.

"It's about forty feet up to the radar antennae," he responded while watching it make its never-ending sweep, wishing to himself that this was the last question.

"Will you be in Buenos Aires long?"

"Only long enough to unload our cargo and refuel."

"You should join us to worship and give praise at the mosque in Ciudad del Estrellas."

"If I had time I would, but I've important work here on the ship while we're docked."

"Nothing is more important than to worship at the mosque with your brothers. It is our strength on the path to victory," the young one chided, his chest swelling with pride.

His voice sounded harsher, more demanding. And while his indoctrination was thorough, he'd mistaken the captain for one of his own, with the same fervor for religious jihad. But Captain Farroque's reason for ferrying these four was strictly financial. He'd decided long ago that religious ideology was a concept for others to haggle over. Besides, what could this young traveler know of work or strength, the captain mused? He could not be more than twenty, the same age his own son would have been if....

The young one continued in a menacing tone, "You are a true believer..., are you not, Captain Farroque?"

"What business is it of yours?" He snapped.

Thoughts of his deceased young son still haunted him, and he was not in the mood to be proselytized by this one's firebrand of Islam. Captain Farroque considered patience one of his few virtues, a counterweight to his temper, but not tonight. The deep furrows above his brow were a testament to his worries of late. Getting his family out of harms way, with no traces, had become a burden on his mind. In addition, the guilt he felt for leaving behind friends and loved ones—both dead and alive—with no explanations, no goodbyes, troubled his conscience.

Leaving his home, a place full of memories, good and bad, would be hard for him. But he would not miss the political turmoil and increasing pressure put upon him and his family by local religious factions. For Fatima, his wife, it would be worse. He had not the ties to Lebanon that she struggled to break free of.

After having spent his early adult life in Egypt, where he had learned his trade at a British-owned shipping company, and the rest at sea or in foreign ports, the bonds that tied him to his homeland had weakened. He needed no convincing that there were better, safer places in the world to live, convincing Fatima and their daughter had been another matter. The pious one continued his harangue, "Captain, I see your faith lies more in material goods."

He nodded toward Captain Farroque's ornate jeweled watch and two, heavy, gold rings on his thick fingers.

"You have spent too much time under the tutelage of Western corruption. What obscene amount are you being paid to deliver us? As if we were some box of goods in the cargo hold of your ship. If you were a true believer, your pay would be the smile graced upon you by Allah for doing his labor. Is it not *haram* to take from your fellow Muslims, giving nothing in return? Your generation has taken whatever crumbs the Western world offers with no regard for your fellow countrymen, other than to climb over them as you clamor for more material wealth."

"I admire your conviction, but what do you know of labor?" Captain Farroque sneered, tapping his spent pipe slowly on a steel support post of the cable railing.

The few remaining sparks of burning tobacco swirled about his hand before being devoured by the moist night air. Smiling, he thought, pay for Allah, indeed. How much money had he paid to his local imam? Money that went for a madrasa to teach young men, like this one standing before him now, to be insolent.

Their irritation with each other's presence was palpable, like two cur dogs circling each other, sizing up the other's weaknesses, teeth bared.

The young one struck first, warning, "Heed the advice of the Holy Qur`an before you suffer the fate intended for infidels, Captain."

He grabbed the captain's coat sleeve for emphasis, catching him by surprise, causing him to lose his grip on the treasured pipe as he was slipping it into his coat pocket. The tobacco pipe bounced off the deck, over the side and out of sight before lodging in the crevice of a cable support brace three feet below the deck's edge.

"Damn you, man. Now look what you've done. That pipe was a birthday gift from my son."

"Ah, but Captain, you know as well as I that it is forbidden, just as alcohol is," he preached, smiling with satisfaction, oblivious to the sentimental value that the pipe held for Captain Farroque.

"The only thing that should be forbidden by Allah is your brash foolishness."

"Captain, must I lecture you about respect for one such as myself?"

"Respect? Hah! Why should I have respect for one such as you?" He scoffed, anger mounting in his voice. "I had enough of your kind back in Beirut. In a few weeks, I'll no longer feel the weight of your oppressive interpretation of our faith. You talk of advice? Allah, be damned! The advice from the Qur`an cost me my young son; an innocent seven year old. The leader of my local mosque instructed my naïve wife that faith in Allah would protect our son, not some polio vaccine from Western medicine. I suppose your answer would have been the same; more prayers for the dying child, his legs limp and wilted as she carried him in her arms to the mosque. And what would you know of a child? Why you've probably never been to bed with a woman."

Captain Farroque finished with a short guttural laugh. How was it just or righteous that his own son was long dead while this one beside him now upbraided him about his faith—or lack there of?

"Your true colors bleed through, Captain. You should be reported to my superiors."

"Reported to your superiors, is that so!"

The captain, unable to control his fury, grabbed his antagonist's cotton gown and, with a savage twist, drew the collar tight around his slender neck. This was what he needed. To vent his frustration, like a volcano building unseen pressure beneath its surface. He was almost fifty, but years of pent up anger had given him a bountiful surge of strength to deal with his young adversary. It felt good, he thought, as he struggled to get traction on the slippery deck, to release his inner demons on such a deserving symbol of life's aggravations.

His red-faced opponent struggled to break free. The captain cursed at the newly minted jihadist thrashing about before him now, blind with rage over his own failures and disappointments.

Fatigue caused Captain Farroque to loosen his grip. His opponent broke free, backing far enough away into the shadows to pull a gilded dagger undetected from his sash.

Captain Farroque could see the feral look in this one's eyes, the hard, determined set of his jawbone as he shuffled back out of the dimness toward him.

Their heads moved in rhythm with ship's motion as the swells increased in size. Here at the stern it was exaggerated, as if they were on one end of a seesaw, each spellbound by the other's predictable up and down movement.

"You are worse than an infidel, Captain," he said, spitting the words like venom. "You move freely about in the Muslim world collecting wealth with no conviction, giving nothing back in return for all that Allah has bestowed upon you."

With both hands behind his back, one caressing the honed blade, the other gripping the handle tighter, he quivered with anticipation. Since being chosen for this mission, some seven months ago, he'd been on edge. His desire was to cleanse the earth of non-believers and apostates; especially apostates. This seemed the perfect time to practice his learned skills as he moved in closer to the captain.

"I'll know *real* freedom in a few weeks when I join my family in America," Captain Farroque bellowed.

He turned, looking wistfully over the edge of the deck where his treasured pipe had disappeared. He'd said too much already, letting his temper get the best of him.

A wry smile crept across the young one's face.

"Ah, Captain, I am afraid that I will see America and you, *inshaa `allah*, never will."

Captain Farroque, kneeling down as he searched over the edge for his pipe, turned back sharply at this comment.

"What's that suppose…."

He saw the weapon glistening with moisture and sprang to his feet just as his knife-wielding opponent lunged at him. Without time to think, he defensively extended his arms to block the blade as it surged toward his abdomen.

In that instant, the ship began to climb another swell and the steepening slope of the deck caused his attacker to move in too close. The dagger, moving in an upward arc, sliced through the side of Captain Farroque's coat just below his armpit. The point exited out the back without penetrating flesh. His extended arms, with his back braced against the two steel cables that served as a taffrail along the stern, had the effect of pushing his assailant's upper body backwards, away from the captain, as if his stiff arms were a pivot point about which the other's body could swing.

Throughout the brief struggle their eyes met fleetingly, both flashing first with anger, then terror, ending with disbelief at what transpired so quickly.

And with the ship angling upward at a steep slope; and with the steel deck slick from rain; and with his smooth-soled sandals almost frictionless: it was inevitable—or perhaps Allah's will—the young jihadist's feet were out from under him. The torque of his momentum carried his taught body over the edge, feet first, one hand still clutching his prized knife, the other making a desperate grab for the cable support pole, blocked inadvertently by Captain Farroque's polished, black Wellingtons. Captain Farroque, because of conditioned reflexes, reached out but not in time. His attacker was gone; snuffed out by fog, wind, and water as quickly as the tobacco embers. No cry came forth. No sounds were audible over the constant rush of wind and waves. All that remained of the young jihadist was a sweat-stained *kufi* he'd worn on his head, which the captain now gripped in his trembling hand.

With one arm wrapped around the support pole, the other extending out into the milky darkness, he knelt there on bended knee, mesmerized by what had just occurred. A nauseous feeling welled-up in the captain's stomach as he let the hat slip from his fingers, watching it fall into the abyss. His mind went blank, unable to fathom the consequences of his actions.

The drizzle became a driving rain, pelting his face, ushering him back to the here and now. Questions began to form in his head: how long had he been frozen there? A few seconds? A minute? With the ship moving at top speed, how far away was his ill-fated passenger? Could he swim?

From a seafarer's instinct, he reached for a life ring hanging on the wall of the superstructure and heaved it over the cable railing into the churning sea. Answers began to form. None of them could swim; he remembered this from their brief conversation that first day at sea, even joking about it with the group's leader, Jamal.

The darkness, fog, and heavy seas would make it impossible to find him even if he could swim, the captain reasoned. Then there was the massive, spinning propeller to consider.

Poor soul, his zealous beliefs had, in a way, cost him his life. Captain Farroque had meant no harm to the young man. Just a harsh dressing down because of his insolent behavior had been the captain's intention. But now, how would he explain the mishap? Yes, certainly a mishap.

Biting his lip, Captain Farroque's concern began to revolve around his own life. He knew he should run to the pilothouse and call for help from any available deck hand, but something stopped him. What would Jamal and the other two passengers think? Captain Farroque was unsure how well this group was connected to the upper echelons of the hierarchy that controlled the mayhem in the Middle East, where, according to their leader Jamal, their journey had begun. How far was their reach? He had been paid handsomely to transport these four that alone brought wrinkles of worry to his forehead. Would the underworld grasp of their "brothers" stretch across the Atlantic to Argentina, he wondered.

He had two more stops on his scheduled voyage after delivering the *Empress's* cargo to Buenos Aires: First, around Cape Horn to the western side of the continent to pick up a load of copper ingots in Santiago, then on to Istanbul to deliver it.

It was there; while the ship was scheduled for three weeks of much needed repairs to her engine that Captain Farroque had made plans to part ways with the shipping company, unannounced. By the time they realized he was not returning to pilot the *Empress of Sayda* on to her homeport, at minimum, three weeks would have passed. That would give him ample time to tie-up a few financial loose ends before leaving Istanbul bound for his new home in America, long before anyone from the company missed him.

The chances of the shipping company finding a replacement for him as captain of the *Empress of Sayda,* before Istanbul, seemed remote based on what he knew of their operation. He had always been paid but never more than two or three times with the same company name on the check. He could not even say for sure who owned the *Empress.* The Panamanian registry was a flag of convenience. This was not uncommon in the shipping world, which appeared to him only slightly less murky than the club his current human cargo belonged to. The few times he had met his superiors, any questions he asked seemed to annoy them and were met with vague answers.

Once, when he fell ill while docked in Manila, the ship sat there for eighteen days until he recovered. Apparently they had no one else to take command of the ship in his absence.

Even the name of the ship, painted on each side of the bow, seemed suspect if one examined it closely. From the deck, the outline of other letters had begun to appear under the fading edges of "*Empress of Sayda* ".

Now, after this tragic incident, to be safe, Captain Farroque thought it best to mail the cash he'd collected for hauling these four as soon as he reached Buenos Aires. Instead of waiting until Istanbul as planned, he would mail it to Fatima as soon as he reached port. Once she and their daughter had settled in St. Louis, she would know to check the postal box he'd set up there.

Captain Farroque had not been entirely truthful with his assailant. On his last trip to America, he'd gone beyond the port at New Orleans. With the ship docked there for five days, he had traveled on to St. Louis to visit a cousin. This was shortly after he first brought up the subject of immigrating to America with Fatima. His cousin had agreed, after a substantial monetary gift, to help the captain and his family relocate.

Wind found the knife hole in his coat as he walked to the starboard side of the ship, sending a chilling tingle down the length of his spine. The rain had soaked him to the bone and he began to shiver uncontrollably. It heightened his senses and forced him to concentrate on the present as he contemplated what to tell the three remaining passengers.

Why tell them anything he decided, albeit with a twinge of guilt. No one had seen them together. He could almost convince himself that it had all been a dream were it not for the gapping hole in his coat. Dream, he thought, laughing to himself, more like a sudden nightmare.

Captain Farroque moved toward the forward deck, frenzied thoughts whirling about in his head, when he was stopped dead in his tracks after spotting a glow of light near the bow. In the captain's overworked mind, the wavering orb had human qualities. It pranced about, helter-skelter, as if doing a pagan dance. Then suddenly, for a few seconds, it would swoop down appearing to hover motionless as if resting just above the obscured deck. The foggy mist produced a halo around the light, and Captain Farroque could think only of the poor martyr's soul, seeking him out to inflict revenge.

He drew nearer the apparition—out of wonder, not bravery—his mouth agape. With each quiet step, his heart quickened. Would not the avenging Jinn know of his presence?

Just as the captain was about to meet his fate, a hand reached out of the fog for the light; a human hand with a wrist, forearm and watch. The captain stood there, not twenty feet from the light, cursing silently to himself for letting his overwrought imagination get the best of him.

The arm belonged to one of his hired crew, a dutiful fellow; the ethereal light—an electric lantern hung from a wire handle. Ship protocol required that the crewman on watch periodically check all deck hatches, making sure they had been secured. The importance of this could not be overstated in rough seas such as they were now experiencing. An open hatch, flooded by seawater, would mean a floundering ship and disaster. The *Empress's* diesel engine was weak at best for the load she carried. Tons of South Atlantic seawater added to her cargo hold would cause a quick rendezvous with land only a few thousand feet below. The ship would breath a sigh of relief when she reached Istanbul, as would her captain and crew.

Captain Farroque was dumbstruck by the amount of time that had transpired. What had seemed like nothing short of eternity from the beginning of his innocuous conversation with.... Damnation! Why couldn't he remember the young man's name? It made him feel more criminal, more culpable in the passenger's demise. Barely ten minutes had passed during which time the man had catapulted over the edge of the ship's deck and the captain had been lured to the bow by the eerie glow of the lantern.

The crewman moved off toward the port side of the ship. In the whiteness that enveloped them, the sailor had not seen him. Captain Farroque pondered this bit of luck for an instant and then slipped stealthily to the opposite side of the forward deck. He reached the railing and used it to guide himself back to the superstructure and the heavy steel door that lead into the stairwell. Standing there, near the door, searching for the wavering light that signified the crewman's position, a plan began to form in his head.

With any luck, the passenger's absence wouldn't be noticed until morning. If he could make it up to his cabin undetected, perhaps he could plead ignorance in the young man's disappearance.

The outside light fixture over the entrance to the stairwell had been broken for some time, but once the door was opened the inside light would shine like a beacon. He caught sight of the crewman's electric lantern, following it with his gaze as it moved aft along the port side of the ship. He waited breathlessly as the sailor disappeared beyond the four-story superstructure, on the opposite side, toward the stern. One virtue— patience—had returned to Captain Farroque.

The stairwell was cavernous and all steel, forcing the captain to go to great pains to avoid any noise. He closed the door quietly behind him and removed his heavy boots. The sharp edges of the expanded steel steps (made that way to give traction to soles in the ship's constantly damp environment) gnawed at his feet up the three flights, but the exhilaration he felt coursing through his veins negated their effect. Reaching his cabin door undetected, a smile appeared on his worn face with the thought that he might get away with the crime. His face flushed as he removed his wet clothes, running his fingers through the added vent in his coat. He chastised himself. Why, he considered again, as he sat on the edge of his bed, should he call the past event a crime? He had done nothing more serious than grab the young man's collar; everything else had been bad luck and of the zealot's own doing. But, he wagered, the other three travelers would not be so quick to forgiveness: retribution and revenge were likely *their* virtues.

A heavy quilt and the steady rhythm of the ship overcame the bone-chilling cold and mind-numbing remorse he felt. Sleep was soon upon him.

A heavy knock on the cabin door woke Captain Farroque. Sunlight poured through the cabin's east-facing window. This meant he'd slept late, and too, the storm had abated. The knock came again more urgently, and he responded while reaching for a pair of dry pants and a fresh shirt.

"Yes, yes, I'm coming. One minute please," he shouted, grabbing a folder of documents off a nearby shelf.

He tossed them on the table to make it appear he was busy, and not asleep, as the cause of his tardiness in opening the door.

"Captain Farroque, there seems to be a problem."

Through the closed door he recognized the muffled voice of his first mate, Ramon, a short, stocky Filipino and was taken aback when he opened the door, finding himself staring into Jamal's cold, dark eyes. Jamal's chest was pressing against the right shoulder of a much shorter Ramon, who stood in front of him, almost causing both of them to lose their balance and tumble forward through the doorway.

"Captain, my friend Monsour, I cannot find him," Jamal said hurriedly.

"What do you mean you can't find him?" the captain asked, a puzzled look on his face as he glanced toward his first mate who had slipped to the side.

So that was his name, Monsour, Captain Farroque mused.

Captain Farroque's heart and head were racing. Now, Jamal's face was inches from his own. His close-cropped hair was partially hidden beneath a black watchman's cap. He looked older than the other three, which made sense, the captain thought, since he was their leader. Was he armed with a knife, too?

"He is missing! We...," Jamal nodded in Ramon's direction, "Have looked all over and cannot find him."

"How long has it been since you've seen him?"

"He was not in our cabin when I awoke this morning. I thought perhaps he had gone out on deck for morning prayers already, but then I noticed his rug still lying on the floor beside mine."

"It's a big ship," the captain offered, reassuringly, with a forced smile. "He is bound to be around somewhere. Ramon, have you looked in the cargo hold and engine room?"

"Yes sir. After breakfast, I sent every available man out to search all corners of the ship."

"Well, go check the cargo hold again," Captain Farroque said, trying to sound annoyed by this turn of events. "There are lots of dark corners down there. Wait a second. Let me put my work away and I'll join you."

He raised the folder off the table to show them and turned to set it back on the shelf. Jamal took a step aggressively into the cabin, uninvited, but more out of frustration than anger as he waited impatiently. The captain gave him time to scan the living quarters for his missing companion since this was the one room that hadn't been searched. Both of their eyes fell upon the puddle of water beneath the captain's coat hanging from a hook on the wall next to the apartment-sized refrigerator.

"Ramon, remind me to have this blasted refrigerator looked at when we lay over in Istanbul. Every time it self-defrosts, water leaks all over the floor."

"Yes sir. I will," Ramon said from outside the doorway, thinking to himself it was the sort of task the captain usually took care of himself.

"All set," Captain Farroque said, after slipping on his boots. "Let's go have a look around the ship for your friend…, Monsour."

The three of them headed down the passageway past the crew's galley. The smell of curry powder wafted on the air so thick that Captain Farroque felt it tingle the inside of his nostrils. How could they eat that concoction, he wondered, having given up on all spicy food in the past year as his departure for America drew nearer and his stomach grew more irritable.

Jamal was right on his heels as they bounded down the stairs to the main deck. The echoing of his boots on the steps made the captain grateful for his sore feet.

Several of the ship's crew and Jamal's two fellow passengers were milling about in the brilliant sunlight as they stepped out onto the forward deck into a westerly breeze. One of Ramon's mates began speaking earnestly to him in Spanish while pointing in the direction of the stern. When he had finished, Ramon turned to the captain and translated.

"He said they have searched the ship several times, including the cargo hold, and can find no sign of him."

"Why was he pointing to the east?" Captain Farroque asked with feigned innocence.

"He said there is a life ring missing from the stern that hangs on the wall of the superstructure. He is sure it was there when we left Lagos."

They headed as a group toward the stern of the ship with the captain leading the way. The Filipino sailor pointed out where the life ring had been mounted, a perfect outline of unfaded paint marking the spot where it once hung.

Everyone began to speak at once: The Filipinos to each other in Spanish, Jamal and his brethren in a middle-eastern dialect. Above the din, Captain Farroque asked Ramon who'd had the night watch.

"Felipe was on from 18:00 until 24:00, then Manuel until breakfast, but he was in the engine room the whole time."

"Fetch Felipe for me, Ramon. Get him out of bed if you have to," the captain ordered, before turning to the three illicit travelers crowding around him. "When was the last time any of you saw Monsour?"

Jamal, their unquestionable leader, spoke for the group.

"Sa'id and myself went to bed early as we were somewhat sick from the rolling of the ship," he confided sheepishly. "Khalib was reading when Monsour decided to go out for some fresh air, but he fell asleep before Monsour returned; if he returned."

"And what time was that?"

"It was some time past ten o'clock," Jamal answered for Khalib.

Captain Farroque was playing detective as best he could while trying to suppress a smile that he couldn't quite explain. Suddenly, it came to him. The idea that he was getting away with something immoral at best, criminal at worst, was exciting him in a macabre sense, like a child getting away with a fib, still naïve to its consequences. Visiting the very spot where his life had flashed before him during the night had a disquieting effect on him.

Ramon returned with Felipe whose eyes were still heavy with sleep.

"Did Felipe see or hear anything last night?" Captain Farroque queried.

"He said once, when he was up near the bow checking the forward deck hatches, he thought someone else was up there, but with the poor visibility and rocking of the ship, it was all he could do to keep track of his light."

Ah yes, the dreaded light, the captain thought. Just then, the crewman who'd noticed the missing life ring knelt down over the edge of the ship's deck next to a support pole. He motioned for Ramon to hang on to him, and then, reaching down, just within the grasp of his fingertips, he pulled loose an object wedged between the cable pole brace and the hull of the ship.

Captain Farroque exclaimed, theatrically, "My pipe! I thought it gone forever. It fell out of my pocket a couple of nights ago. I saw it bounce over the edge, and in the darkness I assumed it was on its way to 'Davey Jone's Locker'. What a good turn."

Jamal gave him a sharp look. The captain did his best to avoid eye contact, fearing his soul would too easily give up the tale.

He stared at his pipe as he spoke. "I have a smoke here almost every evening before going to bed, but the weather was so miserable last night that I opted to stay in my cabin," he explained, feeling compelled to assuage Jamal's damning look.

"We must turn around and search for him!" Khalib announced with a sudden burst.

All three of them had a good command of the English language, but, before the captain could respond to his remark, Jamal declared in a sullen voice that there was no use in doing so. Khalib pleaded with him momentarily, but Jamal only scolded him in a harsher tone in their native tongue. Once done, they both looked at the captain, who'd understood a few words of their conversation, enough to know that he'd been a part of it.

Captain Farroque attempted to explain his own reasoning for not immediately turning the ship around.

"He's right," nodding toward Jamal, then looking to Khalib. "The sea was very rough last night. With the water temperature so low, I'm afraid there would be very little hope of finding him, alive or otherwise, even with the life ring. And then there is the propeller to consider." His voice trailed off for effect.

After a silent moment, for all to reflect on his words, Captain Farroque continued. "Why, if one of you jumped in the water right now with a life jacket…, and escaped the wrath of the ship, it would take the better part of three hours just to turn her around and get back to this same position even with the sea calm as it is now. There is no…"

Jamal interrupted, "Yes, yes, Captain. We have impatient guest expecting us upon arrival in Buenos Aires. We must not keep them waiting."

Jamal said this as much to himself as to the others surrounding him. His eyes were fixated on the turbulent wake while he methodically stroked his goatee, as if trying to picture the circumstances of Monsour's disappearance. Next, the deep-set eyes of his angular face scanned the horizon, as if expecting to catch one last glimpse of Monsour. Khalib, still visibly upset with the inaction on the part of his leader, moved off to confer with Sa`id.

After a few instructions from Captain Farroque to Ramon and the other crewmembers at hand, the gathering broke up, leaving only he and Jamal at the stern railing. He jerked up on the top cable as if testing its integrity for the satisfaction of his companion, wishing he knew what thoughts lurked behind that creased forehead of Jamal's. Just then, as he glanced toward the other's sandals, he caught sight of the last piece of evidence from the previous night's struggle. There, snagged on a jagged weld at the edge of the deck, was a strip of fabric two inches long and no wider than a shoestring. From the captain's perspective, it appeared the size of a national flag flapping in the wind.

He squatted over the cloth and loosened it from its mooring. Try as he might, he could not release it from his grip to let it slip away undetected as he'd done the night before with Monsour's *kufi*. Jamal was hovering over him as he stood up, the cloth fluttering against the sleeve of Jamal's gown; the same type all four had been cloaked in these past few days. It was a perfect match, leaving little doubt as to Monsour's fate in Jamal's mind. For Captain Farroque, it was an eloquent reminder that last night had not been a dream.

He spoke first, hoping to send the conversation in the right direction.

"Why do you suppose he jumped? Was there a problem dogging him? Perhaps the life ring was a misguided attempt to save himself from whatever fate awaited him. He probably knew little of the water temperature and, of course, the propeller."

Jamal shook his head slowly, still stroking his goatee.

"No Captain, Monsour was of a strong mind. He was faithful to our cause and had a just heart. Perhaps it was a misguided attempt to save your pipe," he said with a hint of sarcasm in his steady voice. "Your superiors should know of the dangers on this old, rusting tub of bolts."

Captain Farroque swallowed hard as he considered Jamal's harsh comment and, more importantly, his connections; real or imagined. While it had been an unfortunate incident, he began to feel less culpable; after all, he hadn't pushed the dagger-wielding Monsour over the edge. Besides, his family came first, convincing himself he had to be strong for them. Jamal could surely think it had been nothing more than an accident by a novice at sea; a simple case of falling over the edge in rough seas. Damn that pipe and that life ring and the observant crewman.

Captain Farroque avoided his guests for the rest of the day and night. As had been agreed upon during the initial arrangements, they reached the port at Buenos Aires before daybreak, when less activity and fewer prying eyes would be present. From the bridge, once the ship was secured at the pier and the harbor pilot had left, he signaled to the three remaining passengers that it was safe to disembark.

With the aid of binoculars, the burgeoning light of a new day allowed him to follow their movement along the wharf, amused that their flowing garments and dingy cotton duffels, slung over one shoulder, were a sharp contrast to the shiny, platinum-colored laptop computers Sa`id and Khalib held briefcase-like in their hands. They followed Jamal, looking like a couple of junior executives in step with their mentor, Captain Farroque mused.

The three of them seemed out of place on the docks among the warehouses, ships, and delivery trucks, as if they had stepped into the wrong scene of a movie set. When they reached the end of the long wharf though, as if on cue from the director, a late-model sedan pulled up next to them.

While the driver stepped out onto the cobblestone pavement, Jamal's travel mates piled into the back seat as Jamal embraced the silhouetted figure in typical middle-eastern fashion. The two appeared to talk briefly before Jamal suddenly turned and pointed directly at the pilothouse where the captain held them in his view. The distance between Captain Farroque and these two made it impossible for him to make out any words on their lips through the binoculars, still he felt the heat as his face flushed with embarrassment that they might think he was spying on them. He wondered what Jamal was telling this one of Monsour's disappearance from the *Empress* and of the captain's involvement as he stepped into the shadows of the pilothouse, out of their view. Soon, they were all in the car and the captain watched as it sped away until out of sight past the row of warehouses.

He felt relief that they were gone, yet an uneasiness crept over him. The last words from Monsour haunted him. What had Monsour meant when he said he would see America before me, Captain Farroque wondered.

In his mind, he pictured Monsour, smirking on the stern of the ship, as he said those words two nights ago. Next, he pictured his wife and daughter safely in America. Lastly, he pictured Monsour again, grim-faced, in America, beside his family. He shuddered at the thought as the uneasiness he felt began turning to guilt, not for Monsour's loss anymore, but for the future endeavors of the other three that had just left the ship.

Captain Farroque had heard of the lawless area called "the triple frontier" from some of his previous stowaways before Monsour mentioned it during their quarrel. From the atlas he kept in his cabin, the city appeared to lie in the middle of nowhere some three hundred miles north of Buenos Aires. Any individuals he'd clandestinely transported overseas in the past were either being pursued by the law in their native country or by Israeli authorities. He was sure that wasn't the case with this last gang of four. The money had been too good, their demeanor too secretive, and, with the exception of Jamal, too young to be fugitives, yet.

It took the better part of two days for the cargo hold to be emptied, the ship's fuel tanks refilled, and other necessary supplies loaded onboard. Now that the *Empress of Sayda* was back at sea, heading due south on the next leg of her journey around Cape Horn, Captain Farroque began to relax a bit. He had managed to get his package to Fatima sent without a hitch from Buenos Aires. A last-minute cable from the shipping company had confirmed the layover at Istanbul for repairs after delivering their load of copper ingots with the only change in his itinerary being an unusual stop in Jakarta for a new crew. The freighter, carrying a lighter load, plodded on doggedly toward its next destination—as did its three former passengers.

CHAPTER TWO

"Okay! All together now, let's give a rousing send off to Professor Stevenson," Dr. Brennen shouted as he raised his beer mug and began the chorus. "For he's a jolly good fellow...."

The jovial crowd of graduate students and teachers surrounding the massive oak table joined in, "For he's a jolly good fellow...."

"Bon voyage, Profess...or!" Raymond shouted over the din, slurring the words. "Good luck on your sabbatical. Have a safe trip to Indiana..., I mean Indianola, err Illiopolis."

"India, Raymond! India!" Professor Stevenson shouted back from his end of the table. "It's a good thing you majored in engineering and not geography."

Professor Stevenson smiled, pointing toward the thin, olive-skinned, black-haired young man seated on the bench next to Raymond.

"Perhaps Yussef there could give you a few pointers Raymond since he hails from that part of the world."

Raymond had begun celebrating an hour before the rest of the crowd, having volunteered to get to Perry's Pub in advance of the others in order to secure the large table. The table, pockmarked with cigarette burns and unintelligible carvings, held court along the far wall of this venerable establishment. Perry's Pub, a favorite of students and faculty, was a short walk from campus.

"...Nobody can deny."

The melody came to an end, and those seated next to Professor Stevenson gave him a congratulatory pat on the back. It was a tradition of sorts, when something special happened in the engineering department, for there to be an informal get-together at the pub on Friday's after classes ended for the week. Several professors, most of the graduate students, teaching assistants, and post-doctoral fellows from the department showed up for these impromptu gatherings.

Even Yussef, sitting next to Rachael—by his own design—began attending these events after sweating through a defense of his thesis several months ago. Though still a novice at consuming alcohol—his religion forbade it—he learned to nurse a beer through these social endeavors at the urging of his housemates, one of whom was Raymond. It was a way to make himself feel like an intimate part of the department instead of the stereotypical foreign grad student isolated on the fringe of the collegiate crowd with their nose to the academic grindstone.

Yussef's social life had undergone a dramatic change since moving into the rental house with Raymond and his two roommates, Kenny and Jay, both civil engineering grad students. It had been a year and a half since the fire that destroyed the dilapidated house where Yussef and his deceased roommate, Ahmed, rented a shared room. When

Yussef first came here to the Missouri campus three years ago, there were no other students from Pakistan in the graduate program. He and Ahmed kept to themselves until the devastating fire forced Yussef out on the street with just the clothes on his back.

Raymond, a fellow doctoral candidate in nuclear engineering, offered Yussef a place to stay and clothes to wear. Others in the engineering department gave him replacement textbooks and other necessities. Yussef was not accustomed to this kind of benevolence—with no strings attached—and he was grateful. But even more so, he was grateful, and a little surprised, that his studies and research had not suffered since the tragic fire and resulting mayhem of moving into an unfamiliar house in an unfamiliar culture.

Ahmed had always made a point of "looking over his shoulder", "keeping him on the straight and narrow", like the nanny Yussef had as a child. After Ahmed's death in the fire, it took Yussef several weeks to get over the change from living in isolation to being a part of a more normal society.

Ahmed had strictly enforced this separation, even though Yussef had contact during school with others, they were not of the same ilk. Now, with his hectic schedule since the fire, Yussef rarely missed Ahmed. At times though, when by himself at the research lab, he occasionally thought of Ahmed. He'd never felt a need to mourn for him, and this gnawed at his conscience.

Yussef and Raymond shared an office in the Physics Annex. Like Yussef, Ray was a bit of a wallflower, particularly when it came to social drinking or members of the opposite sex. On the other hand, their roommates, Kenny and Jay, never met a person—especially of the female persuasion—they didn't like, or a craft beer they didn't have a well-informed opinion of.

Yussef would have run into Rachael at stuffy lectures or chaotic lab exercises but only in passing. The end-of- the-month parties, hosted at their house by "K" and "J", as his two other roommates were affectionately known, had brought Yussef into more frequent social contact with Western women, especially Rachael. These kinds of acquaintances were a rarity before Yussef had come to the states. The teachers at the madrasa, fellow Islamist students at the university in Islamabad, and Ahmed before his death; all had tried, with unrelenting vigor, to brainwash Yussef into submission to their fundamentalist social mores.

For Yussef, living with Ahmed had been a double-edged sword. He was a constant reminder of those years at the madrasa. Since Ahmed was working at a local bakery part-time and not going to school, he'd had ample time to continue his studies of the Qur'an. Each evening, when he and Yussef ate dinner together on the floor of their room after prayers, Yussef had always gotten an ear full. Ahmed spewed forth vitriolic rants about his American co-workers, not to mention the female customers that would come into the store and dare to look him in the eye. Night after night, Ahmed hammered on about the decadent Western culture and its eminent downfall. A tree assaulted by woodpeckers must have felt the same way, Yussef thought. Still, looking back, Ahmed was the one tie that anchored Yussef to his homeland and faith. And, if not for the fire, Yussef would not have been able to break this bond.

It was only five o'clock on Friday. Perry's Pub overflowed with the end-of-the-week party crowd. Due to the noise, everyone at the mammoth table moved in close to carry on a conversation. Rachael, on Yussef's right, leaned her lithe upper torso in front of Yussef to talk to Raymond seated on his left. Dense smoke from cigarettes, the preferred prop for conversation in Perry's, could not mask the scent of her perfumed hair below Yussef's nostrils.

Yussef's mind wandered back to his childhood, before the madrasa. It was something he did more often since the loss of Ahmed. His mother's smell no longer registered in his memory. When Yussef was only eight, she and his father had died in an automobile accident; or had been murdered, depending on who was telling the story. Smiling, he took in a deep breath and decided this perfume would be how he remembered his mother. This would be her smell.

"So Ray, how are your experiments going in the lab?" Rachael asked.

"You haven't seen any mushroom clouds in the vicinity of the nuclear physics building, have you?"

"No, and you don't appear to be glowing, either," Rachael said, laughing.

Raymond pointed a finger in Yussef's direction.

"Yussef here has been helping me finish up a couple of my research projects so he can get me out of his way in the lab."

Yussef rolled his eyes, smiled, and joined in the discussion. "That is correct. I need to get Ray out of there so I can finish my own research and blow up the lab myself, before Professor Stevenson gets back from his sabbatical."

Rachael put her hand on Yussef's shoulder to keep from falling off the bench as she leaned in closer to counter the increasing noise. Yussef, once more, had a far away look in his eyes as he tried to remember his mother's touch.

"Ray, I was wondering if I could talk you in to coming over tomorrow and helping me and my roommates move that old car of Tammy's out of the backyard. Tammy says we can get three hundred dollars out of it at the salvage yard. She wants to use the money to buy another car."

Ray laughed. "Why? So she can ignore the 'check engine light' and burn up the motor like the last one. So we can all push it into the back yard where this one is now. No way am I going to let another car suffer at her hands."

"Now, it wasn't all her fault. The *guy* at the QuikLube didn't tighten the oil pan plug," Rachael admonished.

"Says you," Ray snorted, shaking his head. "Besides, I've got tickets to a Blues game in St. Louis this weekend with "K" and "J". The manager down at the liquor store gave them to us."

"Ha! No doubt, since you guys are his best customers, present company excepted, Yussef,"

Rachael said, smiling. "Aren't you taking Yussef here with you?"

She still had her hand on Yussef's shoulder but now Rachael turned and looked into his dreaming eyes. Her raven hair and caramel-colored eyes reminded Yussef of women he'd known as a child; his mother, his aunts—remembered only through an ancient family photograph, now singed around the edges that he'd secreted away before going to the madrasa.

Raymond's sharp elbow to the ribcage brought Yussef out of his self-induced trance and back into Perry's Pub. Ray nodded his head toward Yussef.

"He's still trying to grasp the nuances of the great game of baseball. We don't want to confuse the poor lad with the rules and regulations of ice hockey, too."

Yussef rolled his eyes again in mock distain and spoke rather loudly. "I've just figured out what 'wearing the collar' and 'protecting the plate' mean. I need time to digest all the lingo."

Rachael gave them both a puzzled look; she was not a student of the game.

Yussef continued, "Besides, I have work to do in the lab this weekend, and I promised Professor Stevenson I would supervise the reactor while he's off to India. By the way, Ray, do 'nubber' and 'worm-burner' mean the same thing?"

"You got it, bro!" Ray said proudly, slapping Yussef on the back. "It's a long way from Karachi to the major leagues, but, by golly, you're getting there. Hey, I know. Yussef, why don't you help them move their car tomorrow? I'll loan you my pickup truck since we're taking Kenny's car to the game."

"That would be great," Rachael chimed in, before Yussef could say anything to the contrary.

Rachael liked Yussef. His quiet demeanor and politeness were a refreshing change from the hormone-addled conversations she endured from most college men. And Rachael's on-again, off-again relationship with a friend of her brother's was mostly off since he'd deployed over a year ago. In addition, she knew Yussef to be very intelligent. The casual time they spent together—in places such as Perry's Pub or "K" and "J" parties—made her more comfortable with Yussef's ethnicity and religion.

Yussef weighed his options as he pulled nervously at the end of each of his slender fingers. On the one hand, he would get to see Rachael again at her house: on the other, he would have to interact with her two roommates, Tammy and Jill, whose constant badgering made him consider life long celibacy. When they cornered him at the last "K" and "J" party, they went out of their way to make him feel guilty about the way women were treated by his country and religion. In addition, his driving skills were rudimentary at best since he'd never owned a car and his roommates had only recently begun to teach him how to drive. But, he found himself not wanting to disappoint Rachael.

"Sure…, I'll come over and help move the car," Yussef said grinning as he nodded his head. "Would you like me to wash the dishes, make the beds, and do the laundry while I'm there?"

Rachael poked him on the arm, jokingly. "Come by about eleven o'clock, if that will work for you."

"Yes, my lady," Yussef offered in his best rendition of a servant's demeanor, an American caricature he'd seen in movies recently. Then, addressing Ray he said, "Let's go before you volunteer me for any more projects."

They inched their way toward the other end of the table, through several more minutes of conversations with other students and teaching assistants in the department. Upon reaching Professor Stevenson, congratulatory handshakes were given while listening to his last minute instructions.

"Well, guys, hold down the fort while I'm gone. If you have any problems with the reactor, let Dr. Brennen know about them. I should be gone eight weeks, and I expect Rockledge, Missouri to still be on the map when I get back from India."

Yussef and Raymond smiled at the last remark from Professor Stevenson, nodded their understanding, and then headed toward the door.

"Sorry about sticking you with Rachael and her two blonde buddies tomorrow," Ray offered, as they headed down the street toward campus.

"That's okay. There are worse people I could spend Saturday with."

Ray laughed, "Like me you mean?"

"Now that you mention it, yeah," Yussef said, a smile appearing on his bearded face.

"I'll put the truck keys on the kitchen table when we leave in the morning."

The truck had a manual transmission, which only added to Yussef's already nervous state. Kenny's car—the one he'd been learning to drive—was an automatic. The weather was unseasonably warm for mid-March, and he could feel himself beginning to perspire as he maneuvered the lurching truck the long twelve blocks to Rachael's house. He popped the clutch pulling into the driveway, and the truck shuddered to a stop. Yussef took a deep breath and hopped out, heading for the front door just as Rachael came running out on to the porch, pointing excitedly toward the backward-rolling truck. A massive lilac bush stopped its reverse motion at the edge of the sidewalk just as Yussef jumped back in to hit the parking brake. Rachael was smiling broadly as he carefully drove it back up close to the house.

"Good thing Tammy and Jill didn't see that, Yussef."

"Yes, yes, quite right. My apologies about the bush," he offered, wiping his brow. "Where are your roommates, anyway?" He asked, cracking his knuckles one at a time. He secretly hoped they'd come down with the plague.

"I told them you were here. They said they would be right out. Isn't it a gorgeous day?"

Rachael spread her arms wide before lifting them skyward. With her hair tied back, wearing a long cotton skirt, Yussef couldn't help but reminisce once more about his childhood. His memories were faint, ghost-like, until he saw Rachael, then they would be flooded with a rainbow of colors.

"Yes, yes, I agree," Yussef said, before a long awkward silence ensued.

He thought about how easy it had been last evening at the pub to talk with Rachael; a consequence of the alcohol, he surmised. Now, as was usually the case, he struggled to say anything of interest unrelated to academics.

"Do you miss your home and family in Pakistan?" Rachael asked, leaning back against the stone sidewall of the front porch steps, her figure highlighted by the soft glow of late winter sunshine.

"No," Yussef answered abruptly, caught off guard by the question.

He tried to think of something else to say, something that didn't sound so cold-hearted. Yussef felt a twinge of guilt for not being truthful, looking up toward her on the steps as a gentle breeze tussled her thick hair. The front door swung open before he could amend his harsh tone.

"Hellooo…, Yussef," Tammy said between giggles.

Jill was next out the door. Yussef's mouth dropped open but no sound came forth as he felt the heat rising in his cheeks. Both girls had sandals on their feet, plus white lace panties and bras but nothing more. Nothing more save for mock *hijaabs* constructed from black bath towels that were wrapped around their heads and covered their entire faces except for their eyes and the bridge of their noses. They pranced down the steps, single file, with an exaggerated swing to their hips, bracelets jingling from their wrists and ankles.

In a lilting voice, Jill cooed, "Would you like to go to the casbah with us, Yussef?"

She reached out and tugged playfully on his beard. With her back turned to them, Rachael had not witnessed the theatrics unfold until both girls were past her, down the steps.

"Oh, for God's sake you two, leave him alone!" Rachael protested in an exasperated voice, covering her face with her hands in an attempt to keep from laughing. "Yussef, I'm sorry. These two are one brick shy of a load. Their Women's history class has them ridiculing cultures that they perceive as having a society of domineering men."

Tammy and Jill finished parading around Yussef. Out of the corner of his eye, on his down-turned face, he could see the goose bumps on the backs of their thighs and the jewelry that caressed their elegant, slender ankles as they sashayed back up the steps and exited the stage-porch into the house.

Yussef was frozen in place. His brain was in gridlock. Too many emotions were running through his head at the same time. Anger, embarrassment, and carnal lust fought for control of his thoughts, like the broken ends of an energized power line snapping back and forth at each other. He could have easily stood there forever, eventually merging with the concrete steps, if Rachael had not gently tugged on his sleeve.

She kept apologizing to Yussef, guiding him, like a punch-drunk boxer, around to the backyard for a look at the neglected car. Yussef willed himself out of his stupor, trying to function normally with Rachael again.

"Your roommates dislike me, no?" He said absent-mindedly while checking to see if his beard was still intact.

"No, don't pay any attention to them. It was just a joke. Their idea of humor just lacks a little sensitivity is all. I'm sure they like you, Yussef."

"You know we've had a female Prime Minister in my country. I shall explain that to them."

"Yes, yes that's a good idea," Rachael offered, still leading him.

It was not long before Tammy and Jill reappeared, fully clothed, to help them wrest the car from the clutches of dead weeds and earth that engulfed it. Two hours and a broken towrope later, they had the car out on the street resting on a borrowed two-wheel trailer, headed for the salvage yard.

All four of them packed into the cab of the pickup with Rachael pressed against Yussef, her left arm behind his head clutching the seatback to avoid rocketing into the windshield with each erratic shifting of the gears. The other two girls each had a hand braced against the dashboard for the same reason.

Slowly, Rachael's warmth from her physical presence between him and her two demonic roommates allowed Yussef to relax. Once again, his mind wandered back to his family and his youth, his pre-madrasa youth. He didn't consider those nine years spent in the madrasa as part of his younger life. If anything, they'd stolen his youth, he thought, as if he'd been kidnapped from his real life. Once his parent's funeral was over, his father's devout brother—Yussef refused to call him uncle—had spirited Yussef away to the madrasa. Those nine years were like an ever-repeating tape of Qur'anic verses and study, devoid of the normalcies of youth. He could no longer recall what his father looked like, and his mother now only through the photograph, and through Rachael, his muse.

Tammy leaned forward and turned toward Yussef as they bounced down the oft-patched county road in the direction of the salvage yard.

"So Yussef, were there any girls where you went to school in Pakistan?" She asked with a hint of sarcasm in her voice.

Jill and Tammy were determined to hound him into submission he decided, feeling droplets of sweat beginning to form on his upper lip. But before he could come up with an acceptable answer, Rachael came to his rescue.

She stared at Tammy and began speaking in an exaggerated "hillbilly" drawl.

"For cryin' out loud, Tammy Jo, give the poor boy a break, will ya. Why, Yussef here doesn't think of you as inferior because you're just a woman, stupid," she paused and gave a fake spit before continuing, "he treats you as inferior because you are *stupid*, woman!"

All three girls chortled with laughter. Rachael continued though in a rapid, know-it-all tone.

"Besides, everyone knows they've already had a female Prime Minister in Pakistan."

Now, it was Yussef's turn to try not to laugh. He did not dare let Tammy think he was laughing at her. Rachael's performance had its intended effect as she squeezed Yussef's shoulder and Tammy's harangue ceased.

"Rachael dear, is this the truck we're taking camping and canoeing next month on the Red Oak River?" Jill asked, before whispering something into Tammy's ear that sent them both into spasms of giggles.

"Yes, it is. Raymond, bless his heart, said we could use it as long as Tammy promised to check the oil in it three times a day."

Yussef kept both eyes on the road, both hands on the wheel, and his mouth shut.

"Well, I hope our chauffer has a better command of the gear shift pattern by then."

"I'm going to drive it," Rachael informed them matter-of-factly, raising her eyebrows as she glanced in her two roommate's direction. "And, I guess, if all six of us girls go, *somebody* will have to sit in the back, won't they?"

With the car and trailer unleashed at the salvage yard and the money in her pocket, Tammy became more benevolent, handing Yussef a twenty-dollar bill for the gas and his help in getting the car towed.

Before anyone else had a chance to get back in the truck, Rachael jumped in behind the steering wheel. The other three looked at her momentarily then clamored in beside her with Yussef in the lead. Rachael revved the engine a few times, for effect, before fishtailing her way out of the oil-slicked parking lot while her passengers undulated in unison from the swerving motion of the truck.

"You go, girl!" Tammy and Jill shrieked.

"Where did you learn to drive a stick shift?" Tammy managed to squeeze through her lips as they rounded a curve in the road, doing fifty.

Jill was pressed hard against her and she in turn against Yussef, like falling dominoes. They came out of the curve, and Yussef righted himself as best he could without touching Rachael's body. But before he could grasp a non-living part of the truck, they were headed the opposite direction through another curve with Yussef almost in Tammy's lap.

"I love you too, honey," Tammy yelped.

The girls cackled with infectious laughter. All Yussef could do was relax and laugh along, marveling at how he'd ended up in the middle of a country so reviled by all of his mentors back at the madrasa, not to mention Ahmed. Here he was, sandwiched between three girls in the cab of a pickup truck, hurdling along a gravel road on the outskirts of Rockledge, Missouri.

Rachael, grinning, downshifted as they reached the city limit sign and paved roads, giving all three of her passengers a close inspection of the dashboard due to the instant braking effect of the engine, its exhaust pipes roaring their approval. Tammy and Jill could not stop laughing at the ride, better than any carnival's, while Yussef regained a white-knuckled grip on the overhead dome light. Rachael faked an exaggerated spit out the window and resumed her comic hillbilly drawl in response to Tammy's earlier question.

"My...Granddaddy's got him a pig farm up by St. Joe, (another fake spit followed), he taught me how to drive a truck, slop the hogs, and pluck a chick'n when my brother and me was young'uns just knee high to a grasshopper." Then came another fake spit.

Yussef wasn't quite sure what the fake spitting was about, but he recognized the vernacular from his limited interaction with some of the locals. He smiled, relaxing his grip on the light and moving his arm to the seatback behind Rachael while the other two, laughing wildly, wiped the spittle from their lips.

"Do you still want me to let you ladies out downtown?" Rachael asked, returning to her normal voice.

"Yes, but drop us off at St. Mary's Cathedral," Tammy requested in feigned distress. "I think I just found religion after that wild ride."

"Let us out down at the Women's Center," Jill said in a resigned tone, deciding their fun was over for the day. "We both offered to do volunteer work there until six o'clock this evening."

Rachael downshifted as she wheeled up to the Women's Center, the exhaust pipes rumbling their approval once more. Tammy and Jill said their goodbyes while Yussef scooted over to the far side of the cab.

"So long, suckers!" Rachael shouted out the window, squealing the tires as she pulled away from the curb.

"Man, I love Ray's truck," she said, smiling as they headed up the street.

Yussef nodded. They remained silent, both deep in thought, for the rest of the drive back to Rachael's house. Yussef spoke first when they pulled into the drive beside the mauled lilac bush.

"Are you going to work on your research in the lab this afternoon?"

"No, I think I'll grab a bite to eat, do some laundry, and have a nap. I'm done with school and homework for this weekend," Rachael declared.

Yussef chastised himself for even bringing up the subject of school. He blamed Ahmed and his enforced religious isolation for any ineptness at being able to have a meaningful conversation with Rachael, lasting longer than a few seconds.

Rachael, biting her lower lip, hesitated a moment before hopping out of the truck. She watched Yussef, lost in his own thoughts, as he slid absentmindedly over to the driver's side.

"I guess you'll be eating alone tonight since your roommates left you to go to the hockey game," Rachael contemplated out loud, then added hurriedly, "would you like to go out to eat with me this evening?"

Yussef snapped out of his trance, but—tongue-tied by the unexpected invitation—said nothing at first as Rachael continued.

"I know you've got at least twenty dollars," she added with a laugh, trying to dispel the awkwardness. "You owe me something for getting Tammy off your case on the way out to the salvage yard."

"You are right. I owe you," Yussef nodded and smiled, "and Raymond owes me big time. I'll come by in his truck around seven o'clock, or perhaps six would be better. Would six o'clock be okay?"

Yussef hoped to be to Rachael's and gone again before her roommates got home from work. He'd had enough of their theatrics for one day.

"Sounds good. See you at six," Rachael agreed then skipped up the steps, disappearing into the house.

Yussef backed down the drive in a state of euphoria, narrowly avoiding the lilac bush this time. The lurching movement of the truck as he let the clutch out too quickly served to jog his memory. All the events of the last couple of days had almost erased Mullah Khan from his mind; almost.

Upon first arriving in Rockledge, he and Ahmed had been instructed to call the Mullah on the third Saturday of every other month at eight o'clock sharp Pacific time. Ahmed kept track of when to call and did most of the talking. Since Ahmed's death, Yussef had been on his own in dealing with Mullah Khan who was the head of an Islamic foundation that supplied he and Ahmed with money for living expenses and, in Yussef's case, tuition. Yussef began to have second thoughts about this arrangement even before Ahmed had perished in the fire but had kept them to himself for fear of the consequences.

Now, without the constant onslaught of sermons from his deceased roommate, Yussef had time to clear his mind and open his eyes to a different worldview—a secular view—of Western culture. At this moment though, his mind was too jumbled to see anything clearly. Only a constantly changing kaleidoscope of images containing: Rachael, his mother, Mullah Kahn, and his research papers appeared in his head. After a quick stop at the lab, Yussef headed home and as soon as his head touched the armrest on the tattered sofa he was asleep.

The slanting rays of late afternoon sunlight brushing against his heavy eyelids as it streamed through the threadbare curtains awakened Yussef. He had an hour to get ready for his dinner date, which would give him four hours to spend with Rachael before having to contact Mullah Khan, he calculated. Though Yussef had never met him, he had looked up the area code once and presumed Mullah Khan lived somewhere on the west coast. Still, with cell phones, one could never know for sure where he really lived; that was the whole point, Yussef guessed.

Staring at himself in the bathroom mirror, rehearsing his conversation with Rachael while beads of sweat appeared on his forehead, scissors in hand, he began. The full lips, wavy black hair, and dark eyes looking warily back at him seemed to belong to someone else as the olive-brown skin of his face began to reveal itself. Fifty-five minutes later, he left the bathroom behind, dressed, and grabbed the keys to Ray's truck.

They decided on the Bamboo Garden, a Thai restaurant, for dinner. This secretly pleased Yussef since he'd eaten there for lunch once with Raymond and knew he could afford it. In addition, the spicy dishes they had on the menu were a comfort food for him—a weak link to his part of the world, in contrast to the bland American food he normally ate since moving in with Ray and his other two roommates.

Yussef was determined to steer their talk away from anything to do with school. Life back home, at least his, was another subject he hoped to avoid.

Rachael would have none of it. After being silent all the way to the restaurant, except for a polite hello and a bewildered expression on her face, she was ready for some answers. Once they'd been seated, candles lit, and orders placed, she commenced with the questions.

"Boy! Yussef...., I still can't believe you shaved off your beard. Isn't that part of your faith? I hope it wasn't because of what those two clowns, Tammy and Jill, did this morning. Those two can be so cruel if they get the upper hand on someone, especially a man. I hardly recognized you when I first got in the truck just now, like I'd jumped into a vehicle with a total stranger. I guess I shouldn't have been so eager to get in, huh," she laughed. "Anyway, I think you look more handsome without it."

Rachael smiled and caught her breath before taking a sip of her wine. Yussef, for his part, had already taken a couple of large gulps and its effects were beginning to take hold quickly on his empty stomach as he felt himself beginning to relax.

He kept steering the conversation back to her life growing up in the Midwest of America, and Rachael obliged. She folded and unfolded her napkin several times and it occurred to Yussef that she was as nervous as he, though he'd been taught, and did his best, to keep it bottled up inside. By the time the food arrived, she was up to her freshman year in high school.

"I hope I'm not boring you with my life history, Yussef."

"No, no, not at all. Please continue. I get tired of talking sports with Ray sometimes. This is much more interesting," Yussef explained eagerly, thinking also about the more carnal subjects he and his roommates sometimes discussed.

It was true. Yussef immensely enjoyed listening to her story. In fact, he envied her life. It sounded like a fairy tale or a dream come true. He followed her lips and eyes as she spoke and began to daydream about growing up in America. He saw himself playing baseball, hitting the game-winning home run, driving Rachael to..., what was the word she had used? Prom? Anyway, driving her somewhere in his hot rod car. Too soon, the dream ended.

"I'm curious, Yussef. Why did you say no when I asked you if you missed your family this morning?" Rachael asked.

The food seemed spicier than Yussef remembered as he blotted the moisture from his naked upper lip. He had practiced a half-dozen stock answers to questions about his non-existent family. How many brothers and sisters? How old were they? What did his parents do? Where did they live? But they all escaped him now.

"I bet they wouldn't recognize you without your beard and mustache. I do hope you cleaned up the bathroom after cutting it all off. What a mess it must have made," Rachael exclaimed with a laugh.

Yussef ran his tongue across the edge of his teeth, lips pressed shut; a habit he had when trying to think. He made a mental note to take care of the bathroom first chance he got.

"I do indeed miss my parents," Yussef began, starting slowly, cautiously. "I try not to think about them. But when someone or something reminds me of them, I guess my conditioned response is to deny their existence, so I don't miss them as much. I have to..., to harden my heart. Is that the correct term? Otherwise, I would be quite homesick all the time."

"Ah, that's too bad. I'm sorry if I made you uncomfortable," Rachael offered, reaching across and patting Yussef's clasped hands. "I didn't mean too. That part of the world seems so exotic to me. I would like to hear more about it. Plus, since I'd never heard you talk about your family back in Pakistan, I thought perhaps you weren't close to them, or worse, they were dead."

Yussef gulped more wine before explaining, "No, that's quite all right, indeed. Well, no need to worry about my parents. In fact, I'm calling them tonight. I call them on the third Saturday of every other month at ten o'clock. It's seven o'clock in the morning over there," he added in response to Rachael's quizzical look.

Rachael watched as Yussef shifted in his seat, while his eyes moved between hers and the tablecloth. Since they'd spent more time together in recent days, she had detected a pattern in his speech. His dialect would change to a choppy, British-influenced sort of English, less "Americanized" than she was used to hearing from him. It occurred, she thought, when he was nervous or excited, and this made her smile.

Yussef was proud of himself for the made up response that gave him an out to call Mullah Khan; something he'd been avoiding, though, he felt bad for not being able to tell Rachael the truth. He missed Ahmed, if for no other reason than to have a co-conspirator to confide in. Missed him despite the sharp rebukes and murderous looks Ahmed gave him when Yussef dared to mention his own impure thoughts or questioned Ahmed's interpretation of certain passages from the Qur'an.

Yussef dare not tell Rachael the truth about his parents for fear it would bring him one step closer to telling her the *real* reason he and Ahmed had come to America under the supervision of Mullah Khan.

"Shoot," Rachael replied, loud enough to startle Yussef from his inner thoughts, "I was hoping I could talk you in to going to a movie after dinner, kind of like a real date."

Yussef could sense the disappointment in her voice and he felt his own deep inside. For a moment, he considered the consequences of not calling the mullah, but he feared the repercussions would be too great. Dinner by candlelight with the girl of his fledgling American dreams would have to suffice.

On the way home, the conversation flowed more easily, and Yussef wanted to know more about the concept of a prom. This was foreign to him, and while Rachael explained in detail, he pictured her in a fancy gown, strolling beside him, their arms entwined. He was reminded of a story his mother had told him as a child, about how she had met Yussef's father at a formal dance sponsored by a government ministry of one sort or another years before. There was even a picture of the two, so young, smiling and holding hands. The picture had sat on the dresser in his parent's bedroom. He could recall the picture now, with Rachael sitting beside him. His father's brother had removed it from the house even before he had removed Yussef.

"Would you like to come in for awhile, Yussef?"

Rachael turned toward him, her head tilted slightly to one side, allowing her hair to fall across one shoulder. He wanted desperately to say yes, but he saw movement in the lit up house. Tammy or Jill—or worse, both—were probably home by now. He could not decide who hounded his thoughts more: those two or the deceased Ahmed. In addition, his scheduled contact with the mullah was looming large in his mind, and it trumped any thought of further company with Rachael for tonight.

"I should go home, I'm afraid. Sometimes it takes several tries to make the connection to Pakistan," he explained, unconvincingly.

"Sure, I understand," Rachael offered, the brightness in her eyes and smile on her face unable to mask the disappointment in her voice. "I was hoping to show my roommates how handsome you look without your beard. Not that you weren't before."

Yussef cast his eyes downward with embarrassment, but this time he recovered quickly, albeit with a slight stutter, "P-perhaps we, I mean the two of us, you and I, could go out next weekend for dinner and a movie."

"That would be great, except my Demolition and Explosives Class is going on a field trip next Saturday. We're going to Kansas City to watch an implosion of an old grain silo. We actually get to set some of the charges. I'm kind of excited about it. How about the weekend after next?"

"Indeed, that would be quite nice," Yussef replied.

They settled on seven o'clock, Saturday night, weekend after next. Yussef whistled all the way home, thinking that this must be what it feels like to hit a home run. He felt invincible, and any dread he had of speaking to Mullah Khan evaporated.

CHAPTER THREE

The road from Buenos Aires to Ciudad del Estrellas took the better part of a day to transverse. Their driver, Zahir, made small talk in Arabic about the local scenery and landmarks after picking up his three passengers at the wharf. He spoke passable English and knew enough of the local Spanish to carry on limited conversations with locals he encountered at the petrol stations along the way.

Jamal, in front, with Khalib and Sa'id in the back seat, had little to say at first. Their thoughts were still of Monsour. Zahir warned them as they left the pier not to speak of any specifics of their plans. Only speak in public places away from other people or when you're alone with me, he explained, since agents from hostile countries had infested Ciudad del Estrellas in recent months and few places were safe. As proof, he informed them that an electronic eavesdropping device had been discovered recently in the local mosque.

This information brought venomous rants and epitaphs against the Great Satan from the two in the back seat. Their words brought a smile to Jamal, but a worried look appeared briefly on Zahir's face, before, with a wave of his hand, Jamal quieted their jihadist fervor. After an hour of driving in silence, Zahir modified his earlier statement, saying he was confident the car was not "bugged", encouraging them to talk freely in the car. He proceeded to quiz them on what their plans were for the future, getting no specific details other than the fact that their stay in Ciudad del Estrellas was a temporary stop over on their way to America.

As they drew nearer to Ciudad del Estrellas, Zahir suggested a sightseeing detour to Iguazu` Falls on the Parana River. The stay in Ciudad del Estellas for these three would be short, he reasoned, based on their conversation thus far, and the probability of a return trip seemed unlikely. A little diversion would do them all good, and they could talk more while walking to the falls.

Iguazu` Falls brought dropped-jaw exclamations from all three of the travelers. Zahir explained in tourist-guide bravado how the falls had been formed geologically millions of years ago from a cataclysmic upheaval in the earth's crust; and not from erosion by the Parana River, as Jamal, in a fatherly manner had explained it to his companions. This contradiction brought a sharp look from Jamal.

Khalib would have none of it. Only the almighty hand of Allah could have made a vista of such grandeur, to think otherwise was blasphemous. Sa`id nodded in agreement with Khalib while Zahir shrugged his shoulders but stayed silent, not wanting to anger them further.

The mist from the falls soaked them, and the cooling air of approaching darkness caused all four of them to shiver as they returned to the car. After glancing at his watch, Zahir apologized, saying they would miss evening prayers at the mosque. He had not anticipated the mesmerizing effect that Iguazu` Falls would have on these three, with them having spent four hours exploring the falls from above and below. At least the bridge over the river into Paraguay wouldn't be so crowded by this time of the evening, Zahir thought.

Jamal took Zahir aside and thanked him for this distraction, telling him not to worry about missing prayers at the mosque tonight. The wonder of the falls had pushed thoughts of Monsour out of their heads, especially his two agitated companions. For this, Jamal silently gave praise.

During the short drive on to Ciudad del Estrellas, the car was filled with chatter. Zahir clarified for them why this region was known as the Triple Frontier after they passed a road sign stating they were in Brazil—not Argentina—as his three passengers had believed, and that Ciudad del Estrellas was actually in Paraguay, across the river.

The remaining fleet of *motoqueiros* was dispersing as they approached the bridge. Zahir explained how these motorcycle taxis would ferry passengers across the bridge, between Ciudad del Estellas and its counterpart on the Brazilian side, for a pittance. The motorcycles were much quicker than the cars or buses—brought to a standstill on the clogged bridge—if you didn't mind swerving between the bumper-to-bumper traffic at the risk of losing a limb.

To get a better view of the bridge, Sa`id pulled himself up between Zahir and Jamal, the upper half of his body leaning over their seat back.

The sign to the right as they began to cross was in Spanish, "Puente de la Paz" it read, and Sa`id asked Zahir what it meant. Zahir hesitated as he struggled with the translation.

"It means bridge of uhh…, Peace bridge is how it is pronounced in English," he explained, beaming before apologizing for his mediocre grasp of the language.

Jamal smiled at the name given the bridge, and he wondered if Zahir would be a good candidate to replace Monsour. If not Zahir, perhaps there was someone else among the faithful at the mosque with a good command of English. Someone who knew Spanish as well as "American" English would be an asset on the next leg of their journey, Jamal thought. This was the very reason he'd picked Monsour when assembling his group since, despite his shortcomings, most notably a quick temper, Monsour could speak Spanish. This was a result of Monsour having spent his childhood in Spain, the son of a Saudi embassy official.

They passed the mosque on the way to the apartment where they would be staying for the next several days. Zahir said they could easily walk the short distance to the mosque from the apartment building for morning prayers. He offered to meet them in the morning to show them the way. That would be a good time to talk, he emphasized, reminding them of the discovered electronic listening device, looking into each of their eyes as they nodded in understanding.

Zahir continued the one-sided conversation in the apartment building's lone elevator while Jamal,

Sa`id, and Khalib glanced at each other but maintained their silence, unsure if Zahir was testing them. After a brief tour of their living quarters, Zahir ushered them out on to the balcony of the twelfth-floor apartment. From this height, the Parana River in the distance looked like a dark ribbon, hemmed in by twinkling lights along the bank that guided its journey. To the south, with the help of a full moon, they could just make out the wispy clouds of water vapor that rose from Iguazu` Falls. Zahir bade them farewell, and the weary travelers settled in for the night.

The voice of the *muezzin* chanting the *azaan* floated through the open windows of the apartment. The call to prayer was barely audible in the distance and, from moment to moment, depending on the direction of the morning breeze, would cease for a second only to begin again with a flutter of the curtains.

In the semi-conscious state that precedes waking, Jamal was being gently roused by his father back at his boyhood home in the suburbs of Cairo. As a young boy, he and his father had gone many times to the banks of the Nile, sometimes to fish, other times to stand there in awe of its broad expanse. Due to the demands of his father's ill-gotten government job, these sojourns came to an end and soon Jamal's rebellious teenage years began. Two decades and a multitude of philosophical differences had estranged them from one another. Jamal was about to speak to his father when Khalib's pungent body odor wafted past his nose, waking him from his dream. Khalib stood beside him, gently rocking him by the shoulder, encouraging him to get up lest they miss morning prayers.

"Have we no time to cleanse our bodies before going?" Jamal protested out loud, rubbing the sleep from his eyes before looking toward Sa`id who stood there impatiently next to Khalib.

"Zahir is waiting for us downstairs," Khalib informed him.

Jamal glanced at them in disgust before jumping out of bed. He dressed hurriedly, taking just a moment to step out on to the balcony for another look at the river before leaving the apartment.

The unfamiliar surroundings, seen for the first time in daylight, kept them preoccupied during the walk to the mosque. They marveled at the abundance of trees and dense vegetation lining the avenue. No mention was made concerning the execution of plans that lie ahead for the trio, despite Zahir's subtle prodding.

After prayers, they were invited into the imam's office along with several of his confidants, including Zahir, for sweets and tea. Imam Badawi, wearing a flowing *salwar kameez,* seemed, at first, annoyed by their presence. Despite custom, he warned them to use first names only and after the abbreviated introductions, Jamal spoke.

"Our 'brothers' back at home in the Middle East and around the world wish me to thank the local Muslim community here in Ciudad del

Estrellas for your loyal support and generous financial contributions to our struggle. It has become increasingly difficult for us to obtain money, especially American dollars to buy...."

Before Jamal could finish, the imam interrupted and pointed toward Ali, a short, stocky, moon-faced man with an air of agreeable comportment about him who smiled earnestly at Jamal and the others.

"Ali has been in charge of our money dealings and investments. He has developed a mutually beneficial rapport with local officials."

Ali bowed his head in recognition of the compliment and the imam continued.

"Your cause is ours, and we will continue to do what we can to help. Of course, many of us here have families, so the help we give to you, and your two friends, must be discreet."

Everyone in the room nodded in agreement and prayers were offered for the three new arrivals.

"If you intend to stay with us, we may be able to find work for you," Ali suggested, yet unsure of their reason of coming here.

Jamal reached inside his cloth garment and produced a wrinkled envelope, which he handed to the imam.

"This letter is from a shared acquaintance of ours in Damascus. I trust it will explain the nature of our business and the urgency of our needs," Jamal stated matter-of-factly.

After he finished reading the contents of the letter, the imam spoke with increased deference to Jamal and his companions.

"Our mutual friend," Imam Badawi said, waving the letter, "speaks highly of you and your mission. I hope we may be of service to you.'

Jamal bowed slightly, saying, "Thank you."

"Perhaps, we should go outside and enjoy the garden while we discuss your needs further," the imam suggested, tearing the letter into confetti.

He arose from his chair and ushered the others toward the doorway. It led out to lush flowerbeds adjacent to the mosque. The view of the gardens and its admirers was blocked from the street by a high stucco wall. Only Ali and Zahir followed the imam and his three guests out into the enclosed compound. They strolled three abreast down the paths of the garden, Jamal and Ali on either side of the imam followed by Zahir, Sa`id, and Khalib, all six with hands clasped behind their backs.

The imam spoke in a slow deliberate manner, the same way he walked, as if contemplating each individual step before the next.

"Zahir informs me that you lost a man on the voyage over. Monsour, was that his name? What were the circumstances of his death?"

All three travelers spoke at once, but Jamal silenced the other two with a menacing glance over his shoulder.

"He disappeared during the next to last night of our journey. No one saw him after we went to bed. There had been a storm during the night."

"Perhaps he was swept overboard?" Imam Badawi speculated with the questioning raise of an eyebrow.

"Perhaps, but I don't think so," Jamal said, shrugging slowly. "A life ring was missing near the back of the ship, close to where we found this." He produced the strip of cloth that had snagged on the weld on the aft deck of the *Empress*. "There was a tobacco pipe found near by that belonged to the captain of the ship. He smoked there most nights by his own admission, though he denied being there on that night due to the terrible weather."

"You are suspicious of the captain?" The imam asked, pausing to take in the heavy scent of a flowering rose bush along the path before looking at Jamal. "I believe he has transported other cargo before, both human and otherwise, without incident."

"So he has," Jamal offered, stroking his goatee, "but I sensed a nervousness about him, such as a doe about to kid. Possibly it is just his nature."

With that said, Jamal grasped the imam's arm to halt their progress and turned to face him and the others.

"We have come too far, with too much at stake, to let one of our own betray us now," Jamal lectured.

He spoke in a stern manner intended for all standing there to hear, and everyone nodded their heads in understanding of his meaning.

They continued their walk through the garden for a minute with the silence broken only by the call of a lone dove before the imam finally spoke.

"I will make contact today with our mutual friends across the Atlantic and have them inquire about the captain's allegiance.... I will inform them of the unusual circumstances of your voyage."

Jamal nodded his approval.

"Yes, I think it is worth the risk to make contact. With the loss of Monsour, we are a man short for our mission. I'm not sure if my superiors will think it wise to continue if our plan is compromised. Three of us would be adequate once we reach America, but the trip over here has given me time to think. Too much time, perhaps. Monsour was the only one of us capable of carrying on a conversation in Spanish."

The imam gazed into Jamal's eyes and smiled as if to say he understood. The others listened intently as Jamal continued.

"I am worried about our time in Mexico, before we cross the border. Someone conversant in their language would be a blessing, but they must be of the faith, and...," he hesitated, "willing to seek paradise through martyrdom."

In that instant, Jamal looked toward Sa`id and Khalib, both of whom returned his stare, unflinchingly. Next, he fixed his eyes upon Zahir who had fallen a half step behind the others and had turned away from Jamal, lowering his eyes toward the lush grass beneath his slippers.

On the way here from Buenos Aires, Zahir had been eager to hear of their plans, Jamal thought, but now he seemed more reluctant, more reserved. The air of bravado had disappeared from Zahir's manner since yesterday's trip.

"He must be disciplined and accept instructions from me without question," Jamal added.

A candidate with these attributes might be hard to find on short notice, he surmised.

As they continued among the paths, Ali and the imam conferred intently with each other, gradually leaving the three new arrivals behind under the shade of a large tree as the sun neared its zenith. Zahir lagged even further behind, keeping to himself, not wanting to broach the subject of being a replacement for Monsour. Finally, Ali and the imam stopped their heated discussion, having reached an accord, and returned to the others.

"We own a large piece of property, over two thousand hectares, eighty kilometers west of Ciudad del Estrellas," Ali confided proudly to the guests. "We do much of our work there and also have a fledgling madrasa for the devout to study Muhammad's teachings."

Imam Badawi interjected, "I believe we might have someone there who would be suitable for your needs during the remainder of your journey."

Ali began again, his voice almost a whisper, "It is the location of our airstrip from which you will be able to continue your travels. A training area is available if you wish to practice with any weapons."

A broad smile crossed Jamal's face as he directed his comments toward Ali.

"Your business acumen has served you well. I'm sure members of your mosque are grateful, as we are," he offered, gesturing toward Sa`id and

Khalib as he continued. "They would be quite interested in visiting your school, perhaps even assisting with teaching during our stay."

Sa'id and Khalib nodded in agreement. This was an area in which they held sway over Jamal. He accepted this as a necessary part of their devotion to the mission. It made up for their naiveté of how the world outside a madrasa worked. Jamal deferred all religious matters to them and they in turn acknowledged him as their leader and spokesman. This was what Jamal needed for his plans to succed: blind obedience to his instructions. A trait that had been thoroughly embedded (he hoped) in his two subordinates during the last six months as they prepared for this undertaking. Infidels and injustice to the Muslim faith were what fueled Sa'id and Khalib's jihadist desires. Jamal's reasons for jihad were more complex and not based solely on religious grounds.

Ali, having slipped away momentarily, returned, proudly handing Jamal an envelope containing crisp, new, American one hundred dollar bills.

"This money will work for you in Ciudad del Estrellas and in Mexico, but be careful where you use it once you reach the United States."

Jamal understood. The imam suggested that Zahir take them downtown to the market this afternoon when prayers at the mosque were finished. They could buy western-style clothes, food, and other items they needed for their stay at the apartment. In a day or two, when they were well rested, Zahir would bring them to the ranch, or *hacienda* as Ali liked to call it.

After prayers, Ali and Imam Badawi went their separate ways while Zahir escorted the trio to his car. Sa'id and Khalib were complaining of hunger before he'd pulled away from the curb. Jamal was more disciplined, but he too thought a good meal was in order, having eaten very little since departing the *Empress of Sayda* nearly two days ago. Zahir, eager to steer the conversation away from any talk of a fourth traveling companion, quickly suggested a couple of places to eat in downtown Ciudad del Estrellas, rattling them off in haste. And, before his guests could make a choice, he headed to the one of his own liking.

Upon their arrival at the outdoor café, the four of them sat down at a table near the sidewalk. The owner of the small restaurant, a thin, hyperactive, middle-aged man with a tobacco-stained smile and a regular at the mosque, came out to greet them. Zahir introduced his new companions in Arabic, explaining to the owner what part of the world the visitors were from. The café owner promptly shouted instructions to the nearest waiter, knowing from experience what these hungry travelers would enjoy.

Everyone at the table wolfed down the steaming couscous and roasted lamb as soon as it was placed before them. After a couple of minutes of silent gluttony and observation of the passers-by on the sidewalk, Khalib commented that he'd not eaten food like this since leaving Damascus on their journey to board the freighter in Lagos two weeks past. Sa'id added that if not for the way some of the women passing by were dressed, he would feel at home on this street.

Persian rug vendors, computer and cell phone shops, in addition to money-changing kiosk, lined both sides of the avenue. Wisps of smoke from the open-air grills, laced with the spicy aroma of saffron and marjoram, hung like tendrils from the canopy above the tables. The hazy fragrance seeped out into the street and paused there, trapped between the burden of humidity and the swirls of breeze created by passing automobiles.

The indigo sky formed a brilliant backdrop for the shop signs, colorfully printed in Portuguese, Taiwanese, Guarani, Spanish, and Arabic, which hung above every doorway. Gone were the plain-clothed guards, armed with automatic weapons, who'd fronted many of the buildings the night before when they drove through the city for the first time.

It was early afternoon, and the streets of Ciudad del Estrellas teemed with shoppers who had crossed the bridge from Brazil, hunting bargains from all corners of the world. Taxes were low and duties non-existent on all purchased goods. Local laws governing the maximum value of products that could be taken back across the border were rarely enforced. Everything from Asian silk to the latest American computer software could be found here—authentic and otherwise.

Sa'id and Khalib turned their chairs so as not to face the sidewalk. Still, with each passing woman, their necks craned, food spilling from the corners of their mouths. They gave hard looks of disapproval to the Asian and South American women baring skin and daring to return their stares, but nodded to each other in approval of the women properly attired and deferent to them.

Full stomachs and the warm air, laden with familiar scents, had the effect of opium on the three foreigners. They spoke freely as the underlying current of tension that had kept their talk guarded for the last few days began to unwind. Eddies of nervousness surrounding them, a result of the clandestine nature of their trip and the loss of Monsour, began to dissipate.

The younger two, Khalib and Sa`id, no more than eighteen but with ample facial hair, talked about: the freighter, the waterfall, and, as always, the madrasa; where they'd spent the past twelve years of their lives. It was all they had. Their history, their recollections were all from there, and any opinions or actions on their part in the past or present were forged during the years at the madrasa.

Nearly twice their age, Jamal, after two weeks of constant companionship, knew their short biographies by heart. He was more interested in talking with Zahir. The conversation on the way here from Buenos Aires had been about local people and the mosque, in addition, Zahir had shown a keen interest in their plans for jihad that seemed to be lacking now. Jamal wanted to understand him better. He hoped he'd misjudged Zahir's disinterest back at the mosque this morning.

"You said you had a young wife, Zahir. Do you have any children?"

"Yes, yes, I have a baby daughter," Zahir answered, shifting uneasily in his chair. This was a conversation he had been dreading but had prepared for as he continued with an air of pride. "My wife is expecting another child. I believe it will be a boy."

Jamal nodded his head understandingly as the father-son bond was not lost on him, noting also that Zahir's English was better today.

"That is good news. Congratulations my friend. When is the baby due?"

"In about seven months, I..., I ... mean in less than two months," he stammered. "My first child is eight—no—eleven months old."

Jamal and Zahir smiled at each other.

"I have a wife and son who...," Jamal thought for a second, trying to make eye contact before continuing, "whose age escapes me at the moment." He gave an abbreviated laugh and shrugged his shoulders.

Zahir had his head down, staring into the steaming Turkish coffee the waiter had just placed in front of him, biting his lip as he thought about what to say next to Jamal. He knew, from the imam's response after reading the letter presented to him this morning, that any request of Jamal's would be granted. Zahir wondered what exactly the letter said. He wondered too about the fate of this one's wife and son. He began to speak again, this time in a cowed tone.

"I love my wife dearly. She had much trouble with her first child," Zahir explained convincingly, looking pleadingly into Jamal's dark, emotionless eyes. He added, "I am not as strong of faith as you three are to have traveled this far."

Zahir glanced toward Sa`id and Khalib, who were absorbed in their own discussion. "I fear I would not have the courage when it was most required of me," he confessed, hoping to quell any thoughts by Jamal of asking him to come along on the remainder of their trip.

Jamal placed a hand on Zahir's shoulder before speaking matter-of-factly, "I am not so strong of faith as those two, and one can never truly know one's courage until it is called upon him. What I do possess is an unwavering conviction in my ideology and the methods necessary to bring it to fruition. Perhaps this person that Ali and the imam spoke of will fit our needs. Rest easy for now, Zahir. And take care of your young wife."

They finished their coffee in silence. Zahir swallowed each sip with difficulty as he considered what the consequences might be if he was forced to choose whether or not to go with Jamal and the other two. In addition, he hadn't been totally honest with Jamal concerning his wife, and he hoped Jamal would not find out the truth while he was still here in Ciudad del Estrellas.

Jamal mocked Sa`id and Khalib's eating habits. Pointing out the bits of couscous in their beards that looked like an infestation of nits. Everyone had a good laugh over this, including Zahir, before a worried look reappeared on his face. After collecting the change from a new one hundred dollar bill, Jamal thanked the owner for the excellent meal and tipped the waiter handsomely.

They meandered through the streets of the market for most of the afternoon, picking over the fruits and vegetables piled high on rickety wooden tables that fronted the makeshift booths. In other stalls, leather goods that the region was known for—wallets, shoulder bags, and satchels with intricate stitching—were purchased by Jamal for use during their remaining travels.

In the clothing stores, there was much discussion among the four of them concerning what type of apparel would blend in best once they were in America. Sa`id and Khalib were reluctant to wear anything other than their current robes and slippers as Jamal argued with them impatiently, out of earshot of the other patrons in the store. Finally, they agreed to wear the new clothes but only once they were on their way to Mexico. Jamal could sense the agitation that had resurfaced inadvertently in his young cohorts.

They made their way slowly back to Zahir's car, knowing each day, each hour, brought them incrementally closer to their goal: their end.

The blue tile floor and minaret of the mosque; the taste of the succulent lamb; the fragrances of freshly ground coffee, newly tanned leather, and burning loose-leaf tobacco; the soothing familiarity of veiled women; the carnival-like atmosphere of the market; had all been a lullaby for Sa`id and Khalib. These reminders of home had served to tamp down the omnipresent thoughts of jihad, and its shadow, death, which smoldered inside them just below this temporary façade. The newly purchased clothes were a potent reminder of why they had come here, having the effect of bellows that rekindled those thoughts.

Jamal insisted that Zahir stop by the mosque on the way to the apartment. Zahir, having other plans this evening, protested, using the need to get home to his wife as an excuse and offered to drop them off with all their purchases but not wait on them, saying they could walk home from the mosque. Jamal's own embers began to flare at this suggestion and, using a threatening tone of voice that allowed for no rebuttal, he ordered Zahir to leave the car and its contents at the mosque. Zahir mistakenly argued, and Jamal informed him the only way he would see his dear wife would be to leave the car and walk home at a brisk pace.

Evening prayers restored a level of calmness to Sa`id and Khalib. It was a balm that soothed their irritated psyche. The imam was there to offer soothing words. He, Khalib, and Sa`id talked at length. Their discussion centered on various passages from the Qur`an and the meanings they conveyed to the true believer.

Jamal had finished his prayers long before the others and he stepped outside the mosque into the street. Drawing deeply on a cigarette from a pack he'd found in Zahir's car, Jamal leaned against the front fender, holding his breath, savoring the moment before exhaling. It was the first he'd smoked in over four years, and it tasted exquisite.

He had finished it, as well as a second one, before he heard the voices of Khalib and Sa`id, sounding less disturbed, as they left the mosque. Jamal put away a third one unlit, not wanting to rile his devout companions after them having been calmed by prayer.

Back at the apartment, they spent the remainder of the evening listening to newly purchased tapes of Qur`anic verses they'd found that afternoon at the market. Jamal tolerated the tapes, though they were a distraction as he mulled over the plans he'd mapped out so meticulously for the rest of their endeavors.

The next morning brought a series of storms that kept them in the apartment except for a couple of rain-soaking jaunts to the mosque for prayers. On the first of these trips, Zahir was present, and Jamal offered a brief apology and the keys to his car. Jamal decided that because of the storm it would be better to wait until the next day to see the *hacienda* Ali had invited them to visit.

Sa`id and Khalib kept up their enchantment with the tapes late into the evening, forcing Jamal, still considering his plans, to retreat to the balcony for some peace of mind. The constant beat of the rain on the concrete floor provided less of a distraction from his thoughts. It was also a good place to enjoy one more cigarette. Through the haze of smoke and rain, the distant Parana River now blended into the surrounding landscape. The twinkling lights of Ciudad del Estrellas that had so distinctly marked the river's borders on the previous clear night, blurred into a kaleidoscope of colors, merging into one pattern then, a second later, diverging into many new ones.

Jamal was unaccustomed to a rain like this—a downpour—lasting for hours before easing into a steady drizzle. In his native country, a rain of this duration was a novelty, something to be talked about for days afterward.

He didn't need the enticement of paradise, like Sa`id and Khalib, to wage jihad, still he was curious if it rained there. It stood to reason, he thought, that to have all the lush, tropical vegetation it would have to rain a lot. Wouldn't it? Of course, if it was paradise, maybe rain wasn't needed at all to make the flowers bloom and the trees bear fruit; maybe one never thirsted for water. Several deep breathes in succession cleared the smoke from his lungs and brought into them the cleansed air, heavy with ozone. He decided that a rain of this duration would be a good addition to paradise, regardless of any biological need.

Unlike his two underlings, Jamal did not need the requirement of a constant stream of religion washing over him to keep his hatred focused on the West or on other corrupt governments closer to home. His indoctrination had not come from a single source such as the madrasa, but rather from a multitude of insults and half-truths, presented to his Muslim brothers in the form of morally bankrupt policies from puppet governments whose strings were manipulated by hands in the United States and Europe; illegitimate governments whose sole purpose was to enrich its leaders and their close relatives.

He even despised some of the Mullahs in his own faith who had grown exceedingly rich, though he kept it to himself now. Once, on the freighter, during a long discussion, he'd mentioned this belief to the other three but was met with a cascade of vehement denials and threats that stopped just short of bodily harm. The inequities bestowed upon he and others in the Middle East were everlastingly imprinted upon him. Jamal needed only a little quiet time for reflection on these indignities to stoke the flames of jihad within him.

By sunrise the storm had passed. The air felt crisp and cool with no hint of the moisture that had weighed it down since they'd first arrived in Ciudad del Estrellas. After prayers, Zahir chauffeured the trio to the *hacienda* where Ali awaited them. The silence of their driver went unnoticed by the other three as they marveled at the dense corridor of palm trees and squat shrubs that formed a tunnel of vegetation along the road. Occasional gaps in the greenery offered them a peak at the vast expanse of grassland that lie beyond.

Ali greeted them jovially with a wide grin from beneath his oversized cowboy hat, suggesting they take a tour of the *hacienda* in a much-repaired World War II vintage jeep. Zahir stayed behind at the ranch headquarters. As soon as they were out of sight over the first low hill he headed back to Ciudad del Estrellas.

The *hacienda* had very little open pastureland and consisted mostly of small meadows interspersed among broad reaches of scrub timber and brush that replaced the heavily logged areas. An ideal layout, Ali explained, since most of the profits on the ranch came from endeavors other than livestock. He was particularly proud of the long airstrip that could accommodate larger twin-engine planes.

From the sky, the length of the airstrip appeared much shorter, barely long enough for a single engine plane. This was due to several massive *quebracho* trees on either side of the runway whose canopy completely hid parts of the strip. These trees, along with two moveable, fake hills of ingenious design—flatbed wagons, filled with soil in which grew small trees and bushes, covered with camouflage-painted plywood and netting that could be quickly pulled out of the way by a tractor or jeep—made it impossible for the casual observer to see the runway's true length. Even to a trained eye from above, it appeared to be a short airstrip usable only by small aircraft.

During the tour, Ali also took them to a building that he called the print shop hidden deep within one section of timber. Powered by a diesel generator, it housed sophisticated printers and computers capable of producing high quality counterfeit currency if the right grade of paper was used in the process. Also, transportation documents could be forged here with skill. Before they left the shop, Ali had a feeble old man of European descent, working there alone, take pictures of his three transient guests.

Sa`id and Khalib, both of whom had been silent for most of the jeep ride, were talking heatedly to one another now. During the photography session, Ali gave them a shirt, jacket, and tie to wear over their traditional garments. This sparked an emotional response from both, similar to the outburst in the clothing store two days before. But Jamal would have none of it today, quickly stifling their discontent with harsh words. With their final destination drawing nearer each day, Jamal grew less tolerant of Sa'id's and Khalib's adolescent behavior.

Back in the jeep, Ali told them it would take a day or two before their travel documents would be ready. Jamal nodded his head in approval and inquired about the availability of a plane since they'd not come across one during their tour of the property.

Ali assured him a plane was due to arrive the next day. It would be available to ferry them to Mexico whenever they were ready to go. Jamal tugged on his goatee as they bounced across the rough ground back toward the headquarters of the *hacienda*. He asked if the plane was capable of making it to their destination in Mexico without refueling. Ali suggested it would be difficult, besides, he explained, there would be other cargo on the plane; cargo that needed to be delivered to business associates in Columbia. The plane could be refueled at that stop and easily take them on to the airstrip southwest of Matamoras.

"The pilot knows of our final destination?" Jamal asked, half to himself, lost in thought.

"No," came the quick reply from Ali. "No one besides the four of us in this jeep and, of course, the imam, know any details of your plans."

"Does the pilot speak English or Arabic? How will he know where to take us?" Jamal queried, twisting the long hairs on his chin into a braid.

"The pilot only knows Spanish, and perhaps a little English, but don't worry, he has been to both landing strips before, carrying drugs and other elicit cargo." Ali brought the jeep to a halt as he continued, "He will not know you are going with him until the moment you board the plane."

Ali crawled over the broken door of the jeep that refused to open. He'd parked the jeep next to one of the low-slung, tin-roofed, windowless buildings that made up a majority of the structures around the compound. Beside these, stood a long rectangular building with evenly spaced windows that resembled a dormitory. At the far end of this building, another smaller one sat perpendicular to it. Ali said it housed a kitchen at one end and an open room at the other that served as a mess hall and study area. A short covered porch connected the two buildings and gave them a T-shaped appearance from the sky. He explained how the orientation of the buildings, along with a row of lights on the roof's peak, pointed the way to the airstrip. This made it easier for the pilot to locate the runway both day and night, reminding his guests, with pride, of how well disguised the runway was.

"I'm still worried about our time in Mexico," Jamal confided to Ali as they strolled across the muddy parking lot with Sa`id and Khalib following at some distance behind them. "With none of us able to speak the language, I fear we will be at the mercy of those we hire to smuggle us across the border."

Ali nodded his head to acknowledge Jamal's concern.

Jamal continued, "I have considered asking Zahir to join us, but with his wife and child…."

Ali interrupted Jamal with a chuckle, "Zahir has no child. Why, he only just got married three months ago. He's been lax in his duties ever since, but I believe...."

"Zahir has no children?" Jamal hissed under his breath.

"None at all," Ali reiterated.

Jamal felt his face flush with anger at being deceived. Zahir had seemed sincere, though absent-minded, Jamal thought, and himself gullible at the outdoor café in Ciudad del Estrellas. That would not happen again. It was a weakness. Jamal turned to the other two and started to speak but thought better of it. A show of emotion was a sign of weakness, also; one his younger cohorts had an ample supply of. They hadn't been listening to his conversation with Zahir at the café anyway, he reasoned. Better to take care of this matter himself. Zahir would know his wrath in good time.

"Forgive my interruption. I fear I have been duped, as a joke," Jamal offered, calmly.

"I believe the 'coyotes' in Mexico can be trusted. I've done business with them before and I've paid them well. Their loyalty can always be bought at a price," Ali said, grinning.

Jamal admired the business-like demeanor of Ali and felt he could be trusted, but concern about the trip still gnawed at him. The loss of Monsour so early in the journey haunted him more than he cared to admit, and now this business with Zahir deceiving him. Ali could see the worried look on Jamal's face and responded.

"Please, come inside for lunch,' he offered, climbing the three wooden steps onto the porch that fronted the kitchen. "I have someone here I would like you to meet. Perhaps this one can be of service to you during the remainder of your journey. And, I'm quite certain he has no wife or child." Ali said, winking at Jamal, who was still visibly upset by Zahir's lies.

The screen door creaked as Ali opened it. He ushered the three jihadists past him into the dining area, which doubled as a classroom during other times of the day. He called out to the unseen cook and in a short time the aroma of smoked meat aroused their hunger. Sliced strips of beef and corn tortillas along with chopped tomatoes, sweet onions, and green bell peppers were placed on the table in front of them. The guests had seated themselves on the rough-hewn benches that ran along either side. After blessing their food, Khalib and Sa`id pelted Ali with questions between mouthfuls of food.

They recognized from the contents of the room: a chalkboard that lined one entire wall and displaying verses scribbled on it in Arabic; another wall, lined with shelves, holding neatly placed copies of the Qur`an, notebooks with worn covers and dog-eared pages; a banner with crescent moon and star hanging from the ceiling, that this was a place of religious study. Though smaller and more crudely built than the madrasa they'd grown up in back home, its similarity put them at ease.

Ali excused himself and went to the door of the adjacent building. He stuck his head inside and shouted in Spanish to some unseen occupant, his voice echoing back to his guests in the dining hall. "Ibrahim" was the only word recognizable to them. Jamal, Sa`id, and Khalib leaned across the table, their heads almost touching one another as they peered through the window to get a glimpse past Ali into the connected building. From where they sat, they could see a row of bunk beds spaced between the windows lining the east wall. Next, they heard footsteps on the wooden floor and soon a face appeared beside Ali's. A few inaudible words were spoken between the two, then the new face, devoid of hair, attached to gangling arms and legs, followed Ali back into the dining room.

"*As-salaamu `alaykum,*" were the first words, just above a whisper, out of his mouth when he saw the three guests seated at the table.

"*Wa `alaykum `as-salaam,*" they replied in unison.

Ibrahim sat down at their request and politely refused the food they offered. He'd eaten just before their arrival, he explained in halting Arabic, learned from his studies of the Qur`an. When he couldn't find the right word in Arabic, he would speak fluently in Spanish to Ali, who acted as an interpreter. Before long, it was obvious his English was adequate also. Jamal guessed him to be younger than Sa`id and Khalib by a couple of years.

They finished their meal while Sa`id and Khalib quizzed Ibrahim in earnest about his studies of the Qur`an. He in turn peppered them with questions of his own: Where were they from? Had they made the pilgrimage to Mecca and Medina? Did they hope to become imams themselves? Could either of them be called a *hafiz*, having memorized the entire Qur`an?

An easy bond formed between them. Their backgrounds, though molded on separate continents, gave them an air of familiarity with one another; such as that experienced by childhood cousins, meeting for the first time on a summer outing—neither having seen the other before in the flesh, yet easily recognizable to one another—of the same blood based on looks, patterns of speech, and a family history repeated to them many times by mothers, who, though separated by thousands of miles, had remained close.

Ibrahim, Sa`id, and Khalib continued their banter at the table as Jamal and Ali left the dining hall. Ali had a few more hidden gems scattered about the hacienda he wished to show Jamal. As Ali shepherded him around the mud holes that pockmarked the parking lot toward another tin-roofed building, Jamal inquired about Ibrahim.

"Is Ibrahim native to this area?"

"Yes," Ali replied. "He was born in Argentina. His mother was native to that country, but his father, Mustafa, was from Palestine. Mustafa was a good man, almost a martyr, before the police in Buenos Aires put him on the run. He made it to Ciudad del Estrellas with his family when Ibrahim was no more than two, maybe three. They'd lived here six months before Mustafa disappeared."

"The police?" Jamal asked, uneasily.

Ali shrugged, "Possibly. But there are other groups out there who work with stealth against us."

Ali looked to Jamal who returned his gaze knowingly.

"And what became of his wife?"

"She was young, a recent convert to Islam. Soon, she became lonely for her family. Imam Badawi persuaded her to leave the boy with friends in Ciudad del Estrellas, convincing her that Mustafa would want him reared as a Muslim. At her age, she was easily swayed and eager to return to Buenos Aires—with money in her pocket—to start a new life. Ibrahim lived with my family and others until we started the madrasa here at the hacienda. Once he was old enough, he joined the few other orphans living here."

"He looks young."

"I believe he turned sixteen back in December. I've lost track over the years, quite honestly."

"Is he capable of doing what I ask of him?"

"Very capable," Ali said without hesitation as he searched his pockets for a key to the building at which they'd stopped. "The imam and myself have been involved with his instruction over the years. He has had ample time for indoctrination about the injustice to our faith, and to his father. In addition, he is a hard worker and has become quite good at running machinery around the hacienda."

"I don't plan on sowing the seeds of jihad with a tractor and plow," Jamal was quick to point out.

Ali, undeterred by the sarcasm that hung from Jamal's words, continued, "Ibrahim will do what is required of him. He is loyal. It won't take much to light the fire of jihad in him. And, who knows, his ability to drive a heavy truck or tractor might be needed. Are Sa`id and Khalib capable of that? And, don't forget, he speaks Spanish quite well."

Jamal couldn't make out the contents of the windowless building from just the light filtering through the opened door. But, as his vision adjusted to the dimness and Ali located the light switch, Ali's private arsenal was illuminated before Jamal's disbelieving eyes.

On the wall to the left was a double rack of automatic rifles. Ali boasted that he always kept at least fifty on hand, selling the excess as they came into his possession if the market was profitable. The rifles were complimented by cases of ammunition stacked in metal cases head high. Down the center of the room, several sturdy shelves cradled boxes of grenades, both hand and rocket-propelled varieties. Next to them, in a crate with the its lid askew, were Glock 9mm handguns as yet unpacked, along with three polished-leather, shoulder harnesses hanging from a pointed corner of the lid.

Along the wall opposite the door, at the far corner of the room, was a stainless steel sink and attached countertop ten feet in length. A metal fluorescent shop light hung low over it. Above the counter, at eye level, were three rows of shelves that held a dozen containers each marked with the name of the chemical compound they held at bay. One was marked with the letters PETD, another RDX, and others with skull and crossbones in addition to their label names. Jamal, because of years spent in organized training camps, was well versed in their individual properties, as well as the expected results when a catalyst was introduced. On the other side of the sink, held in place by a metal rod that served as a spindle, were two spools of small diameter, insulated, copper wire. Near by were several switching devices, rolls of electrical tape, and tools need to work with the wire.

Jamal commended Ali on his well-stocked arsenal. Ali, in return of the compliment, wore the smile of a proud father whose son had just kicked the winning goal at a soccer match.

"If any of these will be of help to you, it is yours to use," Ali offered, before heading back toward the rifle rack. "Perhaps, we should go have some target practice."

Jamal nodded in agreement, grabbing a box of ammunition in one hand and selecting a rifle with the other. He slung the rifle over his shoulder and went back for one of the handguns, explaining to Ali that he'd not had much practice with a pistol and probably wouldn't have much use for a rifle. If he had to use a gun during the remainder of the operation, it would most likely be at close quarters where a rifle would be too cumbersome to maneuver and too hard to conceal. They loaded the new weaponry into the jeep, heading deep into the timber toward the firing range.

The sun was a red ball just above the horizon, shimmering on the distant treetops in the evening heat, as Ali steered the jeep back into the gravel parking lot. He pointed out the imam's car parked under the shade of a tree near the front of the burgeoning madrasa.

Imam Badawi was in the dining hall with Khalib, Sa'id, Ibrahim and the other students, but when he heard the jeep pull up outside he headed out to greet Ali and Jamal.

"It is late in the day for you to still be here. It isn't even the right day, is it?" Ali remarked with a puzzled look on his face.

The imam responded, "No, but I wasn't sure of Jamal and the others' plans for tonight; if they were spending the night here or heading back to town. With the problems we've been experiencing of late, I was reluctant to use the phone."

As a rule, the imam came out three days a week usually arriving just before noon and leaving by four. Other volunteers from the mosque's congregation carried out the rest of the students' instruction.

Jamal sensed the uneasiness in the imam's manner and queried anxiously, "You have news from our brothers overseas?"

"Yes, it seems your instincts concerning the captain of the ship may be correct. His wife and daughter left Beirut over two weeks ago, and none of their relatives seem to know how long they would be gone or where they went—but it was discovered their house had been sold."

Jamal and Ali contemplated this news in silence. Before anyone spoke, Sa'id joined them, telling Jamal that he and Khalib intended to stay at the ranch tonight. Jamal, his thoughts elsewhere, didn't register Sa'id's remark until Sa'id had reached the top step on the way back into the dining hall, calling after him, "Ask Khalib if there is anything extra he needs from the apartment. After tonight, I will not be going back into Ciudad del Estrellas."

Sa`id nodded before continuing into the building. Jamal turned to Imam Badawi and thanked him for relaying the information. This news concerning Captain Farroque fueled his paranoia that began with the unexplained loss of Monsour. Jamal decided it best not to delay their plans any longer than necessary, telling Ali he would be back the next day with their clothes from the apartment. Without waiting for Sa`id's return, Jamal left with the imam.

Darkness settled in and the moon was not yet up. For Jamal, the road back to Ciudad del Estrellas—which during the morning drive out seemed so appealing—now appeared as an ominous tunnel built of vegetation. He felt like prey on the run from an unseen predator, waiting just around the next curve in the road. Even if Captain Farroque had turned away from their cause, Jamal wondered, why would he have cause to kill Monsour.

They'd driven for twenty minutes without a word between them. Imam Badawi tried to imagine what was going on inside Jamal's head. The imam was undeniably devout and, based on his sermons, espoused a degree of radicalism, though only as much as he thought his congregation wanted to hear. None who worshiped at the mosque were extremists, voicing their faith stridently to the world, as a counterweight, only when confronted with Christianity's militaristic tendancies.

He could not picture himself giving up his life as Jamal and the others were preparing to do. As they drove on, Jamal continued in his trance, eyes fixated on the road ahead until, finally, the imam broke the silence.

"What are your thoughts on Ibrahim?"

"He is a fine young Muslim," Jamal responded without shifting his gaze. "Ali feels he would relish the roll of a jihadist."

"But what do you think?"

"I was only with him a short time. He seems a younger version of Sa`id and Khalib."

"Not so much younger, and he speaks Spanish well. Was not that one of your concerns with the loss of Monsour? With Ibrahim's history, tracing his origins back to us would be unlikely in the event he was caught or killed."

The imam sounded like a rug merchant in the medina, extolling the virtues of his latest creation to a skeptical buyer, Jamal mused. He dwelled on the word "killed", thinking it was a good thing the other two jihadists were not privy to this conversation. Still, the imam was right. Ibrahim was fluent in Spanish and no doubt trustworthier than Zahir, but he seemed so young. Jamal was already growing weary of babysitting the other two.

"What do you think of Zahir?" he asked, turning toward the imam.

The imam shrugged with indifference. "He has been much help to Ali and myself since his arrival here in Ciudad del Estrellas, though his own well-being is always at the forefront of his thoughts, I'm afraid."

"Yes, I suspect he would make a reluctant jihadist, but perhaps he could be of service to me while we are in Mexico. Just in case Ibrahim should falter, Zahir could step in to help get us across the border. He could return on the plane after we've met our contacts there."

"I see no problem with that if it would make you feel better," the imam answered.

His snowy turban seemed to glow in the dim light of the dashboard.

The imam continued, "It would do Zahir good to be gone from his wife for a few days. He might appreciate her more instead of worrying me with his ideas of taking a second wife so soon."

That settled it for Jamal. Zahir would come with them no matter how reluctant he might be. He was still upset with Zahir for lying to him about having a child, and now he recalled how devoted Zahir had claimed to be to his young wife. Jamal would not tolerate being played a fool by anyone.

"Perhaps you could have Zahir pick me up tomorrow morning at the apartment. I just need to collect our clothes and equipment before heading back out to your property in the countryside. That would be a good time for you to tell him that I will require his services for a couple of days. I suspect it would be better if he heard it from you."

"As you wish, Jamal. I will telephone him this evening."

The imam dropped Jamal off outside the apartment building. They said their goodbyes for what both knew would be the last time, according to Jamal's altered schedule.

The sign on the door of the single elevator declared it temporarily out of service much to Jamal's dismay. By the ninth floor, his new boots felt like they were made of lead, not leather. He stopped on the landing for a moment to rest and unbutton his jacket. Plodding on the last three flights, his chest heaved as the echoing thud of each heavy step resounded through the stairwell. The door leading into the hallway on the twelfth floor was propped open with a fire extinguisher that had been hanging on the wall.

Not until Jamal reached the apartment door did he realize why the stairwell door had been left open. Finding the apartment door ajar, and hearing, in the growing calmness of his breathe, the mechanical whir of the elevator directly across the hall, he knew he'd been tricked.

The faint glow of the single hallway light bulb allowed Jamal to see the numbers of the floor level indicator above the elevator door. It had just reached the lobby. Jamal decided that by the time he could reach the first floor via the stairs, whoever had been here, would be long gone. Then he heard it.

"Click…, click."

Jamal's breathe stopped involuntarily. His heartbeat was like a drum roll as he listened for the sound from inside the apartment to come again. Fear paralyzed him for an instant. Though not one to be frightened easily, he had not calculated any alternative to what the logic of the moment dictated—that whoever had been in the apartment, heard him trudging up the stairs and took the elevator down. The "out of service' sign had been a clever ruse, Jamal conceded. Hearing the elevator moving and the indicator showing it stopped at the lobby, his brain had made the conclusion automatically—that the intruder or intruders had left. He'd been caught off guard.

Jamal grabbed his ear lobe and twisted it severely. Self-inflicted pain was a method he used to discipline himself, to punish himself, in the hope that it would help prevent him from making the same mistake again. Like a slap on the face to keep oneself awake when sleep begins to intrude on a lengthy drive.

"Click…, click."

The sound came again as Jamal slid his free hand onto the knurled grip of his new, but tested, 9mm pistol. The chrome snap on the leather strap holding the gun in its shoulder holster held fast in its newness, until, with an extra surge of his thumb, it broke free. He winced at the exaggerated sound it made.

With the gun armed and aimed at the darkness that confronted him, Jamal moved through the open doorway of the apartment with the stealth of a hunting cat, crouching along the wall, quietly closing the door behind him, not wanting to be a targeted silhouette from the dimly lit hallway.

Jamal waited long enough for his eyes to adjust to the darkness and to discern the whereabouts of the unseen intruder. The infusion of adrenaline magnified his senses. The hum of the refrigerator sounded like a truck. The sweat above his upper lip had the heft of a lead fishing sinker.

The acrid smell of burnt eggs and toast—cooking mistakes of Sa`id's from this morning—tingled his nostrils. Now, he could make out the phases of the moon listed on the wall calendar beside him. And time slowed its pace.

He was sure the sound, perhaps the loading of a gun, had come from the living room. Moving forward, in darkness, toward the sofa a motion registered in the corner of his eye from the direction of the sliding glass doors that led out onto the balcony. Jamal slithered along the length of the sofa, peering around the corner, the barrel of his gun leading the way, its trigger smothered in the flesh of his finger, less than a micrometer from action. At this angle, with his chin almost touching the worn carpet, smelling the dusky odor of mold with every breathe, the bottom of the curtain that covered the sliding door was visible to him and in that moment the sound came again.

"Click…, click."

Jamal lay there motionless, waiting for the sound, to be sure of its source. He remembered now, they'd left the door to the balcony open this morning, because of Sa`id. The curtain billowed open from the breeze that waxed and waned like an unseen giant's breathe. After the rush of air subsided, the curtain fluttered back against the glass door and a weight attached to the bottom made the familiar sound.

"Click…, click."

Jamal relaxed his grip on the gun, muttering a few words to himself. Grabbing the back of the sofa with his free hand, he pulled himself upright, easing out onto the balcony, his gun still cocked.

The only human signs present were the remnants of cigarette ash smeared into the concrete, the only sensation: the cool breeze he felt while running his fingers through his sweat-dampened hair. Rubbing his ear, Jamal decided he'd come to the right conclusion after all. Whoever was here, heard him coming up the stairs and took off down the elevator.

Suddenly, a vision of the computer cases flashed in his head. Where were they, he asked himself? Just as quickly he remembered, picturing them in the back seat of Zahir's car, between Sa`id and Khalib, on the way out to the ranch this morning, and he breathed a sigh of relief. He had chastised Sa`id and Khalib lately for being lax in keeping the computer cases close to them at all times. The intruder was surely disappointed, Jamal thought, smiling. All that was in the apartment were some new clothes for the other two and his *dishdasha*, discarded yesterday for the less noticeable slacks, shirt, and coat purchased the day before.

Now it was time to find out who the intruder had been as Jamal moved over to the phone sitting on the countertop that separated the kitchenette from the living room. Still cautious, Jamal went back and grabbed a wooden chair, wedging it under the handle of the front door since the jamb had been shattered.

Jamal mulled over the events of the last days since their arrival in Ciudad del Estrellas, setting his gun on the counter beside the phone. On a hunch, he called the number Zahir had given him on that first night when he'd dropped Jamal and the others off at the apartment. A lilting voice answered.

"Ola...."

"I would like to speak with Zahir, please."

There was a silence on the other end and Jamal hesitated, wondering if the person on the other end understood him, or for that matter, if he even had the right number. He tried again, speaking slowly.

"Zahir..., is Zahir there?"

"*Lo siento, no hablo Englais muy bien.*" The voice sounded sheepish now, and quite young, Jamal thought. "Zahir...no home. I told already the imam. Out with un *hombre.*"

"Someone from the mosque?" Jamal asked.

"*No, no eh...eh..., un Norte Americano.*"

Jamal understood her meaning. He stared at his muddled reflection in the glossy surface of the refrigerator as he replaced the receiver back in its cradle. The weak moonlight entering through the windows made his image look like a blackish humanoid form surrounded by shades of gray, then, with no movement on his part, it grew bigger. The pace of time seemed to slow again but only long enough for Jamal's one hand to reach an ear lobe while the other inched toward his gun before a savage blow felled him from behind.

Sunlight streamed into the apartment as Jamal opened his eyes. A string of thick saliva connected his lips to a damp spot on the carpet as he raised his face from it. His head throbbed in rhythm with his pulse as his fingers searched the matted hair at the back of his head. Semi-coagulated blood was evident under his fingernails as he held them up to his eyes and his swimming vision.

On hands and knees he struggled toward the sound of rapid footsteps and high-pitched shrieks of laughter coming from the doorway of the apartment. The door to the apartment was wide open, the remains of the splintered wooden chair lying on the floor in front of it. The footsteps halted and Jamal, trying hard to focus, peered into the eyes of a four-year old—eyes that grew to the size of silver dollars upon the sight of Jamal. Jamal just reached the door with his fingertips, flinging the door shut as the rapid footsteps began again, fading down the hallway toward the call of a female voice. One of the other tenants, Jamal supposed, as he tried to think about what had happened, wondering how long he'd been unconscious. He struggled to his feet, his legs rubbery as he wobbled his way to the bathroom.

The phone rang as Jamal stepped out of the shower, still probing the wound on the back of his scalp. Feeling better after the shower plus a handful of aspirin, he walked steadily to answer the phone.

"Hello," Jamal shouted, noticing the ringing in his ears for the first time.

"Hello, Jamal. It is I, Zahir. The imam said you needed my services this morning."

"Yes, yes. I need you to take me out to see Ali and the others, but first I need to pick up a few last minute supplies from a hardware store."

Jamal wondered if the imam had told Zahir yet about his part in their upcoming trip.

"I am almost to your apartment building. I will wait for you on the street."

"You are welcome to come up and visit while I get ready. I've yet to pack up. I was slow getting up this morning after wearing myself out last night climbing the stairs, but I believe the elevator will be working now."

There was no sound from Zahir for a moment.

"No, I prefer to wait in my car. Please, take your time."

"As you wish," Jamal said, smiling as he hung up the phone.

After last night, perhaps Zahir was afraid to come up to the apartment. Though he had no hard evidence, Jamal was more and more suspicious of Zahir.

Jamal dressed quickly, adjusting the shoulder harness to a more comfortable and easily reached level. He reminded himself to purchase emery cloth while securing the gun in place, satisfied it would work to loosen the snap on the holster. After collecting all of their belongings, he headed for the elevator carrying the oversized duffle bags along with a new leather satchel he'd picked up in the market.

As Jamal exited the apartment building, he could see Zahir pacing the sidewalk next to his car, cigarette in one hand and cell phone in the other, engaging in what appeared to be a spirited conversation. Zahir stopped his telephone conversation abruptly and stood upright, as if at attention, when he caught sight of Jamal approaching the car.

"I'm sorry I could not stay at the ranch yesterday. My wife needed me back at home."

Jamal smiled as he spoke. "Yes, that is understandable. It was not a problem. The imam brought me home last night. We had time to talk on the way back to Ciudad del Estrellas."

"And where are the others, Khalib and Sa'id?"

"They decided to stay out at Ali's hacienda last night. In honesty, it was a relief for me. We have not much in common to talk about. They are so young and inexperienced in the ways of the world, unlike you and me. Your company is much preferred as we can talk about our families."

Jamal rubbed the back of his throbbing head, wincing, as he studied Zahir's expensive-looking shoes.

"Did you sleep well last night," Zahir asked, innocently enough.

Jamal nodded as he gazed for an instant into Zahir's narrow-set eyes, thinking perhaps he was wrong about Zahir. He may be more cunning than I give him credit for, Jamal considered, noticing for the first time the fancy leather belt that matched his shoes and the heavy gold chain that hung around his neck. Jamal weighed the circumstantial evidence against his own recognized paranoia as Zahir turned to get in the car. Jamal could see the outline of a holster strapped to the inside of his left shin beneath his well-tailored dress pants.

He tossed the duffle bags and satchel in the back seat and got in, observing the gold rings on Zahir's fingers and the high-end wristwatch as he manipulated the gearshift, wondering if the money to buy these luxuries came from Ali or someone else. Or maybe they were all just good imitations, Jamal hoped.

He felt certain he'd made the right decision in having Zahir come along on the next leg of their trip. Better to have him close by, where he could be watched and dealt with if necessary. Jamal deliberated on how much of what Zahir had told him about the eavesdropping device was of his own doing to gain he and the others confidence.

"There is a store in the neighborhood that carries all kinds of supplies. Electrical, plumbing, building repairs, they have most everything. We won't need to go back downtown to the market, unless you require more clothes or leather goods," Zahir explained.

"No, a local store that carries construction supplies and hardware will be fine. I just need a few things that Khalib and Sa'id requested before I left them with Ali yesterday."

"I am sure the store will have everything you need. The owner is a member of the mosque and carries many items from the Middle East that are otherwise hard to find around here."

Upon reaching the store, Zahir chose to stay with the car. Jamal found the hunched clerk to be a cheerful sort as they wound their way through the store gathering items from Jamal's list. The clerk pointed to the dial on the barometer that Jamal had chosen to purchase, explaining in an excited tone how low the pressure had gone during the storm two days ago.

Standing at the counter while the clerk totaled his purchases, Jamal could see Zahir through the plate glass windows slouched in the front seat of the car with his cell phone pressed against his ear. Why had Zahir given him his home number and not his cell number when they'd first arrived in Ciudad del Estrellas, Jamal wondered. The clerk bent down below the counter and automatically Jamal started for his gun. He stopped when he realized the clerk was only bringing out a hidden cash box. Jamal was nervous and suspicious of everyone considering all that had happened in the past few days. He surveyed the store carefully, a stern look on his face, as the clerk gave him change for the one hundred dollar bill. Afterwards, Jamal relaxed a bit and said goodbye to the clerk.

Zahir had put away his phone by the time Jamal exited the store. He waited anxiously as Jamal added the items to the collection in the back of the car before situating himself in the front passenger seat.

"Well, I believe it is time for us to head back out to the ranch," Jamal announced, glancing at his own cheap watch. "According to Ali, the plane will be arriving today, *inshaa`Allah.*"

"I would like to stop at the mosque before we go," Zahir stated, biting his lip.

"That would be fine," Jamal replied, without protest.

If Zahir thought the imam could persuade Jamal to change his mind about needing Zahir on this trip, he was wrong—dead wrong—Jamal calculated.

Zahir parked hurriedly outside the mosque, opening his door before the car had come to a complete stop.

"May I use your phone, Zahir? I would like to call Ali to see if the plane has arrived yet."

Zahir hesitated, and then tossed the phone back to Jamal, giving his well-rehearsed warning as he turned back toward the mosque, "Remember, I can't vouch for the security of the phones."

Jamal only smiled as Zahir proceeded toward the entrance. After taking note of the expensive case, he scrolled through the recently dialed numbers, recognizing the apartment phone number and the imam's number but none of the others. Of course, why should I, Jamal thought, trying one last time to stifle his suspicions before writing down the unfamiliar numbers Zahir had called in the past two days.

Zahir slammed the car door shut upon his return and stared furiously at Jamal. But Jamal paid him no mind, and they both looked straight ahead in silence for the first twenty miles of the drive. Jamal fingered his goatee, a habit of his when deep in thought. Once, when rounding a sharp curve to the left, so that Zahir's attention was shifted in that direction, Jamal stopped long enough to toss the forgotten cell phone out the window.

Jaml spoke then. "Perhaps, after you get back from assisting me on this trip, the imam will reward you with a second wife, Zahir."

Zahir turned sharply toward Jamal, his face turning red. Caught between embarrassment and anger, Zahir was at a loss to reply. After several more miles of silence he spoke, but by this time, Jamal had already decided that whatever Zahir had to say, it would be of little use; or truth.

"I am truly sorry for deceiving you about my family Jamal, but I thought it might be better than admitting that I'm a coward."

Jamal considered Zahir's explanation before answering; noticing the ringing in his ears was subsiding.

"Don't worry, Zahir. We only need your help in making the arrangements with our contacts in Mexico. As soon as that is settled, you will be back on the plane headed for home. I regret that I cannot speak the language myself, and Ibrahim is so young. I'm not sure he can handle himself as well as you under pressure. Our transfer from Mexico, across the border into the United States, must go flawlessly, and I'll feel more confident with you along."

For the remainder of the drive, they returned to silence with both men contemplating what lie ahead for them.

Sa`id and Khalib met them on the porch of the dining hall as they drove up. They informed Jamal that Ali had gone to meet the plane not more than five minutes ago. Jamal tossed the duffle bags to them before he and Zahir headed down the dirt lane through the pasture toward the airstrip.

Zahir brought the car to a stop next to the runway as Ali was just climbing down to unhook his jeep from the camouflaged wagon. The small trees atop the wagon still swayed from the movement of being repositioned in the middle of the runway. Ali hopped back into the jeep and motioned for them to follow him. They pulled up next to the plane, painted several shades of green. It was parked under the cover of dense foliage and netting strung between the tree branches.

Zahir and Jamal waited in the car while Ali conferred with the pilot. Two young men, whom Jamal had not seen before, began to unload bundles and crates from the cargo bay on to the bed of a two-ton truck whose vintage appeared the same as Ali's dilapidated jeep. After his conversation with the pilot ended, Ali walked over and greeted Jamal.

Ali nodded in the direction of the pilot. "He needs to get some sleep before returning to Columbia. I don't have anyone else capable of flying this plane. He is on loan to me from my friends in Columbia," he said, apologizing to Jamal as he and Zahir followed Ali around the plane to inspect it.

"Yes, I understand," Jamal offered in agreement. "Besides, we need to wait on the photo documents anyway. And, I have need of your warehouse for a few hours."

"I spoke with my man in the print shop yesterday evening, after you left with the imam, and told him of the urgency. He agreed to stay up a good part of the night to get them done. They should be ready later today."

"Does the pilot have any objections to flying at night?" Jamal asked, not sure of how well the plane was equipped with navigational instruments.

"Oh no. We do it all the time," Ali replied confidently, in his ever-jovial mood. "With some sleep, a full stomach, and extra cash, he'll be ready to go home."

"Very well then," Jamal said, feeling the adrenaline begin to flush his cheeks as he considered his plans. "It is almost eleven o'clock now. Perhaps we could leave around one o'clock in the morning. That would give him over twelve hours to rest and still get us to Mexico by...?" Jamal looked to Ali for an answer.

"It depends on how long you are on the ground in Columbia because you will have to take on more fuel there. But you should reach the airstrip in Mexico by the middle of the afternoon tomorrow."

Zahir listened with keen interest to their conversation but added nothing to it. Jamal motioned for Zahir to come along as he headed toward the car with newfound determination. The only thing that Jamal enjoyed more than plotting a course of action was to see it implemented, the end result being proof of his meticulous calculations. He'd made several mistakes these last few days: his trust in Zahir, how to deal with the contacts in Mexico without Monsour, and—rubbing the lump on his sore head—the apartment; mistakes that could jeopardize the mission. From here forward, he was determined that there would be no more.

"I will see you later at the compound," Ali called back to them as he started for the jeep. "We will dine together."

Ali fired up the jeep and whirled it around in a cloud of dust in time to catch Jamal before they drove off.

"Here, you will need these," tossing the keys to the warehouse into Jamal's lap. "I will drop the pilot off at his room and check on your passports before I head back. I should be there within an hour."

At the hacienda headquarters, Jamal discussed with Khalib and Sa'id the change in plans he'd set in motion while Zahir roamed aimlessly around the parking lot. It appeared to Jamal that Zahir was resigned to the fact that he would be going along. Still, as a precaution, Jamal had put the keys to the car in his pocket when Zahir was distracted.

The conversation between Jamal and the others turned to Ibrahim as Jamal quizzed them on Ibrahim's willingness to go along. Khalib and Sa'id were confident that he would be a valuable asset, having been up most of the night discussing with Ibrahim their plight and the desire to seek martyrdom. The dark history of his father's disappearance seemed to make Ibrahim an eager participant, they surmised. Jamal nodded his consent then headed for the warehouse with no mention of the previous nights assault at the apartment or his suspicions about Zahir.

Jamal worked steadily for two hours before Ali poked his head through the doorway of the warehouse. Ali could see Jamal hunched over the workbench, seated on a metal stool at the far end of the building, working gingerly with the explosive compounds and wiring mechanisms. The low-hanging fluorescent bulb highlighted the scene for him: Jamal's jacket and holster lying in a pile on the warped plank floor beside him and the v-shaped sweat stain on the back of Jamal's shirt, outlining where it clung to his muscular shoulders.

While no coward, Ali was a pragmatist. He saw no reason to risk two lives when only one was needed for the task at hand. He was confident that Jamal felt the same way so he called out from the doorway rather than enter the building.

"The cook has prepared a large meal if you would like to eat."

Jamal continued working feverishly for another moment before stopping to rest his hands gently on the countertop. He sat upright, craning his neck in every direction, without turning his body toward Ali.

"You go ahead my friend. I will be there in a little while."

"I will be sure something is saved for you to eat later," Ali offered in return before heading in the direction of the dining hall.

Another hour passed before Jamal was in a position to safely take a break. The sun's heat was pressing down as he walked across the parking lot to the dining hall. Ali was the only one present when he entered.

"Where are the others?" Jamal inquired as Ali went to the kitchen for a plate of food the cook had saved.

"They went to the shooting range. Ibrahim knows the way. Zahir wanted to impress everyone with his new gun."

Jamal proceeded to wolf down the grilled mutton and squash while Ali went back for some drinks.

"What is your arrangement with Zahir?" Jamal shouted after Ali.

"How do you mean?" Ali asked, returning with a tray filled with pastries and cups of sweet mint tea.

"Like, how much and how often do you pay him? And, how well do you know his background before he came to Ciudad del Estrellas?"

"The imam and I have an arrangement where I pay him to make it look like he is an employee of the hacienda, but in reality, most of his time is spent in town helping the imam by running errands and such."

Ali stood directly across the table from where Jamal sat, hands akimbo, his voice portraying a hint of irritation.

"Why all the questions? Don't you think I know how to handle my business? You have just arrived here, yourself, as a guest, might I remind you."

Jamal shrugged and finished eating before continuing. "Truly, I am sorry. It was not my intention to offend you. You have an excellent operation here. And I am most grateful for your help with the money, documents, and, of course, the plane. This is what causes my questions."

He pointed to the back of his head and motioned for Ali to come around and take a look.

"How bad is it?" Jamal asked.

Ali was unsure what Jamal meant until he parted the curly, black hair on the back of Jamal's head and saw the massive bruise with serum still oozing from the cut on his scalp.

"Did Zahir do this?" Ali asked with a gasp.

"I don't know if he did," Jamal said, shaking his head gingerly, "but if he didn't, I suspect he knows who did."

Jamal proceeded to tell Ali about what happened at the apartment last night, and then asked him who had discovered the eavesdropping device at the mosque.

Ali responded, "It was Zahir who found it. Why would he expose his own treachery as you think him capable of?"

"Perhaps to gain your confidence, or perhaps he is playing the other side also; for money. Who else would know of our apartment besides you and the imam?"

"There would be some from the mosque. We have let other people stay there from time to time," Ali explained, still not convinced. "Besides, it could have just been a local ring of thieves."

"That seems like quite a coincidence or bad luck considering we had only been there two nights. Although, I must admit, I've had my share of it so far on this odyssey. Still, why our apartment? And the elevator ruse seems too sophisticated for an ordinary thug."

Jamal warned Ali not to say anything, informing him that Zahir was going with them at least as far as Mexico, adding that he'd taken care of Zahir's cell phone and car keys. Then he gave Ali the paper with the scribbled numbers from Zahir's phone.

"Perhaps there is a way you could find out who these numbers belong to?"

Ali thought for a moment before sticking the piece of paper in his pocket.

"It is getting late in the day, but I will see what I can do. We must get to the bottom of this."

Ali's face bore a grim frown as he began to understand the gravity of the situation if Jamal's suspicions were correct.

Ali left the room at a brisk pace, heading for his office in another of the buildings. Jamal went back to finish his work in the warehouse. Despite whatever Ali found out, he was working on a contingency plan. As he was about to re-enter the warehouse, Jamal could make out the jeep coming over a distant ridge on its way back to the compound from the direction of the firing range. He hoped he was wrong about Zahir, but the dull throb in his head made him think otherwise.

Jamal's watch said seven o'clock when he at last shut off the light over the workbench. Stepping out into the cool night air, he could hear the hoots and hollers of Sa`id and Khalib as he padlocked the door. There was an impromptu soccer game in progress on the grassy field adjacent to the parking lot. Along with his two and Ibrahim, several other students from the madrasa were involved in the game. Zahir stood along the sidelines watching as Jamal approached in the darkness.

"Everyone will sleep well on the plane tonight," Jamal said.

Zahir's feet almost left the ground when he heard the voice come out of the darkness behind him.

"I didn't mean to scare you," Jamal continued as he moved up along side his reluctant cohort. "There is no need to be nervous. I've planned for every possibility."

"I'm not nervous," Zahir stated with an air of defiance. "I just wish you would have planned on learning Spanish. By the way, do you still have my cell phone? I looked in the car, and I can't find it or my car keys."

Jamal chaffed at the comment as Monsour *had* been that part of the plan, but he kept his composure long enough to come up with a plausible excuse for the missing phone.

"I believe I put it in my coat pocket," reaching inside it, in a feigned search, briefly touching the strap that held his gun in place. The emery cloth had done its job. "It must have fallen out when I took my coat off in the warehouse. I will look for it before we leave."

"I need to call my wife before we leave," Zahir said, his voice changing from defiant to demanding. "She will wonder where I am."

Jamal always felt that he was at his cool-headed best when others were becoming agitated, as if an internal autonomic sensor perceived the changing aura given off by others. He could not explain it, but recognized its existence in him and used it to his advantage.

"I am truly sorry for the inconvenience, Zahir. But now that the plane is here and we have set a departure time, there can be no more phone calls, no more contact with anyone other than those of us right here. As you yourself said, who knows who might be listening to our phone conversations? You will be home in a couple of days. If your wife becomes worried, the imam will be able to tell her when you will be home."

He watched Zahir for any sign of aggressiveness, but his only response was to lower his head, releasing a long sigh.

Jamal observed a few more minutes of the soccer match, thwarting any attempts from the others to get him to join in. He needed to find a quiet place to sleep before the one o'clock hour was upon them. Hoping for some news before they left on the plane, he considered looking for Ali, but the tiredness in his eyes, the ache in his shoulders, and the throb from his head needed attention first.

He was forced to sleep on his side, the back of his head too sore to rest it against the flimsy pillows that were standard issue in the dormitory-style room where he found solitude.

He woke several hours later to the feel of a gentle tapping on his forehead. Opening his eyes, he saw Ali squatted down beside his bunk, his moon face not more than ten inches from his own.

"Come, come," Ali whispered, motioning rapidly with his fingers then quickly putting them to his lips, as Jamal was about to protest.

Jamal grabbed his boots from beneath the bunk, his gun and coat from under the pillow, following Ali toward the door. In the bright light of a waning moon, Jamal could make out lumpy silhouettes atop other beds, sound asleep, yet sounding off in a cacophony of somnolent noises: snores, grunts, and moans that resonated from each over the low whoosh of a ceiling fan that served only to stir the smell of sweaty garments in the close night air.

As he exited the room, just behind Ali, Jamal could see through the window into the brightly lit dining hall across the porch landing. He recognized Ibrahim by his closely cropped black hair, and, on either side of him, still dressed in their old clothes, were Sa`id and Khalib. They were bent over an open book their lips moving in time with the movement of Sa`id's finger as it glided across the text. Only a day ago they'd first laid eyes on Ibrahim through the same window, and now, they were as close to him as they'd been to Monsour. For an instant, Jamal envied them, though he knew friendship was out of the question. When the time came his authority must not be doubted.

Jamal sat on the porch steps, briskly rubbing his face before slipping on and lacing up his boots, listening intently as Ali spoke.

"I was able to make contact with someone at the local telephone exchange who owed me a favor," Ali began. Jamal noticed Ali's face, covered in thick stubble, with dark circles under his eyes as he continued. "A couple of the phone numbers on the list were easily traced to local businesses that would be normal for Zahir to call."

"And the third number?" Jamal asked, holding his breathe.

"The third number was untraceable," Ali answered, grimacing.

"Which means what?" Jamal queried, running his fingers through his disheveled hair before delicately probing the back of his scalp.

"According to my contact, it would be very rare for him *not* to be able to trace the number unless somebody wanted it blocked. Somebody much higher up then he would have to approve the secrecy of the number and block its access. Maybe Zahir should stay here with us."

"No, no," Jamal said pointedly, his mind already made up. "I would prefer to keep Zahir close to me. Besides, without his cell phone he has no way to contact anyone now. I hope there is no other access to a phone around here."

"No, I made sure of that after our conversation this afternoon, only as a precaution," Ali offered, still not altogether believing Zahir was a traitor.

Jamal continued his reasoning, "There is a saying 'keep your friends close and your enemies even closer' which I think applies here. I prefer that Zahir stay with me until Mexico. This way we will know where he is, and there will be no chance for my plans to be disrupted. We are too close to achieving our goals to be derailed by traitors. If necessary, I will deal with Zahir, with your permission, of course."

Jamal felt obliged to seek Ali's consent for any punishment Zahir might be deserving of. After all, if Zahir were disloyal, it would be Ali and the imam who suffered as well. Ali's entire operation would be in jeopardy if Zahir sold them out. He wasn't about to risk leaving Zahir behind, though. Once on that plane, I will be in control, Jamal thought, smiling.

Ali responded, "Yes, I understand your concern after last night, plus your friend Monsour, and now the phone number. If we had more time, I would like to pursue the phone number further."

Jamal shook his head slowly.

"I am afraid to delay our departure any longer. After the incident last night at the apartment, we may not be safe here much longer. However, we will not be to the landing strip in Mexico until late afternoon. If you have any more avenues available for tracking down the number, perhaps you could try them in the morning. If you find out anything of significance that seals his fate, relay a message to me through the 'coyotes'. I will allow that much risk, as you have been a valuable friend. If I do not hear from you through the 'coyotes', I will assume Zahir is innocent and allow him to return on the plane."

Ali nodded his approval, turning to survey the buildings that surrounded the parking lot and all that lie beyond before speaking.

"I pray you are wrong about Zahir, or I fear all I've accomplished here will be lost."

Jamal spoke reassuringly to Ali, though in his own mind, he had no doubts.

"Most likely I am wrong about Zahir, and if not, he may well be taking his time selling information to his confidant in order to gain the most money. I suspect your operation will be safe. And what of Ibrahim?"

"Imam Badawi and I have both spoken to him. He has decided that his future is with you and the others. He is willing to do whatever is required of him," Ali said proudly.

Jamal stood up beside Ali. As the glow from the dining hall lights illuminated their faces, the shrill chorus of night sounds from the surrounding forest paused long enough for the voices of the three young jihadists to reach their ears. Jamal felt confident they would succeed and told Ali so. Ali glanced at his watch.

"We should be going," Ali announced as he embraced Jamal. "The pilot and the plane will be ready. Perhaps after the completion of your journey, *inshaa`Allah,* the Muslim world will rejoice at your success."

"You have been a gracious host and quite competent in your business," Jamal offered, patting the gun slung from his shoulder then patting Ali on the back. "Would you awake Zahir and tell the other three it is time to go while I collect my work from the warehouse?"

Ali nodded, "We will pick you up at the warehouse."

The old jeep struggled under the weight of its cargo as Ali drove cautiously across the low hills along the rutted path toward the airstrip. Jamal sat next to him, cradling the bulging leather satchel between his legs on the floorboard. The other four crowded into the back amongst the duffle bags. Sa`id and Khalib had their arms wrapped around the computer cases while their feet, dangling over the side, brushed the tops of the bahia grass that had reached full maturity by this late summer date.

The plane's engines were at a conversation-drowning roar as the jeep pulled up next to it. Ali clamored into the cockpit to confer with the pilot while the others loaded their gear into what had once been the passenger compartment. All the seats were gone and seven, plastic, fifty-five-gallon drums filled part of the space they previously occupied.

Jamal waited for Ali on the ground beside the plane, surveying the aircraft. The turbo prop had been modified extensively according to what Ali had told him earlier. Both engines had been replaced with larger horsepower units, and the fuel tank capacity had been increased for longer-range flights.

After exiting the cockpit, Ali said his goodbyes to the others already in the back of the plane. Over the growl of the now idling engines, he told Jamal that the pilot knew where to take them and had already been paid. He offered Jamal one last goodbye before jumping back into his jeep, heading for the moveable hill dotted with trees as the plane began to inch forward.

Because the cabin was not pressurized, they maintained an altitude of six thousand feet for most of the flight. Jamal wasted no time in telling Sa`id and Khalib to change clothes, since that had been their agreement back at the store in Ciudad del Estrellas, wanting to get it over with while they were still befuddled by the noise and turbulence. They'd been up for the past two days with Ibrahim and would likely fall asleep once they became accustomed to the noise. Times like these made Jamal feel more like a babysitter and less like a jihadist.

Three hours into the flight they were over the jungles of the Amazon Basin heading north from what Jamal could tell of the instrument panel as he crawled into the seat next to the pilot. The four other passengers, as Jamal had predicted, were fast asleep. After one unsuccessful query from the curious pilot, no more attempts at conversation were made between them. For the first time in a week, Jamal felt gratitude for not knowing Spanish, preferring to sit there in silence, as he spied glimpses of water below each time the plane's wing dipped to the east. If not for the moon's reflection off the river and its tributaries far below, Jamal could not tell where the land ceased and the sky began as he stared out the window, hypnotized by the view and the accompanying sound—a steady roar of the engines.

The constant sameness had the opposite effect from the night before when his heart and mind were racing as he entered the apartment. Then, time seemed to slow, but now, with his heart calmed, the hours flew past. Jamal wondered what effect paradise had on time.

During this somnolent state, while he stared dreamily out the window, he registered a flash of green on the horizon. He took it as a sign, a good sign, knowing that it marked the dawn of a new day, as the sun began its rise to power. Jamal had witnessed the phenomenon once before. It was at a training camp in the deserts of North Africa, he thought Libya, though he was never told exactly where he was at the time for security's sake. The first hint of red quickly followed in the eastern sky, spreading slowly north and south, like blood on a tabletop. Would paradise afford him a view like this everyday, he wondered?

A change in the volume of noise coming from the engines followed by a sharp bank away from the rising sun broke the spell Jamal was under. The pilot motioned for Jamal to wake the others. He went to Ibrahim first since he had the best command of the pilot's language.

"He says we'll be over the drop site in forty minutes," Ibrahim explained.

They began a gradual descent that brought a close view of the jungle below them. Jamal was uncomfortable with the mention of a drop site, which had not been spoken of before, but Ibrahim assured him that it was standard operating procedure (based on Ali's tutoring) to drop the barrels into a small lake five miles from the airstrip. According to Ibrahim, the sealed plastic barrels floated and were easily retrieved from the water.

"Why not unload them at the airstrip?" Jamal asked with a perplexed look.

"In the unlikely event that government police were hiding at the jungle runway waiting to ambush them, there would be no incriminating evidence on board the plane."

Jamal pictured this scenario in his mind for a moment as Ibrahim continued his explanation.

"Also, Ali told me once, that if the plane were to crash and burn attempting to land, the expensive cargo would be floating safely back in the lake."

Jamal shook his head in disbelief, chuckling as a smile replaced the worried look on his face.

"Ali is a shrewd businessman. He thinks of everything," he shouted toward Ibrahim who had moved to the back of the plane and began to slide the barrels closer to the side door, which the pilot now shouted for them to open.

By now, the other three were awake and pitched in to help while Jamal stood behind the pilot waiting for his signal to push the barrels out the door. The pilot raised his hand, holding his arm outstretched from his side so Jamal could see as he counted down from five using his fingers until he dropped his arm, signaling the release point.

The first barrel hit the water as the last one left the plane. From the open door, they watched as the barrels bobbed to the surface. Then, suddenly, the green treetops reappeared just below their feet. The pilot shouted for Ibrahim to close the door. No sooner had this task been completed and the five of them had situated themselves on the floor of the plane, when, without warning, their stomachs jumped into their throats, as the pilot dropped the plane abruptly over the edge of the tree canopy and on to a narrow runway carved out of the jungle with barely enough room for the wings to clear the verdant undergrowth on either side.

A half dozen men dressed in various stages of uniform, all clutching automatic rifles, greeted the pilot as he climbed down from the plane. He walked with an air of nonchalance in the direction of a small wooden shack that sported a thatched roof located a few yards from the edge of the crushed-rock runway. The pilot conferred with one of the armed men who then shouted instructions to some invisible figures beyond the shack. In seconds, a pickup truck loaded with barrels of aviation fuel appeared out of the dense foliage.

Jamal and the others climbed down from the cargo door to stretch their legs and relieve themselves. The pilot and armed men continued to talk, away from the passengers, while two men in the back of the truck manually pumped the aviation fuel.

Jamal turned his back to the armed men and spoke to Ibrahim, "Can you hear what they are talking about?"

"No, they are too far away," Ibrahim replied.

Directly, the pilot and two of the armed men approached Jamal and the other jihadists now standing beside him, while the remainder of the armed men hung back a few paces. When they were close enough so no mistake could be made of their actions, the men released the safeties on their guns, pointing them at Jamal and the others. The leader of the group spoke in Spanish to Jamal, but the pilot stopped him long enough to explain Jamal's lack of understanding. But Ibrahim did understand and spoke angrily back to the bandits. In an instant, before he could translate to Jamal, the armed man that hadn't spoken thrust the barrel of his M-16 hard into Ibrahim's gut, doubling him over in pain.

Jamal spoke next, first motioning for his antagonists to calm down, then addressing Zahir who had kneeled to tie a lose shoestring.

"What did they say, Zahir?"

"I believe they said they want more money to ferry us on to Mexico. They say the plane is theirs, and Ali is allowed to use it as long as he is carrying valuable merchandise to them."

Ibrahim had regained his breath enough to tell Jamal they were lying.

"Ali has spent a lot of money on the plane," Ibrahim said, wincing from the pain. "It was he who paid to have the bigger engines put on the plane. I am sure of that."

Jamal seethed inside, but slowly raised his hand and motioned for Ibrahim to calm himself before turning to Zahir, "Your pistol will serve only to get us killed here, Zahir. Hand it over to them as a gesture of surrender. Ibrahim, ask the pilot how much more money it will take to fly us on to our destination."

Zahir started to protest but thought better of it, raising his pant leg and slowly unstrapping the holster before laying it on the ground and pushing it toward the uniformed men with his foot. Jamal hoped this would appease them, thinking they might not check the rest of them for weapons. In addition, it disarmed Zahir should they, *inshaa`Allah*, make it out of here alive.

"They want another thousand dollars. What do we do?" Ibrahim asked in a flustered voice.

"First off, we don't panic," Jamal instructed, looking down the line at his four fellow hostages.

With that said, Jamal reached into the right hand pocket of his pants. Before leaving the ranch, he'd split the money Ali had given him, putting some in each of his front pockets and the rest inside his boots. He pulled the rolled-up wad of bills from his pocket and instructed Ibrahim on what to say.

"Tell them I will give them five hundred now, and they can get the rest from Ali when they return the plane."

Ibrahim did as he was told as Jamal began to peel off the bills. Before he had it counted out, one of the gunmen snatched the entire roll from his hand. The man grabbed the barrel of his gun, money still in hand and rammed the barrel violently into Jamal's mid-section. The gunman counted twelve hundred dollars all told in the roll and then spoke angrily.

This time Zahir interpreted his remarks. "He says they will take this money and ask for another thousand from Ali. The only bargaining done here is with the barrel of a gun."

The pilot and other gunman laughed boisterously.

"Tell the pilot Ali will not be happy with him," Jamal remarked, still bent over, gasping for air.

Ibrahim defiantly translated Jamal's words plus a few extra of his own before Zahir shut him up.

"Maybe we no see Ali again, unless he want plane back," the pilot said with a shrug of his shoulders, smirking at his two cohorts. The three of them laughed in unison at his comment while Jamal just smiled through the pain.

The pilot disappeared into the shack for a few minutes. He returned to the plane, motioning for his ransomed passengers, still under the watchful eyes of the armed men, to get back in the plane just as the fuel truck drove back into the jungle.

The gunmen stood along the airstrip's edge making obscene gestures and laughing at the five who glared at them from the open cargo door as the plane began to taxi toward the end of the runway. Jamal silently wished he'd brought along one of Ali's rifles after all, as he watched their antics before slamming the cargo door shut. As the engines roared to a crescendo and the wheels of the plane broke contact with the runway, he sighed at the missed opportunity, reasoning that even with all the gunmen dead, they'd still be at the mercy of the pilot until they touched down in Mexico; a long six hours away.

As they climbed to their cruising altitude, all five of the relieved passengers shouted epitaphs in Arabic at the pilot and his henchmen back on the ground, knowing he couldn't hear them over the noise of the full-throttled engines. Sa'id and Khalib mocked the pilot's suspected religion with hand gestures of their own, continuing their verbal assault against him as Ibrahim examined his bruised stomach. Soon, he joined the other two in their tirades, each trying to out do the other until all three were laughing uncontrollably. Jamal smiled, thinking it did them good to blow off steam after such a tense situation back at the jungle strip.

Zahir moved off by himself at the back of the plane, sitting down cross-legged with his back propped against the fuselage, ignoring the others. Jamal stretched himself out on the vibrating floor, using his duffle bag as a headrest, cradling the satchel between his legs. He was soon asleep. The younger jihadists continued to talk amongst themselves with Khalib the most agitated of the three. Between several hours of sleep on the plane and the influence of an adrenaline rush brought on by the near-death experience with the armed gunmen, they were fully recharged.

When Jamal awoke, a squat range of barren mountains had replaced the jungle landscape below the plane. He glanced over the pilot's shoulder at the altimeter. Just past the highest of these rounded peaks, the pilot cut the engines back to a quiet idle and began a long descent toward a brown, desolate plateau among the foothills.

Whirlwinds of dust kicked up behind the plane as the wheels touched the sun-scorched earth, and backwash from the propellers churned the dirt into a billowing, dark cloud. Jamal flung open the cargo door, seeing nothing behind the plane but a roiling wall of cocoa-colored dust and ahead, approaching fast, the edge of a sheer rock bluff. The pilot spun the plane around, penetrating the wall of dust as it washed over them. Once past it, in the distance, Jamal could make out another cloud of the same color, hugging the earth, approaching them along the horizon from the west.

As it neared their position, the fast-moving cloud transformed into a late-model pickup truck, the same color as the earth below its tires. The truck stayed upwind, some sixty yards from the plane but directly in its path as the pilot kept the engines running. A stooped old man, his skin wrinkled like a prune by years in the harsh sun, stepped out from behind the wheel and two younger men who looked not much older than Ibrahim exited the truck from the passenger side. With a slicing motion across his neck, the old man signaled for the pilot to cut the engines, but from his position, Jamal could see the pilot shaking his head, indicating he would not.

All the passengers, except Jamal got out of the plane, thankful to be on solid ground again. Zahir headed directly for the old man, and Jamal shouted after Ibrahim to go with him while he began to hand down their duffle bags and computer cases to Khalib and Sa`id. Next, Jamal entered the cockpit, making it clear to the pilot through hand gestures, finger pointing, and the 9mm Glock that he was not to leave until given the okay by Jamal. The truck effectively blocked the plane, backing up Jamal's instructions.

Jamal hopped down from the cargo door, hurrying toward the pickup truck, wondering if the men in the truck held any allegiance to the pilot. Not likely, he decided, based on how they'd parked the truck in the plane's path. Hopefully, Ali was right: money held their trust.

Sa'id and Khalib put everything they carried into the back of the truck with the help of the wary young Mexicans. The old man, standing beside Zahir and Ibrahim, was pointing off in different directions with his warped fingers as Jamal approached.

"He is explaining to us where exactly we are," Ibrahim said, nodding at the withered Mexican. "Zahir wanted to make sure we are at the right place."

Jamal listened to the old man. He talked loudly over the constant thrum of the plane's engines, with more volume then his shriveled body seemed capable of.

"What else is he saying?"

"He says they have a place a hundred miles northeast of here, nearer to Matamoras," Ibrahim paused, glancing worriedly at Jamal before continuing to translate. "He says we'll spend the night there before trying to cross the border tomorrow..., providing that we have the cash payment that was agreed upon."

Zahir, overhearing this, kicked violently at the baked earth and walked a few steps toward the plane with his hands akimbo before turning back to face Jamal.

"Did you plan for this, too?" Zahir shouted. "To leave us stuck here in the middle of nowhere, with no money, no guns."

Ibrahim looked toward Jamal also, bewildered at what they would do with no money to pay the old man save for a few dollars of pocket money he'd brought along; his entire life savings.

Jamal walked calmly to Zahir and stood before him, placing a reassuring hand on each shoulder. He looked into Zahir's angry eyes, his own devoid of any emotion.

"I am not such a fool as you would like to believe, Zahir. We will make do as best we can. I very much wish that you would join us for the rest of our journey." Zahir scoffed derisively at this comment as Jamal continued. "But I gave you my word back in Ciudad del Estrellas. If you desire to return home on the plane, now is the time to go, *ma'a as-salaama.*"

Without a moment's hesitation, nor a wish for good luck, Zahir brushed Jamal's hands from his shoulders and headed for the plane. With Zahir's back now to him, Jamal reached into his boot and pulled out another roll of hundred dollar bills, counting them out slowly, in full view of the pilot, before waving him on his way.

Jamal handed over a thousand dollars to the old Mexican who then spoke to him with a gapped-tooth smile.

"Gracias, Me llamo es Enrique," he said while bowing slightly. Then he motioned for one of the younger ones to move the pickup truck out of the way of the plane.

The pilot, with Zahir seated beside him, angled the plane for the far end of the runway. He throttled up to full power, while holding back its forward motion with all the force the brakes were capable of. After their release, the plane lurched forward in a maneuver to reach take off speed before the bluff and rocky outcropping came into play.

Jamal and the others were enveloped in a miasma of dust and debris. When the visibility was restored, the plane was already a half mile away, its landing gear just disappearing into the bottom of the fuselage as it banked, heading west for a climb over the mountain range.

"Jamal!" Ibrahim exclaimed, "I'm sorry..., I forgot..., the old man..., Enrique, said he'd been contacted by Ali just an hour ago. Zahir was supposed to continue on with us. He said you would understand. Did Zahir not tell you?"

"No, I'm sure he did not," Jamal replied, shaking his head slowly, pleased to hear this information, yet not upset by Ibrahim's mistake.

It was understandable, Jamal thought, what with all the commotion and noise. And, Ibrahim was young but, most importantly, he was loyal.

They all gathered by the truck, shielding their eyes from the afternoon sun as they watched the plane become a speck in the western sky before it disappeared completely from view beyond the last row of foothills. The drone of the engines was still audible for brief intervals, being carried toward them on gusts of desert wind.

Jamal's companions thought of thunder when they heard the deep, distant rumble roll across the barren plateau. Enrique and the other two natives pointed out the cloudless sky as Ibrahim inquired about the sound, speculating that it might have been an explosion from a silver mine, thinking there might be some in the area.

Jamal stood there, lost deep in his own thoughts: about the pilot, who, until they'd reached the jungle strip, had weighed on his conscience, but now, through fate, had been deservedly punished along with Zahir.

Ignoring Khalib's confession, that Jamal's new leather satchel was missing and must still be on the plane, Jamal continued to watch the western sky, stroking his goatee. He was pleased the brilliant sunshine obscured any flash of light from the plane's explosion; not knowing how the "coyotes" might react.

The four remaining jihadists climbed into the back of the pickup, and Enrique retraced the truck's path across the arid landscape, waves of dust billowing in their wake.

Rick Elliott

CHAPTER FOUR

Yussef, in his haste to shave his beard and dress for his dinner date with Rachael, forgot to bring Mullah Khan's phone number. Back at home, he made a mad dash up the stairs to his room, the first of four at the top of the landing. It was a storage room, converted to a bedroom for Yussef when he'd first moved in with his new roommates after the fire. He kept the piece of paper bearing the number hidden in a pair of rolled-up socks at the back of a donated chest of drawers.

Yussef was tempted to call from the house. It was already past ten o'clock, and no one else was home. Mullah Khan berated him and Ahmed if they were more than five minutes late with their scheduled calls. Still, he had always warned them to *never* call from anywhere but a pay phone.

Yussef hurried back to Raymond's truck and started for the twenty-four hour Laundromat that he'd used in the past. The pay phone was on the inside, out of the weather. At this time, on a Saturday night, the place was usually deserted and brightly lit. Only once had this location been a problem.

Shortly before Ahmed's death, four months post 9/11, they had just finished checking in with

Mullah Khan when a carload of locals pulled up outside the Laundromat, apparently in search of a bathroom. From the deserted parking lot outside, the burly roughnecks saw Yussef and Ahmed inside, both bearded, with Ahmed wearing his *dishdasha* and *kufi*.

The five hooligans, wearing dirty baseball caps and flannel shirts permeated with the smell of wood smoke and alcohol, exited the car, heading for the Laundromat. One was too drunk to concentrate on anything but standing. The others began to harass and humiliate the two Pakistanis. They surrounded Yussef and Ahmed, neither of whom weighed an ounce over a hundred and sixty pounds, proceeding to jostle them about before relieving themselves on the two foreigners.

When the "too drunk one" fell down while trying to join in the abuse, distracting the others momentarily, Yussef and Ahmed managed to escape, running out the side entrance of the Laundromat. They crossed the boulevard with no regard to traffic before vaulting over a wooden privacy fence.

Physically, they were unharmed, save for a few bruises from thrown beer bottles and a sprained ankle Ahmed incurred when his robe caught on the fence causing him to land awkwardly. Their urine-soaked shoes and socks left scars they could both visualize right up until the time of Ahmed's death.

A middle-aged, rough-boned woman was doing laundry when Yussef entered to use the phone this time. Without his beard, and with another person in the building, Yussef thought himself somehow less conspicuous and safer. He felt in high spirits, because of his evening spent with Rachael, as he stood there dialing Mullah Khan's number.

The phone rang several times before Yussef began to count. It never occurred to him until this instant that the Mullah might not be there to answer. In three years of bi-monthly calls, he'd never *not* been there.

A recording announced that he should hang up and try his call again. Yussef did as it suggested, bewildered that the Mullah had not answered. The coins clanked loudly into the return bin as he stared blankly at the phone. Emboldened by his new lifestyle, Yussef thought perhaps it would be okay to try another night, maybe next Saturday night. Mullah Khan might be upset but nearly three years without a miss was a pretty good average, wasn't it?

The snap of a towel made him rethink. He glanced at the woman folding the towel, staring at him from across the room, surrounded by piles of laundry with the low hum of a dryer droning in the background. Yussef, despite his recent yearnings to break free from the whole business, still had ties to Mullah Khan, one of which was the link he represented to Yussef's homeland and religion. More importantly though, the Mullah, through an Islamic Foundation, paid Yussef's tuition and living expenses during his time in graduate school here in Rockledge.

Yussef began to worry. What if Mullah Khan was no longer around? What if he'd moved, or worse, been injured in an accident or even killed? What would I do for money? The bond between them began to strengthen while thoughts of Rachael and his three roommates faded from his mind. He dug the coins out and proceeded to try the number again, all the while picturing himself alone, broke, and in a different, difficult predicament with each unanswered ring of the telephone. On the ninth ring, Yussef heard the receiver being lifted on the other end as the ringing ceased but no voice came forth for several seconds until finally.

"Hello, this is Mullah Khan."

"Yes, yes. Hello. It is me, Yu...," Yussef stopped. One of the rules when calling Mullah Khan was to never give out one's name.

"Ahh, my wayward lamb. I thought perhaps you had abandoned the flock."

"No, no. I am truly sorry. I was delayed by some important...."

The mullah cut him off, his tone harsh, "What could be more important than contacting me at the designated time?"

Yussef pursed his lips and tried to think of a plausible excuse; to tell the truth was out of the question.

"I was delayed at the lab. An experiment I was conducting took longer than I thought it would. I could not leave until it was finished."

His cowed tone was met with a long silence on the other end. Yussef thought about the real reason he was late while he waited for the irritated Mullah Khan to reply, smiling as he pictured Rachael in his mind.

"Never forget my young friend, why you are in this country and who provides the money to support you," Mullah Khan stated slowly for emphasis. "You are but one strand in a tightly braided rope. If you weaken…, the entire rope suffers."

"Yes, I understand, and once again, I am sorry. With Ahm…, my old roommate gone, I lose track of when to call." Yussef hoped the mention of Ahmed would soften the mullah. "I have to be more careful about calling since I have several roommates now. It is harder for me to get away unnoticed at this time of night. Working in the lab is one of the times that I can get free to call. Perhaps I should call less often?"

Mullah Khan, ignoring the question, spoke sullenly, "I have never liked this new living arrangement, but it would have looked odd for you to rebuff their hospitality."

"Yes, I agree. It would have looked strange," Yussef offered, trying to appease him.

"I can not stay on the line for much longer, so please listen closely," the mullah ordered.

Yussef knew this to be true from past conversations, which rarely lasted more than a couple of minutes. They always ended with no instructions other than to call back at the proper time, plus a short prayer—tonight would be different.

"There is going to be activity with some of your jihadist brothers unless their plan fails. You must call me back in two weeks at eight o'clock *sharp*.

Mullah Khan paused for a moment. Yussef, stunned by this change in protocol with no further explanation, didn't respond.

"Remember my wayward lamb, eight o'clock..., ten your time, in two weeks. *al-Hamdu li-llah*," Yussef heard him say the time again along with the abbreviated prayer. Then he abruptly hung up.

Yussef wondered as he left the Laundromat what Mullah Khan had meant by "activity". After three years of nothing but the usual brief conversations, and the last months without Ahmed to keep him in line, Yussef had concentrated on his studies and little else. He hadn't picked up the Qur'an in months, hadn't truly prayed in weeks. Ahmed's frequent mention of plots against America that he envisioned Mullah Khan was preparing for them to carry out had been replaced in Yussef's world by idle talk of baseball, girls, and jobs his roommates hoped to acquire when they'd finished with school. Poor Ahmed; how he would have been thrilled tonight.

During the drive back to his house, Yussef's head filled with conflicting thoughts: about Rachael; about Ahmed and Yussef's own guilt at surviving the fire; about Raymond and their close friendship, something he'd never felt with Ahmed due to his constant "big brother" harping; about Mullah Khan and the authority he held over Yussef from such a distance; about Kenny and Jay with their happy-go-lucky attitude toward life; about the five locals and the ugliness at the Laundromat.

A dull pain arose just behind Yussef's eyes and a profound tiredness overcame him as he recalled these past events as well as those of tonight. He ground the gears as he forced the transmission into low range turning into the driveway. The tires chirped against the concrete as he let the clutch out too quickly. Slowly, he let the truck roll to a stop, parking it for the night.

Raymond, Kenny, and Jay returned from their St. Louis road trip after dark on Sunday evening. Yussef had spent most of the day in the lab. There, he found solace from the jumble of thoughts lingering in his head. He had fallen asleep in his clothes Saturday night, not bothering to change before heading off to the lab. Now, back at home, sitting down at the kitchen table for a bit of supper, he looked disheveled when his roommates walked in.

"Holy cow!" Kenny exclaimed when he saw Yussef.

"Wrong religion, dude," Jay countered, stone-faced as he came in behind Kenny with Raymond close at his heels. This comment made Yussef smile for the first time all day.

Kenny started in, "So, how'd you make out with the ladies yesterday, my man?"

"How'd he make out? How'd he make out?" Raymond interrupted before Yussef could respond, rubbing Yussef's bare cheek with the back of his fingers. "Jeez, Yussef, did they shave your beard before or after they tried to rip your clothes off?"

Jay placed a toothpick between his teeth, leaning in close to Yussef before he spoke.

"You didn't give away any of our secrets on how we hold dominion over women, did you? Tammy and Jill can make the Gestapo look like kindergarteners."

Yussef blushed and slowly swallowed the food already in his mouth.

"I told nothing to those two Viragos," he said in mock defiance.

"Virgins!" Kenny shouted, as he winked toward Jay and Raymond standing beside him. "You had your way with those two virgins?"

"Hah, virgins my ass," Kenny interrupted, pointing a finger at Yussef. "Don't let those two girls fool you. They'll say anything to make you talk."

"Ain't that the truth," Jay chimed in.

"No, no…, I had to help the three women…," Yussef tried to explain, digging himself a deeper hole.

"You had three women!" Ray cut in, not wanting to miss out on the teasing. "My God, Don Juan, did you leave any women in Rockledge untouched while we were away? Jay, you better call the police station and see if there are any warrants out for the arrest of a dark-complected, black-haired, bare-chinned gigolo."

"Ask'em if there's a reward for his capture," Kenny added as Jay faked a move toward the phone.

Yussef held up both hands in an act of surrender before explaining in a matter-of-fact tone,

"I helped them take their old car to the salvage yard and nothing more, except...," he *had* to tell them, "I did see Tammy and Jill in their underwear. Oh yeah, and Rachael had dinner with me by candlelight at the Bamboo Garden."

Yussef's three roommates stared at him, their mouths agape. The only sound in the room was from the tick-tock of the Felix-the-Cat clock hanging on the wall, with its incessantly moving eyes, tail, and annoying grin. To enhance its looks, an unlit cigarette hung from a hole drilled into its plastic mouth.

Finally, Jay shook the astonished look from his face and spoke, his voice rising to a crescendo, "Whoa, whoa, whoa. You saw those two goddesses in their...."

Yussef, with a grin on his face, finished the sentence, "Yes, indeed..., frilly, lacy underwear."

"Okay, okay, Yussef, were all adults here. You can say panties and bras without causing undue excitement," Raymond said in a fatherly tone, before adding in haste, "What about Rachael? What was she wearing? Huh? What was she wearing?"

"No, she had nothing to...."

"Nothing!" The three of them shouted in unison.

Yussef stammered, "No, no she had nothing..., I mean, I mean..., she had a dress on but she had nothing to...."

Jay interrupted him again, "She had a dress on but nothing underneath. Is that what you're trying to tell us. Come on, spit it out, ol' man."

He was grilling Yussef like a detective in a homicide case, emphatically pointing his toothpick, now gripped between his fingers, at Yussef as he spoke.

Yussef paused for a moment and took a deep breath. "No, Rachael had on a dress and I've no idea if she had underwear...."

"Panties, bras and panties," Raymond interjected.

"Yes, yes. Tammy and Jill were in their bras and panties, but as far as I know Rachael was fully clothed," Yussef explained, wishing he'd kept quiet.

Kenny, with his hands on his hips, stood there shaking his head in disbelief.

"I don't know how many dollars worth of liquor I've poured for those to girls at our parties and never once got to first base with either of them." He paused in thought for a moment. " What did you do Yussef, buy them a box of chocolates?"

Jay confessed, "Nah, I've tried that approach with them. I struck out, too."

Yussef was confused now, "You've played baseball with Tammy and Jill?"

Raymond rolled his eyes, shaking his head in wonder at Yussef's naivety in the matter of girls. He knew more about Viragos than virgins, and way more about nuclear reactions than relationships.

Kenny continued the grilling. "By the way Yussef, where did you learn the word 'f-f-frilly', anyway?"

Yussef smiled shyly and pointed toward Raymond.

"Frilly, eh?" Kenny said, giving a questioning look of disapproval to Ray. "What are you teaching this kid?"

Now, it was Raymond's turn to be on the defensive. "Hey, come on, man. That's a word we use all the time nuclear physics. It's similar to quark and neutrino. Is it my fault you guys are just civil engineers?"

Kenny countered, "Yeah, right Ray. Uh, my logics a little…, frilly here. I suppose next you're going to tell us those smelly farts of yours in the car awhile ago were subatomic particles left over from the 'Big Bang', eh?"

"Come on, Ray," Jay added, sounding insulted, "We may just be civil engineers, but were not 'Flatlanders'."

Raymond, ignoring Kenny and Jays retort, grabbed a kitchen chair, placing it backwards beside Yussef, putting his arms folded across the top as he straddled it and sat down. Meanwhile, Yussef, thinking the questioning was over, spread a large dollop of humus on another slice of stale bread.

"Okay, buddy," Ray began, "Enough about those two half-naked sirens for now, I want to know more about this dinner date with Rachael. More importantly, I want to know which city park you went 'parking' in with her afterwards."

Yussef, ignorant of this colloquialism, had a blank look on his face as he answered, "I don't know what you are talking about. We had dinner at the Bamboo Garden and came home."

"Uh huh," Raymond grunted as he opened his clenched fist to show what he was holding. "I suppose this lilac flower just jumped into the corner of my truck bumper and got stuck there in the middle of the Bamboo Garden parking lot?"

"Woo hoo, Casanova," Jay said, patting Yussef on the back. "You're smooth Yussef; a fast operator."

"No, no," Yussef, his face blushing, began to explain reluctantly. He'd hoped Ray wouldn't find out about his tangle with the lilac bush yesterday. It was time to confess, he decided. "That must have come from the lilac bush in Rachael's front yard."

"You made out right in their front yard!" Kenny exclaimed while grabbing a cold beer and some unrecognizable leftovers from the fridge before sitting down at the table with the others.

"Hey, moron," Raymond shouted at Kenny, "Put another bottle in the fridge. You know the rules."

House etiquette stipulated that anytime a cold beer was removed from the refrigerator, it was to be replaced by one sitting in the open case on the floor beside the fridge. Raymond said this rule kept the universe in 'harmonic balance'.

"Yeah, yeah. Who made you the Chief of the Beer Police?" Kenny retorted as he started to get up from the table.

"Sit down," Jay said, motioning with his hand as he started for the fridge himself. "I'll take care of it for you. Jeez, first it's 'Flatlander' and now 'Moron'. I suppose next Ray will be accusing us of not being able to count."

Jay proceeded to take one warm bottle from the cardboard case, placing it in the icebox before pulling out a cold one for himself. With an exaggerated motion, he removed the bottle cap, taking a big swig from it, licking the rim of the bottle as he headed back to the table, glancing at Raymond out of the corner of his eye. He produced a mighty belch and, in an unspoken gesture, offered the bottle to Ray who all the while was giving him the evil eye.

"Thanks, Jay," Kenny said.

"No problem, but you owe me one for getting Ray off your ass."

"No way, Jay," Kenny replied.

"You, bastards," Ray admonished, shaking his head slowly. "Is nothing sacred?"

"Relax, Ray. Don't get your shorts in a bind. I'll put another bottle in to make everything right with the world," Jay offered in a soothing tone. "Let's get back to the lurid details of Yussef's and Rachael's rendezvous in her yard."

All three of his roommates were now seated at the table, waiting for Yussef's explanation.

Yussef, resigned to confessing the truth, began. "The truck accidentally rolled into the bush, Rachael hollered and I tried to stop."

Kenny let out a whistle. Raymond followed with his signature guttural laugh. Jay started again, grilling Yussef about the details.

"Things got a little wild in the truck, eh? A little too much passion, maybe?"

Yussef blushed even more at Jay's mock innuendos.

"Sounds like you two were red-hot lovers," Kenny continued, following Jay's lead. He reached for the half-eaten sandwich on Yussef's plate. "What kind of aphrodisiac are you putting in that hummus, anyway? A little ground up rhinoceros horn, perhaps some powdered leopard's claw?"

"Nah," Jay interrupted, stating matter-of-factly, "Black bear bile stones are for love-making. Rhinoceros horn is for constipation."

"Oh, right, right," Kenny nodded in acknowledgement, "Thanks for the enlightenment, Professor Love."

He grabbed the jar, dipping two fingers into the hummus for a taste. Ray erupted with another grunting laugh. Yussef caught on to their teasing ploy. He smiled and reluctantly set the record straight, explaining in detail how the events unfolded on Saturday, beginning with Tammy's and Jill's skit on their front porch and ending, a bit of pride in his voice, with a request to borrow the truck again on the Saturday after next for his second date with Rachael.

Their light-hearted banter continued for another half hour around the table before the four of them dispersed to other parts of the house. Raymond told Yussef as he headed for his room that he would be happy to loan him his truck again.

"Hey, Raymond, what do you think my chances of getting a job here in the United States would be?" Yussef asked sheepishly, standing in the doorway to his own room.

"Jeez, Yussef, I thought you were dead-set on going back to Pakistan. This doesn't have anything to do with Rachael does it?"

"I've been thinking about it for several weeks now. The last few days have made me understand what I like about living here in America."

"What about your obligations to the foundation that pays your tuition? What are they going to say? And what about your family back home? Won't they miss you?" Ray asked, surprised.

Yussef hesitated long enough for the silence to grow awkward before he came up with an answer. He knew what he wanted to say, but he dare not.

"My family…, I will visit my family and then come back to America to start a job."

Yussef felt his stomach churn, angry with himself for not telling Raymond the truth. He wanted to talk to someone about Mullah Khan, Ahmed, and his family (or lack there of), but an invisible force kept his tongue at bay. For a moment, Yussef pictured himself working somewhere in the States, driving a nice car, going to a major league ballgame with Ray and the others.

Ray was waving his hand in front of Yussef's face. "Hellooo…, earth to Yussef. Come in Yussef."

Yussef shook the glazed look from his eyes, snapping his mouth shut.

"Sorry, Raymond. I was just thinking about…, my visa. Yes, my visa. I don't know if I'd be allowed back in this country if I left to go home, even for just a visit."

"Maybe you should talk to Professor Stevenson when he gets back," Ray offered. "He might be able to get you a job at another university as an instructor. With an advanced degree in nuclear engineering, there ought to be a job for you somewhere."

Yussef nodded dreamily, "Yes, yes that is a good idea."

"You know, Yussef, the next time we go anywhere for a weekend, you'd better come with us," Raymond said with a grin, starting back toward his room. "I mean we left you alone for thirty-six hours and look what happens: You shave your beard, you go out on a date, and now you're looking for a job. Next thing you know, you'll be wanting to borrow my pack of rubbers."

Yussef called after Raymond down the hall, "What are you doing with a pack of rubbers? I thought all this time you were being celibate on purpose."

Raymond shook his head and laughed as Yussef watched him disappear into his room.

The next two weeks passed quickly for Yussef. His thoughts alternated nonstop between Rachael and Mullah Khan, with the only break in this cycle coming on Tuesdays and Thursdays, when Yussef taught a physics class during Professor Stevenson's sabbatical. Yussef made up his mind to find work here in the States. With a source of income from somewhere other than the Islamic foundation, Yussef reasoned he would be ready to break his ties with Mullah Khan; to move on with his new life.

Yussef ran into Rachael several times around the engineering campus since their first date, but always there were others present and no chance for any conversation other than a polite hello and a smile. But today, as he left Minton Hall after teaching class on the Thursday morning before their next date, he saw Rachael sitting on a bench near the entrance to the adjacent Mechanical Engineering Building. Yussef stood there for a moment, rehearsing a conversation in his head, one devoid of academia, yet full of wit and humor.

Rachael was seated on the concrete bench in a lotus position, her long print skirt tucked under her legs in an effort to ward off the crisp morning air of a spring day. Her petite sandals and well-worn backpack rested on the ground below her. A stack of papers was cradled in her lap. As she bent forward, tilting her head to one side, her black hair fell forward of her shoulders and a small gold cross hung from a delicate necklace. In rhythm with the ebb and flow of a light breeze, she swept her hair behind her right ear, holding it there briefly until letting go as her concentration returned to the papers. When her hair was back, Yussef could see gold, hoop earrings shimmering in the bright sunlight and the graceful curve of her neck.

As he approached her, his hands were thrust deep in the pockets of his khaki pants while a physics textbook stuffed with loose sheets of notepaper balanced in the crook of one arm.

"Hello, Rachael," Yussef said, timidly.

"Hey, Yussef. How's it going?"

"Very good, very good," He said, rocking to and fro on the heels of his shoes. He stared down at the shiny new dimes Kenny and Jay had placed in the embroidered slots of his loathers. They assured him it was an American custom for good luck.

"What are you doing out and about on such a gorgeous day?" She asked, raising both arms overhead, her hands clasped together, as she stretched her body skyward before releasing a heavenly sigh.

"I've been teaching a physics class over in Minton Hall. I was on my way home and saw you sitting here. What are you doing?"

"Oh, I've just been going over the data I got back from my research project. It's so nice out, I couldn't stay in the grad student offices any longer. I came out here to study for awhile, but I keep getting distracted people-watching and listening to the birds singing."

"May I sit, please?"

"Yes, you may," Rachael giggled. "You're too polite, Yussef. But that's good," she added quickly. "Sit down, relax, and enjoy the beautiful weather."

Yussef sat down on the opposite end of the bench, placing his book beside him.

"Mind if I make myself comfortable? My legs are falling asleep from sitting here."

She turned toward Yussef before he could answer, unwinding her legs and propping her feet on Yussef's book, just touching his leg.

"How do you like teaching a class?" She queried.

"Mmm, it's okay," Yussef said, staring at the rings on her toes. "Although, I don't think I'm very good at it. I get nervous with everyone staring at me. Today seemed especially bad. I kept getting interrupted by people talking to one another."

Rachael shook her head, "That's so rude."

"The undergraduates are so disrespectful. It wasn't like that in Pakistan. Our teachers wouldn't allow it. I'm no good at classroom discipline, I guess."

"I know what you mean. Dr. Jacobs, my advisor, wants me to help teach a class next fall. I'm dreading it."

Just then, Rachael thrust out her arm with her finger pointing toward a flower-drenched dogwood tree just past the sidewalk in front of the bench, exclaiming, "There, did you see them? It's a pair of cardinals singing to each other. They've been in that tree for the past five minutes."

Yussef spotted the pair as they flittered about nervously from branch to branch, the bright red male a sharp contrast to the white flowers of the tree and the rust-colored female.

"It looks just like the one on my baseball cap. The one Raymond gave me," Yussef said.

Rachael rolled her eyes. "Raymond has got you brainwashed about baseball."

Yussef shrugged, still watching the two birds "I wonder why Mother Nature decided to make the male stand out?"

"I don't know," Rachael offered with a finger pressed to her lips. "Lots of species are that way, I believe."

"I suppose that irritates Tammy and Jill," Yussef said with a grin.

Rachael laughed loudly then quickly covered her mouth as people walking by turned and stared.

"Yes, I suppose it does," she agreed, still laughing. "God knows, they've probably complained to somebody about it."

"Are we still going out Saturday night?" Yussef asked, abruptly, holding his breath, waiting on her reply.

Rachael looked at him with a surprised expression, "Oh, my gosh, I'd almost forgot about our...."

Yussef cut her off before she could finish, "That's okay. Maybe another time," he said with resignation.

"No, no," Rachael admonished, leaning toward Yussef, placing her hand on his arm. "I said I *almost* forgot. I had it written down on my calendar. I just hadn't looked at it lately. Going to Kansas City last weekend was so exciting. I'd put everything else out of my mind. You should have seen that grain silo come down. It was pretty impressive, Yussef."

"Yes, I suppose it's hard for me to compete against dynamite and building implosions," he joked, feigning dejection.

"Don't worry, Yussef. I'm not letting you off the hook that easily. You know, there's a movie playing on campus again this weekend. Maybe we could go see it after you take me somewhere fabulous for dinner. It only costs three bucks to get in."

Yussef mulled this idea over in his head for a bit. It competed with ideas on how he intended to deal with Mullah Khan; a problem he couldn't get out of his head.

"Yes, I suppose that would be all right," he half mumbled.

"Well, don't make me twist your arm," Rachael replied.

Yussef was perplexed by this comment, taking a second too long to decipher its meaning, though he'd heard the expression before. He was about to respond when Rachael slid over and grabbed his arm playfully, in an attempt to make good on her threat. "Okay, okay," Yussef said, laughing. "I'll go with you to the movie."

Rachael had his long slender arm bent against the small of his back. Growling, through gritted teeth, in her best tough-guy voice she declared, "You've got to say 'uncle' before I'll let go."

"Uncle? Why uncle?"

"I don't know why. It's just the American custom."

She bent his arm further, his hand almost touching his shoulder blade as he writhed in agony, trying to break her grip.

"Okay, uncle!" Yussef cried out before she released his arm. "I'll go if you promise not to hurt me and you show me how to squeal the tires on Raymond's truck. He said I could use it again this Saturday."

"It's a deal," Rachael agreed. "Hey, would you like to go with me to grab a cup of coffee and a bite to eat? We could walk to the Grind House Cafe.

It's only a few blocks from campus and on the way home if that's where you're headed. I need my caffeine fix to get me through this afternoon."

"Yes, yes, that would be fine," Yussef said, not hesitating in his response. He could go back to lab and finish his work later, he decided.

Rachael gathered up her papers, hopped up from the bench, skipping across the grass to the sidewalk, turning back to address Yussef.

"You know, I was just kidding about you taking me somewhere fabulous to eat on Saturday. We can go back to the Bamboo Garden or somewhere else less expensive if you'd like."

Yussef said nothing as he caught up to Rachael. He hadn't considered the cost of taking Rachael some place fancy for dinner on Saturday night. His mind had returned to thoughts of Mullah Khan.

They proceeded across the quadrangle, lined on all sides with old buildings of brick and mortar, toward Sixth Street and the coffee shop.

"We can weigh our options over a cup of coffee and....," Yussef said before being interrupted by loud voices.

"Go home! To your terrorist brothers," someone shouted toward them from a group of young men passing on the sidewalk.

They were going in the opposite direction, some with book packs slung from their shoulders. Rachael gave Yussef a quizzical look. He continued walking without looking back at the group or at Rachael.

"Were they shouting at us? Did you know them?" She asked.

"No, no, I don't believe so."

Yussef glanced back now that they had moved on a few paces as the Laundromat incident flashed through his mind.

Rachael could see the expression on his face turn from worried to puzzled as he pondered out loud, "Though it seems rather queer. This is the second time I've had it happen today."

"Really! That is strange, but it's probably just a coincidence," Rachael offered, trying to ease his mind. "Most people around campus are open-minded about foreigners. Heck, I'll bet half my undergraduate classes were taught by professors or teaching assistants from other countries."

Yussef shrugged his shoulders as they continued on their way, "Yes, yes, I'm sure they were talking about someone or something else. It's nothing to worry about."

The doors to the quadrangle buildings were like the end of a vacuum cleaner hose, sucking everyone inside just as the carillon began to chime, signaling the top of the hour. The crowded sidewalks were swept clean as classes resumed. A few late-to-class bicyclists whizzed past Rachael and Yussef as they crossed the bike path at the edge of campus. One speeding bike forced Yussef to whirl about to avoid being hit, causing him to almost lose the textbook tucked under his arm.

"I wonder if any pedestrians have been killed by collisions with bicycles?" Yussef said, readjusting his book.

"Oh, yeah, I read an article in the student newspaper a while back about someone who got run over by a bike and was killed. I believe it was at a college over in Illinois. They were talking on a cell phone and walked right into the path of the bicycle."

"You know in Pakistan, everyone has a bell on their bike that they can ring to warn you of their presence."

"Oh, that would never work here, Yussef," Rachael explained with a serious look on her face, barely masking the start of a smile. "When anyone heard the bell ring, they would automatically reach for their cell phone and get clobbered."

Yussef thought this scenario over in his mind before turning to Rachael with a smile, a smile that matched hers as she began to laugh. They both knew she was kidding, sort of.

Turning the corner on to Sixth Street, the doughy smell of a pizza parlor in the middle of the block made them both inhale deeply.

"They have bells on bikes in Pakistan, but do they have pizza parlors?"

"I had never eaten pizza before moving in with Kenny and Jay. They eat it almost every day. Raymond says it's the base of their food nutrition pyramid. I'm sure you could find a restaurant in Karachi that makes it, in an area that caters to Western tourists. Karachi is a large city, very..., what is the word..., cosmopolitan," Yussef explained proudly.

As they passed a bookstore, an older woman putting together a large display in the front window caught Rachael's attention. "WE BUY USED TEXTBOOKS!" it read in bold letters.

"Gosh, I can't believe it," Rachael said, shaking her head. "There are less than two months left, and this semester will be over."

"Are you still going on your camping trip?" Yussef asked, trying to steer the conversation away from academics.

"Oh, you bet, the weekend after next. There are six of us girls going. I'm really looking forward to it. It's a great time. The bugs and snakes aren't out yet. The trees and wildflowers are blooming, plus there are very few people on the river this time of year."

"It sounds nice."

"Have you ever been canoeing, Yussef?"

"No, I'm afraid not. I don't even know how to swim."

"You could wear a life jacket," Rachael stated matter-of-factly. "You should make Ray and the boys take you some time. It's really pretty on the river. I'd ask you to go with us but we do a lot of 'girl talk', besides, Tammy and Jill would make you their slave."

Yussef, laughing, nodded in agreement. At the entrance to the coffeehouse, the acrid smell of fresh roasted beans overpowered any scents lingering from up the street. They stood just inside the doorway, their eyes adjusting to the dimness, as they searched for a place to sit. Several tables were occupied with laptops; their glowing screens highlighting the faces of their entranced owners who stroked their keys. The laptops responded to their commands by fetching new information and then waiting patiently, cursors wagging to and fro, at their master's side, for the next request. Behind the counter, the cacophonic hiss of an espresso machine drowned out the low volume sounds of a local college rock station coming from speakers mounted high in the corners of the exposed brick walls.

Yussef, pointing toward a table near the front window, barren of people but cluttered with news-papers, spoke, but to no avail, his voice drowned out as a man behind the counter bellowed, "TWO CAFÉ MOCHAS TO GO FOR KELLY!"

Rachael understood his gesture though, and they wound their way through the maze to the open table.

"What would you like and I will go order it?" Yussef asked, as they set their books and notes on the table.

"You don't have to do that, Yussef. I'll buy. I invited you, remember."

"No, no, that is quite all right, quite all right. I was going to go somewhere to eat lunch anyway, so this is fine. Please, tell me what you would like."

"Well, okay, if you insist. But I'd really rather pay for it myself."

"I'll make you say 'uncle'," Yussef warned.

Rachael threw back her head in laughter, as Yussef stood there, pleased with himself as he admired the fine line of her face in profile, the ease of her smile, her confident demeanor. She lifted her upper body out of the chair with her arms braced against the table top and chair back, stretching to see the glass countertop display case beyond the intervening tables crowded with coffee drinkers.

"Mmmm, I think…, I'll have…, a cappuccino and a brownie with chocolate icing, please."

Yussef hesitated, enamored by her dark, shining eyes. Finally, he turned to maneuver his way toward a wooden sign—in the shape of a pointing hand—hanging from the stamped tin ceiling. The sign pointed down in the direction of the cash register. It was painted in antique lettering that said, "Order Here". Rachael watched him go before relaxing her grip on the chair back, crossing one foot under her thigh and settling into her seat.

Another shout from the heavy-set, apron-clad young man behind the counter, "FRENCH VANILLA LATTE FOR CHRIS", shattered the low buzz of human voices, satiated by their surroundings. Rachael reached for the front section of the newspaper lying discarded on the wide, condensation-stained, wooden ledge below the window.

Standing in line behind a teenage girl with platinum blonde hair streaked with vermilion and pulled back into a ponytail, Yussef calculated the cost of Rachael's order along with something for himself. The new clothes he'd purchased for his teaching assignment had left him teetering on the edge of insolvency. The check he received monthly from the Islamic Foundation was already three days late and his share of the rent was due on Monday. Perhaps the mullah was sending him a message—in place of the check; all the more reason for him to find a different source of income, he thought. But the teaching stipend wouldn't be paid out until the end of the semester; for now, Mullah Khan still had him under his thumb.

"Hello, what can I get for you?" A willowy, doe-eyed girl behind the counter asked Yussef as he stepped up.

Before he could respond, the trumpeter let go another blast, "TUNA FISH ON RYE FOR BOBBY".

The girl behind the counter cringed, "Sorry about that, we're short a person today so instead of bringing the orders to your table, you will have to come and get it when we call your name."

"Yes, I understand completely. It is quite all right. I would like a small cappuccino, a brownie with chocolate icing, a bowl of your daily special...," he pointed to the rectangular blackboard resting on an easel in front of the cash register, listing in pastel-colored chalks the day's lunch special, "...the corn-potato chowder and a cup of tea, please."

"Would you like black, green, red, or white tea?" she asked, scribbling his order on a notepad.

Yussef smiled at this. Only in America are there so many choices, he thought, then he answered, "I'll have black tea, please."

He counted out the money he'd dug from his pocket while the friendly girl repeated his order as she rang it up on the cash register. There on a rack next to the counter, Yussef glimpsed a folded copy of the front page of today's paper. In one-inch print near the top, he could make out the words,

"PAKISTANI TERRORI", ending at the crease. A weakness came over him.

"Your total comes to ten dollars and thirty-seven cents."

Yussef was almost a dollar short. He glanced quickly over to the table where Rachael was sitting. He could see her leaning over what appeared to be a newspaper laid out on the table, her hair just brushing its surface. He was flummoxed.

"I..., I'm..., sorry. I'm sorry, I think I will just have a cup of the chowder instead of a bowl..., if it isn't too late. I'm not really that hungry," he said hurriedly, as he took another fleeting glimpse at the newspaper.

"No problem," the girl said, still quite amicable.

Yussef handed her all the money in his possession.

"We'll call your name when the order is ready. What is your name?" She handed him his change while reaching for a pen to write his name on the ticket.

"Yussef," he said meekly, pointing for her to put the small amount of change in the tip jar.

"I'm sorry, what...?" She asked again, looking at him over the top of her glasses.

"Joseph, my name is Joseph."

"Well, Joseph, we'll have this ready in just a few minutes."

Yussef nodded sheepishly. He made his way back to Rachael and the paper, wondering what her reaction would be and what questions she would have for him as he spied the paper over her shoulder; the same edition that he'd seen hanging on the rack by the counter.

"They'll have our order in just a moment," Yussef said, trying to sound happy as he slid cautiously into his chair, prepared for the worst.

Rachael acknowledged him with a nod but never looked up from the paper. Yussef could now see the entire headline sprawled out in front of her, "PAKISTANI TERRORIST CELL UNMASKED". In parenthesis at the start of the article, reading it upside down, he could make out the words Phoenix, AZ. on the byline. Yussef wanted desperately to twirl the paper around from in front of Rachael's eyes and read the article himself, but he resisted the urge. Could this be the "activity" Mullah Khan had mentioned during their phone conversation, he wondered?

"Boy, Yussef…," she stopped for a moment.

He watched as her finger moved across the text of the article, the nail painted candy-apple red, matching her exposed toenails. Yussef turned his gaze out the window to a group of people walking past the coffee shop.

"Have you seen today's paper?" Rachael asked.

"No, there is never anything in it that interests me," he replied, trying to sound indifferent.

Rachael continued to read. Yussef bit his lower lip, still watching the group outside: two boys and two girls he guessed of high school age, all four with glistening coal-black hair, the boys' spiked into a single row six inches tall from their foreheads back to the nape of their pale necks. Unrecognizable tattoos adorned the boys' sleeveless arms, their clown-like baggy pants riding low on skinny hips, the girls wearing T-shirts two sizes too small and jeans that rode equally low on more voluminous hips, all with their lips, noses, and ears pierced with rings too numerous to count, each doing their best interpretation of smokers, with cigarettes clenched between lips or fingers.

"Only in America," Yussef said out loud without thinking.

"What's that?" Rachael asked, turning the paper ninety degrees so Yussef could read it also.

"Those four kids walking down the sidewalk. I had never seen anything like that until I came to America to study."

Rachael leaned her head against the window to see them as they moved on toward the end of the block.

"My older brother used to dress like that for awhile when he was in high school, kind of a cross between 'goth' and 'punk'. My parents were half scared of what he was going to become..., then he joined the military and put their minds at ease."

Yussef looked down at the paper, almost reluctant to read it. Rachael returned her gaze to the paper, tapping her finger on the headlines as she spoke excitedly.

"You know, I'll bet this is why people have been yelling at you to go home, since, unfortunately, you do look foreign, although no more than those four that just walked past outside; at least you're tall, dark, and handsome," she said, laughing.

Turning back to the paper, she continued, "They were planning to do some serious damage according to this article."

Yussef scooted his chair around to get a better view and close enough to smell Rachael's heady perfume. He scanned the article, looking for any name he most likely wouldn't know—*huge weapons plant targeted, five Pakistani nationals, outdated visas, neighbors said they kept to themselves, one enrolled in local college, money from Islamic Foundation.* His eyes flickered back to, *authorities looking for accomplices.*

No mention was made of Mullah Khan. Yussef wasn't sure if that was good or bad as his mind raced. Another order was announced from behind the counter.

"Know any of them?" Rachael teased, bumping her shoulder playfully against Yussef's.

"No, no, I don't..., I mean there are a hundred and fifty million people in Pakistan. How could I possibly know any of...."

"I was just kidding, Yussef. Relax, will ya."

"I'm sorry. I've been on edge since someone first yelled at me on my way to campus this morning. I had trouble once, two years ago, with some local hooligans," he confessed.

He proceeded to tell Rachael about the incident at the Laundromat, when he and Ahmed had been accosted by the local rednecks. It felt good to tell someone about the incident, to get some of the secrets off his chest, though he felt a pang of guilt, also; one of the five terrorist's names mentioned in the paper *was* familiar to Yussef. He wasn't for certain, but he thought the one name he recognized had been at the madrasa while Yussef had been there, before he had went off to college.

"Oh, wow!" Rachael exclaimed, turning her attention from the newspaper to Yussef. "What a bunch of Neanderthals. You should have called the police."

Yussef shrugged. "We were happy just to get away from them unhurt. Besides, Ahmed was worried because his visa had expired. If the police found out, he would have been deported."

"I didn't know the person who died in that house fire was your roommate. Was he going to school here at the university?"

"No, he was working at a bakery over on the other side of town, out toward the interstate."

"He came all the way from Pakistan to work in a bakery?" Rachael asked, incredulous.

Another shout came from behind the counter. They both ignored it. Yussef couldn't bring himself to tell her everything, especially now with news of the Pakistani terrorists. In fact, he began to regret that he'd said anything, still, he felt obliged to give an explanation of Ahmed's presence.

"No, no. Ahmed was going to go to school, but he just wasn't ready." Yussef thought of something more plausible. "There was a problem with his admission forms…, he transcripts were fouled up."

Yussef paused, pondering the word "accomplice" in his head. What constituted an accomplice? Would he and Ahmed qualify? Ahmed probably would have gone to school, eventually.

And maybe, if he'd lived here another year or two, he would have abandoned his dreams of martyrdom and realized that America wasn't such an evil place. Perhaps he would have met someone friendly and outgoing, like Raymond or Rachael. Still, the Laundromat had been a setback. Ahmed had never known the good side of human nature, not like himself, who at least had vague memories of a mother and father; a family. Ahmed had told him once that he was raised in an orphanage from the time he was a baby, with no recollection of a mother; then, when he was old enough, he was sent to the madrasa.

"LAST TIME! ORDER UP FOR JOSEPH!" The voice bellowed from behind the counter, loud enough this time that everyone, including Yussef and Rachael, paused to look in the direction of the bass voice. Yussef saw the girl who'd taken his order standing beside the announcer, pointing over the counter in his direction. He leapt to his feet and made his way to the counter.

She pushed the tray toward Yussef, smiling, wiping her hands on the stained apron hanging from her neck, looking again over the top of her glasses as she spoke, "I was about ready to throw a dishcloth at you to get your attention."

"I'm sorry, I was busy talking."

"It looked pretty serious over there," she said, tossing the dishcloth back on the edge of the sink. "Well, enjoy your lunch."

"Yes, yes. Thank you."

Yussef moved back to the table carrying the tray. Faces that seemed to be burning holes in his flesh moments before as he walked toward the counter had resumed ruminating with their tablemates or playing fetch with their trusty computers.

"Joseph?" Rachael said with a quizzical look.

"She thought she misunderstood me, I guess. It has happened before," he explained with a shrug of his shoulders, placing their food and drinks on the table before setting the empty tray precariously on the wide window ledge.

"Thank you, Yussef."

Rachael stirred her cappuccino and watched discreetly as Yussef's lips said a brief prayer before eating.

"Do you say a prayer before every meal?"

"I am supposed to but I don't always. I'm afraid I've been slack in my religious duties of late, especially when I'm around people who aren't of my faith. I fear it makes them—and me—uncomfortable."

"What about just now with me?" Rachael asked, gazing steadily at Yussef.

Yussef hesitated, "...I must apologize. I didn't mean to offend you."

"Oh, no," Rachael said, shaking her head adamantly, "no, you didn't upset me. I was just curious, that's all. I'd never seen you do it before. Are you comfortable with me?"

Yussef blushed. "I didn't think you would mind."

"And I don't. I think it's nice that you feel you can pray in front of me without feeling ashamed or uncomfortable or whatever," Rachael offered apologetically. "But you're absolutely right, most people in this country, I think, feel uncomfortable praying in public. Yet, I'm sure a lot do it at home. We always did growing up, just like you, before every meal."

"May I ask what religious faith you belong to?" Yussef queried, before another spoonful of his chowder.

"I guess I like to think of myself as an agnostic," Rachael explained with indifference. "When I was young, we went to a Catholic church, but my parents weren't very dedicated to it. And now that I'm in college, it seems out of vogue with my friends and me."

Yussef stopped for a moment, a puzzled expression on his face. "I know about Catholics and Protestants, but I'm not sure I know what it means to be an 'agnostic', though I've seen the word."

Rachael giggled, rolling her eyes, "I'm not sure I know either, but I guess it means that I believe in a God but not in organized religious faiths. It just seems like so many people have died in the name of religion through the ages. You know, like Northern Ireland or the Holocaust."

Yussef nodded, matter-of-factly, "Yes, like the Crusades or the Spanish Inquisition or Palestine."

"Right," Rachael acknowledged, deciding it was time to change the subject. "Hey, you know those plastic explosives they mentioned in this article about the terrorists? We used the same type last weekend in Kansas City when we were bringing down that concrete grain silo. That's such a wild class. Later this semester we're going to Ft. Wilson, to a demonstration of different types of explosives and to go through their museum."

"Ahmed and I went there a couple of years ago; not long after we moved here."

"Really? Did you like it?"

"Yes, it was interesting. A friend of ours came down from St. Louis..., he was going to school up there. He drove us down to see the museum. I liked the Arch in St. Louis better, though. I saw it when we took a bus to St. Louis and he drove us there, to the Arch, and a few other places."

"Oh, yeah, I've been there a couple of times," Rachael said. "Did you go to the top?"

"Yes," he answered sheepishly. "It almost made me sick. I guess I'm scared of heights."

"Not me," Rachael replied, wiping crumbs from her lips. "I like going to high places. In fact, I'd like to go to your country some day, or at least next-door to India, to see the Himalayas."

"Most of the Himalayas are best approached through Pakistan," Yussef informed her. "And there are some other mountainous regions in Pakistan as well. The Hindu Kush range in the Northwest is quite impressive. I've been there several times, to the base of them anyway. Have you been to any mountain ranges here in America?"

"I've been to the Rocky Mountains. And, I've been to the Grand Canyon."

"I would like to visit the Grand Canyon some day, before I leave this country," Yussef declared with a sigh.

"Yes, the Grand Canyon is a must-see if you get the chance. Have you been anywhere outside of Missouri since you came here to go to school?"

Yussef shook his head briefly then stopped, "Well, we did go across the Mississippi River into Illinois that weekend we went to see the Arch. We went up to see the lock and dam on the river above St. Louis."

Rachael raised her eyebrows mockingly, "Wow, now I bet that was exciting. Don't they have any dams in Pakistan?"

"Of course, but not on a river *that* big, "Yussef said defensively. "It took a lot of engineering, just like the Arch."

"I suppose so," Rachael conceded with a sly smile, adding, "but I think it would be more fun to blow them up."

Yussef was silent for a moment, thinking.

"I'm joking, Yussef. Watching those silos come down was just so…, so…," Rachael had the palms of her hands turned upward, along with her gaze, searching for the right word. "I don't know…, exhilarating I guess."

"Yes, yes, I get the same feeling when I see a mushroom cloud."

Rachael, reaching for her coffee cup, almost spilled its contents as she burst out laughing.

"Okay, okay, it sounds crazy, I admit it. But it was such a feeling of power when they came down. You atomic scientists are so over the top with your thermonuclear reactions."

Yussef tipped his cup to get the last spoonful of chowder then took a long sip of tea as he considered her statement thoughtfully before responding.

"I suppose it's the same feeling for a jet pilot when the after-burner kicks in, or a motorcyclist when he opens the throttle all the way on a straight stretch of road; raw power at the flip of the switch or flick of the wrist, just barely under control."

"Yeah," Rachael nodded, "something to do with being able to harness all that pent up energy and having command over it."

They sat there for a minute in silence both drinking their preferred stimulant, lost in thoughts that included the other. Rachael preoccupied herself by thumbing through the rest of the newspaper, stopping after each section for another sip and to glance at Yussef.

"Ray told me the other day that you were thinking about trying to find a job here in America," Rachael disclosed, disaffected, folding the paper and placing it back on the window ledge. "You could go see the Grand Canyon then."

"Ray is about to get his research project sabotaged," Yussef replied sternly. "I'm glad I didn't tell him any of my deepest, darkest secrets."

"Oh, you would have told me sooner or later that you were thinking about staying in America, wouldn't have you?" she said, playfully grabbing his arm. "Besides, you told him about our dinner date."

Yussef could feel the heat rising in his cheeks, "Well, I…, I bloody well had to tell him so I could borrow his truck again."

He tipped his cup back for one last swallow, satisfied with his quick response.

"Uh huh, blabber mouth," Rachael chastised, followed teasingly, with both hands on her hips, mimicking Yussef's brogue, "Aye, there'll be no sex for you ol'chap."

Now Yussef was trying to suppress a laugh. Caught between a swallow and a gasp, tea trickled out both corners of his mouth as he lowered his cup quickly, trying to catch the dribbles off his chin.

Rachael, not letting up, patting Yussef on the back, continued, "Don't give up hope, laddie. Maybe some day, when you have a few more whiskers on ye chin and the Queen comes out in a miniskirt, you'll get lucky."

Their table bounced with laughter as the newspaper and empty tray tumbled to the floor.

"CAFÉ MOCHA FOR JERRY! ER…, I MEAN JENNY. CAFÉ MOCHA FOR JENNY!" echoed through the room.

Rachael, between laughs with Yussef, blurted out, "They are having trouble with names, aren't they? What happens when they get to Lois or Louis?"

They grabbed their books and headed out the door, stepping around a lonesome bike chained resolutely to a rack just outside the café.

"Are you going back to campus?" Yussef asked, hoping the answer would be yes so they could talk, maybe laugh, some more.

"No, I think I'm done for the day. My brains fried. I think I'll head for home. How about you?"

They had reached the corner of the block and Yussef paused for a moment. There was nothing for him to do at home except wait and worry about why the check hadn't arrived. He needed time to think and his grad student office at the lab was his place, his sanctuary.

"I need to go back to the lab. To check on some experiments."

"Well then, Yussef, I guess I'll see you on Saturday night."

"Yes, yes, I'll see you Saturday night at seven o'clock, correct?"

"Correct," Rachael confirmed.

"No sex, huh?" Yussef asked, turning to go, a big grin appearing on his face as he looked back toward Rachael.

"Not a chance, mister."

CHAPTER FIVE

Jamal and his three fellow passengers in the back of the pickup truck talked first about what lay behind them: the gunmen at the jungle airstrip, meeting Ibrahim for the first time at the *hacienda*, the market in Ciudad del Estrellas, the voyage over on the *Empress of Sayda*, and the unexplained loss of Monsour. Ibrahim had been told by Sa`id and Khalib about the parts of their trip he'd missed before joining them on the plane that brought them to here to this desolate, desert, plateau in northern Mexico.

Wincing as he rubbed the back of his scalp, Jamal was thankful the throbbing had stopped during the night. A picture of Zahir flashed through his mind, feeling satisfied with the decision he'd made concerning Zahir and the pilot's fates. With any luck, Ali's operation would not be compromised. A lost plane would be a small price to pay for that, he calculated.

The blazing afternoon sun bore down as they sat on their duffle bags, huddled close enough to hear each other over the rush of air that swirled past the cab and gave a degree of relief from the heat. They were repeatedly ejected from their makeshift seats with each pothole encountered and tossed side to side as the old Mexican swerved to avoid the brick-sized rocks that peppered the dirt road. A pump-action, twelve-gauge shotgun tapped against the back window in response to every bump as it hung from a homespun gun rack held together with braided, hemp, baling twine.

Sa`id inquired of Jamal how they were going to get across the border into America. In response, Jamal nodded toward the old man and his two younger cohorts—grandsons—as he spoke.

"They have prepared a way for us to get across the border undetected, according to Ali," Jamal looked at each of their faces before continuing. "Someone will meet us in Brownsville...."

Khalib interrupted with a quiver in his voice, "Is that..., is that in America?"

Jamal waited before responding, watching Khalib who had lowered his head and was picking incessantly at a loose thread in his new jeans with one hand while the other, displaying a mild tremor, vibrated on his duffle bag. Jamal reached out and put his hand firmly on Khalib's.

"Yes, Khalib, it is in America, in the state of Texas, across the river from Matamoras. Our contact will meet us there and take us on to Houston. I believe there is a mosque," Jamal offered, looking intently at Khalib, who nodded in response. "We will wait there for a week before going on to our final destination."

He instantly regretted his choice of the word "final".

Ibrahim calmly made designs in the film of dust blanketing the edge of the closed tailgate. Sa`id sat idlely beside him, his beard spotlighted by the glint of sunshine reflecting off the computer case resting on his lap. The three in the cab sat motionless, save for the movement inherent from the rocking truck.

They spent only a short part of the four-hour trip on a paved, two-lane highway. The rest consisted of long-neglected, oiled roads, cross-hatched with cracks that resembled spider webs; gravel roads wash-boarded by infrequent rains and even less frequent maintenance; and dirt paths with a layer of powdered dirt so fine, it appeared suspended above the surrounding earth until the force of the tires exploded it in every direction.

The sun hovered above the western horizon as they rolled slowly through a small town. It was the first settlement they'd passed through since leaving the airstrip hours ago. Their driver, Enrique, shouted back to the four of them that his farm was only a few miles beyond the little hamlet, based on the translation by Ibrahim. Shadowy outlines of faces were visible just inside the open-doored thresholds of sun-bleached houses as they drove by on the main street, past a small store and petrol station.

The farmstead was comprised of a square-shaped clapboard house whose front porch appeared slightly off-kilter; two long, squat pole barns open to the south with undulating rooflines; a chicken coop; and an outhouse. Each of them was topped with the same covering of corrugated metal that was being coated with the uneven brushstrokes of advancing rust.

Thirteen bony cows and a herd of anemic-looking goats grazed in a fenced lot at the penumbra east of the barns, their heads haloed in the sun while the remainder of their bodies cooled in the shadow, keeping pace with its slow advancing march.

The four of them dismounted from the back of the pickup while Enrique and his grandsons climbed out of the cab. He led the way to a water well close to the house, its pump handle polished from years of steady use. After a few rhythmic up and down strokes, water gushed from the lip of the pump into a communal tin cup he offered to his paying customers.

With everyone's thirst quenched, Enrique reached into his shirt pocket, pulling out the roll of sweat-dampened bills given to him by Jamal. Peeling off the outside one hundred dollar bill, he handed it to the young Mexicans, instructing them to go back to town for supplies that included food, beer, diesel fuel, and a salt lick for the cows.

Without hesitation, the two grabbed several nearby, empty five-gallon fuel cans, tossing them haphazardly into the back of the truck before speeding away in a shower of gravel and dirt. Everyone left behind turned their heads, squeezing shut their eyelids and mouths to avoid the flying debris propelled toward them by the spinning tires. As the cloud of dust dissipated, Enrique uttered a few words in Spanish before heading up the steps onto the sloping porch and disappearing into the house.

Jamal had Khalib busy himself by checking through the duffle bags and the outside of the computer cases for any signs of damage from the punishing truck ride. Ibrahim and Sa'id were intrigued by the tarnished, silver-colored windmill that spun slowly in the corner of the barn lot, thirty feet from the nearest of the two barns. A couple of vanes missing from it made the wheel rotate in an awkward fashion. The reward of its constant effort was a trickle of water that sputtered out of a horizontal pipe into a circular cement trough eight feet across and three feet high that was braced against the base of the four-legged windmill. Ibrahim explained to Sa'id how it served as a source of drinking water for the farm animals. This became apparent to Sa'id as a goat sauntered over to the trough, hopped onto a tree stump butted up beside it, placed both front hooves on the wide concrete lip of the trough before lowering its head into the pool of water that came within inches of the top.

"I believe goats are smarter than cows," Ibrahim proposed off-handedly with a nod of his head in the direction of the creature.

The parti-colored goat, satiated, smacked its lips, twisted its neck toward them and returned their gaze, water dribbling from the long hairs under its chin.

"I wonder if they taste better," Sa'id considered out loud over the growl of his empty stomach.

He'd eaten the last of his food on the plane not long after their departure from the jungle airstrip in Columbia, some ten hours ago. The thought of food brought pangs of hunger for Ibrahim, too.

"Maybe the old man would let us butcher one this evening. A *cabrito*."

"A what?"

"A young, tender, succulent one," Ibrahim explained, licking his lips.

"If Jamal has any money left, we could buy it from him."

"If Jamal won't, I will. I've brought along a little money," Ibrahim insisted.

Both decided this was a reasonable idea, and they headed back to their cohorts with it. Sa`id described to the others he and Ibrahim's idea for the evening meal as Enrique came out onto the porch with bottles of cola in each hand. His broad grin revealed several missing teeth as he passed around the warm drinks. Sa`id pointed out to the others, in Arabic, that the old Mexican's mouth and the wheel of the windmill had a lot in common. A boisterous round of laughter ensued from the four, and Enrique looked to Ibrahim for an explanation but was ignored. Not wanting to be left out on the joke, he followed suit by grinning widely as he let out a weak laugh, bringing on another chorus of laughter from the others.

They stood in silence for a minute, tipping their bottles skyward one by one as the sun vanished behind the blistered hills. Enrique, with a motion of his arm, beckoned them to follow him as he tossed his empty bottle into a patch of stunted weeds next to the porch before making his way toward the nearest of the pole barns.

With twilight approaching, the air cooled rapidly. Jamal rummaged through his bag for a jacket while the others hurried after Enrique. Having removed his gun from the waistband at the small of his back, Jamal put on his shoulder holster and repositioned his gun into it; a more comfortable, better concealed, and easier accessed position.

In his mind, Jamal could picture his own grandfather with the same pattern of missing teeth as Enrique. He'd died when Jamal was thirteen, but Jamal could still remember the stories his grandfather told of how he'd lost them during interrogations by the Egyptian State Police in the early days of the Muslim Brotherhood. He wondered how the old Mexican had lost his, catching up to the others, as Enrique was about to show them their method of transportation across the border into the United States.

Parked in the barn, clearing the eave by less than an inch was a tandem axel, refrigerated truck over thirty feet in length from bumper to bumper. Enrique opened the door at the back that allowed access to the cooled compartment. A warm, stale, musty odor, not of mold, but of an organic, almost earthy quality was released into the night air surrounding them. He explained, through Ibrahim, that there was a false ceiling where the insulation had been removed, leaving a space just wide enough between the roof and ceiling for a man to lie flat.

Jamal, with a skeptical look on his face, interrupted, "Ask him, Ibrahim, if there is room enough for all of us to go across in one trip."

Sa'id added, "Won't we cook up there with the sun beating down on the metal roof of the truck?"

Everyone nodded his head in agreement at Sa'id's observation. Ibrahim voiced his and Jamal's concerns to the old Mexican. They stood there with uneasy, questioning looks, waiting for a response.

Enrique reached inside the refrigerated unit, flipped a switch, and stepped up into the empty cooler. A dim light bathed the interior compartment in a jaundiced pallor. Reluctant to go further, the four jihadists stuck their heads simultaneously through the open doorway, with Khalib kneeling at the step leading into the cooler, Sa'id leaning over him, a hand resting on Khalib's shoulder, while Ibrahim and Jamal stood on either side, craning their necks around the edge of the open doorway to peer inside.

The outlines of faint, pinkish stains were visible on the smooth, white vinyl walls while darker ones were apparent on the floor next to where Enrique stood. He pointed to a metal vent in the ceiling near the back of the compartment. According to Ibrahim's interpretation, there was a duct that passed through the insulated—formerly insulated—ceiling that went from the vent to the refrigeration compressor mounted over the cab of the truck. It cooled the entire compartment; in addition, he explained there were multiple holes in the duct that let cooled air escape into the concealed area. He assured them that there was room for all four of them to fit, and they would go across the border together.

This gave Jamal a measure of relief. He didn't want to be separated from the others from this point forward, especially Khalib who seemed increasingly nervous.

Enrique went on to explain that they would stop in Matamoras to pick up a load of goat carcasses from an unlicensed slaughterhouse, pointing out four rows of thick metal rings attached to the ceiling from which the carcasses hung. Most of the border crossing guards, he said with a laugh, were reluctant to spend any time inside the cooler looking for stowaways when it was packed full of fresh goat carcasses. After crossing the border, he would take them to a warehouse in Brownsville.

"There will be no problems with papers or inspections at the border?" Jamal asked.

Enrique shook his head. Normally, he hauled meat across the border to Mexico, he explained. And for that reason no one would question him going the other way. He assured them everything would go smoothly. His big toothless grin gave Jamal little solace.

Ibrahim, with permission from Jamal, asked the old Mexican if they could buy a goat from him to slaughter and roast for supper, eagerly adding that he had money to pay for it. Enrique was quick to ask how much money. They settled on thirty-five dollars, which Ibrahim paid for gladly out of his own pocket, anxious to assuage the growl coming from his stomach.

After pocketing the money, Enrique led them to the other dilapidated pole barn. A pen of young goats, being fattened with grain, clamored to the fence in an effort to see who was going to feed them tonight. Ibrahim and the others did likewise. Sa'id pointed out a plump one pushing its way to the front of the pack. Khalib, his own hunger pushing to the forefront of his thoughts, hopped the fence made of discarded wooden pallets and grabbed the one that would join then for supper. He lifted the squirming kid over the fence to the others, its panicked bleats sending the remaining cabritos scurrying in random directions as they bounced off, or over, one another like bowling pins. Ibrahim and Sa'id each held a back leg while Enrique unsheathed a knife hanging from his cracked leather belt. The young goat gave one more high-pitched cry and then there was silence, save for the steady drum of blood pulsing against the packed-earthen floor.

A rising, orange moon provided them with ample light for the gutting and skinning. Enrique told Jamal where to find a pile of mesquite wood, just west of the house. With Khalib's help, they brought back armfuls of dry wood, placing it in a shallow pit not far from the windmill. The pit was surrounded by large flat stones and filled with the gray ash of previous fires. Ibrahim and Sa'id, following Enrique's guidance, hoisted the fresh carcass onto a metal rod that served as a spit over the fire they were beginning to build.

The cabrito had been over the fire for more than an hour with Jamal turning it every few minutes while stirring the coals and adding wood as needed. Enrique, after bringing out seasoning for Jamal to sprinkle on the roasting meat, vanished back into the farmhouse. The other three recited their evening prayers and read from the Qur'an by the flickering firelight before turning their discussion toward more mundane topics. Questions, directed toward Jamal, concerning his training in the deserts of North Africa came from Ibrahim and Sa'id. Khalib withdrew into his own world, his arms wrapped around his knees that were pulled up against his chest as he rocked to and fro on the ground, his eyes staring blankly at the night sky.

A few minutes past before a glow of light became visible in the east only to disappear for an instant before reappearing. Jamal noticed it before the others as he stood up from his kneeling position beside the fire, glancing over at Khalib who seemed almost in a trance.

"There must be a million stars in the sky," he pronounced, stretching his arms over his head toward the heavens. The shaft of light grew brighter but disappeared again. "I suppose they are not the same stars as those we saw just last night at Ali's ranch. What do you think, Khalib?"

Jamal was trying to subtly draw Khalib's attention to the intermittent light.

"What is that?" Khalib asked, pointing an unsteady finger in the direction of the light he now caught a glimpse of as it reappeared briefly.

Jamal, pretending to have just seen it, answered in a serious tone, "Why, I have no doubt it must be Allah, come to answer your prayers, Khalib. I saw it once, after prayers in the deserts of Libya, during the training camp I was just telling Ibrahim and Sa'id about.

"They'd dropped me off, blindfolded, in the middle of nowhere. I had to find my way back to camp as part of a survival exercise. Thirsty all the time it seemed, day turned to night. I prayed for water to soothe my burning throat and for guidance to find my way back to camp."

Sa`id and Ibrahim began to take notice of the light. It seemed to point heavenward, as Jamal told his story over the sound of the spitting, hissing fire and the constant creak of the windmill, kept in motion by a steady breeze out of the west.

Wide-eyed, nerves frayed, Khalib responded, "And Allah heard your prayers and brought you water, yes?"

He was on his knees, leaning forward almost out of his sandals, looking dreamily at Jamal for the answer he knew must follow but needed to hear it anyway.

"No." Jamal stated abruptly as the light grew still brighter and the serious look on his face was replaced by a devious grin. "A jeep, with several of my comrades in it, brought me a jug of water."

Khalib's intense gaze had been replaced by a puzzled expression. At that moment, a pair of headlights topped the last of the low hills to the east, revealing the source of the illumination— Enrique's grandsons in the pickup.

Jamal laughed, turning toward Ibrahim and Sa`id who were both smiling. Khalib, quivered momentarily with anger, having been duped, then he lunged at Jamal.

"You are a non-believer! You ridicule our faith in Allah," Khalib shouted as he knocked Jamal to the ground. "An infidel, you mock us. I will not be led by the likes of you!"

Sa`id and Ibrahim pulled Khalib away from Jamal. Jamal struggled to his feet, grabbing at Khalib's shirt with one hand, the other clenched into a fist ready to strike.

"Don't be so naïve, Khalib," Jamal shouted angrily, before pausing to catch his breath. "You can not run to Allah every time you are scared, like a child hiding behind his mother's apron. The moment is fast approaching when we will not have time to pray for direction before each move as we complete our mission. Don't expect Allah to give you guidance every time you are confused or scared. You must get hold of your emotions, Khalib," Jamal chastised. "All of you must," he continued, glancing at Sa`id and Ibrahim to be sure they too understood his meaning. "I can not hold your hand through all of this. Pray to Allah now, but once we start for the border don't hesitate or appear nervous in your actions to anyone. Use your own judgment; your own common sense."

Khalib seethed with anger as he shook loose from the grip of the other two. Jamal wondered if he'd heard a single word just spoken to him. Sa`id stared at Jamal with the same look he'd given him back on the freighter when the four of them argued about the different branches of their religion.

The pickup truck reached the driveway and pulled up toward the fire in the same manner it had left the farm, blinding the four Muslims with its headlights and choking them with dust as it screeched to a halt.

Enrique's grandsons had already begun to deplete the purchased supplies lying in the back of the truck as evidenced by the bottle of beer each held in his hand plus two empty ones on the seat between them. The driver, Jose`, lowered the tailgate and hoisted a snow-white salt block on to his shoulder, still clutching the nearly empty bottle in his hand as he walked toward the paddock where the cattle and goats were grazing. His brother took a couple of bags of groceries and headed for the house, calling out boisterously for his grandfather as he stepped on to the slanting porch.

Enrique appeared and, after helping unload the rest of the supplies, he joined Jamal and the others by the fire. He brought along more cola, tomatoes, peppers, and a stack of stale tortillas. Jose` turned the truck around, backing it up close to the fire pit so its tailgate could be used as a table. Pablo, the other grandson, soon joined them carrying a broken cooler, bound with duct tape and packed with iced bottles of Mexican beer. He offered everyone a bottle, but Ibrahim explained to him that their religion forbade the drinking of alcohol. Jose`, his inhibitions melting away with each new bottle, grabbed another one and shouted, "*Mas para nosotros.*"

Pablo, nodding in agreement with his brother's assessment, shouted skyward, "We will drink it ourselves." Then, he handed a bottle to his grandfather.

Jamal continued to turn the spit. With each rotation, juices from the cabrito fell into the fire, urging it higher. The seven of them stood there quietly for a time, staring into the flames as reflections of glowing embers shone in their eyes. The hiss of dripping grease upon the hot coals, a forlorn call from a distant wolf, and the erratic windmill were the only sounds. As the breeze calmed, smoke drifted aimlessly toward the star-filled sky, its movement broken up by quivering waves of heat emanating from the blue flames.

The incessant stroking of Khalib's hand against his pant leg broke the spell for Jamal. This nervous tick had only begun today, Jamal thought, and he worried more and more about Khalib's mental state as he watched him out of the corner of his eye. Perhaps he'd been wrong to joke about the lights with Khalib and then to chastise him about his constant need for prayer. Though Sa'id was similar in his constant indulgence of prayer, he demonstrated no outward signs of falling apart the way Khalib was. In any other place, under any other circumstances, Jamal would have punished Khalib severely for attacking him as he'd done a short time ago. Of his three subordinates, Ibrahim seemed to be the most comfortable with their situation so far. Most likely it was because he could speak to the three Mexicans in their native tongue, Jamal surmised.

"*Bastante...*, *ehh...*, *stop*," Enrique commanded in halting English as he raised his hand toward Jamal and the turning spit.

The old Mexican waved his knife through the hottest part of the fire. Then, with the aid of a charred stick to steady the carcass on the spit, he sliced a piece of meat from the loin, holding the filleted meat against the knife blade with his blackened thumbnail. A few seconds passed as he allowed the meat to cool, cautiously nibbling on the end before he devoured the whole of it.

"*Mmmm, muy bien cabrito. El es un cocinero bueno,*" he said in the direction of his grandsons as he pointed at Jamal with his knife.

"You're a good cook, according to the old man," Ibrahim said with a smile as Jamal looked toward him with a questioning expression.

Jamal shrugged, rotating the spit a few more times while Enrique got a plate from the back of the pickup. He sliced long strips of meat, letting them fall into a pile on the plate.

Following the lead of their host, Jamal and the others grabbed tortillas, layering them with peppers, tomato, and mouth-watering meat. Khalib said a prayer out loud, which was ignored by the three Mexicans and only briefly acknowledged by Sa`id, Ibrahim, and Jamal before they began to devour their bounty. Khalib chastised them in Arabic for their greediness to eat without giving thanks to Allah, but only Sa`id stopped long enough to offer a sincere apology.

"I gave thanks to Allah," Ibrahim explained, barely coherent with a stuffed mouth, "during evening prayers for our safe journey and the food we were about to eat."

Khalib chewed methodically as he stared into the flames, giving no recognition to what Ibrahim or the others had said. Jamal continued to observe Khalib while he finished his own food before washing it down with another cola.

Jose` borrowed his grandfather's knife and carved off more meat from the cabrito. Everyone, except Khalib, indulged in another round of feasting. Pablo cleared a spot on the tailgate and sat down while Enrique stood leaning his full stomach against the truck, his arms dangling over the side into the bed where one hand grasped the lip of his empty beer bottle. Jose`, in a mix of two languages, began to quiz Ibrahim.

"*Donde ustedes* learn to *usar una* computer? Will you get jobs in *Los Estados Unidos usaando* them?"

Ibrahim shook his head, pointing a finger at himself, "*Me no uso la computadora. Ellos usan los computadoras.*" He pointed to Khalib and Sa`id as he finished.

"Can I see them," Pablo asked, in good English, surprising Ibrahim.

Before he could answer, Jamal interrupted with a shake of his head.

"No, the batteries have run down. The computers will not work until we recharge them," Jamal explained.

Pablo and Jose` both took hefty swallows from their bottles of beer.

"Can they not run off the truck battery? If you have a charger, we could do it," Pablo demanded.

"No," Jamal said abruptly, staring into the fire, searching for a plausible excuse, but in the end said nothing more.

This silence irritated Pablo as he wiped his mouth with his forearm. "Aren't we good enough to use your equipment? You don't have any problem eating our *cabrito, amigo.*

"We paid for the goat," Jamal admonished, pointing a finger at Enrique who was spinning the empty bottle in the bed of the truck, oblivious to the conversation.

"Thirty-five dollars," Sa`id added, "and we had to cook it."

This brought a laugh from Jamal and Ibrahim while Khalib continued to brood. Jose` and Pablo took turns speaking in harsh tones to their *abuelo* in Spanish. Their deference to their grandfather had begun to vanish along with each bottle of beer. Jamal looked to Ibrahim for an explanation.

"They are complaining to Enrique about the money we gave him for the goat. They say their father sent them the money to pay for the goats and to buy feed for them."

Just as Ibrahim finished, Enrique pulled thirty-five dollars in crumpled bills from his pocket, tossing them onto the tailgate and gesturing for his grandsons to take the money. Pablo and Jose` each took part of the money, ignoring their grandfather's mutterings of how he'd looked after the two of them the past four years.

"Where is your father?" Ibrahim inquired, after Enrique had finished his discourse on raising two ungrateful grandsons.

"He is in America," Pablo stated proudly. His chest was jutting out like a strutting rooster as he continued, "or he was there. Now he is in Kuwait or maybe Iraq."

Khalib eyed him intently from the edge of the hissing fire as he continued.

"He and my mother, along with our little sister, have been in America for almost four years. My father joined the military last year after the meat-processing plant he worked at closed its doors. As soon as he gets discharged from the army, he will be able to obtain his citizenship papers much quicker and we will go live with them in *Los Estados Unidos.*"

"Is your father killing Muslims?" Khalib's voice was just above a whisper, his eyes were fixated on his trembling right hand that moments before was incessantly strumming a loose thread on his jeans.

"Is your swine of a father killing Muslims?" he repeated, louder.

Then he shouted the question a third time, loud enough for the ruminating cows, visible in the distance when the flames peaked, to stop chewing their cud and take notice of his voice.

"Khalib, we are guests here," Jamal admonished sternly.

Khalib ignored him.

But Pablo didn't. He wasted no time in answering Khalib with an invective tirade of mixed Spanish and English, which ridiculed their Islamic religion and their prophet Mohammed, adding he hoped his father killed many, as he crouched in front of Khalib, taunting him.

Khalib flung a handful of dirt at Pablo's face before grabbing an empty cola bottle lying beside him. He smashed it on the flat rocks surrounding the fire pit. Still bent over, he lunged at Pablo driving the jagged-edged neck of the bottle deep into his thigh.

The force of Khalib's body slam sent Pablo back against the tailgate as he tried to regain his balance. He toppled over into the bed of the truck with Khalib on top of him shouting incoherently, ready to plunge the bloody glass a second time.

Sa`id grabbed Khalib's arm before he could do more damage and began to wrestle him off of Pablo. Jose`, cursing at the four jihadists, his reaction time slowed by alcohol, reached for the knife used in carving the cabrito and swung it around wildly at Khalib as Sa`id pulled, and Pablo pushed, Khalib off.

Jamal watched the blade, smeared with grease and sinew, as it disappeared into Sa`id's shirt just above and behind his elbow. He could see Sa`id's legs buckle; and in that moment he remembered how he'd been taught, at the desert training camp, to bring the knife up under the ribcage from behind for an unobstructed path to the heart in an effort to inflict a quick and hopefully silent death.

It was a lucky stab by Jose`. Sa`id never uttered a word. Jamal could see the life draining from Sa`id's eyes, the puzzled grimace on his face as Sa`id's grip on Khalib went lax. He watched as the crimson color spread in a glistening wave across Sa`id's shirt as he folded up onto the ground.

The report of Jamal's gun echoed across the night. It brought Khalib out of his mindless rage. It brought Jose` to his knees as the knife, now coated with a thin sheen of blood, dropped with a dull thud onto the dirt as he crumpled lifeless on the ground against Sa`id. It brought Ibrahim, who'd been watching in open-mouthed disbelief, scurrying across the ground on all four's to Sa`id's side. It brought Enrique's right hand frantically across the side of his face as he wiped remnants of Jose` off his cheek while the rest of him moved stealthily toward the cab, his left hand searching discreetly for the shotgun hanging behind the seat.

The next shot from Jamal's 9mm left a shiny, paint-less hole in the steel cab support adjacent to the back window of the pickup.

"No!" he shouted at Enrique over the screams of Ibrahim and now Khalib, who just realized that his brother—if only through religion—had been felled by the knife intended for him.

"Move back away from the truck!" Jamal ordered, adding the universally understood language of a pointed gun barrel, motioning it toward the old Mexican.

With his gun trained on Enrique, who understood, Jamal squatted down beside Jose's corpse and flung the knife into the fire. He pulled Jose`corpse off of Sa`id and, as he let go, Jose's limp body fell from its sitting position onto its side, exposing the missing parts of his head that Enrique had wiped from his own face moments before.

"Jose`! Jose`!" Pablo cried out as he took a step toward the body but stopped short as the pain shot up his leg. He turned away from the grotesque sight of his brother's mangled head.

Jamal pressed his gun hard against Pablo's ear. "Unless you want to look like your brother, get down on your knees with your hands behind you."

"Ibrahim," Jamal called out in a calm voice as Ibrahim continued to kneel by Sa'id, not responding.

"Ibrahim!" He called out again, nudging him forcefully with his boot. "Tell the old man to sit on the ground with his legs crossed and his hands behind him."

Ibrahim did as he was told, mechanically, his voice devoid of inflection, still stunned by the events.

"There is a roll of insulated wire in my duffle bag," Jamal ordered, his gun trained alternately on Enrique and his one grandson. "Get it out and bind their wrists behind them..., hobble their feet also, Ibrahim."

Ibrahim did as instructed in silence while Jamal, keeping a wary eye on Enrique, removed the shells from the loaded shotgun, pocketing them in his jacket before removing the keys from the truck and locking it.

Khalib, with breathless rapidity, whispered Qur'anic verses into Sa'id's deaf ear as he knelt beside him. When Jamal returned to the bodies, Khalib ceased his prayers and looked up into Jamal's cold eyes.

Perhaps because of the tears that blurred his vision, or perhaps from a desire for punishment in some manner, as a form of redemption, he made no attempt to move as Jamal kicked him hard in the side. In almost the identical spot where minutes before Sa`id had felt the cold steel blade of a knife. Khalib rocked forward on his knees, his head propped against the dirt, gasping for air as Jamal kicked him again, like a master punishing his problematic dog.

"You fool! You imbecile!" Jamal shouted angrily as he brought the butt of his gun down on the back of Khalib's bowed head. "I've played nurse maid to you for weeks and now this…, this is how you repay me."

Khalib offered no resistance as Jamal grabbed him by the hair, picking him up and slamming him against the edge of the tailgate.

"Stop! Jamal stop! No more, please."

The cry came not from Khalib but from Ibrahim as he reached Jamal and pulled him away. Jamal staggered backwards, panting, then turned and walked off into the darkness beyond the fire.

Ibrahim helped Khalib, heaving with sobs, to his feet, "Come, Khalib, we must dig a grave and bury Sa`id before morning."

Ibrahim and Khalib found a pickaxe and two blunt-ended shovels in the barn where the goats were kept. They decided on a low rise west of the barns and, after considering the direction the grave must face, began digging. They'd been at it for thirty minutes before Jamal spotted them silhouetted against the night sky. The moon hung low behind them as clouds, blued by its glow, languished about, keeping quiet company.

Enrique and Pablo had crawled to the side of the pickup truck with Ibrahim's permission. When Jamal returned, both were propped against the tires, their hands and feet diligently bound, fast asleep. He'd wandered aimlessly across the low hills for more than an hour before his anger receded enough that he could face Khalib without harming him further. In addition, he'd had time to formulate a new plan in his head since Enrique could not be trusted now. With one grandson dead and the other wounded, Jamal was sure he wouldn't take them across the border willingly for *any* amount of money.

Jamal took up the rough-handled axe. He worked out the remainder of his anger on the rocky soil beneath his feet in silence: save for his grunts, the dull thud of the axe upon hard earth or its frequent "chink" when encountering rocks that produced a shower of sparks. Jamal worked feverishly at one end while the other two rested, panting and soaked with sweat, at the other end. When he was spent and out of breath, they changed places with not a word spoken between the three of them until their heads had disappeared below the earth that surrounded them, as had the moon.

"That will be deep enough," Jamal said to no one in particular, his voice wavering between breaths. "We must get some sleep before morning. Tomorrow will be a critical junction in our journey."

"We need a burial shroud for Sa`id," Khalib said timidly, still unsteady from the beating, as he climbed out of the hole.

Jamal glanced his way, anger beginning to flare again. He was ready to berate Khalib once more but thought better of it as he looked at the back of Khalib's bent head. There was a streak of dried blood mixed with sweat and dirt tracking down the back of his neck. Jamal was reminded of the soreness at the back of his own head and the lump still prominent at its base.

"I'll go look in the old man's house and see what I can find. Bring some water from the well to cleanse Sa`id's body with," he instructed Ibrahim.

Ibrahim and Khalib nodded their approval.

Khalib chanted a litany of prayers while Jamal and Ibrahim began to shovel dirt onto the mummy-like, white bed sheet. Once the hole was back-filled, Jamal took a second sheet he'd found while rummaging through the house and wrapped it roughly around Jose`. With Ibrahim's help, they carried the stiffening corpse to the barn and packed what was left of the ice from the cooler around it.

They could see Khalib's dark form sitting atop the mound of dirt as the two of them headed for the well to clean up before any attempt at sleep.

"Jamal, what happens if no one is there to meet us in Brownsville?" Ibrahim asked.

Jamal shrugged before answering, "They will be there. If not, we will make our way to Houston." Jamal sounded more determined then ever, "I have the address of our contact there. You must have faith in your fellow jihadists…, except for Khalib. I am worried about him right now," Jamal confided. "I fear he may not have been the right choice for this journey. Mentally, he is showing signs of weakness, and now, with Sa`id gone, I don't know what he will do next. We must keep a close watch on him, Ibrahim."

Jamal slept in the bed of the pickup, in case Enrique or Pablo made any attempt to escape. The crow of a rooster woke him sooner than he would have wished, and, for a moment, he struggled between sleep and consciousness. A slight movement of the truck brought him fully awake to the lighting sky of dawn.

Jamal peered over the side of the truck and saw one of his captives, Enrique, beginning to stir. Pablo, his left pant leg encrusted in blood, was still sound asleep, most likely a result of the alcohol as much as the blood loss from his wound, Jamal mused. Though not as devout at abstinence as Khalib and Sa`id, he could plainly see why alcohol was forbidden. It had played the demon's role in Sa`id's death.

From his vantage point, standing in the back of the pickup, Jamal could see Ibrahim asleep on the wooden porch of the house. Farther away to the west, on the horizon, was Khalib's profile, prone against the mound that marked Sa`id's final resting place.

Jamal was resolute in what had to be done as he completed his survey. Every calamity that had befallen them on this trip made him more determined to see it through to its end. He hopped down from the truck and with long strides headed for Khalib.

"Come on, Khalib. It is time to go."

He tapped lightly on Khalib's forehead with his boot, too stiff to make any attempt at bending down. Khalib woke with a start but offered no complaint, following Jamal obediently back to the others. Enrique was wallowing around on the ground as he tried to rise. The awkward position in which he'd been forced to sleep had rendered his legs numb.

"*Tengo sed por favor unos aqua,*" Enrique asked, his voice gravelly from the phlegm and dust in his throat. He finally managed to stand, shaking one leg and then the other in an effort to regain the feeling in them. Not sure if Jamal understood him, he asked for water in broken English.

Jamal, despite the steady trickle of fresh water from the pipe, plunged an empty beer bottle into the algae-tinged water trough and brought it back to the old Mexican whose chin was tucked in against the wattles of his neck.

It's time to take us across the border, old man," Jamal pronounced.

He proceeded to tip back Enrique's head, pouring the water on his captive's face and in his mouth.

"You can drink the same water as the other old goats around this place," Jamal said, looking off in the direction of the herd grazing south of the barns, "then you will drive us to Matamoras."

"I no take you Matamoras," he vehemently insisted, barely above a whisper, shaking his head slowly before spitting toward Jamal. Jamal did nothing except smile from ear to ear after hearing the old man's belligerent remark.

Khalib, indifferent to where the knife had been the night before, fished it out of the cooling ash and sliced off a piece of meat from the cold carcass hanging on the spit.

Jamal shouted toward the house, "Ibrahim! It is time to get up. We must be on our way."

Enrique repeated, defiantly, louder this time, "I no take you Matamoras."

"Oh, I think you'll take us where we want to go," Jamal informed him with a nod of his head toward Pablo, "or you'll be short *two* grandsons."

With that, Jamal grabbed Pablo by the hair and brought him abruptly out of his deep slumber. Pablo shrieked in pain as he was forced to bear weight on his injured leg.

Enrique said nothing more as Jamal went to the water trough, bringing back a drink for Pablo, whose face was ashen from pain with beads of sweat appearing on his upper lip and forehead. Ibrahim gathered up his belongings while Khalib washed himself under the hand pump.

"Make sure we leave nothing behind," Jamal shouted toward Ibrahim. "Hurry, we must not be late to our contact point across the border. They will know it is too risky to wait on us for very long."

Jamal grabbed Enrique and Pablo by the arm, one on each side of him, escorting them to the refrigerator truck. Pablo drug his leg, wincing with every step as he and Enrique shuffled along, their feet still shackled with wire.

Unable to stand any longer, Pablo sat down on one of the five-gallon diesel cans that had been emptied into the truck. Enrique stood behind him, telling his grandson to rest against him. Jamal and the others busied themselves with stuffing their belongings into the false ceiling of the cooled compartment.

Enrique repeated himself, louder this time, *"No voy con ustedes para Matamoras."*

"He says he's not...," Ibrahim began to translate.

Jamal, sounding annoyed, interrupted Ibrahim before he could finish, "I know what he's trying to tell us. Go ahead and start up the truck, Ibrahim, while we finish loading our gear in the back."

"But I don't know where we are going."

Jamal shouted back at Ibrahim, making it plain to him not to question or back talk again when given an order. Khalib increased his speed at loading the truck and, after an apology, Ibrahim hopped into the cab, firing up the diesel engine. Jamal searched the barn and, after a minute of rummaging, found what he needed: some rusty number nine wire and a rickety wooden stepladder.

He shouted over the idling engine for Khalib to come help him.

Jamal instructed Khalib to steady the ladder while he proceeded to the top rung, looping the heavy gauge wire over one of the barn rafters. He motioned for Ibrahim to come help, also. The three of them, with Jamal's guidance, lifted Pablo up onto the top of the ladder. A cloud of exhaust fumes enveloped them as Jamal fashioned the wire into a noose around Pablo's neck. Once finished, Jamal jumped down, a satisfied look on his face, and looked at Enrique who was watching with a dejected look of surrender.

"Now will you take us to Matamoras?" Jamal asked him directly, no translation necessary, an impatient tone in his voice. He kicked the ladder and it swayed precariously as Pablo scrambled to shift his weight and keep it upright.

"*Si! Si!*" The old Mexican said, nodding his head, helpless to steady the ladder.

"Untie him, Ibrahim. Tell him the quicker he gets us across the border, the quicker he can get back here. Any tricks that delay us will make it that much harder on his grandson."

Ibrahim did as he was told.

"You ride in front with the old man, Ibrahim. Remember, stay calm," Jamal added, handing him the knife he'd put in his pocket after Khalib's earlier use of it.

Khalib and Jamal crawled up into the narrow space above the cooler while Ibrahim replaced the panel, tightening the screw that held it in place.

Enrique backed the truck out of the barn. He shifted gears, gunning the motor as he gave a glance at Pablo, still perched on top of the unsteady ladder while shifting his legs in tiny increments to find a comfortable position. In an instant, he was lost from Enrique's view.

The ride to Matamoras for Jamal and Khalib was punishing with one jolting bump after another. They managed to stuff articles of clothing from their duffle bags between their heads and the roof of the truck. At least, Jamal thought, it kept Khalib's mind off what was ahead for them.

The reefer unit that cooled the compartment made it impossible for the two stowaways to hear anything from the cab or the compartment below them. They were stopped in Matamoras just long enough to fill the truck with goat carcasses. The dusky smell of freshly skinned meat permeated their hidden compartment. This smell along with the renewed motion of the truck meant they would soon be at the border crossing, Jamal calculated. He raised his voice above the din to reassure Khalib of their progress. With no response from Khalib, Jamal twisted his neck to get a look at Khalib whose face was only inches from his own but barely discernible in the dark enclosure. He could make out Khalib's eyelids squeezed shut, his lips moving rapidly with no audible sound. He was praying.

The motion of the truck stopped for what seemed longer than what Jamal considered normal for a traffic light or stop sign. Jamal could hear the door to the refrigerated compartment open and then muffled voices directly below him. Next, Jamal felt a couple of light taps on the ceiling below him and he reached for his holstered gun. He released the safety aiming the barrel between his legs at the vent they'd crawled through. Now he regretted not lying prone on his stomach facing the other direction for a view of what was going on below, though the ride would have been intolerable in that position. Just as he cocked his gun, he heard laughter followed by the slamming of the door. Before he could holster his gun, they jolted forward. The truck was moving again.

Ten more minutes of jostling about in their hiding place and once again the truck came to a prolonged stop. This time the diesel engine was turned off and the hum of the refrigeration motor ceased also. The door opened again and this time he could hear the screws being taken out of the ventilation cover.

Khalib inched his way toward the opening with no regard to Jamal who was actually closer to it. He squirmed down through the opening while Jamal pushed all their bags and computers out behind him.

Jamal slid out feet first, holding his gun and holster above him. A pair of hands grabbed his legs and waist as he was lowered to the floor. The first sight to greet Jamal's blinking eyes were the rows of goat carcasses, their deep red muscle and white seams of fat glistened in the light. He turned his head, both hands still overhead, obscured from view. Next to him, inches away, was a ruddy-faced, blonde-haired young man that Jamal guessed to be in his early twenties. His hair hung to his shoulders in unkempt braids, his goatee was the color of wet sand. Jamal tightened his grip on the pistol as he looked past the man toward the open door.

Before he could decide on a course of action, his blonde counterpart spoke, *"As-salaamu `alaykum `akh marHaba `ilaa `amriikaa."*

Jamal released his grip on the holster, proceeding to shake hands gently and making eye contact while his other hand rhythmically squeezed the knurled handle of his gun.

" `es-mee Joshua, you can call me Josh for short. I am sorry that I don't know more Arabic. I was told you would be fluent in English."

"You were informed correctly. My name is Jamal."

The puzzled look on Jamal's face negated the need for a verbal question and Joshua was ready with an answer.

"They sent me to pick you up, perhaps because I don't look like a foreigner. You know, less conspicuous," he explained in an apologetic tone, before boasting, "I have been a devout member of the mosque in Houston for three years."

Jamal holstered his gun and followed Joshua out of the truck into a large warehouse. Ibrahim and Khalib stood beside the vehicle, conversing about the ride as Ibrahim recounted the cargo inspection by the border agents. Enrique was still seated behind the steering wheel; a black cloth sack had been pulled down over his head as a blindfold before Joshua brought his car into the warehouse.

"How long will it take us to get to Houston from here?" Jamal asked, after ordering the others to load all of their belongings into the trunk of the midnight blue, Grand Prix now parked beside the truck.

"It will take four or five hours, depending on how fast I drive. We have a safe house prepared for you just off Telephone Road, near the old airport. I was told to deliver you there."

Jamal took a deep breath, strapped on his shoulder harness and smiled, satisfied that he and his crew were safely in America. He stopped Ibrahim as they were about to pile into the car and guided him over to the driver side window of the truck. They both stood on the metal step leading up to the cab, level with their reluctant driver's cloaked head.

"Tell him I am truly sorry for the loss of his grandson. I wished him no harm. He and our Sa`id will be in my prayers."

Ibrahim lowered his eyes for a moment before translating the message to Enrique as Jamal dropped several one hundred dollar bills onto his lap.

CHAPTER SIX

Captain Farroque looked on with distain from the bridge of the *Empress of Sayda* as more pallets were loaded into the forward cargo hold. The telegram from the ship's owner lay before him on a bank of navigational instruments. A faint breeze, the first since they'd docked here in the stifling heat and humidity of Jakarta, pushed the paper onto the floor at the captain's feet. He reread the cable before folding it neatly and placing it in his shirt pocket. When he'd last talked to the shipping company, before leaving Buenos Aires, no mention had been made of taking on more cargo, only a new crew, which by itself made the captain lose sleep for several nights.

Ramon had been his first mate for five years. The entire crew of sixteen had been with the ship for that length of time. Although only Ramon could speak passable English, the others had been hard workers and diligent in their duties. Too diligent sometimes, Captain Farroque thought, as he recalled the missing life ring; the life ring, which had been brought to everyone's attention when the passenger, Monsour, was discovered missing during the first leg of the voyage from Lagos to Buenos Aires. Still, they were a good bunch, which he was thankful for, asking no questions of Captain Farroque or the illicit passengers that padded his bank account.

It took a long time to become comfortable with a new crew, many of whom had come and gone over his years as a Captain. But that had always been the arrangement with the *Empress's* owners. The captain had no say in who they hired to work on the ship. His only concern was to pilot it from port to port and make sure the crew did whatever was necessary to get them there.

His old crew had only left the ship this morning. Captain Farroque was already missing them as he watched what appeared to be the entire new crew milling about on the deck.

"A days work for a days pay" had always been Captain Farroque's mantra with any crew during his years at the helm. Several of this crew appeared to be arguing with the first mate near the forward cargo hold as another pallet of bagged ammonium nitrate descended below deck. The captain could see the crane operator gesturing toward the men on deck, who, in turn, seemed agitated with what he was implying. Captain Farroque decided it was best that he go down and see for himself what the problem was.

When the new first mate spotted Captain Farroque coming across the deck, he shouted orders to the other crewmembers nearby in a dialect unfamiliar to the captain. When he'd introduced himself upon boarding, the first mate spoke English, though he appeared of middle-eastern descent, which eased Captain Farroque's apprehension of fielding a new crew that couldn't understand his commands. This new discovery upset him, but no more than the way his old crew was rudely ushered off the ship without a chance to say goodbye.

And worse yet was the content of the telex, informing him to take on three hundred tons of ammonium nitrate fertilizer here in Jakarta. The ship's engine already struggled under the partial load of copper ingots carried from Santiago, seemingly getting weaker each day. Captain Farroque had thought it a wise decision on the part of the owners to take on the smaller load of copper. Now, he wondered if they even had a clue—despite his multiple warnings—about the condition of the engine or the qualifications of this new crew.

"What seems to be the problem…, Nicolas?"

The captain struggled with the pronunciation, not because of the sound, but because it struck him as an odd name for someone from the Middle East as Nicolas had informed him and attested to by his thick accent.

"There is no problem, Captain Farroque."

"Then why does the crane operator seem so upset?" he asked abruptly.

Captain Farroque's irritation with the changed situation came through in his voice. He had meticulously planned this trip—his last—and now everything seemed to be out of his control. First, the constant struggle with the failing engine, forced to make one to many trips before a much needed overhaul, then the death of Monsour followed by Jamal's disbelief that it was an accident and now the changing of the crew, plus an additional three hundred tons of cargo.

Nicolas hesitated in his response, taken aback by the captain's harsh tone. "The crane operator says the last pallet completed the manifest, but I am quite sure we are still several tons short, at least ten pallets."

Captain Farroque kneeled at the edge of forward cargo hatch, knowing full well the tricks of the dockworkers, including crane operators. One of which included shorting a load and selling the remainder to someone else. He peered into the gloomy hold. From the row of lights, half of them not working, he could see the pallets of fertilizer stacked to the top around every bulkhead. All he could think about was the added strain of this weight on the engine.

"It looks full to me down there, perhaps it was you who miscounted and not the dockworkers," the captain said.

"I'm quite sure we are still short ten pallets," Nicolas insisted.

"Good God, man! We're already carrying a load the engine is struggling to handle. If we run into rough seas, we'll be lucky to ride through them as it is."

"But Captain, won't the owners be upset if we don't haul what's been paid for?" Nicolas suggested, showing the captain his integrity.

"Less so, I'm sure, than if we don't make it back at all," Captain Farroque shot back.

The insistence in the first mates manner was exasperating to the captain's raw nerves. Nicolas cared not what shape the ship's engine was in despite informing him of it when he first boarded.

Still, Captain Farroque mused, I've always dealt honestly with the shipping company and I won't end my career by being discredited for shorting a load of cargo. A man has his pride in a job well done if nothing else. He took a deep breath, letting out a long sigh.

"Very well, Nicolas, bring it on board but stack it on the mid-deck and cover it with tarps. Put nothing more below deck, understood?"

Captain Farroque radioed the crane operator and demanded they send over ten more pallets.

When he'd finished, he turned back to Nicolas, "Be sure the pallets are strapped down tightly so there is no shifting of the load. I've hauled those pallets of fertilizer before. They have a tendency to move about in heavy seas." At least on deck they could be thrown overboard, the captain thought with a laugh. "And be sure all of our fuel tanks are topped off. We may have to take a longer route, staying closer to shore in case we have trouble."

"Yes, Captain," Nicolas answered swiftly.

The first mate's oblong face broke out in a smile as he watched the captain leave the deck. He ordered several of his shipmates to the mid-deck while others fumbled about looking for straps, turnbuckles, and tarpaulins.

Captain Farroque watched the renewed bustle of activity from the stairwell door, always glad to see his crew busy. Despite the ill-advised addition of more cargo, he felt the familiar twinge of excitement that always came to him at times like this when the ship was being made ready for departure from its berth, leaving the safety of a protected harbor behind for three thousand miles of open sea. He puzzled over his future. Would he be content to stay on land for the remainder of his days with Fatima and his daughter, with no family, save for his cousin in St. Louis?

He shrugged, knowing the answer would come in time since the winds of change had already begun. By now, his wife and daughter should be safely in America. He had another twelve days at sea before the ship arrived in Istanbul; his last port of call before joining them in the states.

Not having had time to leave the ship and not wanting to risk a phone call, Captain Farroque had sent a letter with the out going mail, carried ashore by his departing crew. The unscheduled stop in Jakarta, coupled with the slow speed of the ship would delay his arrival by a week, and he knew Fatima would be worried.

"Captain Farroque!" Nicolas called after him as he was about to head up the stairs to the bridge. "I was inspecting the life boat earlier and there are no provisions on board. Also, one of the oars is missing. Should we not do something about it?"

"Absolutely not, the owners of the ship will try to take it out of my paycheck if I purchase anything not critical for the running of the ship. I can not squeeze an extra dime from them with a vise," Captain Farroque added light-heartedly, trying to get a laugh out of his new first mate.

"But Captain, you said yourself the engine is in dire need of repair."

The captain's smile left his face at this reminder. Perhaps this new first mate wasn't so bad, he thought. Maybe he's a little too serious, but at least he's thorough. And besides, what did he care about the owner's pocketbook now. If they were going to squeeze every last dollar out of the *Empress* by hauling this extra cargo, then he would spend some of their profit. The bill for these new provisions wouldn't find its way to the shipping company until after he'd left their service, paycheck in hand.

"Yes, you are right, Nicolas. Prepare a list of everything that is missing or broken and order them. Be sure they arrive by late afternoon and are properly stowed prior to our departure. The tugs are scheduled for seventeen hundred hours. Make sure there is fresh gasoline for the lifeboat's motor. Allah help us if we have to row that boat on the open sea. Oh, and by the way, Ni…, Nicolas, there is a life ring missing from the wall of the superstructure on the aft deck, go ahead and order a replacement."

"Yes, sir. I will see that everything is taken care of," the first mate replied, obediently.

As he climbed the stairs toward the bridge, Captain Farroque puzzled over the sudden interest in the lifeboat and its provisions. Perhaps, he thought, the sight of the rust-streaked hull of the freighter, along with his comments earlier concerning the over-taxed engine had inspired the first mate's due diligence. The first mate, an experienced seaman, assigned to an unfamiliar ship, most likely inspected the lifeboat and other safety equipment not long after boarding the worn out *Empress,* just in case it would be needed.

The *Empress of Sayda* trudged through the blackness, laboring to be on the upside of twelve knots. She'd left port on schedule, and now, with it past midnight, the lights of Jakarta were far behind. Thick, low hanging clouds snuffed out any celestial illumination from above. An occasional pinpoint of light could be seen off both starboard and port sides of the ship; their source being the running lights of other ships sailing the Java Sea or shore lights from the many inhabited islands that rimmed the Indonesian Archipelago.

Instead of taking a straight-line course for the Gulf of Aden and brushing only the Maldives in the middle of the Indian Ocean, Captain Farroque had charted a course north by northwest, hoping, most of the time, to stay within several hundred miles of shore, in case the ship's engine failed completely. He explained this to Nicolas as the two of them stood over the computer screen and gauges that cast a red glow onto their faces. They would cross the mouth of the Bay of Bengal, skirting Sri Lanka, before taking a more westerly route across the Arabian Sea through the Gulf and into the Red Sea.

"Well, Nicolas, I believe I'm ready to head for my cabin for a few hours of sleep. Do you have any questions before I relinquish the helm?"

Captain Farroque had quizzed his first mate off and on through out the evening. He was confident of Nicolas's knowledge, that it matched the credentials he'd presented to the captain when they'd first met. He couldn't say the same for the rest of the crew. Many, he thought, judging by their actions, appeared to be novices when it came to the workings of a ship at sea. Why the company had hired them, he couldn't say, though money most likely played a role he wagered, figuring the good captain could deal with their minimal skills.

With the former crew, he would have been in bed at his usual time, leaving Ramon in control of the ship. But with the unease he'd felt ever since receiving the news of an unscheduled stop in Jakarta, sleep had been fleeting. Most nights he lay in bed for hours, going over scenarios of what his new life would be like in America before drifting back to memories from past years. Nothing but smooth sailing ahead with rough seas far behind, he kept telling himself. It was easier to look forward most nights, until now.

"I have everything under control, Captain. The *Empress* is in good hands with me, sir."

"Very well then. The maritime weather reports show nothing of importance in our immediate area. There was only the mention of a disturbance some two hundred miles due west but not likely to cross our path."

"Should be an easy sail, Captain," Nicolas commented.

The captain nodded in agreement ready to leave.

"Do you have any family, Captain?"

The question was innocent enough, and though the captain was too fatigued for any more small talk, he felt obliged to answer.

"Yes, I have a wife and lovely daughter. And you?"

"No, I am single with only the sea as my mistress."

Captain Farroque smiled at this remark, remembering his younger days.

"I shall be back at 0600 hours to relieve you," Captain Farroque said, looking at his watch as he turned to open the door.

"And your wife and daughter, do they live in the Middle East?"

"Yes, in Beirut."

He'd said this so many times out of habit that it came out before he could correct himself. Though better to say Beirut than where they actually were, he thought.

"Ah, yes, Beirut. It is a lovely city," Nicolas remarked.

"You've been there, then?" The captain queried, tightening his grip on the doorknob.

"Yes, ...and I have friends who still live there. It's too bad we won't be stopping there on this trip. We'll be passing not far from Beirut. You could see them..., I mean your family, of course, and I could visit my friends."

The tone of his voice seemed off, probing, Captain Farroque thought, or perhaps he was just tired. It had been a long day.

"I'm afraid," Captain Farroque answered, wearing he's best smile, "once we exit the Suez Canal, we will be heading straight for Istanbul. This isn't an excursion boat."

218

"No, of course not. It was just wishful thinking on my part. We have a schedule to keep. Besides, you will have time to go see them during our long layover in Istanbul, won't you."

Captain Farroque was annoyed by Nicolas's continued interest in his family, yet he felt compelled to answer, cautiously he thought, in an aloof and unconcerned manner.

"Once the *Empress* is unloaded and we have her docked at the maintenance facility, I intend to spend a few days in Istanbul visiting old friends before catching a flight back to Beirut."

"I'm surprised, Captain. After months at sea, I assumed you would be eager to get back to see your wife and daughter."

Captain Farroque, becoming agitated, stared at his first mate. He seemed reluctant to make eye contact. Was he fishing for something? He hesitated before replying, feeling the heat rise in his cheeks as a picture of Monsour, slipping over the edge of the deck, flashed through his mind. Then, taking a deep breath, he answered calmly.

"They went on vacation, more like a get-well visit, to see a sick relative in Cairo. My daughter had never been out of Lebanon so they planned on spending a few weeks there. Hopefully, they will arrive back home at about the same time as I do," the captain explained, satisfied with his response, thinking two can play this game as he continued. "What about you, Nicolas? What will you do while the ship's engine is repaired?"

His first mate shrugged, "It's only three weeks."

"Hah! I'll wager it will be more like six weeks before they have the engine overhauled. Repairs go at a snail's pace in those shipyards. Istanbul's is notoriously slow. Doesn't it seem odd to you that they would put on a new crew for such a short time before forcing you into a long layover?" He didn't give Nicolas time to respond. "Do you have friends to stay with in Istanbul, also? You probably won't get paid until the ship returns to its homeport, if you get paid at all. They may well leave you stranded in Istanbul. What will you do for money?"

"I'm not worried about getting paid," Nicolas answered.

"Not worried? My, you are enamored with the sea if you care not for getting paid," Captain Farroque opined.

Captain Farroque was more and more anxious to know why indeed the ship's owner would change crews at such an unusual time. To save money? That was always a possibility. By dropping off the last crew in Indonesia they didn't have to spend much getting them back to their native Philippines. And this new crew? Maybe the shipping company *was* going to stiff them. Though Captain Farroque thought this a little too underhanded even for them.

And why all this curiosity from Nicolas about his family, the captain wondered. Had Jamal and the others that disembarked in Buenos Aires been in contact with someone who'd made inquiries about him? Every answer from Nicolas about his experience on ships and his training seemed legitimate to Captain Farroque. Perhaps he was legit and the rest of the crew was counterfeit, yet the first mate had made no comment to him about the crew's ineptness. And what little he'd watched them interact today, Captain Farroque thought the first mate and the rest of the crew seemed familiar with one another. A week of sleepless nights and endless worries about his new life in America fueled the captain's paranoia. He needed time alone to think, to sleep.

"Don't hesitate to wake me if there is a problem," he instructed Nicolas.

Captain Farroque swung open the door, ignoring the next question from Nicolas. Before heading to his cabin, the captain took the stairs down to the main deck, stopping to pack the scrimshaw bowl of his pipe with rum-scented tobacco. The match flared in the still air at the base of the stairs and he took a long draw. Seeing his wavering shadow on the metal walls produced a startled cough that echoed up through the cavernous space. Moisture-laden air filled his lungs as he stepped out into the darkness, a refreshing change from the smell of diesel fuel that wafted up the stairwell from the engine room below. A couple of deep breathes and he could feel his heart rate begin to slow.

"One more passage," he'd told Fatima before he left home. "One more chance for a big payoff for ferrying shadowy figures to a new continent. That would help insure they had plenty of money to start over in America," he'd said.

She'd tried to talk him into leaving the ship before this last journey, but he'd been confident in his plans and wouldn't hear of it. The glow from his pipe waxed and waned with each breath as he reminisced. She had been the reluctant one for so long, but then, when the time had drawn near, he'd been the one to insist on one last voyage, one last big paycheck.

Captain Farroque let out a muffled laugh and wandered about the deck before coming to a stop in front of the lifeboat. Nicolas had informed him, shortly before the tugs arrived, that the replacement oar had been stowed along with provisions and a fresh can of gas for the small outboard motor attached to its stern. This brought another chuckle from the captain. He wagered the motor had ceased-up long ago from years of neglect and non-use. In all his years at sea, Captain Farroque had never the misfortune of needing to use a lifeboat. Not unusual in this day and age, he considered, with regulations and maritime laws. Though the *Empress's* owner neglected as many of these laws concerning the safety of ship and crew that they could get away with.

The ship had been under his command for fifteen years. He knew the ship to be about forty years old. She'd had her share of patchwork repairs but had always gotten him and the crew home. But now, he wasn't so sure. All she had to do was get him to Istanbul where it would be easy for him to slip away with a hard trail to follow.

Captain Farroque eyed the off-color smoke trailing out the exhaust stack—a testament to the condition of the diesel engine vibrating the deck below his feet. Even the Bosporus seemed a long haul for the ship now.

A close inspection of the frayed cables and hand-operated winch that held the twenty-eight foot skiff suspended by davits off the deck gave little solace. With his penlight, Captain Farroque could see the locking mechanism on the winch was rusted to the crank handle. He guessed it hadn't been moved since first being mounted on the *Empress*. Perhaps some solvent would loosen the mechanism, he thought, making a mental note to have one of the crew put some on it tomorrow. He tapped his spent pipe on one of the braces to empty it. The last remnants of burning tobacco drifted down onto the deck and were extinguished into the darkness. The pipe safely in his pocket, Captain Farroque made his way toward his cabin for what he knew would be another fitful night of sleep.

The refrigerator in his cabin was empty except for a can of juice and a few sliced apples; their cut surfaces an unappetizing brown. He decided on a quick trip to the galley for whatever the cook had prepared as dinner for the rest of the crew. But first, with a bit of trepidation, he fumbled with the combination to the small safe anchored to the wall next to his bed. He opened it rarely; only when a crewman needed cash for some compelling reason on shore leave, or, on even rarer occasions, when the ship's documents were to be scrutinized by suspicious port authorities.

The gun he removed from the safe, a two-shot, pearl-handled derringer, had been a trade, more like a gift, from a passenger he'd befriended many years ago. The captain's part of the trade, a silver cigarette case and three packs of menthols—the last he would ever own—made it easier for him to switch to a pipe. This had pleased Fatima to no end. She insisted it made him look more dignified despite his substantial weight gain.

A "fair trade and a great equalizer", his illicit passenger at the time had stated as he handled the cigarette case, wishing to change his lifestyle or at least the cause of his future death.

With the leather holster clipped to the inside of his polished black boot, Captain Farroque stepped out into the passageway, heading for the galley. The holstered derringer took some getting used to as he walked, and Captain Farroque considered taking it back to his cabin. He'd never fired a gun in his life and yet something about it made him feel less vulnerable. Since the new crew arrived this morning, for reasons he couldn't quite explain, he'd felt uneasy, almost as if he were a prisoner on his own ship.

The lingering aroma of curry and grilled onions greeted him, leftovers from the evening meal. Besides finding food, he hoped one of the new crewmen might be present, taking a break from their nighttime duties. Captain Farroque thought he might be able to extract more information from them than what he'd gotten out of his first mate. Finding anyone who could speak understandable English or Arabic would be the trick.

He discovered the room where they ate to be empty, not even a pot of coffee was present; a sure sign the new cook was a novice to the seaman's way of life and the drink that sustained him. The pantry in the galley offered a few snacks he could take back to his cabin, and after grabbing a can of soda pop from the double-door, commercial-sized refrigerator, he turned and faced the first hard evidence that the new crew might be more than just a bunch of cut-rate sailors. It made his heart sink.

There, adjacent to the six-burner stove, hanging on a rack suspended from the ceiling, between pots, pans, spatulas, and a much-stained apron, was an automatic rifle. The stock consisted of a shaped metal rod that was folded back against the blued barrel, making it the same length as a pair of large cooking tongs positioned farther along the rack of utensils. The banana-shaped ammunition clip jutting from the rifle made Captain Farroque believe it was an AK-47, though he was admittedly unschooled when it came to types of firearms. One thing even he was sure of—the three inch, chrome-barreled pistol holstered to the inside of his boot was no match for this weapon. How many other guns, he wondered, had come aboard with this new crew. Maybe the new cook was just extra-sensitive to criticism, he joked nervously to himself, trying to allay his mounting fear.

Though worried, Captain Farroque felt an inexplicable outward sense of calm. Now, at least, his puzzlement over the changing of the crew had been answered. Nicolas's methodical questioning about his family had *not* been innocent small talk. Most likely, he thought, his mind racing, they knew that Fatima had sold the house in Beirut but, hopefully, was nowhere to be found. If Nicolas came right out and asked him point blank about the house, it would do little good to feign innocence and argue his own wife had deceived him since he'd signed the papers himself. For a moment, Captain Farroque checked his paranoia.

Maybe they had no connection to Jamal and the Middle East. Maybe Nicolas's questions *had* just been innocent small talk. Perhaps it was just bad luck that a criminal crew, on the last leg, of the last voyage, of his career, would board his ship. Maybe they were just pirates after the cargo. The copper ingots were worth hundreds of thousands of dollars on the black market if you could find an unscrupulous middleman. Though, it didn't matter, he surmised. His life would be in danger whatever their plans might be.

Lifting the rifle off the rack, he pictured the cook—or what ever his profession was—struggling with the weapon slung across his back, trying to do the chores in the galley. He probably hung it there while he finished his work and then forgot it, Captain Farroque decided.

His first instinct was to take the gun with him back to his cabin, but, if all the crew were in this together, it wouldn't take them long to deduce where to look for the missing rifle. If he threw it overboard, they would accuse him of hiding it and throw him overboard, too. His head was spinning. Lack of sleep was taking its toll on his ability to think clearly. He stood there daydreaming, imagining the faceless cook pointing the rifle and pulling the trigger, sparks flying as the bullets hit metal, then, just as vividly hitting him, with the splatter of blood replacing the sparks.

Captain Farroque's tired eyes stared ahead unfocused. When his vision readjusted to the sights in front of him, the first thing he saw was a ragged, steel wool pad lying on the corner of the cast iron griddle atop the stove. They might miss the rifle, but they wouldn't miss the coil of unraveling steel wool and, with no further hesitation, he began packing it into the end of the barrel, first with an ink pen from his pocket, then with a blunted ice pick he found from one of the cabinet drawers.

The gun took the whole coil, being careful to leave the last three inches unpacked so anyone looking casually at the end of barrel would see nothing amiss. In another drawer, he found a bottle of glue and, for good measure, squeezed its content into the gun, watching with his penlight as it seeped through the steel wool.

A sensation of satisfaction came over him, replacing the feeling of helplessness from moments before. Captain Farroque hung the rifle back on the rack beside the dirty apron, using it to wipe the glue from his fingertips and outside of the barrel. Chances were good, he thought, that no one would ever know the gun had been sabotaged until they pulled the trigger. He didn't know if it would stop the bullet, but it might throw off its trajectory or, if lucky, even backfire.

He scooped up his food and walked briskly to his cabin, sitting on the edge of the bed, thinking, while he polished off the last of his drink. Calling for help was probably out of the question. Most likely, this bunch had already disabled the radio transmitter based on several maritime warnings that had crossed his desk over the years concerning hijacked cargo ships and there outcomes. The Java Sea was notorious for such episodes.

The warnings had gone unheeded by him for the most part, though he had to admit, hijackers had been in the back of his mind when he made the trade for the derringer. Most of the piracy cases he heard of ended in a bad way for the captain and legitimate crew of the ship. Captain Farroque wondered how ruthless this crew on his ship would be. He would be shark bait before any of them would think about letting him off the ship alive, he surmised.

Much to the captain's chagrin, it occurred to him that he'd probably hauled a few of this type over the years. Monsour's and Jamal's faces flashed before his eyes. If this new crew weren't random thugs, but somehow related to the likes of Jamal, others of his wife's extended family back in Beirut, through a sinister web of connections, would be punished, too. Part of the very reason he'd wanted to leave his homeland.

Captain Farroque decided the best thing to do for the time being would be to play along and be patient. It might buy him more time to find out what their plans were and perhaps thwart them. For now, he would do nothing out of the ordinary and wait for Nicolas and the others to make the first move.

The leaden sky was ominous-looking and the sea much rougher than when Captain Farroque had left Nicolas in command the night before. Nicolas was examining a nautical chart when the captain entered the bridge to relieve him.

"How goes it, Nicolas?" He asked cheerily.

He was determined to keep a calm demeanor, hoping that if Nicolas didn't think anything was amiss, he would be allowed to stay onboard, and alive, a little longer. Nicolas probably wasn't even his real name, Captain Farroque mused. No wondered he'd had such a hard time associating the name with his new first mate.

Before answering, Nicolas folded the map haphazardly, shuffling it amongst others in the drawer.

"The sea was calm until an hour ago. Now, it looks as though we may be in for some rough weather. The storm that was west of us, changed direction during the night and is about to overtake us."

Captain Farroque nodded, knowingly, "Yes, I noticed the sea kicking up a bit when I first awoke. I trust you have the crew preparing for whatever may come our way?"

Nicolas hesitated before answering," I..., I believe everything has been taken care of."

In truth, he'd been too busy sharing the details of his plans with the others the crew, too preoccupied to tend to the ship's normal protocol.

"I will take the helm for the rest of the day, until we've weathered the storm," Captain Farroque said, anxious for Nicolas to leave so that he might see which chart the first mate had been perusing. "Before you go to your cabin for rest, perhaps you should double check that the crew has fastened all the hatches and make sure the cargo is secure so as not to shift in heavy seas."

"I am sure everything is in order, Captain, but I will check everything myself."

"Thank you, Nicolas," Captain Farroque offered, knowing full well, based on what he'd seen so far, that the crew had probably missed something important.

No sooner had Nicolas left the helm before Captain Farroque began his search through the nautical charts. Ramon was meticulous with them, and the captain hoped that in his haste to re-file the chart, Nicolas had misplaced it. It may be of little value, he thought, but if he knew anything more about their plans he might use it to his advantage in prolonging his time on the *Empress*.

It was a map of the Persian Gulf. It had been folded wrong and was not completely embedded with the rest of the charts. Captain Farroque examined the map closely, noticing a faint circle of pencil lead surrounding Bahrain and Qatar. He knew all the ports that bordered the gulf from countless deliveries of cement he'd made over the past few years. Dubai, Doha, Bahrain: he'd called on each of them. All with bustling harbors due to the frenzied rate of construction in the cities. The Strait of Hormuz was choked with freighters delivering all manner of supplies to the region. In addition, fully loaded supertankers plied the waters, sailing in the opposite direction.

Captain Farroque crowded his girth into one of the tall swivel chairs. They allowed him to see over the instrument panel and controls. He gazed across the deck below him, and in front, the endless miles of ocean. There was not a vessel in sight. He estimated the waves crashing against the bow of the *Empress* to be twenty feet in height. She lumbered through them as if the water were made of molasses. After changing her heading, to confront the waves from a safer angle, he went back to contemplating the chart Nicolas had so hastily put away. If indeed Bahrain was the destination his derelict crew was bound for, there would be no need to change course for several days, he reasoned. Why, of all places, he wondered, hypnotized by the ship's lethargic movement, would they go there unless they had already made arrangements with a disreputable middleman to handle the dispersal of the cargo of copper ingots and ammonium nitrate?

A chill ran down his spine, like the histamine release after a wasp's sting, as another answer came to him. There was one other element, which he'd overlooked, that led to the congestion in the Strait of Hormuz: Bahrain was homeport for the United States Navy's 5th Fleet.

A new, ill-trained crew; three hundred tons of ammonium nitrate fertilizer; the naval fleet; Nicolas's concern about the life boat; an aging freighter with costly repairs awaiting it: all the pieces fit.

Captain Farroque shook his head slowly in disbelief, rubbing his face with both hands as thoughts raced through his mind. How could he have been so naïve to think that after all he'd done: transporting shadowy passengers, hauling illegal cargo; that he would not be silenced, muted out of the picture someday. His fate had been sealed long ago, before the start of this last voyage; before he had decided himself that it was time to get out.

If not for the storm, he would have been tempted to fling himself overboard right then and there. Of course, what difference would the storm make, he thought, laughing out loud. Heavy seas or no, it wasn't like he would be able to swim the three hundred miles to the nearest shore.

Staring blankly at the thundering waves, entranced by their unceasing march across the ocean, he struggled with the likely results of confronting Nicolas and the rest of the crew. The results were no different then what he'd calculated the night before. He felt doomed.

For the sake of Fatima and his daughter, Captain Farroque had to do something. Politics and religion aside, he couldn't conceive of letting this bunch onboard carry out such a sinister plot unchecked. His newly found conscience wouldn't allow it.

Monsour's last words haunted the captain now more than ever as he sat watching the storm's intensity increase. Whatever Jamal and the others' plans were in America, he now felt a sense of guilt for assisting them in their travels. He'd looked the other way on too many occasions, pocketing the money without complaint, corrupted by it just as Monsour had accused him.

Still, the answer, he concluded, wasn't to help these radicals that were a vocal minority of the Islamic faith but to stop them. It was too late to disrupt Jamal's plans, he knew. And he wasn't the hero type. But he felt obliged to stop this crew's scheme. If he was going to die, perhaps he could do something to make his wife and daughter proud of him, he mused, longing to see their faces, hear their voices, one last time.

Captain Farroque decided that whatever plan he devised to thwart Nicolas and his crew, it would only succeed through stealth with the *Empress of Sayda's* last port of call being the bottom of the Indian Ocean. He calculated at best they had three days before they would need change the ship's heading if he'd deduced correctly about their plan; then the moment of truth would be at hand. Nicolas and the others would have to enact whatever fate they had in mind for the captain. Maybe less time, if they suspected him of knowing any inkling of their scheme, figuring he'd outlived his usefulness to them and their floating bomb. With these thoughts in mind, he put the chart back in the drawer, approximating where Nicolas had placed it.

Captain Farroque spent the remainder of the morning desperately seeking a solution that would, first and foremost, sink or disable the ship and secondly, however remote the odds, give him a chance at survival. It took his mind off the strengthening storm. The white froth at the pinnacle of rogue waves lapped at the gunwale, now and again, sending a torrent of effervescent foam cascading across the deck.

Twice, before Nicolas came back on duty, a different crewman had approached the captain on the bridge, despite the language barrier, inquiring nervously with gestures and garbled words about the fury of the storm and if anything else needed to be done to ensure the ship's safe passage. It gave Captain Farroque a queer sense of satisfaction as he smiled at their unmastered fear of the sea, knowing that for the moment at least, he held *their* fate in *his* hands. Once the storm passed, as well it should, he would be back under their invisible thumb; a free roaming prisoner on his own ship. And while the sea was rough, especially to a novice, the *Empress* had survived more ferocious storms, though granted, her diesel engine had been running smoothly on those occasions.

Captain Farroque realized he'd forgotten all about the decrepit engine these past hours, replaced by new worries. Too bad it didn't fail now of its own accord, then at least one of his worries might be over. However, sabotaging the engine was no guarantee that the ship, adrift in the water, would sink. No, he had to be sure that the *Empress* never reached shore. Captain Farroque tried to focus on his family as a melancholy feeling enveloped him. Losing the ship was the main goal now, but he was becoming more resolute in his desire to survive as well. He had to try, for Fatima's and his daughter's sake. And the novice crew, save for Nicolas, gave him an idea.

The storm abated by late afternoon when Nicolas came back to the bridge to take his turn at the helm. Captain Farroque informed him that a change of course was necessary.

"With the engine struggling as it is, I think it would be wise for us to take a more northerly route once were past the tip of the Indian subcontinent, staying closer to shore. We have plenty of fuel on board to take a longer route."

Nicolas nodded, smiling as he replied, "I agree one hundred percent. We were quite sluggish passing through the middle of that storm. To lose the engine during another storm would leave us helpless."

Captain Farroque smiled, too. Perhaps the change would buy him a little more time as it played directly into Nicolas's plan—a more direct route toward the Persian Gulf. He wouldn't suspect the captain of knowing anything. Captain Farroque hoped the failing engine would be a blessing in disguise.

"We'll skirt the western Indian coast as far north as Mumbai before steering for a westerly heading."

Captain Farroque traced the path as he moved his finger along the chart laid out before the two of them; still secret adversaries. If he could get within a couple hundred miles of shore, he pondered furtively, then maybe there was a chance he could pull off his scheme.

"Yes, Captain, I will make the adjustments to our course. It is a wise move."

A toothy grin spread across the first mate's long face, leaving the captain satisfied that he was not suspicious of the real reason for his change of course.

"Very well then, I will leave the *Empress* in your hands while I do some paperwork in my cabin and grab a bite to eat." Not able to help himself, Captain Farroque added, "The new cook's abilities leave a little something to be desired, don't you think, Nicolas?"

Nicolas shrugged, paying little attention to the captain's remark, as he went about the business of charting a new heading.

Captain Farroque began in earnest to collect items he would need when the time came for him to abandon the ship—willingly or not. The lifeboat had fresh provisions, Nicolas had seen to that. Apparently their plans included escaping from the floating bomb themselves. The captain spirited away all the empty soda bottles he could find, filling them with drinking water before stowing them in his cabin.

Surrounded on three sides by land, albeit some distance away, with scores of ships plying its waters, there were worse places than the Arabian Sea to be marooned in a small boat. If things went as planned, Captain Farroque would have the ship within a reachable distance of shore before he abandoned her. With any luck, the currents would carry him toward shore. He figured, once safely on shore, his optimism growing, Mumbai or Karachi would be within reach. He had enough money in his possession for a plane ticket on to Istanbul from either of those ports. If he made it that far, arrangements were in place for him to make his way on to America.

The *Empress of Sayda* was three hundred miles west and only a hundred miles south of Mumbai when Captain Farroque took the helm for the last time from his unsuspecting first mate. The only changes in the past two days were the increasing noise and vibration coming from the engine room. Nicolas was making more noise, too. The captain's goal was to keep him at the helm as much as possible of late, hoping the long hours would make him unduly tired when he was finally relieved. Captain Farroque was confident that Nicolas was the only one of the entire crew who would be able to tell by the stars in the night sky, if they were heading in the wrong direction. Luckily, the moon would not rise until well past midnight.

"Our course will change in a little over an hour, Captain," Nicolas informed him, yawning.

He didn't bother to apologize. His demeanor grew more insolent with each passing day, enough so, that under normal circumstances he would have been upbraided by the captain. But Captain Farroque, knowing what the consequences of such action might be, ignored his behavior or only mildly commented.

Nicolas quizzed him several times about the Persian Gulf. Had he traveled there? Which ports were best? Was access easier at Dubai or Qatar? Did he have to fear getting too close to American naval ships? Captain Farroque played along. The questions only reinforced his suspicions while his eager answers perpetuated the ruse between Nicolas and himself. Captain Farroque was thankful they'd left him on board this long, unaware of his own plans.

It had been dark for an hour, with no sign of Nicolas or others of the crew on the foredeck below the bridge. Earlier, Captain Farroque had begun a slow turn, in the opposite direction than was charted, back toward the east, toward the nearest shore. He was confident that only Nicolas would notice the turning of the ship, and, if below deck, wouldn't perceive which direction.

The *Empress* stayed on her eastward course undetected well past midnight, lessening the distance to Captain Farroque's salvation. With the stealth of a thief, he left the helm, making his way back to his cabin to collect a makeshift survival kit: bottles of water, packaged snack food, a compass, and some extra clothes purloined from the laundry room, not sure how long the provisions already aboard the lifeboat would last. As he passed the galley he paused, considering whether to raid the pantry one more time. A loud conversation that sounded like the whole crew coming from inside made his decision an easy one.

His last foray into the galley for a cup of coffee had been an uncomfortable one. Several of the ignorant crew were sitting closely around one of the two tables having what appeared to be a heated discussion that ended abruptly upon his entrance. As he'd left the room, he felt the hairs on the nape of his neck bristle as all eyes followed him out the door. There were provisions for a whole crew on the lifeboat so why risk another confrontation, he decided. What a relief it would be to get off the ship he told himself, fully aware though that being stranded alone in a small boat on the ocean was not without a multitude of dangers, only a few of which he felt confident to handle.

Out on the main deck, undetected, he swung the skiff out over the water forty feet below, cursing under his breath at every screech of the rusty swivels. After stowing the extra gear, one last trip to the helm was required to reset the heading of the ship back to the west, away from the nearest land and the direction he intended to be going in the lifeboat. The moon had just begun to appear directly in front of him as he reached the controls. These last six hours under full throttle had brought him closer to land, estimating the *Empress* was now within two hundred-fifty miles of the Indian coastline, due east of her current position.

From the bridge, there was nothing to see in any direction save for the vast dark sea below him, shimmering in the reflected moonlight, and a plethora of stars; stars that were rotating their position in the sky. Captain Farroque swallowed hard, knowing his safe arrival on shore was no sure bet. A sudden squall capsizing his boat, an unseeing ship bearing down on his small craft, or gunfire from his shipmates were all distinct possibilities. Thoughts of the latter made his stay on the ship any longer, untenable. One last stop, by the hopefully unoccupied engine room with a box of matches, and then a rendezvous with the sea awaited Captain Farroque.

After leaving the engine room, he hesitated on the stairs up to the main deck, thinking he heard other footfalls in the stairwell above him. The oily smoke coming from the engine room forced him to go on. Reaching the door that opened onto the deck, hands trembling, he pulled his derringer from its nest.

Salt spray and time had seized the electric motors that powered the winches used to lower the boat into the water. Captain Farroque was prepared for this inevitability, knowing the hand-cranks would substitute in their place. Nicolas had seen to their working condition. The noise they made was still intolerable as was their slow speed, then, three-quarters of the way down, one of the handles twisted off in his hands. Exasperated and out of breath, he stood there sweating, staring down at the skiff swaying easily in the breeze, just ten feet above the undulating sea.

A low clank, barely audible over the unsteady drone of the engine, then a glow of light came with clarity to Captain Farroque's heightened senses. He turned awkwardly in his cumbersome life vest in the direction of the noise and light. There, not fifty feet away, was one of the crewmen. He wore a white cloth, evidenced by its flagging in the breeze as its bearer leaned forward, searching the darkness with his unadjusted eyes for the source of the sounds coming from somewhere along the edge of the ship.

Kneeling in the shadows, taking stock of his predicament, Captain Farroque nearly cried out when he saw who was stalking him. By God it was the cook.

The cook stood still, scanning the deck. Behind him, wisps of black smoke seeped out from under the closed door of the lighted stairwell. Captain Farroque remained motionless, not sure of his next move. He caught a glimpse of the rifle barrel held in his stalker's hands as a glint of moonlight reflected off of it.

The cook panned the deck slowly, the rifle held out in front of his body at waist level like a spear. Could it be the rifle he'd sabotaged the first night out of Jakarta, Captain Farroque wondered. It looked like it, which meant it looked like a thousand others of the same design, he mused. Still, it was the cook, the captain was sure as he inched toward him and the lifeboat. Crouched in the shadows, Captain Farroque, hearing shouts from somewhere within the ship, knew he was running out of time. It was now or never as he stood up. In that instant, the cook caught sight of him and the rifle flashed. The odd recoil tore the gun from the cook's hands, but the captain was untouched by any bullets, only scared out of his wits. A fair trade he thought, as the crewman, cook, pirate, or whatever he truly was, cried out and pushed the fire alarm on the wall beside the door. Next, he rushed at the captain, stopping short when he saw the chrome-barreled gun pointed at him.

Stopping one of them, or even two, depending on his marksmanship, which most likely was poor, would do him no good, Captain Farroque reasoned. He would not make it to shore with only a life vest and no boat, either. He glanced at the pistol almost swallowed by his big hand. Indeed, he thought, it probably looked like a toy to the cook who was creeping closer. Damn those two seized-up cables, he muttered under his breath, feeling defeated.

And there it was, the answer: two. He turned to the aft cable next to him, keeping a sharp eye over his shoulder on the cook. With the barrel of the two-shot derringer against the cable, he squeezed the trigger, sending the once-tense cable slicing through the air. With a loud splash, the keel of the boat was in the water. Captain Farroque turned back, pointing the gun at the silhouetted cook who had advanced another step closer, freezing him in place. Perhaps now the cook realized the gun was no toy, the captain thought, feeling a burning sensation, then a trickle of blood running down his neck. When it snapped, the taut, aft cable had left its mark. He moved to the forward cable, keeping the gun trained on the cook.

This time he kept himself at arm's length as he swung the gun back to the cable, pulling the trigger a second time, preparing himself for what would happen next.

The last thing Captain Farroque saw as he sailed overboard, arm-in-arm with his would be assassin, was the smoky light from the stairwell as the door burst open, hearing frenzied shouts and curses until he and his embraced opponent hit the water. The impact of the water broke the death-like grip that Captain Farroque and the cook held each other with, and that was the last the captain saw of his unwilling, diving companion.

He was already clear of the *Empress's* stern when he reached the skiff bobbing leisurely in the freighter's wake. It was not until he'd clamored aboard that gunfire rang out. In the ensuing chaos, others of the crew who'd come on deck were slow to realize what had happened. He heard dozens of bullets whistle by, some came close overhead or singed the water beside him as he lay lengthwise beneath the gunwale for over a minute trying to catch his breath. By now he was a quarter of a mile behind the ship and almost out of range.

He struggled from the life jacket, his back muscles cramping repeatedly, a result of the impact with the water from a drop of forty feet. The salt water stung at the wound on his face, but he was alive and off the ship, he thought, rejoicing, whispering a reluctant prayer to Allah.

Distressed voices from the ship carried ominously across the tranquil sea. Among the shouts and commands that Captain Farroque could make out, were the words "fire" and "explosion" in two languages. Nicolas was back in charge of the ship.

He watched as the *Empress of Sayda* sailed westward, away from him, its speed slowing gradually until it appeared dead in the water. What few deck lights it possessed had been extinguished. A dark silhouette was all that marked its position on the horizon from the captain's vantage point in the lifeboat. But above it, coal-black smoke was blotting out a widening section of the star-filled sky, like a bottle of spilled ink spreading unchecked in space.

Struggling with the outboard motor, Captain Farroque paused as a low rumble came from the direction of the distraught ship. Now, as he looked to the west, an eerie, throbbing glow had replaced the ship's dark outline. He stood in the small boat as it rode over the gentle waves, watching as a series of explosions rocked the freighter, illuminating the night sky. His mouth agape, he was astounded at how quickly the ship's bulk evaporated, leaving behind only the ink-spot as a memento of its existence.

In triumph, Captain Farroque cried out to Fatima across the unfathomable miles that separated them, promising her that they would soon be reunited.

The first shoulder-wrenching tug on the motor's pull starter sent the captain reeling backwards, grasping at the gunwale to prevent his falling overboard as the rotted cord disintegrated in a shower of cotton dust. First a grimace, as the pain in his back returned, then a smile crossed his face as he positioned the oars, one of them brand new, in the oarlocks and began the long haul toward an unfamiliar shore.

CHAPTER SEVEN

Saturday morning arrived, and still no check in the mail. Yussef spent the previous night lying awake in bed, mulling over his options. On Friday, he hit upon the idea of donating platelets at Life Services, a business downtown, near campus, that paid a small sum each time you gave blood, it being used for research purposes.

A small bruise marked the spot in the crook of his right arm where the nurse had finally hit pay dirt in her search for a blood vessel under his olive-colored skin. Twenty-five dollars for being a first time donor wouldn't put a dent in his share of the rent payment, but it might be enough to pay for his date with Rachael tonight.

Yussef decided the best thing to do would be to get a loan at the check-cashing service he and Ahmed had used for the past three years. They knew him there, and no doubt, had made a tidy sum off the percentage they took from the foundation checks he cashed there. Borrowing the money from Raymond, assuming he had some to spare, would be a last resort. He was already borrowing Ray's truck for the second time not to mention all the generous help Ray and the others had given him these past two years. Yussef was determined to get by on his own without anyone's help. If he was going to break his ties with Mullah Khan and the Islamic Foundation, financial independence was the first step to leaving them behind, he reasoned.

Yussef made a mental note to fill the truck with gas this time after using it, assuming he had some money left after paying for dinner. After dressing, he made his way to the kitchen, his stride bouncing with confidence, having decided on a plan that would set him free.

"Yo, my man. What's happening, bro?" Ray greeted him in his best pseudo-gangsta dialect, having watched too many music videos on television of late.

He was hunched over a bowl of cereal at the kitchen table with the daily newspaper spread out before him. He had a spoon in one hand and a pencil in the other, part of his never-ending but always futile attempt to finish the crossword puzzle while eating breakfast. Kenny and Jay joked it was a sure sign of his mental pathology from having stood too close to the reactor, too many times.

"Hey, Yussef, what color is closely associated with Islam? It has five letters."

"Green."

"Boy, it's a good thing you came down this morning. I thought I was going to have to come up and get you out of bed to finish this one. I swear they get harder every week," Ray said, scribbling frantically with the pencil. "Okay, how many players are there on a cricket team?"

Before Yussef could answer, Ray dropped his spoon into the bowl of cereal with a resulting splatter of milk across the page, elated as he cried out with glee, filling in another word he'd just come up with.

"How do you spell crochet?"

"How should I know?" Yussef said, laughing, trying to make the vintage 50's era toaster work. "Kenny and Jay say I shouldn't encourage your illness."

"Screw those two pinheads. They're just jealous 'cause they can't spell anything with more than one syllable."

"You need to find another hobby, like girls."

"Oh yeah, right. Like you've been on one date and now you're an expert."

"Two after tonight. Can I still borrow your truck?"

"Well, excuse me, Mr. Cassanova. Sure you can borrow it, if...you correctly tell me the number of players on a cricket team."

Yussef thought for a moment, before answering with a smile, "I'll tell you, *after* you give me the keys to your truck."

"You whore. Don't make me beg for the answer. What's the Pakistani word for scumbag, anyway? It has six letters and starts with Y-U-S."

Yussef laughed, crumbs of toast spilling from the corners of his mouth. Ray dropped his pencil and reached for an envelope lying on the corner of the table.

"By the way, Kenny said to remind you that the rent is due today."

"Yes, yes. I'm on my way down to the check cashing-service right now to get some money."

"So your check finally arrived, eh?"

Yussef didn't answer as he stood at the kitchen sink with his back to Raymond washing down the dry toast with a glass of water.

"I don't know why we pay that money-grubbing landlord, anyway," Ray added in disgust. "I think I'll put some mouse turds in the rent envelope when we pay him today. Maybe he'll take the hint. And Christ, it sounds like there's a whole subdivision of squirrels up in the attic above my room. If his not going to get rid of the furry varmints around here, he should at least make them pay their share of the rent. Either that, or I'm going up to the attic with my deer-hunting rifle. Too bad if the house ends up with holes in the ceiling or roof. I'll wait 'til you guys are out of the house, of course."

"That would be very considerate of you," Yussef said laughing as he headed for the front door. He just made it to the bottom step of the front porch when Raymond hollered after him.

"Hey, I almost forgot to tell you. Professor Stevenson called yesterday while I was at the lab; all the way from Karachi. I thought he was going to India."

Yussef nodded and held his breath, afraid of what was coming next.

"Anyway, he said he was making an unexpected side trip while on his sabbatical and was going to look up your parents. He said he was having trouble locating the village they lived in. He wanted you to give him a call if you got the chance. I left the phone number on my desk at the lab."

Yussef waved at Raymond in acknowledgement and resumed his rapid gait down the sidewalk, biting his lip without saying a word.

They had moved, simple as that. I will make up some excuse for not calling Professor Stevenson and when he gets back to Rockledge, I'll just tell him they moved.

Once he had the rent money, Yussef thought he would buy a paper, stop by the lab, and look through the help-wanted ads before going home. Perhaps he could find a part-time job. That money, along with a weekly visit to Life Services would keep him going until his paycheck from the university for teaching the physics lab became available. He could just hear the mullah's deliberate voice, castigating him for leaving the fold. He shrugged it off, thinking a great weight had been lifted off his chest as he took in great gulps of the fresh spring air, almost skipping down the sidewalk on his way to the check-cashing service for a loan.

A distant bell from the direction of campus signaled the noon hour.

"You look like you're dragging a fifty pound ball and chain," The voice said from above him.

Yussef slowed his pace from a shuffle to a crawl as he came to the front steps, raising his bent head to see where the voice had come from. Kenny was sitting on the waist-high wall that surrounded the front porch, leaning back against one of the support columns of the roof with his legs stretched out in front while he perfected his smoke ring blowing technique. Yussef stood there not knowing what to say.

He'd only managed to float a loan for seventy-five dollars, and at an interest rate that would make a shylock flinch. Nothing in the help-wanted ads had looked too promising, either.

"Just a tough morning at the lab," was all he could muster.

Kenny stubbed out his cigarette on the cement floor of the porch. "Well, you're all in one piece and you're not glowing, so it couldn't have been that bad."

"No, I suppose not," he replied, not sure it wasn't as bad. He resigned himself to the fact that he would have to ask his roommates for help with his share of the rent money.

"I'm getting ready to go to work, and I was going to drop off the rent at the landlord's office along the way. Have you got your share of the money?" Kenny asked.

Yussef thumbed through the mail he'd dug out of the mailbox before running his hand along the inside corners in case an envelope was stuck along the side. There was nothing for him. A Playboy magazine, addressed to Raymond, held his attention for a moment.

"Kenny, I...," Yussef hesitated. "I don't...,"

"Hey, let me see that," Kenny interrupted, holding out his hand, pointing at the shrink-wrapped magazine.

"It's addressed to Raymond."

"Yeah, yeah, yeah," Kenny motioned again with his fingers for Yussef to hand it over. "Let me see it. It's contraband material, which means it's available for anyone's closer inspection that lives here. That's a hard and fast rule, just like the cold beer in the fridge doctrine. Oh yeah, I almost forgot, there's a manila envelope inside, addressed to you. I tossed it on the sofa on my way out for a smoke. It was lying on the porch floor beneath the mailbox."

"What was it doing on the floor?" Yussef asked, already flying through the front door as Kenny tore off the plastic wrap from the magazine.

"I have no idea. Maybe the mailman was preoccupied with Ray's contraband material and dropped it."

"I believe our mailman is a woman," Yussef shouted back from the living room.

He recognized the postmark, but the return address was not the same. He'd never heard of the business name from which it had been sent, either.

"Yeah, so?" Kenny said, his face buried in the magazine. "Remember, this is America, Yussef, anything goes."

Yussef nodded, thinking about the black-clad teenagers he'd seen at the coffee shop with Rachael as he opened the bulging envelope. Normally his check from the foundation arrived in a plain white envelope, so his hopes weren't too high. When he saw the contents of the package, he was bewildered.

Kenny finished perusing Ray's magazine, purposely wrinkling some of the pages before shouting in to Yussef, "Well, I have to be going. Have you got the money?"

"Yes, yes, I have the money. I'll be right back down with it."

Yussef bounded up the stairs, dumping the contents of the envelope on his bed: six thin bundles of one hundred dollar bills and a folded piece of paper. He snapped the rubber band off one bundle and grabbed two of the bills before heading back down to Kenny waiting for him at the base of the stairs.

"I don't have the exact amount, just two hundred, even," Yussef said, trembling.

"Jay paid his share in cash so I can get you some change," Kenny offered, as he searched the rent envelope. He pulled out a couple of wrinkled twenties and a ten. "Jeez, he must sleep with his money," he grimaced, handing the worn bills to Yussef before placing the two crisp ones in the envelope. "Well, I'm out of here. See you later."

As soon as Kenny was out the door, Yussef was headed back to his room, leaping three steps at a time, the floor shaking under his feet as he reached the doorway to his room. This time though, he hesitated before crossing the threshold, eyeing the package's content scattered on his bed. As he shut the door behind him, Yussef had the sinking feeling he'd just traded one problem: paying the rent, for another problem: Mullah Khan and his "brothers".

Yussef began counting the money, observing the trembling in his hands. He'd noticed this once before, at the Laundromat with the townies. Fifty-eight bills! He counted it again, thinking there could be no *good* reason for this money. How relieved he'd been when he first opened the envelope and realized his rent problem was over. But now, now the folded letter lying there beside him was like a snake in a wicker basket, waiting to strike when he opened it.

Yussef leapt from the bed, startled by the scurrying sound of rodent feet across the attic floor above him, while at the same time a check fluttered onto the bed from inside the folded letter as he grasped it. The slim hope that the cash money was some kind of mistake, some kind of lottery winnings, some kind anonymous benefactor, evaporated from his mind when he saw the usual name on the check. After a couple of deep breaths, he sat down and read the letter:

You will not be able to reach me at the old phone number. If this letter does not reach you by the date we set for our next phone conversation, call me on the first night you receive it, at our normal time. This new phone number replaces the old one. Enclosed, you will find your check, which you should cash in the normal manner. If for some reason you are unable to contact me, there has been a change in plans. Sometime in the near future, You WILL be contacted by "brothers of our cause". As soon as possible, use a portion of the money in the envelope to rent them a safe house. They will be in need of the remainder of the money and your loyal service. Allah Akbar!

Yussef sat on the edge of his bed, staring blankly at the wall, feeling the poison from the letter coursing through his veins. He read the letter twice more; to be sure his eyes weren't playing tricks on him. Ahmed's face drifted through his mind. He would have been pleased, ecstatic even. It was what he'd prayed for right up until that night when the fire consumed him. Ahmed had been raised, educated, and indoctrinated for martyrdom. Yussef wasn't sure about himself anymore. He had drifted away from their dreams of jihad against America. In fact, he wasn't sure he'd ever bought into their plans. It seemed as if he'd been brainwashed by the unceasing diatribe from the teachers at the madrasa, from Ahmed, and from Mullah Khan.

With Ahmed gone, the relentless preaching had stopped. Yussef was able to think clearly about his future. Ahmed never gave himself a chance to open up, to go to school, to see America the way Yussef saw it now.

Sure this country had its decadent side, but not everyone was that way. Rachael did not run around half-naked like the women Ahmed always railed against after coming home from work at the bakery. And Ray, Ray was a decent fellow: quiet, intelligent, and certainly not decadent—except for the "girlie" magazine as Kenny and Jay always called it. But now, now this deathly envelope had shown up.

"You will be contacted soon by 'brothers of our cause'" Yussef read the last part of the letter, thinking.

How soon? Was it to late to call Mullah Khan and tell him the truth? To tell the mullah that he desired to disassociate himself from the Islamic Foundation and the "brothers". And what price would he pay for doing so?

Yussef tried to bring into focus the jumbled mix of scenarios revolving in his mind. He felt a dull pain in his gut as the view became clearer.

He was able to answer each question. Sure he could leave Mullah Khan and the others of his ilk behind, that would be easy enough. But the price, most definitely the price would be high. He would have to pay them back all the money, thousands of dollars over the past three years. And where would he get that kind of money when he could barely get a loan for seventy-five dollars? Even if he could get the money, would that be all it took to satisfy them and let him just walk away? The honest answer to that question made his empty stomach churn even harder.

Despite having met only the two "brothers" from St. Louis and no others from this secretive tribe in the past three years since his arrival in America, Yussef realized, too late, that he knew too much for them to just let him walk away unscathed. The more he considered it, the more Yussef realized what a bad predicament he'd created for himself.

Why had they left him here, alone since Ahmed's death, no mosque within a hundred miles? Did they not think he would drift away from their ideology? They couldn't expect him to maintain his jihadist fervor, not without Ahmed here constantly reinforcing it. In the dark recesses of his mind, despite his denial, he knew the most important answer of them all; that to Mullah Khan and the others on their way to meet him, in their jaded eyes, it would be an unpardonable sin for Yussef to leave the fold. In their view, he would be a traitor, an apostate.

What about contacting the police? It would save his life, but it would be a short reprieve, Yussef calculated. Without citizenship, without completely truthful information on his applications, and with his past associations, the best he could hope for would be a one-way ticket back to Pakistan. No engineering research, no camaraderie with Ray and his other roommates, no freedom, all of which he enjoyed more every day, and..., no Rachael.

Within a short time back home in Pakistan he would be hunted down and killed, perhaps by someone from the madrasa, or even his own uncle, to save face—and his own life.

Yussef knew how it all worked. He had just ignored that side of his existence since being released from Ahmed's control, convincing himself that here, thousands of miles from the tribal regions; here, in the middle of the United States, not close to any iconic landmarks, that he would never be called upon by Mullah Khan. Ahmed's death had made it easy to ignore this possibility.

These thoughts along with the arrests in Arizona made him decide to double check for any images of the Arch, the lock and dam system on the Mississippi, or the baseball stadium that might still be on his computer from their one visit to St. Louis.

Yussef paced the floor, trying to make a decision. He put ten of the bills in his pants pocket and hid the rest under the shelf liner in his chest of drawers just to get them out of his sight. What to do? What to do? Call Mullah Khan. Tell his roommates. Rent a house as instructed for the new arrivals. Run away and never look back. The room began to spin as the dull pain in his gut turned into a full-blown retching as he lunged for the wastebasket next to his bed.

How could his life have changed so fast? Two days ago he was sitting with Rachael on a bench in front of Minton Hall, her bare feet touching his leg. Now he was sitting on the edge of his bed, alone, pondering how much time he had left to live.

More headache-inducing contemplation forced Yussef to give up, at least temporarily. For the rest of the day he would follow Kenny and Jay's motto: live in the present. Whatever happens is Allah's will. Besides, unable to shut off his mind completely, didn't the paper on Thursday say the jihadists had been arrested in Phoenix? Yussef realized the postmark on the envelope indicated that it had been mailed the day before the arrests. If the "brothers" were in jail, they couldn't come here, could they? He had money. He had a date with the girl of his fledgling "American Dream" tonight. And, all of a sudden he was hungry. Yussef left his worries behind in his bedroom and headed for the convenience store ten blocks away to load up on food.

Two blocks before the store, Yussef noticed a "For Rent" sign in the front yard of a grey, single story wooden house with fish-scale siding. A car was parked on the two narrow ribbons of cracked concrete, separated by still-dormant, knee-high weeds that led to a broken down garage behind the house. The stale aroma emanating from the wide-open front door attested to the age and condition of the home. The request in Mullah Khan's letter resurfaced in Yussef's head.

"Hello…, is anyone about?" Yussef shouted as he stuck his head through the doorway, rapping loudly on the wall.

He heard a muffled response from the back of the house followed closely by footsteps. A short, wiry woman with snow-white wisps of hair peaking out from under a cap emblazoned with "Big R", the name of a local farm supply store, appeared in the hallway. Her faded overalls were a size too big and Yussef noticed her intermittent head tremor that seemed worse as she spoke.

"Can I help you, young man?"

"Yes, yes I am interested in renting your house."

Yussef decided at the last moment, upon seeing the "For Rent" sign, the best approach was to follow Mullah Khan's instructions; live in the present he kept repeating to himself. After all, he had plenty of money, so what if the house sat empty. And, if by chance he was somehow connected to the terrorists captured in Arizona, or to Mullah Khan, he might need a place to stay that no one knew about, though that idea seemed far fetched to him as he slid back into denial of the whole business. Also, if by chance these "brothers" did show up, however unlikely, they would be in this house, buying Yussef time to make alternative plans.

"I don't like to rent to foreigners. I can't understand them," she informed him as her head shaking became more pronounced. "There was a house here in town that got burnt down by a couple of foreigners 'bout a year and a half ago."

"But I have lived here in Rockledge for three years. And I speak English."

"Yes, I guess you do."

The elderly lady continued to stare intently at Yussef who was trying to make eye contact but to no avail as her tremor intensified.

"Where are you living now?"

"I live over on Elm Street..., with three Americans."

"Don't you like them?"

"Oh yes, they are my friends."

"Then why are you wanting to move here?" She snapped, her voice wavering in conjunction with her movements.

Yussef thought for a moment, telling her he was renting the house for some foreign friends bent on jihad was probably not the best option.

"I am..., I'm getting married next month, ... to an American! And we need a place to live."

"Well, that's nice. What color is she?"

"Pardon me," Yussef answered, stumbling with a response, not quite sure of the question—or the proper answer. "She is black...," he watched as the landlady shook more violently. Her mouth opened and her tongue made a clucking sound against the roof of her mouth. "She is black-haired with skin as white as ivory," he added quickly. "And she grew up right her in Missouri."

"Well, that's nice!" she said, as a vibrating smile appeared on her wrinkled face. "I'm a Baptist. I don't believe in any shenanigans."

"Shenanigans?" Yussef wasn't sure what that meant, but from the tone of her voice he decided it best to change the subject. "How much is the rent?"

"It's five hundred a month, unfurnished, with a stove and refrigerator. Well, I suppose there are an old table and four chairs in the kitchen. I was going to throw them away but if you want them, I won't charge you anymore."

"I'll take it," Yussef said loudly over the growl of his stomach, which reminded him of why he'd come this way in the first place.

"But you haven't even looked at the other rooms yet. And I'm not even sure I want to rent it to you, anyway. How do I know you're not a fire bug?"

Yussef was becoming annoyed, partly from hunger, but mostly because it seemed like nothing was going smoothly in his life of late. Always before he'd had a strict regime, kept specific hours at the lab, at home, or at the library for study time. Now, it was if chaos ruled. Entropy, too much entropy was the problem he felt as he thrust his hands deep in his pockets, frustrated. But then, the stiff one hundred dollar bills scraped against his fingertips.

"I have cash. I can pay cash, including the deposit, if there is one," he offered, fishing out the money as he watched her tremor disappear for an instant.

"Well, if you want it that bad," she said in a friendlier tone, motioning for Yussef to follow as she turned and walked toward the kitchen.

The transaction was completed in short order and Yussef was back on his way to the store, folding the rent contract along the way as the house keys jingled in his hand. Best of all, she'd not asked for an ID and had only wanted a half month's rent for the security deposit. There were aspects of business in America that weren't much different from those in Pakistan, Yussef mused, as he caressed the remainder of the money in his pocket.

Back at home, after ravaging the bag of groceries he'd bought at the store, Yussef laid on his bed staring at the ceiling. The next order of business was his date this evening with Rachael, and where from to call Mullah Khan. Yussef considered not even calling. How would I know when I got the envelope with the instructions on when to call, he considered, finally deciding that he wanted it all over with.

He would call Mullah Khan and tell him that he wouldn't be associated with the Islamic Foundation any more. That he'd done as instructed in renting a house, but after the "brothers" showed up, if they showed up, and he'd given them the rest of the money, then he wanted no part of them any more. Yussef was emboldened by thoughts of breaking free, banking that they were probably all in jail.

He arrived at Rachael's house just after seven o'clock, a little better versed in the operation of Ray's truck than the last time, two weeks ago, when he mauled the lilac bush. Much to his chagrin, Tammy opened the door when he knocked, but slowly enough for him to quickly hide behind his back the single red rose he'd purchased at the store this afternoon. At least she was fully clothed, he observed, with mixed relief and regret.

"Well, hello handsome," Tammy cooed, holding the door open as Yussef side-stepped her, his back brushing against the door, already forgetting the rose in his hand that he was hiding.

"Good evening," Yussef mumbled to her toes.

"Come on in and make yourself comfortable," she implored, taking a draw on the cigarette in her hand. "I won't bite, unless you want me too."

With that said, she exhaled slowly, blowing a long trail of smoke in his direction as she turned to walk past him to the sofa. Yussef held his breath, wondering if Tammy or Jill had ever been to the bakery where Ahmed worked.

"Is…, is Rachael here?"

"She's still upstairs getting beautiful," Tammy answered, leaning forward over the coffee table to crush out her cigarette in the stained ceramic ashtray set precariously on a stack of textbooks.

"Hey, Rachael!" she shouted in the direction of the stairs, "your lover boy is here."

Startled, Yussef opened his mouth and just as quickly closed it without uttering a sound. Instead he hurriedly wiped saliva from the corner of his mouth with his dominant hand, forgetting about the rose until it scratched his nose.

"Woo hoo! Yussef, you romantic dog, you. A flower, is that what that is?"

He looked at the remnants of the red rose in his hand, half the petals either torn or missing, with the stem crushed and tilting at a forty-five degree angle.

"It is a tradition in my country," Yussef explained, trying to swallow, his mouth now dry as a desert in a determined drought, "to bring a single rose to the house of the woman you are calling on; to ward off evil spirits," he added, proud of his quick response to this teasing viper as he waved the wounded flower before him. Two can play this game, he thought.

Tammy responded without missing a beat, "The tradition in our country is the same, except we usually expect at least a dozen."

Tammy winked at Rachael descending the stairs as Yussef, oblivious to her presence, calculated the cost. Suddenly he thought it seemed very warm in the living room.

"A dozen what?" Rachael asked, feigning innocence of the conversation between Tammy and Yussef.

Yussef was embarrassed for not being familiar with this American tradition. But the sight of Rachael relieved him, like a shield separating one from a stinging scorpion. With her flowing black hair pushed back onto her shoulders with a white, silk headband, her lips candy-apple red, Yussef had already forgotten Tammy was in the room.

"Roses!" Tammy's voice jolted him out of his trance. "He was going to bring you a dozen roses but *that* piddly thing was all the store could muster." She nodded her head in the direction of the lone feeble flower. "Can you believe that lousy flower shop," she continued, as Yussef was about to forgive her, letting his guard down. "What store did you buy it at anyway, Yussef?"

"Oh, isn't that sweet," Rachael said, ignoring Tammy's banter as she took the flower from his hand.

Yussef saw his chance for an exit and headed for the door.

"Well, have fun studying, Tammy, dear," Rachael taunted, gliding past Yussef holding the screen door open for her, "Yussef, what did you do to your nose?"

"Nothing, nothing. It is just a scratch," he explained, watching out of the corner of his eye as Tammy got up from the sofa, heading for the door. Distracted as she lit another cigarette, Yussef made a point to swing the door open to the limits of its springs before letting go.

A cigarette-in-mouth mumbled, "You two lovebirds have a good ti…" and then the "SMACK" of the screen door closing were the last sounds he heard as he escorted Rachael down the steps to the pickup.

He concentrated on backing down the driveway, paying special attention to the lilac bush that was beginning to bloom. "Relax, relax," he kept telling himself, thinking of what to say to Rachael. Then, with the chirp of the tires on the pavement, they were on their way.

"You look quite lovely, indeed, tonight," Yussef offered without a stutter.

"Indeed, you look bloody well handsome yourself, Yussef."

He smiled; beginning to like the way Rachael mocked his British-legacy vocabulary.

"Thanks for the flower. It was a nice gesture," she continued, sliding across the bench seat toward Yussef, "and don't believe anything Tammy tells you. I heard what she said about the dozen roses. She's just pulling your leg."

Yussef felt relieved. This was one Americanism he was familiar with, thanks to his roommates.

"Although, if you have thirty or forty dollars to spare some time, don't hesitate in buying me a bouquet."

Yussef looked at Rachael; even in profile, he could see the smile on her face.

"Where shall we eat tonight?" He asked, hoping she knew of some place expensive and special.

"Oh, let's go back to the Bamboo Garden. It's not too pricey and we can get a glass of wine."

"But I have money tonight," Yussef protested. "We can go anywhere you like." He felt pride in the fact that he didn't have to "pinch pennies" for a change, followed quickly by guilt for how he had come to possess the money.

"I like the Bamboo Garden," Rachael countered as she wrapped her hand around his forearm, "and I know you can't have that much money. Besides, I like to think of the Bamboo Garden as *our* place."

Her smell intoxicated him as she leaned closer and squeezed his arm tighter. He couldn't argue with her logic.

Rachael requested a booth, and they got the last available one back in the corner without waiting. Yussef liked the way she took charge, and yet, at the same time he felt a sense of his own inadequacy, or perhaps ignorance, in the ways of American courting rituals. What little he knew of dating, he'd gleaned through conversations with his roommates. He knew little more about the way it was done in Pakistan, except that to his recollection there was no courting at all; the parents did all the choosing.

We would like a bottle of red wine," Yussef blurted out, almost before the waiter had stopped to give them their menus.

He was determined not to let Rachael talk him out of it for lack of funds, though he was stumped when the waiter asked him which type he would like. He looked to Rachael for help, but none was forthcoming as she buried her face in the menu. Giddy with the excitement of a second date, and not to be deterred, Yussef's mind was in overdrive as he turned back to the waiter.

"What do you recommend? Something special I hope."

"Well, we don't have a large selection, but we have a nice Chianti that's only thirty-two dollars."

"Yes, yes that sounds good. We'll give it a go."

Rachael lowered her menu just far enough so that her big, dark eyes peered over the top at Yussef. The waiter lit their candle and left before she spoke.

"Yussef, are you crazy?" She whispered across the table. "That's more than our entire meal cost last time." She gave him a stern look before continuing, "I'll tell you right now; I'm allergic to dishwater."

Yussef puzzled over the meaning of her comment before laughing. "No, no, I've got plenty of money to pay for it."

"Are you sure?" Rachael asked with a pleading look.

With staccato speed he replied, "Yes, yes. Don't worry. Don't worry. Everything is fine. Everything is fine."

Yussef felt uneasy after her response to his big spending. He thought it best to slow down. Thinking, sooner or later, if he kept splurging, she might broach the subject of where the money had come from. And, despite a quick mind, he had no idea how to answer that question.

"I'm sorry, Yussef. I don't mean to nag, but you don't have to buy me a bottle of wine or a bunch of flowers to impress me."

His eyes met hers and lingered there. It was as if he was glimpsing an incredible vista for the first time, wanting to avoid the embarrassment of staring, yet unable to pull his eyes away from the beautiful view for fear of it disappearing when he averted his gaze,

"Hey, would you like to get the dinner for two? It's got calamari and shrimp," Rachael asked, thinking it sounded romantic.

"That sounds good to me. Is that what you like to eat?" He asked, not knowing what calamari was.

"I've eaten it a couple of times. It's good," she said, nodding her head.

Yussef paid no mind to his own menu or anything else, except Rachael. He realized just how little he knew about her and the world at hand. His world, until Raymond, Kenny, and Jay interceded, had consisted of textbooks and the Qur'an. He decided that whatever they were going to eat, if Rachael liked it, it had to be okay.

Rachael sighed deeply, leaning back in the booth as she surveyed the restaurant crowd. The waiter reappeared, opened the bottle of wine, setting the cork in front of Yussef along with a sample of wine in the glass for his approval. Yussef sat there staring, mesmerized by the graceful line of her neck, the sensuousness of her bare shoulders, until finally the waiter gave up and filled both their glasses.

"So, would you like to see a movie after dinner?" Rachael asked, after a sip of wine.

Yussef switched from a sip to a gulp in midstream. "I would like to but I have to make a call at ten o'clock."

"Another phone call. To your family?"

Yussef could hear the exasperation in her voice.

"No, no I need to call the foundation that pays for my tuition, room, and board. They made a mistake in their payment to me, and I must get it corrected."

"But why ten o'clock at night?" Rachael asked, rolling her eyes.

Yussef hesitated before answering, "Be…, because of the time difference."

"Yes, but won't it be Sunday over there? Would there be anyone in the office on a Sunday morning?"

Yussef was slow to answer, confused by his own lie and her response. He had meant west coast time, where Mullah Khan lived. She was thinking Pakistan, and then, a more plausible fib fell into place.

"Yes, indeed it will be Sunday, but to us of the Muslim faith, Sunday is just a normal day. Our holiest day of the week is Friday."

Rachael shook her head slowly, gritting her teeth, a little embarrassed. "Ahh, I'm sorry. I didn't know that. Maybe, if you feel like it, you could tell me more about Islam. It interests me to know about other religions, and I'm obviously ignorant about many of them. But back to the movie, how long will your phone call take? Maybe you can make your call and then we could go to the late show. I think it starts at ten-thirty."

Yussef nodded his head in agreement but said nothing as he tried to formulate a plan in his head, not wanting to disappoint her again.

Rachael added, "I wish I'd brought my cell phone. You could have called from here."

Yussef stopped nodding. Another roadblock had just appeared: how to explain to Rachael he needed to call from a pay phone.

"I'm not sure a cell phone will work on international calls," he offered cautiously, not wanting to contradict himself or get caught in another lie. And he wasn't lying. He'd never made an international phone call on any kind of phone; there was no one for him to call.

"Oh, yeah they will," Rachael responded eagerly, before Yussef could come up with another reason. "I call overseas to talk to my brother on it. The one I told you about who used to dress Goth in high school before he joined the military. He's been overseas for the last sixteen months. In fact, his company just got rotated back home a week ago. He and a dear friend of mine are supposed to come by any day now for a visit. I'm going to be so excited to see them again."

"Perhaps we could stop at a pay phone on the way to the movie theater. I could call from there. It shouldn't take more than five or ten minutes," Yussef offered.

"It's hard enough making a local call from a pay phone," Rachael admonished, waving off Yussef's idea, "let alone an international call. Let's just go back to my house and you can call from there. It's not far out of the way. We'll still have plenty of time to make it to the movie."

Yussef spoke slowly, searching for a way out, "I don't believe I should do that. They...."

Rachael interrupted, Oh, don't worry about Tammy. As soon as Jill got home from work, they are going to a party at some friend's place. They'll be long gone by the time we get there. We'll have the whole place to ourselves," Rachael said, fluttering her eyelashes teasingly as she stroked Yussef's hand with her finger in mock lust.

Forget about calling Mullah Khan from a pay phone, Yussef told himself. He wasn't going to miss a chance to spend more time with Rachael tonight. Besides, the mullah wouldn't know where he was calling from anyway, plus he wasn't calling from his home phone, not that he thought it really mattered any more.

"I suppose…, that would be okay. I will pay you back for the long distance charges."

"Oh, don't even think about it big spender. It won't cost that much, and if it does…, Rachael grabbed his index finger, bending it backwards, "I'll torture you until you pay me."

Yussef squirmed to break free of her grip, and then he remembered the magic word. "Uncle, uncle!"

Rachael released her grip, both of them laughing as they drank more of their wine.

The rest of the evening at the restaurant was a blur for Yussef. They talked about everything, including school, though in such a casual way that academics seemed interesting to both of them. He told her about growing up in Pakistan, his make-believe mother and father, the university on the outskirts of Islamabad where he'd obtained his undergraduate degree, and the fundamentals of Islam.

She told him about growing up Catholic, her much beloved older brother, and her grandparents livestock farm. By the time they arrived at Rachael's house after dinner, the wine-induced euphoria was at its peak effect. So much so that Yussef almost decided to neglect calling Mullah Khan—almost.

Rachael handed him her cell phone, and after instructing him on how to navigate the steps for making international calls from it, plus a quick peck on the cheek, she headed upstairs to change shoes, leaving Yussef all alone on the sofa, grinning at the phone.

With a newfound confidence, fortified by wine, he dialed the number that tethered him to Mullah Khan these past three years. Now was as good a time as any to let Mullah Khan know that he wanted out. That he no longer felt a bond to the jihadist beliefs he'd been indoctrinated with since his earliest days at the madrasa in Peshawar. That he would not..., "The number you have dialed is no longer in service, please hang up and try your call again."

Yussef had forgotten to use the new number that had been sent to him along with the money. He jerked out his wallet and found the new number, dialing it as he sat on the edge of the sofa. Suddenly he felt alone in this new world he was creating for himself. Letting go of his previous life was not so easy.

The voice on the line said "hello" several times before Yussef leapt to his feet, at first not hearing it, in part due to the noise from his own deep breathes, in addition to Rachael's footsteps overhead.

"Yes, yes this is…, I'm sorry if I'm late." He paused. It was a woman's voice. "Is…, err may I…, speak to Mullah Khan, please."

Yussef looked at his worried reflection in the mirror hanging on the wall at the foot of the stairs, unsure of the person glaring back at him with furrowed eyebrows.

"Let me see if I can get him for you. Just a moment please," the voice said politely, in a manner similar to the secretaries that worked in the engineering department office at the university. He stared into his own eyes, fascinated by the bewildered look in them. Did they always look that way? How would he reconcile the fact that he'd called the west coast and not Pakistan when the phone bill came to Rachael? Still, it was a woman's voice, he considered. Too many thoughts were spinning about in his head. Waiting nervously, not knowing quite what to make of all these changes in his life, at least a minute had passed.

"Hello. Hello!" Yussef raised his voice, as if the long distance made it harder for them to hear him on the other end.

"Yes, I'm still here," the woman's soothing voice offered. "I believe Mr. Khan is on his way. It should be just a moment or two now. How's the weather where you are? What did you say your name was again?"

"Yus…," He watched his eyes turn wild, flickering about in their sockets. His arms and legs felt weak, made of putty, as he willed himself—in what seemed like slow-motion—to make his thumb press the disconnect button.

Deep breath, deep breath, his brain told his lungs, which were resisting any movement at all. Finally they responded. The perspiration in his hair gave it the sheen of a raven's feathers.

"So, did you get everything straightened out?"

Yussef whirled about as he heard the voice behind him, losing his grip on the phone. It was Rachael, standing at the base of the stairs. Instinctively, they both reached for the phone as it fell from Yussef's hand, bumping their heads against one another in a futile attempt to catch it before it hit the floor.

"I'm sorry, I didn't mean to startle you," Rachael apologized, wincing as she rubbed her head and watching Yussef do likewise. "We make a great team, don't we?" She laughed. "So romantic, I'm such a klutz."

"No, no. It was my fault, my fault," Yussef stammered as he retrieved the phone, still in one piece. "I was daydreaming, I suppose."

"You looked like you'd seen a ghost," she said, still laughing. "Well, shall we shuffle off to the picture show, love?" She asked, holding out her hand to Yussef.

"Indeed, we better hurry along. We mustn't be late," he replied.

He wiped his sweaty palms on his pants, took her hand, and headed out the door, glancing back briefly at the phone he'd laid on the stand below the mirror.

For Yussef, the remainder of the night was a constantly blurring dream, appearing at times like a relentless, wind-driven snow, blinding his thoughts. A "white-out" of sorts, with odd instances of calm when the wind would lie down, offering glimpses of himself and the road ahead, only to be blinded again by a new rush of thoughts, a new road to follow. He was mesmerized and terrified by the visions swirling about in his head, unable to separate them from reality.

Throughout these visions, his mind grasped: Rachael leaning against his shoulder, her warmth, her fragrance lingering, and then blown away; the intense heat of the fire and the oppressive, thick smoke; Ahmed, still alive; the relentless cry of the muezzin as Yussef and unrecognizable others went about their dark business under the approving gaze of Mullah Khan; parties yet to come at the house with Ray, Kenny, and Jay; the humming fluorescent glow of the nuclear physics lab; the vibrating head of the white-haired landlady; a uniformed figure with a rifle hunting an unseen quarry in the attic; bits of dialogue from the movie; the moist, softness of Rachael's lips, the velvet feel of her skin, the curve of her hips, the sultry sighs of pleasure.

When quizzed the next morning by his roommates, Yussef couldn't recall the name or plot of the movie. This brought hoots and catcalls from the others, along with more sober warnings about falling in love.

In truth, the only thing Yussef could remember clearly from the night before was the white, commercial van, with three silhouetted figures inside, parked on the street across from the driveway as he drove Ray's truck up to the house. It was a memory he dare not share with his roommates.

CHAPTER EIGHT

Ibrahim did the bulk of the driving, spelled only once by Jamal for a quick nap before reclaiming the driver's seat. A torrential rain plagued them for most of the trip since leaving Houston early that morning after prayers.

The heavy traffic borne by the highway had worn a depression in the pavement that collected rainwater. It pulled at the vans worn-out suspension, requiring constant corrections by the driver. Jamal had never driven in rain this heavy. He shifted in his seat and thanked Ibrahim for his steady hand at the wheel. Ali had been correct in his description of Ibrahim's skills back at the *hacienda* in Paraguay.

Khalib sat in the back seat, alternating his view between the open pages of the Qur'an that he held firmly in his lap and the rolling hills of northeast Texas, which were covered with towering pine trees and lush grass. He'd been pacified, in part, by the four days spent in Houston. Those days found them either at their safe house or a local mosque a few blocks away. The travails of the journey and the inevitability of his fate had worn him down to emptiness.

First Monsour, and now with friend and fellow jihadist Sa'id already in paradise, he felt more duty bound then ever to wage jihad, to avenge their deaths and join them. He knew also, deep down inside, that Jamal was right; that he'd been responsible for Sa`id's death at the hands of the alcohol-fueled, young, and proud Mexican. Not being used to pondering his own thoughts too deeply, Khalib returned to the safety of the Holy Book. He was determined to follow through with the plans laid out by Jamal and to control his emotions. He had prayed for four days, and, *inshaa`Allah*, he would soon join his fallen "brothers".

Letting Khalib drive was out of the question, though Jamal had to admit that since reaching Houston, Khalib had settled down. His habitual nervous tics had subsided to a degree. Once they'd heard the news from Arizona, Jamal knew they should move on without delay. He did not like waiting now that they were in America.

For his part, Jamal would have gladly parted ways with Josh—their Islam-converted chauffer whom he could not bring himself to trust—as soon as they'd reached Houston and kept right on going to their predetermined destination. He felt like he'd been waiting all his life for this final act to play out, and he was ready for it. But word had come through their contact in Houston to wait, plus Jamal was not sure what to do with Khalib who, at the time, appeared to be falling apart mentally.

The four days had not been a total waste though, Jamal decided. They'd had time to familiarize themselves with an American culture so different than anything they'd known. No amount of satellite television could prepare you for what it was really like here: the way women dressed, the incessant billboards, convenience stores on every corner, live news broadcast not just a talking head staring sternly at you. In addition Jamal had time to read through all the newspaper and online accounts of the jihadist's arrest in Arizona, which occurred on the day after they'd crossed the border from Matamoras to Brownsville. From these articles, he gleaned what information he could concerning which sleeper cells might be compromised.

Within a day after the arrests, the local cell leader noticed increased traffic in the neighborhood around the mosque. This was enough to prompt Jamal to move quickly. Their reasons for stopping in Houston were to obtain a vehicle suitable for their mission and to receive the name and address of their final contact, which had arrived in a sealed envelope on their last full day in Houston. Such was the structure of their organization; rarely did one individual cell know the names of any others outside their own cell and never their location. Even Jamal had been privy to only a few important contacts, names and numbers, in case an emergency arose.

They stopped at fast food, drive-up windows and twice at gas stations for fuel and nature breaks. Wanting to be seen by as few people as possible, Jamal had Ibrahim pay each time since he spoke with the least obvious accent. Khalib desired to go in and sit down at the restaurants but Jamal refused, afraid that, even though they wore American-style clothes, they would look suspicious to locals. The newspapers were filled with stories related to the arrests in Arizona, along with pictures of the jihadists and their intended target; a weapons plant where missiles were manufactured. Local people would have a heightened awareness of foreigners, Jamal reasoned.

Once, at twilight, Khalib insisted, frantically, that they pullover near a scenic overlook not far from the Arkansas-Missouri border. He didn't want to admit it to Jamal, but the curving road with its steep hills and switchbacks made him car sick. Jamal could hear him retching just out of sight among some pine trees while he and Ibrahim studied the road map. The faint squeal of the tires and the fishtailing effect as they lost their grip on the pavement took a toll on Khalib's stomach. None of them were used to these kinds of roads, and Jamal, himself, felt a little queasy on a couple of the s-curves that Ibrahim had approached too fast.

According to the map, Jamal thought they would reach the university town, Rockledge, where their contact lived in another three hours.

"At least the rain has stopped. I can see better," Ibrahim commented, regarding the past four hundred miles.

Jamal and Khalib shared a laugh at this observation, something they'd rarely done during the past three weeks.

Since it was getting dark, Jamal suggested Ibrahim drive a little slower as they were not familiar with the roads. Khalib agreed with a vigorous nod while Ibrahim shrugged his shoulders but complied. It was sage advice, as twice during the remainder of the drive they encountered whitetail deer sharing their side of the two-lane highway. Both times, the slack-jawed expressions on their faces were a testament to their amazement at sighting an abundance of wildlife so close up.

They sat side-by-side in the front seat after the emergency stop for Khalib. In the darkness Khalib couldn't read and having the dome light on was out of the question after Ibrahim confessed it made seeing the road difficult. Khalib demanded that he sit next to the window, hoping it would quell the churning of his stomach.

Thirty-five miles from their destination, according to the sign along the interstate highway they were now traveling, Jamal saw the exit ramp that lead to his intended target. No smile, no shout of joy, just a deep sigh of relief at having finally reached a concrete symbol of his efforts. It was as if he'd just been handed the keys to a building that took nearly three years to complete. It is almost finished, Jamal mused, knowing it would be just a matter of days now before he produced tangible results.

Since his early twenties it had been his goal—his dream—to avenge the wrongs perpetrated against members of his family, against his "brothers and sisters", by a puppet government that did America's bidding; to punish the hand that pulled the strings. So many things he'd learned since joining the Muslim Brotherhood, Jamal reminisced, not the least of which was patience, and patient he'd been. His mentors had taught him well. Not just bomb-making and marksmanship, but leadership skills and anger management. He had learned, above all else, to channel his anger into patience, to bide his time until the goal was attainable; this was the mantra of his organization. Now, time was just about up.

Jamal read the name—Yussef—and address of his contact out loud, repeating it several times until he and the others had it memorized. He then instructed Khalib to toss it out the window.

Just past ten o'clock, they pulled off the interstate, moving slowly through the lighted streets of Rockledge, Missouri. They stopped at a convenience store for a map of the town. None were available for sale. Jamal tore the street map out of a borrowed phone book while Ibrahim kept the clerk—a leather-skinned, middle-aged native of India—occupied with questions.

Khalib, tired of waiting outside as instructed, came in and joined the conversation with the clerk, who it turned out was a cousin of the store's owner. Khalib offered that he was from Pakistan without thinking, or, more to the point, thinking what a coincidence that they were from neighboring countries. Born less than three hundred miles apart—the clerk said he was from a northwestern province—and now, ten thousand miles away from home, they had something of a shared history, something to talk about. Soon though, the conversation turned to what had brought Khalib to this corner of the world, and he stumbled for an answer.

The clerk, whose black hair and dark, round face mirrored that of Khalib's, minus the bearded youthful appearance, flashed a look of mistrust at the trio. Ibrahim had purchased a fifty-cent piece of candy and the other's, nothing. Jamal had joined Ibrahim and Khalib at the counter, handing back the phone book to the clerk. He tried to cover for Khalib by answering quickly that they were planning to enroll at the university. The distrustful clerk scoffed at this answer, irritated with them for not buying anything more. He shook his head in disbelief, asking why they were here now when the summer semester was almost three months away.

"Can't you read a calendar?" he said, half joking.

Jamal shrugged, saying nothing in response as he discreetly tugged on the back of Khalib's shirt while moving toward the door. Khalib stood his ground, staring at the Indian clerk, paying no heed to Jamal's physical hint. The clerk had turned away from Khalib, ignoring his presence, busying himself with another task, brushing Khalib's innocent attempt at benevolent talk aside.

Ibrahim followed Jamal obediently out the door, leaving Khalib standing there alone, feeling snubbed. With the other's gone, the surly clerk gave Khalib his full attention, telling him to buy something or leave. Khalib uttered a series of derogatory remarks about the clerk's native country followed by threatening insults concerning the disputed region of Kashmir as he stepped outside. Looking back through the plate-glass window he could see the clerk staring at him, lips moving. Khalib could easily guess the words he spoke.

Back in the van, Jamal chastised the other two for talking too much. Ibrahim protested that he was only doing what he'd been told to do—keep the clerk distracted. Both turned to face Khalib who'd been regulated to the back seat again by Jamal. Khalib frowned but said nothing as Jamal continued to berate him. He was tired of apologizing, tired of the trip, and tired of being told what to do by Jamal. He admittedly didn't have the strength of discipline nor the worldly knowledge that Jamal possessed, but he was not going to be a deaf-mute that Jamal could do with as he pleased. Jamal, nor anyone else, were going to order him around anymore, Khalib decided, picking at a loose thread in his slacks.

Ibrahim was tired, too, physically tired from all the driving. Jamal, though, had newfound energy since seeing the exit sign for Ft. Wilson back on the interstate. He turned his attention from Khalib to the street map, instructing Ibrahim on which direction to go as they left the lighted parking lot of the store.

Eleven o'clock was early enough for carloads of teenagers and college students to be cruising the streets that bordered the campus and downtown. Some were riding in pimped versions of older vehicles that made the van look less conspicuous. Jamal rolled down his window, resting his arm on the door as he held the map with both hands, deliberating on which street to take next.

The bawdy street scenes of young adults, most no older than himself, diverted Khalib's attention from the store clerk. He stared out the window with open-mouth wonder, the same as with the head-lighted deer they'd encountered earlier in the evening.

Ibrahim slowed to a stop in front of the address that belonged to their contact. When a car came up the street behind them, Jamal, ever wary, ordered Ibrahim to drive around the block and park twenty yards up the street from the driveway.

They sat there in silence for ten minutes, watching the house, waiting, before Jamal got out and headed toward the front door. The other two watched as he slowly climbed the steps to the front porch and peered through the window into the lighted room, masked only by crookedly hung, threadbare curtains. Ibrahim and Khalib could see him knock on the door and, after a moment, a silhouetted figure standing in the doorway talking to Jamal. In less than a minute, Jamal was headed back down the steps and along the sidewalk on the opposite side of the street from where they were parked. He went to the end of the block before doubling back to their van. Jamal climbed into his seat, informing the others that they were at the correct address but, according to the red-haired American who answered the door, their contact had borrowed his truck for a date and had no idea when Yussef would be home.

Khalib turned on the dome light and began to thumb through pages of the Qur`an. Without a word, Jamal dislodged the plastic cover and removed the light bulb, dropping it on the floor and crushing it beneath his boot. Ibrahim could see Jamal's cheeks sucking in and out as he sat there brooding by the light of a waxing half moon. Khalib quietly laid his Qur`an on the seat beside him.

No one spoke for a long time; long enough for Khalib to have fallen asleep in the backseat. Jamal, in a somber tone, finally spoke as he stared through the window at the house.

"We will take shifts watching for his return. Go ahead and get some sleep, Ibrahim. I will take the first watch."

Ibrahim nodded, "Jamal..., what if he doesn't show up?"

Immediately, Ibrahim regretted asking the question, as Jamal glared at him for a moment stone-faced before he answered in a cold, calculating manner.

"We will watch until daybreak and then go find a motel room. After we rested for six hours, we will hunt him down."

Ibrahim avoided eye contact with Jamal, closing his eyes instead, trying his best to sleep.

Jamal woke Khalib at one o'clock, telling him to watch for the truck that their contact would be driving. Nearly an hour passed with Khalib staring into the darkness outside the van. He pressed his forehead against the window while his hands twitched repeatedly. The house at the end of the driveway had gone completely dark. Headlights of a slow-moving vehicle pierced his wavering eyelids. The lights belonged to a pickup truck that slowed almost to a stop, facing the van, before turning onto the driveway.

"Jamal," Khalib whispered, nudging him forcefully on the shoulder, "a truck just pulled in the driveway. I think he may have noticed us."

Jamal awoke in time to see the red glow of the truck's tail lights fade and then merge with the surrounding darkness. Ibrahim, resting his head against the steering wheel, was sound asleep."

"Stay in the van, Khalib. Understand?" Jamal ordered as they both began to get out. Khalib, reluctant to obey, got back in the front seat as Jamal took a step toward him. "And keep quiet," he hissed, as Khalib rolled down the window.

Jamal sprinted across the street, staying in the shadows of the neighboring house, coming up silently along a row of evergreen shrubs that separated the house from the driveway, contra lateral to the pickup truck and street.

Yussef moved toward the porch, all the while looking back in the direction of the van parked on the street with Texas license plates. From the shine of his headlights, a moment earlier, he could see three silhouetted human figures in it. The night with Rachael filled his mind. Though the feel of her lips was gone, the taste of her lipstick and the smell of her perfume lingered on. Worries of Mullah Khan only now began to creep back into his thoughts after the euphoric drive home.

"*As-salaamu` alaykum*," Jamal announced as he moved out of the shadows and approached Yussef.

Yussef did not turn to see where the voice had come from, and Jamal thought for an instant that perhaps he had the wrong person. Surely his contact would know Arabic or at least the proper words of greeting. Even Joshua, the newly minted, American jihadist who picked them up in Brownsville knew that much.

Yussef stood there, still looking toward the van, holding his breath. He'd heard the greeting from Jamal and, with a sickness in his stomach, knew what it meant. Knew that his life was about to change. He closed his eyes, seeing Rachael once more, waiting for his heart to slow before he turned and answered.

"*Wa `alaykum `as-salaamu.*"

They faced each other, three feet apart. Yussef saw the close-cropped hair, the goatee, and the intense, dark eyes set deeply in an angular face. They embraced—stiffly, hesitantly—and made customary kisses on each cheek.

Jamal detected the fragrance of a woman, perhaps alcohol too, and was surprised by the youthful look of his clean-shaven counterpart. They were the same height, though Jamal was heavier, more muscular, compared to Yussef's slender build.

Before Jamal could say anything more, Yussef motioned him toward the street, away from the house and his disintegrating life. Plausible explanations as to why this man was here raced through Yussef's head for the benefit of his roommates should any of them see him standing here. Upon reaching the sidewalk and stepping behind a giant sycamore, Yussef spoke.

"I did not expect you so soon."

"No, that is quite apparent to me. We've been waiting here for three hours," Jamal snarled.

"I only received a letter from Mullah Khan this morning, stating you were on your way here, but nothing about what day you would arrive. I wasn't sure after what happened in Arizona if you would even come." He proceeded to pull the folded letter out of his back pocket for Jamal. "I had already made plans for tonight. I have experiments in my lab that I must attend to."

Jamal glanced quickly toward Yussef before returning to the letter as he tried to read it by the yellow haze of a streetlight half a block away.

"Have you contacted Mullah Khan as he requested in the letter?"

"Yes, yes. I tried this evening at the usual time."

"You tried?" Jamal interrupted, letting his hand holding the letter drop to his side as he stared at Yussef with a questioning look.

He didn't know what to think of Yussef. Didn't know if he could be trusted. Still, he had a letter from Mullah Khan. Jamal had pictured someone else as his contact when driving up from Houston; someone more resolute in his manner.

A dog barked close by. Yussef kept moving deliberately further up the sidewalk from the house, and Jamal obliged, directing him with subtle awareness toward the van. Looking back, longingly, at the house, Yussef felt as if he were caught between the gravitational pull of two forces.

"I called both numbers, the old and the new, but I got only a woman's voice. She kept telling me he was on his way to the phone; after awhile..., I hung up."

"You hung up. Why?" Jamal had gone back to re-reading the letter, but now he stopped again to look at Yussef.

"I'm afraid I may have stayed on the line too long."

Jamal gave him a quizzical look, and then nodded slowly, understanding Yussef's meaning. When their eyes met this time, Jamal could sense the fear in them.

"Did you call from a pay phone?"

"No," Yussef answered quickly, without thinking, "but it was not a phone that could be traced directly to me or this house," he added.

They paused directly across the street from the van as another dog joined the chorus. Ibrahim was awake now, and along with Khalib, watched, waiting for instructions from Jamal as he and their new contact approached the vehicle in fits and starts.

"The letter mentions money. How much was sent?" Jamal asked, making his way around to the passenger side as he motioned for Yussef to get in.

Following Khalib as he crawled into the back seat, Yussef's response, "six bundles", was drowned out by the engine noise as Ibrahim started the van.

"How much?" Jamal asked again.

"Sixteen hundred dollars is what I have left," Yussef replied, looking first at Khalib now seated beside him then glancing at Ibrahim's face in the rearview mirror, avoiding Jamal's glare. "I used some of the money to rent a house for the three of you. It's just a few blocks from here, and there is a garage you can park the van in. I had to pay a deposit in addition to the rent, but I used a fictitious name," Yussef continued, hoping to appease Jamal, who he already discerned to be the ringleader as he steeled himself for a harsh response.

Yussef's mind was in overdrive as he tried to keep his lies straight, doing his best to find the right answers to keep these three, especially Jamal, happy with him.

For the moment, Jamal seemed satisfied with the information. He instructed Ibrahim to follow Yussef's directions to the rented house while he continued to size up their new companion.

It took three of them to get the rusty-hinged garage doors open. Ibrahim waited behind the wheel while the others surveyed the inside of the dilapidated shack, illuminated by the van's idling headlights.

Yussef, hungry and in a hurry, had not bothered to check the garage's condition during his afternoon visit. The roof was caved in on one side to a level five feet above the ground. By using two-by-fours strewn about the dirt floor, they managed to prop the roof up just enough for the van to fit under it. After removing their gear from the back, Jamal used an uprooted cinder block he'd tripped over in the tall grass to pin the garage doors shut.

Yussef escorted them to the front door, fumbling for the key. The closed-up smell of the old house greeted them as they entered. The only overhead light as best Yussef could remember, stumbling forward through the darkness, was in the kitchen where he headed now in search of the switch.

The harsh light, from two, one-hundred watt, bare light bulbs, sent an armada of cockroaches and silverfish scurrying for cover under the curled edges of the etched linoleum floor. At last, the four of them stood there in the naked, shadowless light, examining one another. They took stock of each other, moving hesitantly around the chrome-legged table and mismatched chairs, each one a different color, the seats and backs composed of brittle plastic with cracks that exposed yellowed tuffs of padding in various stages of escape.

Yussef, for the first time in two weeks, wished he still had his beard, feeling naked under the strong light and distrustful glances from the others. It was as if two different species, unknown to one another before, had met in the forest, sizing each other up before deciding on their next move. Yet, they weren't so different, he thought, and he felt drawn to them by their commonalities: religion, language, and ethnicity. Something he realized he'd missed, at least a little, since the loss of Ahmed. Jamal broke the silence by introducing Khalib and Ibrahim. They greeted each other with ceremonial hugs and kisses as Yussef began to let his guard down. For now, familiarity and curiosity had trumped fear. Yussef began the questioning.

"Where have you come from? ...I mean today."

"We left Houston early this morning, after prayers," Ibrahim offered, "and drove all day plus half the night through steady rain to get here."

"We've been here since ten o'clock; over three hours we waited for you," Jamal reiterated.

"I am truly sorry. As I said earlier, I did not know when you were coming. I had work to do."

"That's not what the red-haired one at your house told me," Jamal said, eyeing Yussef carefully for a response.

Yussef pursed his lips, trying not to respond. He heard the comment but ignored it as thoughts spun about in his head. Of course they would have gone up and knocked on the door. Be careful, he chastised himself, quickly directing a question to Khalib who seemed anxious to join in the conversation.

"How long were you in Houston?"

Khalib started in, "We crossed the border three days before at Brownsville, after just a little over a day in Mexico."

"So you've heard about the trouble in Arizona?" Yussef interrupted, wondering if they'd been involved. He assumed not since the only response from them were somber nods.

Khalib continued, reviewing the entire itinerary of their trip, eager to get it off his chest. His voice wavered at each juncture of the journey where Monsour and Sa'id had been lost.

Yussef was amazed by the distance of their journey and the indirect route they'd taken to get here; here in the middle of America; here, where a newspaper article a few weeks earlier had stated was the geographic center of the country's population as it slowly inched its way south and west. Why here, he asked himself. He wasn't prepared for the answers.

"I lost my roommate two years ago in a house fire," Yussef explained, looking at Khalib and Ibrahim, avoiding Jamal. "His name was Ahmed. We spent several years together at the same madrasa in Peshawar. After I finished at the university in Pakistan, he joined me on my studies here in America."

Khalib had heard of the madrasa Yussef attended. It was less than a hundred miles from the one he'd attended in Quetta. Khalib mentioned the encounter with the Indian convenience store clerk despite the sour look on Jamal's face.

"Where do you go for prayers? Is there a mosque nearby?"

Yussef shook his head. He hadn't prayed at a mosque in the past three years. Lowering his eyes, he answered sheepishly, ashamed to admit his answer—out of guilt and fear, "No, there isn't a formal place of worship here. The closest one is in St. Louis."

"Will we be going there soon?" Khalib asked, turning to Jamal.

"No, I told you before this is our *final* destination. It is time to begin preparations for our sole purpose in coming here. It is time to begin preparing for your martyrdom," Jamal's voice was resolute. "Our martyrdom," he added, strongly.

Jamal's gaze left Khalib who was bowing his head and sinking slowly into a chair. He looked to Ibrahim—the youngest among them—who was leaning against the ancient-looking, gas, cooking stove and staring at the floor; then he moved on to Yussef standing by the enamel sink.

Yussef started to speak but couldn't. His lips parted but no sound came forth. He felt frozen in place. Thoughts flowed through his brain as if they were floating in a river of slush, almost ready to coalesce into solid ice and cease their flow altogether. He had convinced himself since first receiving the letter from Mullah Khan that when the "brothers' showed up, if they showed up, this would be just a stop over point for them—a way station in route to some big city destination, some inspiring target, and, if asked to join them, he would be able to come up with a plausible excuse to stay behind.

Ibrahim moved toward one of the empty chairs and this visible movement brought Yussef's mind back into focus. Thoughts began to flow again, but now it was as if the current was gaining strength, and he could not slow its speed.

Yussef's voice betrayed his calm demeanor. "You are not going on to another destination from here?"

"No, I chose this place over two years ago. Myself, and the others that I trained with were asked to pick one of several locations, determined by our leaders to be the best targets based on various factors. I chose this one."

"But why here?" Yussef asked, bewildered at his choice. "Why not Chicago or Los Angeles or St. Louis? I have pictures of the Arch. Or better yet, the lock and dam system on the Mississippi River. It would paralyze shipping on the river for months, maybe even years."

Yussef was trying to sound convincing, wanting to make Jamal see the folly of waging jihad in sleepy Rockledge, Missouri. Inside, he was in turmoil. First, he'd deleted all the images from the trip he took to St. Louis with Ahmed. He hoped there was a way to retrieve them if pressed by Jamal. Second, he felt guilty—two-faced—for suggesting any place at all. Why America? What was so bad about it? Why not Israel or Pakistan, specifically the part of Pakistan where his despised uncle lived?

Jamal raised his hand with one finger pointing toward the water-stained ceiling, rubbing his chin with the other as if thinking about what Yussef had just said, not quite sure of the appropriate answer, such as a lecturer contemplating an unforeseen question from a student. At last, Jamal explained.

"Others have thought of your plan—for the lock and dam I mean—but we have no cell in St. Louis."

Yussef interrupted, trying not to sound desperate, "Yes, yes, Ahmed and I went with them to take pictures. We made drawings and took measurements."

Jamal waved him off, and then continued, "They are no longer there. They were eliminated."

"Eliminated?" Yussef whispered.

He looked at Jamal, but Jamal paid him no mind. Jamal wasn't quite sure whether to trust Yussef with all his plans and knowledge of their organization. Still, his pride of accomplishment in reaching Rockledge with his payload, his determination to follow his plans to fruition, made him ever more bold as he explained why he chose Midwestern America as his target.

"I had several reasons for choosing this location. Number one: our cause is ridiculed, and perhaps rightly so, for bombing soft civilian targets. Therefore, I chose a military target, the one we passed on the way here to your home."

"You mean Ft. Wilson!" Yussef nearly shouted, looking at Jamal in disbelief. "But there are thousands of soldiers there. They have guards...."

Jamal patiently raised his hand again, "Please, let me finish."

He was looking directly at Yussef. There was no emotion showing on his face, Yussef thought, as if he were lecturing to a group of students about World History.

"Number Two: At the time I made my choice of targets, I was told we had operatives already planted close to a military base in the Midwest, waiting to sow the seeds of jihad; one of whom had expertise in nuclear physics; both willing to die for our just cause. Was I misinformed?"

The lump in Yussef's throat was choking him. He couldn't breath, and he dare not look at Jamal or the others who had turned their gaze to the newest jihadist among them. All Yussef could think of was Ahmed. If he'd been here, how eager he would have been to dispel any notion of their unwillingness to participate in whatever plot Jamal conceived. With no answer from Yussef forthcoming, Jamal continued.

"Number three: For the very reason you just asked, 'why not Chicago or Los Angeles?', in my opinion, striking a blow in the very heartland of this evil country will send a message a hundred-fold louder than anything we could do on either coast or in a large metropolitan area. They would know that we could reach them anywhere, that nowhere in this country are people safe from the sword of justice.

"Finally, there are few of the Muslim faith in this part of America. With the nearest mosque over a hundred miles away, hopefully, few if any of our 'brothers or sisters' will perish."

Ibrahim nodded his approval as Jamal finished, stating, "It is an excellent plan Jamal. It will be totally unexpected, and I will do my part to see it happen, whatever you wish of me."

Khalib nodded slowly but said nothing. His left hand rested on the worn cover of his Holy Book, his right hand trembled on the tabletop. Yussef moved closer to the trio, not sure what was expected of him or what he expected of himself. His plan to stall for more time until they went on to another destination had tumbled like a stack of cards. His earlier intuition, after reading the letter and seeing the bundles of money was proving true; they—at least Jamal—wouldn't let him walk away unscathed. For now, he decided it best to play along. With all the bravado he could muster, he pledged his allegiance to them.

"What else do you need from me, Jamal?" He asked boldly.

"We need the rest of the money sent to you from Mullah Khan."

As Jamal spoke, he spread a large map across the table. "We also need materials from your engineering department to make the explosive device."

Yussef could not help but laugh out loud. Finally, a loose thread had appeared in Jamal's plan that would make it all unravel. Jamal eyed him with increasing disdain, bordering on anger. Before Yussef could explain the fallacy in Jamal's scheme, Ibrahim asked how close they would need to get to their intended target. Using his index finger, Jamal, leaning over the wobbly-legged table, began to slowly circle the military base on the creased map.

"Ideally, I would like to get onto the base itself, but we must at least get within a radius of…"

Yussef interrupted again, "You have miscalculated my abilities. There is not enough available fissel material at my lab, indeed, on the entire campus to make a thermonuclear device. The reactor we have is a small experimental one. Even standard chemical explosives for a radioactive 'dirty' bomb are not easily accessed by me."

His mind wandered for a moment, picturing Rachael in a hard hat, blowing up the abandoned concrete grain silos. A smile spread across his face.

Jamal, mistaking his smile for insolence stood up and faced Yussef. He threw off his coat, exposing his gun and then released the strap that held it in place. The stone-faced look from Jamal along with the sight of the gun reminded Yussef of his own miscalculations.

"We don't need *any* radioactive material from your lab. What we need is your expertise, minus the arrogance, in assembling the material that we've carried ten thousand miles at the cost of two of our devoted 'brothers' lives."

With that said, he picked up one of the two polished stainless steel computer cases propped against the table and opened it. The fake keyboard came out to reveal no internal components, but instead, a lead shield covering a tightly wrapped package of weapons-grade uranium. Jamal recited the figures concerning the amont of radioactive material present in each of the two cases. For Yussef, it was as if Pandora's box had just been opened; the proverbial genie let out of the bottle. Yussef's knees began to buckle and he just managed to sit on the edge of the table, breaking his fall, one rubbery leg touching the floor, too weak to support his weight. He hoped they mistook his sitting down as a form of nonchalance about the revelation placed before him. His back was now turned away from the others and they could not see the expression of terror on his face. It would take a heavy mask to shield it from them, he mused.

Yussef knew the others, especially Jamal, were waiting for a response from him. Facing the wall, he spoke out in a low, calculating voice, stating the amount of explosives needed to detonate the fissile material present in the two cases and the radius of destruction it would cause if triggered at ground level. The numbers rolled off his tongue as if he were reciting the alphabet. Years of study were beginning to bear a bitter fruit. After three minutes of oral calculations he paused, collecting himself with a deep sigh before turning to the others. He looked at each of them, settling at last on Jamal before he spoke again.

"I know where we can get enough explosives. It will require breaking into a building, but I believe there will be enough material there to do the job."

Jamal nodded slowly, warily as he watched Yussef. The other two, eyelids drooping, were too fatigued from the trip to respond. Jamal was tired also, but still suspicious, he was unwilling to let Yussef leave the house on his own; at least not without further instructions. He motioned for Yussef to come with him as he moved from the kitchen, through the dark hallway toward the front door. Jamal put his arm around Yussef's neck, gun in hand, and guided him outside the house, away of the others. He explained to Yussef what was expected of him and what would get him killed.

"Your American roommate told me you were on a date when I came to your house, not at some lab doing an experiment as you stated earlier. Are there lots of Muslim women around here?" Jamal sneered.

Yussef stuttered, trying to think of an explanation but Jamal cut him off. Jamal's face was inches from his own. He could feel Jamal's hot breath on one cheek and the cold steel of his pistol on the other.

"Don't take me for a fool, Yussef. I am not convinced of where your loyalties lie but to help guide you, remember this. Your roommate gave me her name and where she lives. No harm will come to either of them if you do as you are told. But I *will* be watching. Go home and sleep in your own bed for what's left of the night. Be back here at nine o'clock in the morning with the money."

He holstered his gun, and Yussef nodded before walking away without another spoken word between them. Jamal watched him go until the darkness had made Yussef's outline its own. Wary of the new addition to their group, Jamal considerd going after Yussef and bringing him back to spend the night here under watchful eyes. He reconsidered, thinking it might cause suspicion, deciding instead he would watch Yussef's house from the van. He went back inside to tell the others but Ibrahim and Khalib were already sprawled out on the living room floor asleep.

On his own, Jamal managed to get the van out of the garage, driving it back over near Yussef's home and parking a considerable distance away to wait and watch. Though he was tired, sleep was evasive.

Jamal's mind wouldn't shut down as he sat there watching the dark house. The smell of a woman on Yussef's clothes revived memories of his own wife. Jamal had not seen her since being sent to prison in Egypt, sentenced to twenty-eight months along with six of his cohorts. He was only nineteen at the time. When he was released, the first thing he'd been told was that his wife's family had persuaded her and their young son to disown Jamal and to leave him for their own safety. Once, nearly a year after his release from prison, Jamal had managed to make contact with her via a phone conversation. She told him the authorities had indeed come to their apartment, multiple times, making threats and offering money for her to spy on him.

He couldn't blame her for leaving. It was for the best. The time he'd spent alone in prison only helped to cement his relationship to the Brotherhood. By the time he was released, his indoctrination was complete. The years spent incarcerated had earned him a higher rank within the organization. He traveled a lot in those early days after prison; it would have been a burden on his young family.

Year after year his focus had sharpened, and when the opportunity had come to be the leader of a terrorist cell, he was ecstatic. The plan had gestated for two years. Passing the sign at the exit to Ft. Wilson marked the beginning of the fruition of his labor. Now, it was just a question of the precision of the operation. How cleanly the plan could be pulled off was just a matter of aquiring the explosives and building the bomb. He thought it could be done in less than a week. With self-discipline and working fourteen hours a day it should take no more than five days, he calculated. Discipline had become his strong suit. It had allowed him to survive, to thrive in prison, to endure the desert training camp, to carry out the orders that included the elimination of those accused of betrayal.

As he entered the final stages of the plan, he was confident it could be executed so long as his fellow jihadist did not falter. Except for his one outburst at the jungle airstrip, Jamal could tell Ibrahim had self-discipline, also. He had done well, so far. Perhaps it was the hardships thrust upon him at such an early age. It appeared to Jamal that Ali and the imam had treated Ibrahim more like a slave than a son, but it wasn't his place to say anything. Maybe, Jamal mused, his own son would grow up with ample self-discipline. He hoped this act of jihad would inspire him and others to continue the fight against the West. That was always an underlying goal of the organization: to inspire others to action. They would not throw off the shackles of oppression in his lifetime—since it was near its end. But in his son's life time, *inshaa`Allah,* albeit with his own plan a success, the tide would turn in their favor. The Western powers would quickly crumble and his son's generation would taste a freedom Jamal could never attain, he hoped.

Khalib had been the big disappointment so far, Jamal thought. He needed the constant crutch of the Qur`an to keep himself propped up. In the end, he was sure Khalib would falter but by then it would not matter. He had been a mule, trained to obey the commands of his leader. So far, he had carried the load, though stubbornly at times.

Yussef was the one unknown, Jamal considered, his eyelids growing heavy. He was not sure what to expect from this college-educated contact before they met a few hours ago. Yussef seemed aloof and not enthusiastic when they greeted outside his house. He had shown little emotion except when the intended target had been mentioned. It was a bold plan, Jamal conceded, allowing himself a moment to gloat.

Still, Yussef had rented the house on short notice and seemed genuine in his concern about the phone conversation—or rather lack of one—with Mullah Khan. And he had the intelligence to call from someone else's phone, which should buy them time if indeed the call was traced. Tomorrow, Jamal decided, he would spend more time with Yussef to be sure of his allegiance. The fatigue that was clouding his judgement would be dissipated by a few hours of sleep, he decided.

Jamal began to take inventory in his head of the materials they would need for the bomb, nodding off just past heavy steel cylinder and acetylene torch.

CHAPTER NINE

The next morning, Yussef took the ribbing from his roommates in a good-hearted way. He was quieter than usual, offering no details as Raymond and the others let their imaginations run wild based on the time he'd returned home.

"Technically, he hasn't spent a whole night with a woman," Ray concluded.

"I suppose your right," Kenny agreed. "When I heard the front door shut, it was only four o'clock."

"He looks like he's been rode hard and put up wet. And he can't even remember the name of the movie they went to see," Jay chuckled.

Yussef looked disheveled, but not for the reason they suspected. After returning home, minute by long minute, during the remaining hours of dread until dawn, he hadn't slept a wink. With Jamal's warning fresh in his head, he lay there, his head spinning, the bed turning, his stomach churning, as he reached for the wastebasket repeatedly. What should he do? Who should he tell? Where should he run? The answers seemed just beyond his reach.

The silence from Yussef had its intended effect. The banter from his roommates ended as they went their separate way, leaving him alone, searching the cabinets for anything that would quell his stomach and stop his headache. Under his breath, he prayed to Allah for guidance, something he hadn't done in a long, long time.

Medication eluded him, but as he grabbed his shoes, left by the front door to avoid detection of his early morning return, Ray stopped him.

"Hey listen, Yussef. Professor Stevenson called again last night."

"Oh, yes, yes. I'm sorry, I forgot to call him," Yussef confessed, tying his shoelaces without looking up at Ray. "I will call him tonight."

"Don't bother, bro. He said he was leaving today, heading back to India. Said he'd be back to the states in another two weeks."

Yussef nodded, stood up, ready to head out the door, wishing to avoid any conversation for fear of what he might blurt out.

"Also, there was a guy that stopped by here last night, like after ten o'clock, looking for you. He said he was a friend of yours, or knew a friend of yours, something like that."

Yussef feigned ignorance, "Maybe he'll be back today."

"Maybe," Ray continued, searching his friend's face for an explanation, "but also, Tammy called over here. She said someone called Rachael's phone looking for you late last night. You're in demand big guy."

All Yussef could do was shake his head and muster a weak laugh, grabbing his jacket hanging from a deer's antlers mounted on the wall.

"Is…, everything cool, man?"

"Yes, yes. I just had a problem getting my stipend this month from the foundation is all."

Yussef paused, biting his lip, and then brushed by Ray as he headed out the door.

Ray called out after him, "Hey, are you going to the lab today? I needed some help with my research project if you are?"

Without looking back, Yussef shrugged his shoulders and kept walking. Where, he didn't know. All he wanted was to be alone for a while, to sort things out. Should he go back and tell Raymond before he left for the lab, before Kenny and Jay left for work? Or maybe Rachael would be the one to talk to, she would listen to him; or did he just want to see her again? Either way, the end result would be a trip to the police station, and then on to prison or deportation to Pakistan: or both. And was Jamal bluffing? Would he try to harm Yussef's unsuspecting friends? It was already ten minutes until nine o'clock. Before getting out of bed this morning, Yussef had made up his mind to tell someone, but downstairs, when he saw his roommates, he couldn't do it. He wasn't ready to throw everything away, still looking for a way out with no one else knowing. He felt like he had a noose around his neck.

In a daze, he continued walking, calculating all the inputs, checking the results of each possible outcome. He felt most comfortable talking to Rachael. He'd told her things about himself these last two times they were together alone that he'd never told Raymond. Yet—as Professor Stevenson flashed through his mind—he hadn't told her the truth about his parents or any particulars about the group from which his money came or the real reason Ahmed had come with him to America.

He decided that now was the time to tell her. He would screw up his courage, invite Rachael to the coffee shop, and confess all. The two of them, together, would figure out what to do.

He felt his spirits lift with the breeze, realizing he was already walking in her direction. Wrapped up in his own thoughts, he hadn't noticed Jamal following him slowly, at a considerable distance, in the van.

Yussef nearly fell as he tripped over a broken section of sidewalk. He paused for a moment as the undulating sections that went on for nearly the entire block caught his eye. He contemplated their mal-postioned lie, forced upon them by the unrelenting power of the gnarled roots that nourished the majestic trees towering above him. Was it so different from his own experience, he wondered? His own life seemed to have been under the contol of others since the death of his parents, molded to fit the needs of an organism bigger them himself. In some way he had to change the intended outcome for himself, but he didn't yet know how.

Spring—after starting as a trickle: Jonquils erupting, azaleas ablaze with color, and the shrill trill of tree frogs—had begun its head long rush into existence. Redbud trees along with pink and white dogwoods were in full bloom. The intoxicating scent of the massive lilac bush in front of Rachael's house caught Yussef's attention from a half block away. It lingered on a gentle rush of air before fading into the cornucopia of other sensations that signaled the arrival of another growing season. Blades of slender grass thrust up from the thatch into the forefront, marshalling the faded, brown fescue of the previous year into the background, while the sun-warmed, moist earth had the smell of a fresh beginning.

A forsythia bush marked the farthest corner of the lot on which Rachael's house stood, its flaming yellow leaves already morphing into thick green foliage. Next came an ill-maintained, head-high, deciduous hedgerow that occupied the remaining distance to the lilac bush at the edge of the driveway. The hedge was sprouting new leaflets, their color a mix: of maroon, the shade of old blood, as if the buds had hemorrhaged in giving birth to the leaflets; and sickly pale green, the color of sun-starved grass under a fallen log.

The new curtain of growth obscured walkers on the sidewalk from anyone's view standing on the porch of Rachael house. But for Yussef, suddenly stopped by the sound of voices on the porch, the view was quite clear as he peered through the new greenery.

He saw an unfamiliar car with out-of-state plates parked on the rain-washed, white chat driveway. He saw the two she-devils standing side-by-side with their hands clasped in front of them, chest high, as if the recipients of a surprise birthday present. He saw two muscular young men dressed in military uniforms, with wool berets not quite covering the close-cropped hair above their ears, wearing boots, not the familiar shining black ones worn by soldiers in his native Pakistan, but instead they were tan, the color of sand.

Even from this distance, Yussef could tell the handsome young man standing beside Tammy and Jill was Rachael's brother, his facial features almost identical. Yussef saw Rachael, her dark hair swaying to one side of her face as the other uniformed soldier lifted her in his arms and pirouetted her around on the front porch next to the others. Yussef, from seventy–five feet away, could hear her laughter and the clapping of hands by Tammy and Jill.

The last thing Yussef saw was the couple embracing, followed by a full-lipped kiss. A multitude of emotions filled his head, overflowing, spilling down his body to his trembling hands. The witnessed scene was like a punch to the stomach from a schoolyard bully, taking Yussef's breath away. He turned away, stumbling blindly over the broken sidewalk, going in the opposite direction— away from Rachael, thinking harshly that perhaps Jamal's plan for Ft. Wilson wasn't so bad.

"Ahh, our wayward Yussef. I have been looking out for you, my friend, in case you strayed," Jamal growled menacingly, patting his gun. "You were supposed to be here at nine o'clock," he continued as Yussef shut the front door upon entering the rent house.

"Perhaps he overslept," Ibrahim offered, trying to diffuse the anger that had been building in

Jamal since his return in the van some thirty minutes ago. "You were sleeping in a nice warm bed, dreaming of virgins, while Khalib and I slept on the cold living room floor, wondering if Jamal had deserted us."

Khalib kept his head lowered, not wanting to be the recipient of Jamal's wrath as he had in Mexico. His bruised ribs and head were just beginning to heal. He feared Yussef and Ibrahim were about to feel the same wrath now.

Instead, Jamal glared briefly at Ibrahim to silence him before turning back to stare at Yussef with his arms outstretched, the palms of his hands turned upward, the 9mm resting obtrusively in the right one, searching for an answer from Yussef with the unspoken gesture.

"I had to wait for my housemates to leave," Yussef explained, shifting Ray's rigid rifle case to his other arm, glancing at his watch. "I didn't realize it was getting so late. I thought we might have use for the rifle, but the owner would not have let me taken it if he'd been there."

Yussef *was* telling the truth, about not realizing the time. After leaving the scene on Rachael's front porch behind, full of bitterness and dispair, he had wandered aimlessly for a time, eventually returning to his own empty house. The last hours of his life seemed to have passed by in slow motion.

His world had changed. It had been seismically shifted; his priorities re-aligned. Confusion, dispair, disgust, and guilt mingled in Yussef's head, while the oily residue coating the barrel of Raymond's deer-hunting rifle still lingered in his mouth. Slowly, a new plan had begun to emerge. Strands of remorse and regret had been twisted into a braid of revenge. If Yussef could have seen the face that the other three jihadists were staring at, he would have recognized a face dazed by a lifetime full of last-minute disappointments, following brief episodes of happiness. Now he was determined to see no more came his way.

Yussef opened the gun case, handing the rifle to Jamal, its sharp-edged sight at the end of the barrel speckled with dried saliva and a fleck of blood. Yussef sat down on the floor, leaning back and resting his head against the peeling wallpaper of his new home. Jamal methodically inspected the new weapon. It wasn't the automatic rifle he'd left behind in Ciudad del Estrellas in favor of the pistol, but its long-range capabilities gave them one more option when, and if, it was needed. Khalib asked what needed to be done next, relieved that Jamal had been distracted from his mounting fury.

"I'm sorry, what did you say?" Jamal asked, staring through the scope at Ibrahim, then Khalib, and finally Yussef, whose legs were pulled up against his chest, elbows resting on his knees as he cradled his head in the palm of his hands

"What do we do now? Since there is no mosque close by," Khalib repeated.

Jamal ignored the question, again, putting the rifle back in its case as he turned his attention back to Yussef.

"Did you bring the money?"

Yussef reached inside his shirt and pulled out the manila envelope. Before Jamal could count the money, Yussef offered an excuse for the discrepancy.

"There is a thousand dollars more than what I told you last night. I miscounted it," he explained, having decided before leaving his old house for the final time, to hide some of the money as insurance since Jamal had no idea how much Mullah Khan had sent.

Jamal looked into the envelope, then back at Yussef who added, "It only came yesterday, and I was in a hurry. I had to find a house to rent in addition to my normal routine."

Jamal took out two of the bills and handed one each to Khalib and Ibrahim without taking his eyes off Yussef.

"Yussef and I are going for a ride, to do a little sight-seeing. You two take the money and go get some food plus whatever else we need to get by for several days here in the house. And try to keep a low profile," Jamal instructed, his voice rising as he turned to Khalib, adding, "no conversations with any store clerks like last night. *Yafham?*"

Khalib nodded that he understood, itching to do something, anything, to keep his mind busy and off of what was to come. Since there was no mosque to mollify him, he was becoming agitated again.

"Is there a store near here, Yussef?" Ibrahim asked.

Yussef hesitated, worried about being left alone with Jamal, and going where? "Just a couple of blocks down the street there's a convenience store. There are a couple of supermarkets, but they are on the other side of town. It would be a long walk."

"Go to the one up the street," Jamal commanded. "First, help us get the van out of the garage. It collapsed on me this morning when I pulled in."

Ibrahim and Khalib pushed up the collapsed roof while Jamal guided Yussef who was driving. The four of them freed the vehicle from its ungainly hiding place. Yussef breathed a sigh of relief as Jamal got in the van and called out to the other two.

"We'll be back in a few hours."

As much dispair as he felt over Rachael and the precarious position he was in, Yussef discovered back at the old house, in the closet with Ray's rifle, that he couldn't pull the trigger. Maybe, he was just a coward, but he still wanted to live, no matter what the consequences. He wasn't so sure Jamal felt the same way.

The van's tires crunched over dead leaves and twigs lying across the twin, cracked, concrete strips that led out to the street from the garage. Yussef, out of habit, started in the direction of his old home of the past two years before asking Jamal where they were going.

"We are going to survey are intended targt," he answered, matter-of-factly.

"You mean Ft. Wilson," Yussef asked, wide-eyed as he glanced at Jamal who began nodding his head. Yussef had not yet come to terms with Jamal's grandiose plan.

"We also need to begin buying the items necessary for the operation. Cell phones, a heavy steel tank, more electrical wire...," Jamal counted off the items on his fingers as he spoke. "I was writing up a complete list..., while I waited for you in the van this morning," he said, pausing to look sternly at Yussef before continuing, "We'll need steel springs, an acetylene cutting torch with a brazing tip, a video camera..."

"A video camera?"

Yussef had only been half listening, trying to concentrate on his rudimentary driving skills as Jamal rattled off the list, until "video camera" caught his attention. He corrected the steering wheel just in time to avoid a speed limit sign as he turned the corner and drove by the old house he'd shared with Ray and the others.

"Why do you need a video..."

Yussef stopped in mid-sentence, turning suddenly as he slowed the van to look at a plain, dark-colored sedan parked in the driveway. Two burly men wearing sunglasses, tight suits, and polished shoes were just climbing out of the vehicle. The license plate was stamped with the words "U.S. Government" and a series of numbers. Yussef, out of instinct, slouched low in the seat as he drove on by.

"What is going on?" Jamal demanded.

He sensed Yussef's apprehension as he also caught sight of the two men wearing uniforms universal to government police around the world. But he had a different instinct: to reach inside his jacket for the Glock 9mm.

"Do you know them?"

"No!" Yussef snorted.

"Don't even think about stopping or drawing their attention with the horn," Jamal warned, pressing the gun against Yussef's side. "They look like government security goons. How did they know to come to your house? Did you contact them?"

Yussef shook his head emphatically.

"No, no. Perhaps it was the phone call to Mullah Khan," Yussef thought outloud, trying to appease Jamal. "The letter told me to call a new number, as if the old one had been compromised. And the new number..., I waited a long time, too long, for Mullah Khan to come on the line, but he never did."

"Stupid! You made the call from here?"

"No, no. I made the call from someone else's phone. I told you that last night..., but it wasn't from a pay phone."

Jamal stared at him with distain before looking back at the car still parked in the driveway.

"Does anyone know of the house you rented for us?" He demanded.

By now they were far enough away that his hidden gun no longer pointed at Yussef's abdomen, but instead, he had it pressed against Yussef's right temple. Jamal's voice sounded calm, measured. Yussef thought his own sounded higher pitched, his speech too rapid as he cringed, trying to get away from the cold hardness of the barrel, but there was nowhere to go.

"No! No one knows about it. Please, I just rented it yesterday; with cash."

"Not the red-haired roommate, or the girl…, is it Rowchell?" Jamal persisted.

Yussef began shaking his head from the start of the question. He stopped for a moment at the mispronunciation and held his breath. Jamal didn't miss much, Yussef realized, and he remembered everything.

"No one knows but the four of us," Yussef reiterated forcefully, attempting to sound indignant at being questioned again about his loyalty, even with a gun pointed at his head.

"This means your contact, Mullah Khan has been compromised; or worse. I can't believe they got here this fast. We must move along with our plans quickly," Jamal emphasized.

He pulled the gun away from Yussef's head as he began to ponder the situation at hand. Yussef had brought the rifle and rented the house, Jamal considered, trying to decide what to do with him. But he'd lied initially about the amount of money, bringing an extra thousand dollars. Jamal wondered if there was even more. And he'd lied about where he'd been last night, with a woman, and calling from a phone that could be traced no less. What else was he lying about?

"I suppose the arrests in Arizona has everyone on heightened alert," Yussef offered, worried about Jamal's silence.

Yussef was quivering from fear, his mind racing. At least I don't have the problem of telling Mullah Khan that I want out, he thought, suppressing a laugh. No more wondering when the next check would arrive. No more calling from the pay phone at the Laundromat. No more getting pissed on. Maybe, those rednecks lived within the radiation lethal zone, close to the military base.

Even if it was a military base, it was a crazy idea, wasn't it? To do the unthinkable. Yussef had heard all the rhetoric before—from Ahmed and the madrasa. Jamal's speech at the kitchen table sounded almost identical. Still, Yussef rationalized, the American military was in cahoots with the Pakistani government, weren't they? Even Yussef, who paid little attention to politics of late, thought it to be true. He shook his head, clearing his mind, trying to concentrate on the present and his driving.

"What's the matter now?" Jamal asked, resting his gun on his lap.

"Nothing," Yussef answered. "I guess the police will have pictures and know what we look like."

"Only you, brother," Jamal remarked slowly, "only you."

At least my picture was with a beard, Yussef thought, and black horn-rimmed glasses. He'd managed to squirrel away enough money during the past year and a half, through starvation, to get contacts.

"Is there a hardware store around here?"

"There is a Lowe's out by the interstate," Yussef answered, having gone there with Raymond a couple of times.

"They will have what I need?" Jamal asked, unfamiliar with the name.

"I believe they will have some of it: the torch, wire, bolts, but not the camera or cell phone."

"Let's go there and then on to Ft. Wilson."

Yussef glanced at his watch. "They won't be open, yet. It's Sunday. It is their day of worship. They open at noon, I think."

"Their day of worship only lasts for half a day?"

"Well, some may last longer. I'm not too familiar with that, but most of the stores and businesses are closed all day on Sunday unless it is a grocery store or a big chain store like Lowe's. I believe it is a religious law. Except that during Christmas season in December, a religious holiday; then they're all open on Sunday."

Jamal thought about this, confused. They were only a few blocks from the interstate when they passed the Springhill Baptist Church. The time of worship services and the guest pastor's name scrolled across the electronic marquee beneath the fanciful sign. Jamal noted that the parking lot was full, the expansive lawn beautifully manicured and landscaped. When Jamal inquired about the other houses of worship they'd passed, Yussef tried to explain, with what limited knowledge he possessed on the subject, about the differences between this church and the two others a few blocks back: United Methodist and Sacred Heart Catholic.

"They sound much like our Sunni and Shia divisions, I imagine. Not to mention the different sects within each," Jamal commented, eyeing the Community Church of Christ sign along the access road as they merged on to the highway.

"I'm afraid I don't know much about religion in this country. I've only been out of town twice since Ahmed and I were placed here," Yussef replied. "I've spent all of my time studying and doing research here at the university in Rockledge."

"Except last night," Jamal reminded him.

Yussef tightened his grip on the steering wheel as he felt the heat rush to his cheeks. Last night's dinner and movie flashed through his mind, and then what he'd witnessed at Rachael's house this morning. He offered a careful explanation, hoping to appease Jamal.

"The girl is a fellow engineering grad student. She is taking a demolition's class this semester, and I thought it would serve our purpose to get to know her better."

"And she will help us get the explosives we need?" Jamal quizzed, his interest piqued.

"No, but because of her I know where the explosives are kept," Yussef clarified.

Yussef knew it was a lie, but one Jamal could not uncover, and it had succeeded in arousing Jamal's interest as well as holstering his gun. A "white lie" as Raymond had explained to him once. Yussef already knew where everything in the engineering department was stored.

"So, no romantic attachment to her? I must admit my friend. I was…, am still, suspicious of your commitment to our cause; your trustworthiness."

"No," Yussef shook his head, feeling a burning sensation in his gut, "no attachment whatsoever."

"You smelled of romance when I greeted you outside your home last night."

Yussef said nothing, focusing on the road ahead, but Jamal wasn't done.

"Is she a Muslim?"

"No, Catholic," Yussef answered, regretting it as he raked his teeth across his lower lip before continuing. "Look, we are friends, no different than my roommates, who are also my friends. I have no choice but to intermingle with women, of all faiths, at school. That is the way it is done over here. It is just part of their culture. I had to try and fit in, especially after Ahmed died, or I would have been shunned and looked at with suspicion. I've lived here for three years, half of that time alone. I mean at least in the sense that I've had no one to discuss our faith or our jihadist plans with, other than a five minute phone call every other month with Mullah Khan."

Yussef was talking rapidly, his palms sweaty upon the steering wheel.

"These people helped me after the fire. I had no clothes, no money, and no place to stay. The check from the Islamic Foundation barely gets me by. I couldn't just ignore their generosity without arousing suspicions."

"But are you still committed to our cause? That is the question I have to be sure of," Jamal confessed, staring at Yussef with eyes like laser beams. "I..., we are so close to realizing the impossible. I will not tolerate any dissenters or deserters."

Yussef glanced at Jamal. Seeing his arm outstretched, his hand braced against the dashboard as his jacket swung free of his body, the correct answer was staring at him from its leather harness.

"Yes, yes, very much so. I have waited three years. I watched Ahmed die before his chance at martyrdom. My hatred of American soldiers grows every day. The decadence of the people in this country astounds me. Young people in the class I teach are lazy and arrogant. The women shameful in the way they dress. I've been humiliated here and threatened because I am a foreigner and my skin is not ivory in color."

Yussef's voice was strong, fiery even; thinking his imitation of Ahmed was thorough, and partially true, as he considered what he'd just said.

Jamal stroked his goatee as they drove in silence for a few miles before Yussef backtracked.

"There are some decent people here, though. Most of them are associated with the university. That is why I was taken aback by your bold plan last night; to destroy the military base so close by will cause much radioactive fallout, with sickness and death here in Rockledge."

Jamal replied in a philosophical tone, "Yes, that is always the case. Sometimes good, innocent people must die because of their close proximity to the evil, guilty ones." Jamal chuckled, then continued, "That sounds like something their Air Force would say when they kill innocent Muslims with their so called 'smart bombs' and *highly* accurate missles, doesn't it? Still, we must never lose sight of our cause, for it is a just one. And, just as you explained last night, Ft. Wilson is far enough away the fallout won't be so bad, not everyone here will perish. After seven, or perhaps double the time to fourteen days and then they can crawl out from under their rocks safely without so much risk from radiation poisoning."

Picturing those he knew in Rockledge, Yussef tried to wrap his head around the words "innocent must die" and "fallout not so bad" as they drew closer to the exit at Ft. Wilson. There was nothing more he could say to Jamal. And the next question took him by surprise.

"How did you manage to survive the fire and not Ahmed?"

Yussef steered the van back off the shoulder of the highway. No one had asked him that question since the day after the fire when someone from a state agency had inquired about his recollection of the tragic event.

His answer back then, "I awoke to see the room engulfed in flames, including Ahmed. He had apparently fallen asleep in a chair against the far wall next to the hot plate that we used to cook on," was the same as it was today. It satisfied the fire official and it would suffice for Jamal, Yussef decided.

The moist palm marks on the steering wheel had yet to disappear and Yussef felt barely in control of his emotions as they approached the main gate at the base entrance. Jamal fastened his coat. A young man stepped out of the guardhouse. Younger than Yussef, Jamal thought, as he examined the soldier's clean-shaven face, pock-marked with pimples, the helmet covering too much of his head. He was wearing a baggy uniform that seemed as if it belonged to someone else, someone bigger; an adult. Yussef rolled down his window as the guard spoke.

"Good morning. I need to see your drivers license, please." His voice sounded like his face looked, too young for the job.

"I..., I don't have a drivers license only a university ID card," Yussef stammered while pulling it out of his wallet. It slipped from his fingers as he looked at his bearded, bespectacled self in the photo on the laminated card. Who is that person in the picture, Yussef wondered.

"It is my vehicle, sir," Jamal stated in a calm, reassuring manner.

He reached across and handed the guard his own license before discreetly finding Yussef's ID on the floorboard and pushing it further under the seat.

"I'm letting him drive for practice. He just arrived here from India. It's a miracle we made it over here from Rockledge," Jamal said with a laugh.

Yussef shrugged.

"Y'all are from over at the university in Rockledge?"

The guard handed back Jamal's license as Jamal nudged Yussef, prompting him to reply.

"Yes, yes, I..., we are with the engineering department. We came over to tour the military museum."

"Do you know how to get to the museum from here?"

"No." Jamal's voice echoed Yussef's.

"Hang on, I'll get you a map of the base," he said, turning to re-enter the guardhouse. "I'll need to inspect the back of your vehicle, also."

Yussef fumbled with the key chain while the soldier's back was still turned. Jamal put his hand on Yussef's and squeezed hard.

After a brief exam of the empty van, while a second guard materialized to inspect the undercarriage with a mirror, the young soldier shut the back door. Leaning over, next to the driver's side door, he handed the keys and map to Yussef. Yussef grabbed the keys with a trembling hand while Jamal reached across, grabbing the map fluidly, and resting it on the steering wheel, covering Yussef's hands in the process.

"Just follow the main road, Independence Boulevard, to where it 'T's'." His scrawny, freckled finger traced the path on the map. "You turn left at the 'T'. After that, y'all will go by the hospital. The museum is the next place on the right."

"Thank-you, sir," Jamal called out as the soldier stood up, motioning for Yussef to take off. "This will be easier than I imagined. I wasn't sure how hard it would be to find our way around the base."

"No problem, drive safe," they heard the soldier say, already looking toward the next car in line.

Yussef drove slowly down the broad, four-lane street, lined on both sides with majestic trees. He was oblivious to the cars and trucks speeding by him. He waited for instructions from Jamal who was studying the map, comparing it to the one he had etched in his memory from months of study. When they reached the "T", Yussef looked to Jamal. He motioned with the wave of his hand for Yussef to turn left, as the soldier had instructed, without uttering a word or lifting his eyes from the map.

They passed housing complexes and an open field several hundred yards in length, marked with a sign designating it as a training area. By the far end, in the corner next to the road ditch, Yussef recognized a pair of soccer goals, their nets fluttering in the breeze. At one point along this narrower road, Yussef slowed almost to a stop as he came upon a painted crosswalk and the words "school crossing". He looked toward Jamal who'd glanced up to see why they'd slowed, showing only indifference as he returned to the engrossing particulars of the map lying across his lap.

"There is the museum, Jamal."

Yussef pointed at the sign out in front.

"Yes, I see it. If there is no one behind us, keep going straight on this road for a while. I shall tell you when to turn."

Yussef looked in the mirror and kept going. More training fields and buildings passed by. Camouflage-painted tanks with bulldozer blades attached to the front were parked in a lot with freshly dug earth. A platoon marched by in front of them and Yussef slowed the van to a stop, far enough away so as not to distinquish any faces, save for the one turned toward the van in the middle of the road with their arm outstretched in front, halting traffic while the rest of the unit marched by in unison.

"Don't run over them, okay?" Jamal said, looking up from the map with a smile.

Yussef glanced at him but said nothing in return. Instead, he exhaled, relaxing his strangled grip on the wheel.

"Go through this next intersection, but then take the next left. It will eventually lead us to another exit gate."

"There seems to be more civilians here than I remembered from before. Did you see the school crossing sign back there?" Yussef insinuated, waiting for Jamal's response.

"Most of them are off-duty soldiers or retired military personnel, masquerading as civilians," he replied in an off-handed way, ignoring Yussef's implication.

Yussef turned as instructed. Ahead on the right, inside a twelve-foot high, double row of sparkling, chain-link fence topped with concertina wire, they saw a group of ten soldiers being lectured to by an officer.

"They have some of our brothers imprisoned in cages like that," Jamal snorted, pointing at the mock-up training prison, his voice tinged with anger. "Some have been locked away for years. Have you ever been in prison, Yussef?"

Yussef shook his head. "Perhaps, if your plan is successful, they will be released," he offered.

The landscape changed from wooden barracks, brick buildings, and fenced compounds to forested hillsides, glades, and greening meadows.

Traffic was minimal as they made their way down the winding road, allowing Yussef to creep along in the van, observing Jamal as he worked. Jamal continued his study of the map, making notations in the margins of distances and topography. He smiled, occasionally nodding his head as if in answer to some unheard question. To Yussef, Jamal looked like someone who had just been given the birthday present he'd always wished for.

"I never dreamed there were so many trees in one place; endless kilometers of trees. The pictures we received from our former cell in St. Louis didn't do justice to this place," Jamal observed.

"It is a big country," Yussef commented in response as they passed the exit gate, manned by two, bored-looking sentries. "It's easy to be overcome by its vastness. Which way do we go now?"

Yussef eased the van to a stop at the intersection outside the base, waiting for a reply. Acres of hardwood forest still dressed in a brown monotone, dotted by the occasional deep green of a red cedar or white pine, surrounded them.

"The map ends here at this crossroad. An arrow points straight ahead to the Red Oak River. Turn left, the road winds around and will take us back to the interstate."

The Red Oak—Yussef had heard of it before, from Rachael. "Perhaps we should go straight and cross the river. It might be a better escape route should we need one," he proposed.

"No," Jamal answered tersely.

"Yussef followed the road north past several abandoned houses, each being slowly engulfed by the forest that surrounded them. Just past one, Jamal sat up suddenly in his seat and shouted for Yussef to stop the van.

"What's the matter?" Yussef asked, braking hard, harder than he intended, startled by Jamal's sudden command.

A pickup truck, approaching fast from behind, honked and swerved around them, just avoiding a collision. A hand protruded from the passenger-side window and gestured at the van's occupants as it accelerated away from them.

"I'm sorry," Yussef muttered as Jamal pushed himself back up into the front seat.

"You and Ibrahim must have attended the same driving school."

"You shouted for me to stop."

"I didn't mean for you to throw me through the windshield. Turn around *slowly* and go back to the last house we passed."

"Why?"

Jamal, in a flash of anger, grabbed Yussef by his hair and pulled him over, inches away from the taut muscles of his own face, before speaking through clenched teeth.

"My patience has grown thin on this trip. Because of that, I am tempted to shoot you right now; either that or we must come to an understanding my college-educated friend. I am in charge here, and you will do as I say with no backtalk or second-guessing. I can see you have spent too much time in the presence of Western disobedience. Now...turn...the...van...around."

He released his grip on Yussef, strands of black hair wedged beneath his fingernails. Yussef carefully turned the van around, before rubbing the top of his head.

"And by the way," Jamal added, "I saw the school crossing back on the base. For what it's worth, I have a child of my own, a son. But neither that, nor anything else is going to hinder our mission here. In fact, it's the very reason I'm here."

Yussef drove back to the last decaying house they'd passed along the road. After making sure no one was approaching from either direction, he turned and drove around toward the back of the house, out of sight from the road, as Jamal instructed. Tree limbs buried in the overgrown weeds that had once been a yard thumped against the underside of the floorboard. Each one sounded like a gunshot to Yussef's heightened imagination as he backed up directly behind the house.

"Come with me," Jamal ordered, nodding his head in the direction of the house as he hopped down out of the van.

Yussef followed slowly, thinking. Could he out run Jamal—and the bullets—if he fled into the woods. Then what would he do?

Jamal disappeared around the corner of the house, leaving Yussef somewhat relieved that atleast they weren't going into the house where his body might not be discovered for months, if at all. He stepped gingerly around the corner, squinting his eyes, expecting Jamal to have his gun cocked and aimed at his head.

Instead, Jamal was eagerly inspecting a pair of one hundred gallon gas cylinders standing upright next to the rotting carcass of the house. A pitted brass pipe that disappeared under the house connected the steel cylinders to one another. The tanks, still partially coated with flaking, silver paint, were being overtaken by rust and moss. On one tank, Yussef could make out "Ozark Propane Co." on a cracked and faded label.

These should do nicely, don't you think?" Jamal said, grimacing as he tried to loosen the pipe from the tanks.

Yussef knew what he meant but kept quiet, his heart rate just beginning to return to normal. Jamal had a keen eye and a quick mind, Yussef thought, to spot these tanks from the road and realize their potential at a moments notice. Yussef hadn't even considered where they were going to get the casing for a bomb. Jamal's mind was focused on one thing and one thing only.

For Yussef, the events of the past two days had left his mind in a fog of conflicting thoughts that came to him in no particular sequence. He felt drugged as he stepped back from the side of the house to examine it while Jamal worked feverishly to loosen the tanks from their pipe attachments. Its gapping, windowless frame reminded Yussef of jack-o-lanterns he'd seen every fall since his arrival in America. Did Jamal really have a son, he wondered.

"We'll use the cutting torch to split the tank, and then, after the components have been put in place, we'll braze it back together and reinforce it with parts of the second tank," Jamal explained, out of breath.

Yussef continued to gaze at the house, only half listening to Jamal, thankful he was still alive. With no tools of any count in the van, Jamal bent the tubing back and forth until it gave way at the crimp. He struggled with moving the first tank, finally stopping long enough to look at Yussef with distain then back at the heavy tank. Taking the hint, he helped Jamal wrestle the tanks into the back of the van, noting that Jamal's anger had subsided. He was like a kid in a candy store with this lucky find.

The trip back to Rockledge was one of prolonged silence. Jamal marveled to himself at the scenery. Though admittedly not an authority on Islam, he couldn't help wonder why Allah, some fourteen hundred years ago, had chosen the barren sands of the Middle East as the center of Islam instead of here: the land of plenty. Plenty of timber, plenty of grass for livestock to graze, plenty of rain as evidence by the abundance of vegetation, and plenty of fresh water, he thought, as they crossed a bridge spanning the steady flow of the river far below it; the Red Oak River, the sign at the edge of the bridge announced.

Yussef was still in a haze. His brain was thinking of nothing precise, but of a thousand possibilities all at once. He was trying to connect the dots of why things had turned out this way, but the dots kept moving, rolling about in his brain like beads of mercury. Finally, just before their exit, they coalesced into a question.

"How old is your son, Jamal?"

"Fourteen, I believe," he answered, as he continued to stare out the window at the rolling hills.

"And..., and you have a wife?"

"Yes, you will learn that is a necessity for a child."

"Will you see them again?"

Jamal shrugged, now looking toward Yussef, "Not likely, but it doesn't matter."

"What I mean is, do they think you're coming back?"

Jamal shrugged again. "It does not matter. I have not seen my wife or child for a very long time. They were taken from me when I was in prison."

"Who took them from you?" Yussef demanded, thinking of his own childhood.

"Her family, but they were coerced by an illegitimate government, propped up by spineless American agents. They get others to do their bidding while keeping their own hands clean. It has been done time and time again across the Middle East and elsewhere.

"Your own country, Yussef, has felt their heavy hand. Money and weaponry are their methods of persuasion. You yourself have been affected. Was not the government involved in the death of your parents? It is not just Islam they offend. What they offend are our rights as Muslims, or any other religion, or any other political and economic belief to be governed as we see fit, without their interference and corruption."

Yussef thought about this for a minute before answering. He'd talked purely religion with Ahmed, without the political bent of Jamal's ideals; and for the past year and a half—no talk at all. He now understood the saying "ignorance is bliss".

"I must admit," Yussef started as he tried to sort out his thoughts verbally, "as I stated earlier, the problem I have with waging jihad here is that not everyone is evil. Most of the people I'm around wish me no harm. They are wrapped up in their own lives, apathetic toward their government. Why should we punish them?"

"It is not enough that they wish you no harm, Yussef. A man on shore causes no physical harm when he watches another drown in the water without helping. It is their very complacency in allowing their government to carry on as it has for the past five decades that has brought us to this point. Even longer, if you consider how the British were allowed to carve up the Middle East. Most of the world wished no harm when they gave Palestine to the Jews. They closed their collective eyes and looked the other way as Muslims were forced from the homes they'd occupied for centuries. The people have been asleep *too long*. We must wake them up. And I have chosen this place, right here, right now, to sound the alarm."

Jamal was pointing his finger emphatically downward.

"The people of the Western world must know that we will never give up. That we are relentless and will attack them anytime, anywhere: until they change their leadership. I will make this point clear in our video."

Yussef swallowed hard. Two questions— what need did they have of a video camera and how would they escape—begging for a response in his subconscience, were answered in one breath. After this morning's attempt with the hunting rifle, Yussef feared he was not ready for death or cut out for martyrdom. Though Jamal had said last night that this was their final destination, Yussef had hoped he meant before going home.

"Jamal, what if I fail?"

"You will not fail. You have expertise in nuclear engineering, and I have ample training in rigging detonators for explosives. If the materials are where you say they are, everything will work according to plan," he replied in a business-like manner.

He went on to explain the wiring procedures and triggering mechanism he would employ as if giving a Power Point presentation at a corporate meeting. Finally, Yussef interrupted him.

"No, I mean what if I can't go through with killing myself?"

"Oh, rest assured," Jamal replied without hesitation, considering it a non-issue as he patted the outline of his gun underneath his jacket, "I will not let that happen."

They pulled into the parking lot of the big box hardware store and began filling the rest of Jamal's wish list.

Rick Elliott

CHAPTER TEN

Jamal decided they would get the explosives that night. After seeing the two men in the government car at Yussef's house this morning, he knew they should waste no time in obtaining the needed equipment and explosives. Jamal felt sure the police were following the links—Yussef and Mullah Khan—in search of any other terrorist cells.

On the way to the campus building where the explosives were stored, Jamal instructed Ibrahim to drive toward Yussef's old home, being sure to turn the corner before it instead of going right by. As they approached, Jamal and Yussef saw the same dark sedan parked on the street, in almost the identical spot they'd parked the van last night during their wait for Yussef. Two silhouettes were seated in the car; waiting, not knowing Yussef had left for good.

Security in the campus engineering building, while adequate for local criminals and mischevious students, was no match for Jamal's expertise. Ibrahim waited in a nearby fast-food restaurant's parking lot. Thirty-five minutes later he picked up Jamal, Yussef, and Khalib, all three gingerly carrying heavy, unmarked, wooden boxes, placing them carefully in the back of the van.

The next four days were a blur for Yussef and the others. Jamal worked tirelessly on the two steel cylinders; first removing the valves on top before filling each with water, as a precaution, and then slicing them in half with the just-purchased cutting torch. Yussef explained to him the design for proper placement of the explosives in relation to the radioactive material and the force required from the explosives to trigger the chain reaction.

Yussef and Ibrahim took turns grinding rough metal edges in a shower of sparks while the other watched from the living room window for anyone passing by on the sidewalk. When no grinding was needed they practiced loading and unloading the rifle, studied the map of Ft. Wilson, or read from the Qur`an. At night they listened to taped verses brought along by Khalib who Jamal no longer trusted to work in the kitchen.

The kitchen became their workshop. It was the only room with adequate lighting. They ate their meals surrounded by cut pieces of copper wire, clumps of hardened solder, shards of metal, and rubber hoses running across the floor to the acetylene-oxygen tanks. A haze of smoke lingered near the ceiling. The acrid smell of burnt metal mixed with the aroma of boiling rice and beef hotdogs as it permeated the entire house.

Watching Jamal work, it was obvious to Yussef that he was well versed in the handling of explosives and the rigging of detonators. And Yussef, a quick study, was becoming more comfortable working around the dangerous mix.

Yussef thought often about Rachael during these times, picturing her there in place of Jamal, wearing a hard hat, her black hair spilling out from under it while her long slender fingers manipulated the wires into their proper positions. He longed to see her one last time, but Jamal wouldn't let him out of his sight.

They'd left the house only once after obtaining the explosives, on Tuesday, to buy a video camera and packaging material, along with a few remaining components for the bomb. After their return, Jamal informed them that there would be no more leaving the house until they left for Ft. Wilson in three days, the exact time depending on their progress in the kitchen.

The only exception to this decree, which reinforced Jamal's reasoning, was Ibrahim's daily trip to the convience store each morning before daylight to get a newspaper. Because there, on the front page of Thursday's paper was a bearded and bespectacled picture of Yussef; the same one that was on his university ID card. Yussef stared at the newspaper for a long time, hardly recognizing himself in the photo.

The brief article that accompanied the photograph said he'd been missing for three days and that university officials became alarmed when he hadn't shown up to teach his physics lab earlier in the week. No mention of any terrorist plot was made, and nothing connecting him to the break-in on campus reported in the paper a day earlier. He was simply a missing person.

Yussef wished it were that simple. That he could just show up to teach his class this morning; that all would be forgiven. But he knew better, thinking back to that day when all the money first arrived, before he'd been intimately introduced to Jamal's 9mm Glock.

He tossed his ID card onto the front burner of the cooking stove, watching it melt into oblivion, its sickly vapors mingling among the others that were accumulating in the kitchen-turned-bomb-making workshop.

Culpable because of the stolen explosives, and realizing he had been since the moment he and Ahmed first set foot in America, Yussef resigned himself to the fact that there was no going back. Now, he'd diagrammed the proper assembly of the bomb. "In for a pint, in for a pound" was how Raymond always put it, Yussef remembered.

The dark half circles under Yussef's eyes, in juxtaposition to his smooth brown skin, were a testament to how he'd slept the last three nights. His brain ached from lack of sleep as he moved about the house in a stupor. The others, save for Jamal, looked as Yussef did—like zombies.

With each passing day, Jamal seemed more buoyant than the preceeding one. Each morning, while the other three lolled about on the living room floor, staring blankly at the water-stained ceiling, having just woke, he could be found seated at the kitchen table sipping sweet mint tea as the steam curled about his face. The dented pot creaked and popped with displeasure as it cooled on the stove while Jamal went over the previous days work, looking for mistakes or loose wires. He'd slept like a baby.

As the week wore on, Khalib became more agitated and unreliable, despite the pledge he'd made to himself before leaving Houston to honor the deaths of Monsour and Sa`id. He was loosing his grip on reality, and the others knew it. Yussef and Ibrahim left him alone to read the passages from the Qur`an he most enjoyed, either silently or outloud, in an attempt to appease his moodiness.

Other than to ban him from the kitchen, Jamal ignored him. He dare not allow Khalib to help any with their work as it neared its completion. And he couldn't just be sent home. He was home. Rockledge, or more precisely, Ft. Wilson would be his final resting place.

Khalib's shaky hands reminded Yussef of the landlady and of his own hands though he willed himself to steadiness while he labored at the kitchen table with Jamal. At other times, when they weren't helping Jamal, Yussef and Ibrahim took turns keeping an eye on Khalib in the living room while watching for passersby out front. They feared he would do something stupid, upsetting Jamal and bringing his wrath down on all of them, or worse: get them all killed.

On Friday, near dusk, Jamal announced the bomb was ready. The entire day had been spent rigging the detonator and brazing the tank back together. The smoke and fumes hung so heavily in the air that their eyes watered and their lungs burned from the noxious gases. Jamal would not allow them to open any windows until after they were done each day for fear the noise they made pounding the heated metal into shape would arouse the neighbor's suspicions. The kitchen's linoleum floor was littered with debris and pockmarked where red-hot scrapes of metal had burnt through it.

Now, with the cloak of darkness and a warm night—for mid-April—the three of them loitered about on the porch as a light southerly breeze sucked the toxic air out through the open windows. Khalib remained cloistered in the house.

The last pack of cigarettes, purchased by Ibrahim for Jamal, at the convience store, was shared between the three of them. The otherwise quiet night was broken up by the violent coughs of two virgin smokers, laughing as they tried to catch their breath.

Jamal, seated on one of the chairs brought out from the kitchen, commented on the space between the houses, the abundance of trees along the empty streets, the wide sidewalk, and the largeness of the yards—which to a native would have been considered "postage stamp" size. He had spent most of his life in the cramped, grassless quarters shared intimately by millions of his bretheren in a different part of the world; a different universe.

Ibrahim, having spent the past ten years on the *hacienda* outside Ciudad del Estrellas, couldn't understand his marvel. Yussef, for his part, since his arrival in Rockledge, had lost any and all amazement about the way things were in this country. He'd grown accustomed to the "American Dream", having been brought up to speed by his roommates and more recently by Rachael and her stories of growing up here in the rolling hills of Missouri. To Khalib, a *hafiz*, the moon would have seemed no more foreign.

Not a soul strolled by on the sidewalk during the hours the three jihadists occupied the front porch. All of these fond things: the yards, the trees, the sidewalks were wasted on these ungrateful Americans, Jamal thought. Thrice, they moved quickly back inside the dark house when headlights signaled the approach of a vehicle on the street. All this lack of commotion made Jamal uneasy. With no plot to consider, no aggrieved to avenge, no bomb to build, he was out of his element sitting there attempting small talk with Yussef and Ibrahim.

It was just past eleven o'clock when Jamal motioned them to go back inside.

"We should finish our videos," he said, adding sarcastically, "Khalib, it is your turn to make a statement if you can stop reciting and grace us with your presence in the kitchen."

Ibrahim and Yussef looked fleetingly toward Khalib who was tugging painfully at his beard. Jamal set up the makeshift camera stand using one of the chairs placed atop the table as Khalib shuffled into the kitchen followed closely by his two fellow martyrs.

"Would you like to hold the rifle or pistol as you speak?" Jamal offered. "Make sure they are unloaded before he takes either one," he directed toward Ibrahim and Yussef with a laugh. "Or you can stand next to the finished bomb if you like, just keep your hands off it."

Khalib took a deep breath, holding it, while his hands moved from his beard to the thick, unruly hair on his head, stroking it backwards, painfully, with such force that his raised eyelids exposed a disproportionate amount of his blood-tinged sclera. He had not uttered a word to the others.

"You will need to clean yourself and remove all of your body hair, preferably with a razor, before we leave in the morning," Jamal goaded, still laughing.

"Leave him alone a minute, Jamal," Ibrahim shouted.

Yussef moved a chair next to Khalib just as his quivering legs began to buckle. Ibrahim guided him by the arm into the seat.

"We can not leave you behind, Khalib. You owe it to Sa'id to be strong," Jamal commanded. "Don't be a burden."

These last words were too much for Ibrahim, and he lunged for the pistol, still in its holster, lying on the table. His hands trembled with anger as he fumbled with the snap that held it in place. Five straight days in the house, watching the mechanism of their death being built piece by piece before their very eyes was the real burden, Ibrahim thought, aiming the gun at Jamal.

Ibrahim screamed, "If you don't shut up, your own video will have been a waste. Can't you see he's sick?"

"He's a coward. In the name of Allah," Jamal responded, lifting his eyes heavenward as he spoke calmly, mocking them, "why did I choose you two as my mules? Such weaklings; give me the gun, Ibrahim."

"I am not too weak to pull the trigger, Jamal. Forget about Khalib's video. If we are successful, the news coverage will supply all the propoganda needed to bring others to your..., to our cause. I came because there was no future for me in Ciudad del Estrellas, except to avenge my father, but I have no affiliation to your organization, only to Allah, the same as Khalib. He has done your bidding, must you continue to antagonize him?"

"I am the leader and, as I have warned Khalib many times, I will not tolerate dissention nor can I afford cowardice among you. Not now. Not when we are so close."

"But you don't need Khalib or me in your video. It is your plan," Ibrahim argued.

"Without the video no one will know of your glory."

"You can have the fame, Jamal. Khalib and I will seek glory in our own way. Yussef can speak for himself. Just mention our names in your video, that is all the recognition we need."

Ibrahim laid the gun back on the table, his anger spent. Yussef was in agreement though he stayed silent. He wanted no record left behind of his achievements, but also, he wanted Jamal to have no more reasons for mistrusting him.

"But what about your family, your father?" Jamal pleaded, keeping eye contact with Ibrahim while he reached across for the gun.

"I have no real family. Ali and Imam Badawi raised me for one purpose, and I am about to fulfill whatever debt I owe them. As for my father, *inshaa` Allah*, I will see him soon enough, and we will be contented," Ibrahim concluded.

Jamal re-holstered his gun, slinging the harness over his shoulder, secretly pleased that Ibrahim had joined them on this trek, despite this last moment of insubordination. With Sa`id gone, it was Ibrahim who'd kept Khalib from falling apart any sooner than he had. He'd kept his cool for the most part, Jamal considered. He couldn't be angry with him because of this one outburst, the stress had been building in all of them. Next, he turned his attention to Yussef.

"And what of you, my university friend? As a soon to be martyr, do you wish to make a *shaheed's* video?"

Yussef nodded confidently, seating himself at the table with a pen and paper. An idea had surfaced in his head.

"Yes, I would like to make a statement. Give me a minute to prepare."

It had occurred to Yussef, during his muddled thoughts of the past few days, that perhaps, in his own way, he could repay his uncle for sending him away to the madrasa after his parents' death, and, in a more sincere way, Ahmed too could be honored.

Jamal persuaded Ibrahim to run the camera while he put the finishing touches on his own video statement, leaving Khalib seated in the corner, catatonic, facing the peeling wallpaper. In his video, Jamal announced succinctly that he and his fellow jihadists, mentioning Ibrahim and Khalib by their full names, had smuggled refined uranium into

America though he gave no details as to their method or route. This morning, Yussef had filmed him working on the bomb as he thanked his "brothers" in the Middle East for their thorough training, while encouraging young Muslims from around the world to join the struggle.

Finishing his video tonight, Jamal focused on the reasons for their terrorist attack. Most of them Yussef had heard before: the villainous American government, the puppet regimes of the Middle East, propped up by American and European monies, the Jews bent on world domination and trespassing in the land of Palestine, vowing attacks would not stop until all infidels were driven out of the cradle of Islam, from the Arabian Sea across the Persian Gulf to the Red Sea and around the rim of North Africa. Finally, he spoke of his son and his hope that this act would help lay the groundwork for him to see true freedom in his lifetime, without the yoke of arrogant Western manipulation.

These last sentences were spoken with a wavering voice that caused Yussef to pause with his own speech writing in order to scrutinize Jamal's face. Was he sincere? Or was it a well-orchestrated attempt to tug at the heartstrings of those he wished to inspire?

No sign of an answer appeared on his face that Yussef could discern. But the tone in his voice *had* changed. Before, when he'd spoken of his wife and son, the bitterness had shown through like a beacon, his voice rising to a crescendo of anger. This time it was different, Yussef thought. Jamal's voice was melancholy, almost tearful for those last few words.

How could he have feelings for a child he'd never seen, a wife who'd deserted him some fifteen years ago, no matter the circumstances? Yussef was sure if his own father were still alive, he would have scoured the earth looking for his young son, had they been separated.

With his part finished, Jamal went scrounging for one last cigarette to smoke outside in solitude. Khalib continued to rock unceasingly in his chair, staring blankly at the wall in front of him, the only sound a rhythmic squeaking of the chrome chair legs against the brittle linoleum.

Yussef prepared himself for his own speech, eager to get it done before Jamal returned. Ibrahim picked through the last of the cold rice.

"I am ready, Ibrahim," Yussef announced, tugging at the knit stocking cap that doubled as a facemask.

He'd borrowed it from Khalib's duffle bag, thinking Khalib wouldn't mind as he stretched it below his chin. It smelled old; of earth and cooking oil, of familiar spices, of mint tea, wood smoke, and perspiration. Yussef fancied these were the smells of his native Pakistan.

"Why are you wearing the mask?" Ibrahim asked, grains of rice spilling from the corners of his mouth as he prepared the video camera.

"Our cause should be an anonymous one, no fame or heroes. Jamal is too vain, too proud of his accomplishments that we all struggled to help him with," Yussef explained, nodding in the direction of the front door, glad Jamal wasn't in the room to see or hear him.

Ibrahim just shrugged, "Okay, the camera is ready."

Ibrahim was sluggish from lack of sleep, and Khalib's condition weighed heavily on him. At the ranch, he'd been the eldest of the students attending the newly formed madrasa. Having looked after the younger ones when they first arrived, he was used to seeing someone paralyzed by fear, but this was the first time he'd seen it in someone older than himself. The two deaths in Mexico had been a first for him, also. And Khalib had confided they were the first for him as well. Now they reappeared nightly in Ibrahim's restless sleep; what little he slept.

"Do you want to hold the rifle? The one you brought us?" Ibrahim interrupted, as Yussef was about to begin.

"No, I just want to get this done before Jamal comes back," Yussef said abruptly. Ibrahim looked at him with a puzzled expression and, without explaining, Yussef offered a quick alternative. "I will stand next to the bomb, just as Jamal did."

Ibrahim focused the camera on the redesigned propane tank as Yussef positioned himself next to it. The crisscrossing welds on the surface reminded Yussef of a patchwork quilt made of steel. At its top, wires emerged and arched down to a switch duct-taped on its side. Soon after they'd brought the tank inside, Khalib, with his artistic hand, had drawn skull and crossbones on the side of the tank with the slogan "Death to the American Infidels" beneath it. This had been his sole contribution to its manufacture.

Yussef addressed the camera by first identifying himself, using Ahmed's full name. He spewed epitaphs about Western decadence and recited Qur'anic verses. Verses that had receded from Yussef's mind over the past two years, replaced by scientific data and baseball statistics, until reintroduced these past six days by Khalib's incessant recitation and Ibrahim's more sporadic readings. Yussef stated that he was grateful for the friendship from his "brothers" at the religious madrasa where he trained after being orphaned. In particular, he thanked the uncle he loathed; carefully enunciating his name plus the town that Yussef knew to be his last address from years before. He hoped it would suffice since he had not a word from his uncle after being left at the madrasa as an adolescent.

Smiling, Yussef walked away from the camera, removing the wool mask from his irritated face. No matter the outcome tomorrow, he hoped his uncle's fate had been sealed.

"Would you like to review the recording," Ibrahim asked, bewildered by Yussef's statements but too spent to question them.

Yussef shook his head, "Just put the entire video in its case and we'll mark it. We can leave it in the kitchen for someone to find."

"No," Jamal said, coming through the doorway. "I have a large envelope. We will drop it at the post office on our way to Ft. Wilson in the morning. It might not be found here."

Yussef quickly gathered up the video and sealed it in the brown envelope Jamal had pointed out lying on the kitchen counter, not wanting him to see the video using Ahmed's name.

"What should we write on it?" Yussef asked, reaching for a felt-tip marking pen next to the cutting torch.

"I'm not sure, professor, but wouldn't it have been smarter to write on it before you put the video in?" Jamal answered, grabbing the package from Yussef's hand.

Yussef shrugged, handing him the pen as Jamal continued to eye him with disdain.

Midnight had come and gone. After taking turns in the bathroom to shave their hair and bathe, they had turned out the kitchen lights and moved into the carpeted living room where they'd slept since setting up shop in the house. Khalib refused to budge from his chair and Jamal, after Ibrahim's earlier outburst, left him alone. Even Ibrahim, who'd tried to coax him into joining them in the living room and had formed a bond with him and Sa'id before leaving Ciudad del Estrellas, grew weary of defending Khalib to Jamal. It was all he could do to defend his own sanity.

Tonight, like each night before it, sleep was elusive for Yussef and Ibrahim despite their weariness. On previous nights, after prayers and bedding down on the living room floor, the conversation went on for hours while they waited for sleep to overtake their adrenaline-fueled thoughts. When sleep finally arrived for them, it was in fits and starts, prefaced by uncomfortable dreams. This last night was different only because the voice of Khalib whispering verse as he lie beside them was replaced by the steadfast creaking of the chair rocking on the kitchen floor, and too, Jamal, the one normally sound sleeper among them, was restless as well.

Before, Ibrahim was amazed by Yussef's description of college life during the long nights as they talked. Yussef, in turn, liked to hear about life on the ranch, as well as Ibrahim's description of Ciudad del Estrellas. He was fascinated by the diversity of cultures in this city he'd never heard of until this week. During the past nights, each had pestered the other with many questions, along with intermittent queries from Khalib for both of them, and admonishments from Jamal to shut up and go to sleep.

Tonight it was Jamal who did most of the talking: about his training in the deserts of North Africa, growing up in Cairo, fishing on the Nile with his father and grandfather, life in prison, and, after prodding from Ibrahim, physical loving of a woman.

Yussef begged silently for dreamless sleep, receiving only half of what he wished for. Once, he woke, sure he'd heard Rachael calling his name before drifting back into a fantasy of his adult life in America.

When he next awoke, it was to the sound of birds chirping outside in the bushes that fronted the house; a signal dawn was near. Also, he could hear a faint grunting sound coming from the direction of the kitchen, puzzling over its source as he became more fully awake.

Raised on his elbows he could see Ibrahim asleep beside him, but Jamal was not there. In addition, a smell he'd first notice as he opened his eyes in the darkness grew stronger. As he approached the kitchen door cautiously, the grunting sound stopped for a moment.

In the red glow before sunrise, Yussef, straining his eyes, could make out two bodies on the kitchen floor between the table and the stove, one hovering over the other. He scraped his hand along the wall, groping for the light switch just as the grunting began again.

"Don't touch that light switch," Jamal hissed, startling Yussef. "Go open the window and the front door."

"What is wrong?" Yussef asked, standing there dumbfounded in the morning twilight, trying to focus his eyes and his mind. "Where is that smell coming from?"

Breathless, Jamal tried to shout. "Open the windows and doors to the outside, but don't..., don't turn on any lights. The smell is gas from the stove. Please, no sparks," he begged.

Bewildered, Yussef opened the kitchen window, and from that vantage point, he could see the open oven door. Jamal was pressing his interlocked hands against Khalib's ribcage. The grunt Yussef heard from the living room coincided with each of Jamal's forceful presses.

"Has..., has he tried to kill himself?" Yussef stuttered, his mouth agape.

Jamal stopped his rhythmic pressing and blew into Khalib's purple lips once more. Yussef watched, frozen with fear, as Khalib's chest rose then collapsed. Jamal leaned back with his hands on his thighs.

"No, professor, he hasn't tried; he has succeeded."

Yussef bent down on his haunches, oblivious to Jamal's sarcasm, gingerly touching Khalib's shoulder as if he were infectious. He shook Khalib gently, disbelieving what had happened, hoping he was just asleep. But when no response came, Yussef shook him violently, begging Khalib to wake up. Jamal snorted at Yussef's futile attempt, climbing over the two of them, heading toward the front door.

The sulfurous, rotten-egg smell, the blank stare of Khalib's eyes; it all began to register in Yussef's brain. He'd never seen a dead body, not in the flesh so to speak—Ahmed's remains had been identified only by some jewelry. The skin was cooler than his own but rebounded when pushed with his finger. When the muscles in Khalib's forearm twitched involuntarily, Yussef jumped back, banging into the table. Gouging his knee on the oven door as he lept over Khalib's body, Yussef reached the sink just as he began to vomit.

Yussef stood at the sink, watching through the curtainless window as the sun forced its way above the horizon, his breath coming unevenly. He could not help but envy Khalib; at least he was intact. In a few hours, Yussef mused, he would be vaporized alongside Jamal and Ibrahim, their body ash swirling together as the plume moved heavenward. The school crosswalk flashed before his eyes.

Yussef had rinsed his mouth and was standing resolutely beside the bomb when Jamal returned to the kitchen.

"What will we do now?" Yussef asked.

"We will go on as planned, of course. Khalib had become a liability, anyway. He was apt to do something stupid, exposing us before we made it onto the grounds at Ft. Wilson," Jamal explained, already discounting thoughts of Khalib.

"Have you no sympathy?"

"He was weak!" Jamal shouted angrily at Yussef, loud enough to wake Ibrahim. "He has been a headache for too long. I am tired of babysitting you three; or two now."

"What will we do with his body?"

"We'll burn it with the house. I intended to anyway," Jamal said, glancing at Yussef. "Burn the house I mean, as a diversion."

Yussef was thankful he'd seen Jamal trying to revive Khalib; otherwise he might have been suspicious of Jamal's intentions.

"We can't do that. Ibrahim won't stand for it. I won't stand for it," Yussef countered.

"Won't stand for what?" Ibrahim asked, sleep still apparent on his face as he pushed the door open into the kitchen.

Yussef pointed to Khalib's body lying on the floor next to the gas stove. "Khalib…, Khalib…," was all Yussef could muster before he had to leave the room.

Yussef, his legs wobbly, sat down against the wall in the hallway adjacent to the kitchen and listened as Ibrahim raged, shouting Khalib's name repeatedly between bursts of Spanish and Arabic that Yussef could no longer decipher.

"We are lucky he didn't kill us all," Jamal suggested, pointing toward the open oven door, trying to calm Ibrahim now that the windows were open.

"You killed him," Ibrahim exploded. "Your constant badgering and mocking; you treated him like a child."

"He acted like a child," Jamal countered calmly. "He was falling apart before we left Paraguay. You did not see it because you are too much like him."

"You're wrong, Jamal. You've made mistakes leading us here. Why..., you've no one left that started this journey with you. They're all dead," Ibrahim said, finishing with a sardonic laugh.

Yussef heard the slap of flesh on flesh, heard Ibrahim curse, but, from the sound of Jamal's voice, he dare not interfere.

"All of them are dead because of their own stupidity. If I made a mistake, it was in choosing Khalib to accompany me on this mission. If he'd kept his head in Mexico, Sa'id would still be alive. And Monsour was swept overboard or perhaps even killed by the captain of the ship that we came over to South America on."

Ibrahim scoffed, "And what of Zahir? If you knew Khalib was not up to the task, why not leave him behind and bring Zahir along in his place?"

"Zahir was a traitor in our midst. Ali found proof of it."

"And you let him go?" Ibrahim retorted, disbelieving.

This time it was Jamal's turn to laugh, a derisive and sinister laugh that continued as he explained.

"No, my young, ignorant friend, I did not let him go. The leather satchel with explosives; the one I mistakenly left on the plane? It was wired to a barometer; set to detonate when the air pressure dropped as they climbed over the mountain range. That was *not* the sound of thunder or a nearby silver mine that you heard." Jamal shook his head slowly, sneering at Ibrahim. "And what about you, Ibrahim? Your mouth and misplaced bravado could have easily gotten us all killed back at that jungle airstrip. Khalib, Sa'id, and perhaps even you, Ibrahim, know training only from the Qur'an.

"Strap a bomb on them and send them out the door of the madrasa and they would do fine in a local market or police station. But to strike an enemy in a distant land requires patience, discipline, the ability to think rationally, the need to adapt to conditions at hand, and, most importantly, to obey orders. Khalib could do only the latter with any proficiency, and, in the end, not even that.

"Yes, Ibrahim, you are right. Everyone I brought along on this journey has died…, or will die. Those already dead, died because of the reason I just said: stupidity. And if not stupidity, than of its relative, weak-mindedness, or, in Zahir's case, greed."

Jamal's voice slowed and dropped in volume. He unsnapped the leather strap holding his gun in place as he continued, "Ibrahim, you and Yussef, must decide where along the remainder of our time together you wish to die. There is no other choice."

"I am no coward, Jamal," Ibrahim stated, defiantly. "I will see it through to the end as I said I would. I just think you should have eased up on Khalib. It might have nade a difference in how he acted. Now he can not be a martyr."

Yussef sat in the hallway, hearing the entire conversation, thinking about his situation as Jamal spoke to Ibrahim. He should run, run as fast and as far as he could. But his legs felt like they were made of lead, indeed, his whole body refused to work. He laughed to himself, picturing his heavy legs dragging along, his feet too heavy to lift off the ground, his arms the weight of anvils as he tried to lift them from his side. The only thing moving swiftly was his brain as his thoughts turned to Rachael, his roommates, and that crosswalk.

Jamal, so cool and collected, had an answer for everything. He'd had years to forge his convictions, hardened in the fires of experience, Yussef thought. He was probably right about Ibrahim and the others; they knew nothing of the outside world and were not prepared for it, or, in Ahmed's case, wore the blinders of his faith and chose to ignore it. Yussef was reminded of himself and Ahmed when they'd first arrived in Rockledge. Their solace had been the Qur`an. All of them had been separated from their families for one reason or another, and then off to the madrasa for religious indoctrination. It seemed to be the common thread connecting all of them, except Jamal.

Of all of them, besides Jamal, Yussef thought himself the only one with meaningful experience away from the fenced-in yard of religion. These last three years in America had taught him things the others could not understand.

"We must bury him before we leave this morning." Ibrahim insisted, as Yussef still sat in the hallway.

"Where? In the backyard, with the neighbors help?" Jamal retorted. "We will leave him here and burn the house."

"He is a Muslim, Jamal. We cannot do that. We must clean him and bury him in a white shroud, facing Mecca, just as we did Sa`id."

Had he not listened to a single word I just spoke, Jamal wondered, about to unleash a torrent of epitaphs at Ibrahim. Instead, Jamal took a deep breath, held it, and then slowly released it. The look in Ibrahim's eyes had made him stop. Loyalty was a must among their tribe, and Khalib, despite his breakdown, had been loyal, as had Ibrahim. Jamal yielded to the demands of the Holy Book one final time.

"We have nothing to wrap him in here. We will bury him somewhere along the way," Jamal offered.

Ibrahim nodded his head, assuaged.

"Go get the van out of the garage, Ibrahim, and bring it around as close to the front door as possible. It is time to be on our way."

Ibrahim moved past Yussef who was still propped against the wall, his head resting on his drawn up knees, feigning sleep until Jamal kicked him in the thigh.

"Come help me move everything to the front door," Jamal commanded. "We must load the van quickly while no one is about."

With the tank on dollies, the two of them were able to roll it to the front door. Before they could go back for Khalib's corpse, Ibrahim returned, requesting help in maneuvering the van out from under the collapsed garage roof. Jamal went to help, leaving Yussef alone with Khalib and the bomb.

As much as he wanted to, Yussef could not leave now. Like Ibrahim, he would see it through to the end. He dragged Khalib's limp body to the front door, laying it beside the bomb. Yussef inspected his own work one last time while watching through the window as Jamal guided Ibrahim and the van up against the low porch.

Jamal checked the street and the house next door for prying eyes before giving the okay to Ibrahim and Yussef to bring out Khalib's body. After placing it on the floor against the wheel well, they went back for the explosives-packed tank. Try as they might, the three of them could not lift it up into the van. Yussef came to the rescue by removing the front door from its hinges, using its seasoned oak planks as a ramp. Jamal secured the tank in place with chains and turnbuckles, after which he packed the remainder of the stolen explosives around its base, connecting them with a delayed timer to the detonator, running the wires up to a switch he'd placed on the front seat.

"Will the nuclear device not be adequate for you? Yussef asked, sarcastically, trying to hide a worried look creeping across his face.

He turned away, clamping his eyes shut, hunching his shoulder as if that was all it took to protect him from a misconnection.

Jamal ignored him, concentrating on attaching the wires correctly to the switch.

"In case your calculations and alignment are incorrect, this secondary explosion will help to disseminate radioactive material in the immediate area," Jamal explained, matter-of-factly.

The three of them said final prayers side-by-side on the mildewed carpet before Jamal ordered them out to the van. Then, just as Jamal was setting fire to the shabby curtains in the living room, Yussef ran back inside, insisting they should bring the rifle case along.

Jamal, furious, called after him, "If we get stopped, the uncased rifle will be the least of our problems."

"It means something to have it with me," Yussef insisted, not able to think of a better excuse as he hustled into the kitchen to retrieve it.

The smell of cooking gas was stronger than ever since Jamal had turned on the stovetop burners as well as the oven. They met in the hallway as Yussef came out with the rifle case slung under his arm. Jamal reached for the case, but he would not give it up.

"You will get us all killed and blow up the entire town," Jamal shouted as he shoved Yussef toward the front door. "You're beginning to act just like Khalib—crazy."

Flames from the curtains were beginning to lick at the ceiling as Jamal slammed the front door shut behind him. Next, with complete calm, Jamal reminded Ibrahim to drive slowly as he climbed into the van: Jamal in front with Ibrahim, Yussef in the back seat, putting the rifle in its case, with Khalib and their weapon of destruction in the cargo area behind him.

"Where can we go to find sheets and a shovel?" Jamal asked as they pulled away from the house.

Ibrahim glanced at Yussef in the mirror, waiting for directions.

"Wal-Mart would have everything," Yussef answered, struggling with the directions on how to get there.

Jamal's impatience began to grow with each wrong turn, until finally, they turned into the vast parking lot, having deposited the envelope containing their *shaheed* video in a mail drop box along the way. He instructed Ibrahim to park well away from any other vehicles, equal distance between the superstore and an adjacent Burger King while he searched his pockets for some money.

"Go in and get whatever we need to wrap Khalib with and to dig a grave for him," Jamal ordered as he handed a one hundred dollar bill to Ibrahim.

"I will go help him," Yussef offered.

"No," Jamal stated flatly, staring at Yussef. "No, Yussef and I will wait here," he said, turning back to Ibrahim. "Go, and be quick about it. Leave the keys with us in case there is trouble.

Ibrahim did as he was told, walking briskly toward the store. A cloud of black smoke marred the horizon in the direction of the house from which they'd just come. The far-off sound of wailing sirens could be heard as Jamal rolled down his window.

Yussef and Jamal waited in the van without a word spoken between them. Jamal tapped his foot non-stop on the floorboard. Yussef, for reasons he only vaguely understood, was at peace.

He watched as a school bus pulled up next to the restaurant. A stream of exhuberant, high-school age students poured out. Yussef recognized the name on the side of the bus. It was from a private academy in the St. Louis area. They had brought prospective students through his lab at the engineering school on several occasions in hopes of enticing the best and brightest to come here for their education. Most exiting the bus appeared to be boys, Yussef observed, though one girl with black hair and skin as dark as his own caught his eye.

Jamal's foot tapping had been joined by the steady drum of his fingers on the dashboard. Yussef heard him whisper "finally" under his breath and he turned his attention away from the bus to see Ibrahim coming across the parking lot. His arms were full of garden tools: two shovels, a pickaxe, and a mattock. In addition, he held a bag containing white cotton sheets, pointing out to Jamal, as he handed the tools back to Yussef, that the sheets were made of Egyptian cotton.

"Ibrahim, my young friend, there are only three of us in here capable of using tools," Jamal chastised.

"You, my old friend, have not dug many holes," he retorted.

Jamal shook his head, tossing Ibrahim the keys.

"Besides, after today, we'll have no more use for money."

Yussef was smiling as they headed out of the parking lot in the direction of Ft. Wilson. He liked Ibrahim and wished they'd met under different circumstances. He neither liked or disliked Jamal, and decided that was probably the way that Jamal wanted it. Yussef did not envy him, nor could he understand his leaving a wife and son behind. Still, he admired his conviction and his unwillingness to compromise—except in the case of Khalib's burial.

It had to have taken years of planning, Yussef considered, and with the ultimate goal so far away, it must have seemed like a mirage in the beginning for Jamal. And yet, here he was. Yussef still had trouble believing it. His own world had been turned upside down in the span of a week. These events had come upon him in such a blitz that he realized what he was experiencing was a sort of "shell shock". But now, he was on the mend.

There were several exits before the one to Ft. Wilson. Ibrahim picked one with a boarded-up gas station and drove north a few miles and then back east on a deserted gravel road, lined on both sides by a mix of cedar and oak trees just beyond a collapsing, rust-eaten, woven-wire fence. He found a grassy lane with no gate and pulled far enough down it to be obscured from the road. After a brief discussion concerning the direction the grave should face, the three of them set about digging a final resting place for Khalib.

"There is not enough room in here for the three of us," Jamal said, as they approached a depth of four feet. "Let's rest a minute and bring the body out of the van. Yussef can prepare the body while Ibrahim and I continue digging."

"I can not do that, Jamal," Yussef stated, shaking his head. Just thinking about the body was making his stomach queasy again. "Please, let me keep digging."

"Very well then, keep digging," Jamal said, eyeing Yussef coldly. "Dig it big enough for two people."

"I will prepare the body," Ibrahim offered, quickly. "Come on, Yussef. Help me get Khalib's body out, and I can do the rest."

Yussef watched Ibrahim during breaks while Jamal shoveled out the rocky soil that Yussef had broken free with the pickaxe. Khalib's corpse was beginning to stiffen, and Ibrahim struggled to remove his soiled clothes.

"What a lonely place to be interred," Yussef murmured so quiet that Jamal didn't hear, or heard but didn't care.

In the greening valley below them, Yussef spotted a herd of wild hogs rooting about beneath a row of patchy, white-barked, cottonwood trees growing along the banks of a sparkling stream. He remembered Raymond's description of hunting wild hogs the summer before, using the very rifle Yussef had stolen at the beginning of this odyssey. Ray said the hogs were destructive, digging deep holes and wallowing about in them, tearing up the pastureland. The farmers and ranchers were more than happy to let Ray hunt them.

Wielding the mattock with newfound energy, Yussef insisted they go deeper yet with the grave as he glanced again at the hogs. Jamal obliged him for another ten minutes before ordering him out of the hole unless he intended to keep Khalib company there.

They made short work of covering the body with loose dirt. Ibrahim and Jamal rested while Yussef searched frantically for the largest rocks he could find to place on top of the grave. A mix of sweat and dirt dripped from his chin as the vision of rooting, wild hogs stuck in his head.

"Get in the van, Yussef. We must be on our way," Jamal ordered.

"Perhaps I should practice shooting the rifle. I've never actually fired a weapon," Yussef suggested, thinking of a good target down in the valley.

"No, the sound might attract somebody. If all goes as planned, you will not need to use it any way. But make sure it is loaded just the same."

Jamal moved behind a tree to relieve himself. Ibrahim went to Khalib's grave to say a final prayer and a heartfelt goodbye. With their backs to him, Yussef did as he was instructed, removing the rifle from its foam rubber-lined case, briefly rummaging underneath the padding before unloading and reloading the gun, and, at last, releasing the safety.

Rick Elliott

CHAPTER ELEVEN

Back on the Interstate, Jamal busied himself by checking the ammunition clip in his 9mm handgun repeatedly. Next, he placed the detonator switch on his lap while Yussef untangled the wires that were caught on the edge of the seat.

Ibrahim, after reciting verse at the top of his wavering voice, grew silent. He inhaled with an increasing cadence of one deep breath followed by a series of rapid, shallow breaths as they approached the exit for Ft. Wilson.

Yussef could feel his own heart racing beneath his sweat-soaked shirt, but his mind was crystal clear for the first time in days.

"Pull off and stop on the shoulder, here," Jamal directed.

Ibrahim did as he was told, pulling off to the side of the road half way up the exit ramp. Jamal produced several heavy plastic cable ties from beneath his seat and proceeded, in a series of interlocking loops, to bind Ibrahim's hands to the steering wheel. Now, Ibrahim was panting like a fat, mongrel bitch on a hot, thick August afternoon.

He sputtered, "H…, H…, How will I shift?"

Yussef could see Ibrahim's eyes in the rearview mirror. They were the size of saucers and glazed in terror.

"I will shift for you, brother," Jamal said calmly.

He placed his hand on Ibrahim's shoulder before taking a deep, resolute breath, and then he leaned across, kissing Ibrahim on both cheeks.

"*Inshaa` Allah*, we will meet in paradise with others who have gone before us."

Jamal reached back, and Yussef met his embrace.

"Remember, we will not stop at the guard post. The closer we can get to the center of the grounds, nearer the barracks, the better. Yussef, you will shoot anyone who tries to stop us once we get inside the base's perimeter," Jamal commanded with false bravado.

Yussef nodded in acknowledgement as he made eye contact with Jamal, knowing full well that he was too nervous to do any such thing.

"Now close your eyes," Jamal instructed.

He hunched down in his seat and, with all his force, kicked out the windshield glass.

For the third week of April, it was an unseasonably warm day. Yussef turned his head toward the open side window and closed his eyes. The breeze, stirring out of the south, dried the sweat on his forearms and cooled him. It carried with it the sound of the highway traffic below them and the odor of urine from the front seat. He felt the jerk of the van as it started in motion. Life as he knew it, as he dreamed it would be with Rachael and his American friends, was about to end.

At least they were away from Rockledge and the university, Yussef considered, pleased. And the breeze; Yussef consoled himself with the fact that the wind was blowing away from the place he'd called home for the past three years; two of them, the happiest years of his life.

Three vehicles were stopped in the lanes at the entrance to Ft. Wilson, next to the guardhouse. Ibrahim slowed his approach accordingly and, when one car blocking a lane moved ahead, he accelerated toward the opening. He was back to chanting incoherently at the top of his lungs. The soldier on duty waved his arm, signaling for the van to slow down, finally shouting for them to halt. Three other MP's loitering nearby heard his shout, looking up just as the van raced by. Ibrahim was forced to swerve to avoid hitting a second vehicle just pulling out from the adjacent lane. In doing so, he sideswiped a humvee parked along the road beyond the concrete block guardhouse, slowing the van's momentum.

Yussef could hear the shrill wail of a siren as Ibrahim brought the van back onto the road. Through the back windows, Yussef saw the muzzle flashes from the direction of the guardhouse and heard a triplet of pings as bullets ripped through the rear door before encountering the reinforced steel propane tank. He saw more soldiers run toward the dented humvee before disappearing from sight as the van topped a hill, thinking, as he turned back toward the front, that the bomb had just saved his life.

Yussef was met with a fine spray of blood that peppered him across the face. A fourth bullet had glanced off the tank before penetrating the front seat and Jamal's right hand. The bullet had torn a hole the size of a quarter as it exited through his palm. A thin stream of arterial blood pulsed from the wound, sprinkling the headliner and blowing back onto Yussef's forehead, nose, and lips. It tasted of salt and iron.

Ibrahim struggled mightily with steering the van, muttering what few curse words he knew, as they lurched from one side of the road to the other. A bullet had blown out the right front tire, and, as he tried to gain speed, the front end shook with such violence that he lost control of the van.

Jamal, bent over in search of the detonator switch that had been torn from his bloodied hand, was unprepared as the van began to tip going fifty. Yussef braced himself between the seats as the van left the road, rolling several times down a steep embankment before coming to a rest against a hickory tree and a thicket of multifloral rose.

Yussef pushed his way out from between the crumpled seats, crushed by the shifted propane tank. He could hear the sound of one wheel still turning slowly as it rubbed against a bent fender. The van had come to rest on its side, and, between the tangle of legs, Yussef caught sight of Ibrahim's blinking eyes. He could make out the audible moans of Jamal's voice, but Yussef could not see where the sound had come from since Jamal's head was nowhere to be seen. Thinking his own head was playing tricks on him, still experiencing vertigo from the wild ride down the hillside, Yussef climbed hesitantly over the front seat, situating himself next to Ibrahim.

With a pocket knife, given to him by Raymond once for no special reason other than his admonishment that every red-blooded American should carry one, Yussef cut the plastic ties that secured Ibrahim's hands to the mangled steering wheel.

"Come on, Ibrahim, hurry. We must get out of here."

Yussef grabbed him under each arm, hauling him out from under Jamal's limp legs. Ibrahim was stunned. He winced with pain and screamed in agony as Yussef pulled him over the shattered dashboard and out away from the wreckage, both of them collapsing onto a pile of decaying leaves and weeds that had been shoved along in front of the van as it skidded to a stop two-thirds of the way down the hill at a small outcropping of rock.

Yussef stood, bent over, clutching his pant legs, trying to catch his breath. His view of the road above them was blocked by the van, resting on its side, acting as a shield. But he could hear unfamiliar voices shouting in the distance and coming closer.

Ibrahim had managed to get to his knees, and it was then that Yussef could see the jagged ends of a bone poking through Ibrahim's tattered shirtsleeve between his shoulder and what should have been his elbow.

"Please, Ibrahim, get up," Yussef pleaded.

"Where is the bomb? Did we trigger the bomb? Are we dead?" Ibrahim asked in a high-pitched tone, still dazed.

"No," Yussef began, shaking his head, "I don't think it will go off."

"It will not go off? ...It will not go off?" Ibrahim repeated, confused and reeling from the impact of the wrecked van and the intense pain in his limp arm. "But where is Jamal?"

He began to crawl as Yussef prodded him along, bent over by his side, trying to lift him. Yussef half-guided, half-shoved Ibrahim toward the thicket of brambles at the edge of the outcropping where the hill began an even steeper descent toward its base. A rustle of leaves and snapping branches coming from the side of the van caught Yussef's attention. There lay Jamal: alive. He'd been thrown part way through the passenger side window. Only his head, chest, and upper torso had made it clear. He was pinned just below the waist by the top edge of the van, still holding his gun in his good hand, clumsily searching for the detonator switch with his wounded hand as blood spritzed the debris surrounding him, painting it a crimson red.

Ibrahim was standing now, though wobbly and not yet fully coherent. He looked back to see Jamal lying there just as a volley of bullets shredded the tree bark above his head. He started for Jamal, but Yussef caught him, spinning him back around and through the wild rose thicket.

Yussef took one last look back at Jamal and followed his eyes toward the detonator now exposed among the leaves inches from his fingertips. One more desperate stretch, clawing at the ground, and the detonator slid into Jamal's trembling grasp. Without hesitation, he flipped the toggle switch to detonate the nuclear bomb but nothing happened. He worked the toggle back and forth in a frenzy as his eyes locked on Yussef, standing there, shaking his head slowly. Jamal uttered a guttural cry of frustration and rage as he twisted his shoulders, trying to level his gun at Yussef.

Yussef dove through the bushes, their barbed stems tearing at his clothes and exposed flesh. The last sounds of gunfire he heard were too close to come from anywhere but Jamal's pistol. He also knew the explosives Jamal had packed around the modified propane tank when they left the house were rigged to the same switch but with a ten second delay that Yussef had no opportunity to disarm.

The concussion of the blast sent Yussef tumbling down to the bottom of the hill. All of the gunfire had ceased. The only sound now was a ringing in Yussef's ears. He found he could stand despite a terrible burning sensation in his back; the result of embedded shrapnel.

Catching up to Ibrahim at the edge of a paved road, they crossed it on the run and scurried down another hill before plunging into the thick cover offered by a grove of cedar trees. Yussef reasoned that the explosion had bought them a little more time. He stopped alongside Ibrahim to consider their plight, both of them panting and pale-faced.

He made a sling out of his own shirt for Ibrahim's mangled arm as they stood there inhaling deeply of the heavily scented air, listening as best they could.

Ibrahim, regaining his alertness, asked again, "Why didn't the first bomb, the big one, detonate?"

"I don't know," Yussef replied straight-faced. "Jamal must have wired it wrong."

"Jamal was too thorough for that to happen," Ibrahim answered abruptly, between gasps, shaking his head.

"Then perhaps a wire got jarred loose as we rolled down the hill. That thing almost crushed me," Yussef countered, "or a bullet may have severed one of the wires. I heard several hit the tank before we crashed."

Ibrahim seemed satisfied with this explanation and returned to thoughts of their immediate predicament.

"Where do we go from here? We should have brought the rifle."

Yussef laughed.

"I know there is a river east of here, the Red Oak River. Jamal and I drove by it when we scouted the base earlier in the week."

"Poor Jamal, we should have tried to help him."

"No, Ibrahim, there was nothing we could do for him. The van had him pinned. The soldiers would have shot the three of us if we'd stayed with him any longer, or we would have been killed by the explosion."

"But I wanted to die," Ibrahim said breathlessly. "I was prepared to die."

"Then go back there now," Yussef retorted, standing over Ibrahim, pointing up the hill. "I'm sure they will be happy to oblige you, you fool. Besides, they will soon be searching to see if anyone survived the blast. If they pick up our trail, they'll hunt us down like dogs. The explosion has just bought us a little time. We are not out of the woods, yet."

Ibrahim was licking his bloodied lip as he spoke, "Then what do we do now, Yussef."

Yussef didn't answer right away. He was smiling, thinking to himself that Ray and his roommates wouldn't have let that unintended pun slip by without a laugh or groan. A wave of relief washed over him as they stood in the dense cedars deciding their own fate. They were thirty-five miles from Rockledge and the nuclear blast threat was over. No radioactive fallout for miles and miles downwind. At worst there would be some radioactive debris in the immediate vicinity, resulting from the back up blast but certainly no catastrophic loss of life. All of his friends at the university would be safe. It made his heart ache to think of them. Ibrahim was right though, Yussef thought; the two of them might as well be dead. Yussef had lost everything he cherished just as sure as if he'd been killed.

"Let's head for the river. It can't be more than four or five miles from here."

"Then what?" Ibrahim asked dejectedly.

"I have some money," Yussef divulged, producing the remainder of the hundred dollar bills he'd hidden under the padding of the rifle case. "We will follow the flow of the river. Maybe will we find a log we can float on for a day or two, and then, who knows," Yussef shrugged. "Our best bet might be to go to Houston. You think you could find the safe house the three of you stayed in on the way up here?"

Ibrahim nodded, a glimmer of hope in his voice, "Perhaps, I could."

Yussef figured any plan was a start. It gave Ibrahim hope, something to work toward, no matter how implausible it might be.

"Perhaps, if we survive, we could change our identity, and I could go to college," Ibrahim said with an eager smile.

"Maybe," Yussef offered, patting Ibrahim on the back for encouragement but thinking again about all he'd thrown away himself. "We could go to Ciudad del Estrellas. You could go to school, and I'll get a job at that hydroelectric plant you talked about. We'll find nice, pious, dark-haired Muslim girls to take as our brides and live happily everafter."

Ibrahim grinned, and they started off at a trot through the dense undergrowth in the direction of the Red Oak River. Yussef laughed silently. He could almost convince himself that it would work, almost. If you're going to dream, dream big, Yussef figured. It was the American way. One thing was for certain, he'd decided. He wasn't going to give up just to be taken prisoner and have to face all those people he'd so thoroughly let down.

They reached the river just as night was falling. After stumbling along its banks in the twilight, over down trees and brush, for more than a mile, they stopped, exhausted. Ibrahim sprawled out on a rocky ledge that jutted out into the river, leaning his throbbing shoulder down, submersing his entire arm into the cold, spring-fed water. To placate his empty stomach, Yussef gathered handfuls of deep-green watercress along the mouth of a small spring to nibble on. Next, he amassed a pile of dried leaves and grass, big enough for both of them, before collapsing into a dreamless sleep.

A combination of bright sunlight filling the sky above him and the rumbling of hunger pangs woke Yussef. Ibrahim was fast asleep beside him, a cluster of brown leaves clinged to the dried blood surrounding his wounded arm. Serum drained along the jagged edge of the exposed bone. Was it already infected, he wondered?

A chorus of birdcalls echoed above him. Layers of fog hugged the river, extending upwards several feet above its glassy surface. As Yussef watched, the fog drifted aimlessly, splitting into individual clouds, and then coalescing back into one continuous blanket of whiteness, moving in the same direction with the flowing water as if they were somehow attached to one another. He leaned over the ledge that Ibrahim had been on the night before, taking a long draw of water, splashing his face and matted hair. Its coldness shocked his senses.

He stood up, one moment enveloped in a chilling fog, the next warmed by the rays of a mounting sun. The smells were of damp earth and river water. The only sounds: the gurgle of water as it rippled over the submerged rocks, the steady, deep thrum of a woodpecker, and the harsh, staccato chatter of a kingfisher winging its way up river along the limestone bluff on the opposite side.

Looking further upstream, during breaks in the fog, Yussef caught sight of a blue heron struggling awkwardly to take flight, gliding silently past him, disappearing, and then reemerging from the wispy white vapors that hung above the river.

Yussef had no idea where to go from here as he stood along the river's edge, trying to think. Some primeval instinct told him to follow the river. It seemed the most logical and easiest thing to do.

The rustle of leaves behind him caused Yussef to turn as Ibrahim stirred from his sleep. How long could Ibrahim go with his arm in that condition, he wondered. Then, there was another sound.

Yussef cocked his head and held his breath, willing himself to hear better. Perhaps, it was just the water tumbling over the rocks, he thought, moving away from the river's edge, toward their bed of leaves, stopping to listen again. He heard it once more: the distant sound of baying hounds, coming from the direction they'd traveled last night.

"Ibrahim, you must get up," Yussef said in a panic.

He helped lift Ibrahim from the ground, taking note of his ashen face, a testament to the pain he was enduring.

"We need to get in the water and drift down stream for a while," Yussef insisted, steadying Ibrahim as he relieved himself near the crushed leaves that had been their bed. Steam rose from where his fevered urine made contact with the chilled earth.

Ibrahim shook his head adamantly, explaining as he shivered, "I cannot swim, and the water will be so cold."

"I cannot swim either, but we can hang on to a log and float," Yussef implored, desperate to convince Ibrahim.

Ibrahim was still hesitant about the idea as he looked at the fast-flowing river.

"We have no choice, Ibrahim. I think they may be tracking us with dogs, listen."

Yussef motioned with his hand for Ibrahim to be still.

He cocked his head and held his breath as before. Ibrahim did likewise. This time, the forlorn baying of one hound was answered by another.

"Did you hear that?"

Ibrahim swallowed hard, nodding.

"They are getting louder since I first heard them a few minutes ago. Maybe in the water they won't be able to pick up our scent."

With no more hesitation, the two of them searched for a substantial, fallen log that would float with their weight added to it. Just past a gravel bar, Yussef found one he thought might work, calling for Ibrahim to come help him. Yussef carried most of the load, his arms wrapped around the log, fingers interlocked, the rough bark scraping his bare skin as he strained with all his might, sliding it toward the shimmering water. Ibrahim did what he could with his good arm, half carrying, half dragging the other end until finally, their energy spent, Yussef dropped his end into the water with a splash.

"Climb on and straddle the log," Yussef instructed, holding on to it against the pull of the current.

Ibrahim did as told, cautiously inching his way out to the middle third of the log only to have it roll sideways, twisting free of Yussef's grip, sending Ibrahim plunging into the water. Yussef pushed his end of the log back onto the bank, wading into the waist-deep water to grasp Ibrahim's flailing arm.

The coldness of the water took their breath away as they stood there in the water pressed against the log, gripping it as best they could. Yussef's feet ached from the chill as he pushed them away from the bank, holding on to the log with one hand and Ibrahim with the other.

After one more attempt, they were floating downstream with the current. They clung desparately to any nub or split in the log that they could reach with their fingers, draped over the half-submerged timber like inverted "L's", their feet dragging along the gravel bottom or floating freely beneath them, depending on the depth of the river as they drifted along.

The bright sun, having burnt away most, left only a few remnants of fog still hovering above the flowing water. Its warmth felt comforting on Yussef's bare, scabbed back in contrast to the heavy feel of his numbed, stiff legs. Another quarter mile down river put them in the shadows of towering cliffs that blotted out the sun, sending goose bumps down the length of their arms.

They floated slowly down the river. Yussef estimated they'd been on it for an hour. He watched Ibrahim shivering uncontrollably in front of him on the log, wondering if he would have the strength to pull him back on if he lost his grip.

"Hang on a little longer, Ibrahim," he shouted, repositioning his own hold on Ibrahim, "and we'll get out of the water to rest."

Spoken through chattering teeth, Ibrahim's reply was incomprehensible.

They moved through a series of riffles, beating their knees and ankles against boulders and sunken tree limbs jutting up from the river's bottom. The crystal clear water made it easy to see the water hazards, but with no way to control it, they were at the mercy of the log's own course.

After another series of rapids, they floated into a pool of slower, deeper water. The sluggish log bobbed below the surface from the extra weight it carried, submerging Ibrahim and Yussef momentarily before its buoyancy brought them back up, gasping for breath. Yussef's body arched involuntarily each time the cold water stung at the shrapnel wounds in the small his back.

He guessed they'd traveled three miles, when, rounding a bend in the river, a down tree blocking half its width produced a current that forced them against a gravel bar on the far side. Unable to stand, their numb legs refusing to work, they crawled ashore to rest.

"I can't go back in the water, Yussef," Ibrahim announced, shaking his head dejectedly. "My good arm is too weak to hang on any longer."

Yussef agreed. "It's just as well. I could not save you if you fell in. But we have gone a fair ways. Perhaps, it will be enough to lose the dogs that are tracking us."

The sun-warmed gravel felt like a heating pad as they moved their stiff legs back and forth, feeling slowly returning in them.

"When we get warmed up a bit more, maybe we should go on foot a while," Yussef suggested.

They lay there several minutes, the sun's heat coaxing them toward drowsiness. With Hurculean effort, Yussef picked himself up before helping Ibrahim to his feet. He led the way, moving along the shoreline until they reached a draw that angled away from the river between a break in the tall bluffs that served as sentinels along this stretch of the Red Oak River. A small stream meandered out of the draw, becoming one with its larger counterpart.

Yussef, hoping for easier walking conditions, followed the draw for three-quarters of a mile, slowly rising in elevation until they'd reached the summit. It was the first and lowest of a series of wooded hills, each a little higher than the one before it. The forest floor was littered with the previous year's decaying leaves but otherwise was free of undergrowth, making travel faster and easier. The occasional warning bark of a squirrel was the only indication there were any living animals present beside themselves.

Yussef waited at the ridge as Ibrahim struggled to the top of the last hill. They could see a clearing through the trees ahead as they stumbled over a fallen limb, continuing in the direction of the sunlit plateau.

Coarse, tan, sage grass; small, low to the ground, green cacti no bigger then a spread hand; and a rainbow of wildflowers in bloom, covered the glade. The sun, directly overhead, brought a glow to everything below.

Neither had an inkling of which way to go, standing there chewing absentmindedly on brittle stems of last summer's grass before deciding on straight ahead, toward the treeline on the opposite side of the meadow a quarter mile away.

Just as they re-entered the forest, having crossed the glade, the sharp report of a rifle echoed after them, immediately a second bullet sizzled the air overhead. Yussef looked back in disbelief as more gunfire followed. A bullet tore through his turned cheek, exiting his open mouth as it smashed through the tips of his front teeth.

Ibrahim was already moving off the top of the hill, running down its steep slope. Yussef, spitting out blood as he went, followed closely, running and tripping, then running again until reaching the bottom. With his tongue probing at the hole in his cheek, picturing Jamal's mangled hand, Yussef swallowed, tasting blood as the sting from the side of his face was usurped by the burning ache in his legs as they propelled him up to the crest of the next hill.

One more ridgeline and, in the distance far below them, they could see a ribbon of water. Ibrahim glanced at Yussef with a puzzled expression.

"We have been going in circles."

"No," Yussef replied, breathless. "I think the river made a sharp turn after we left it back there at the mouth of that little creek."

"But which way do we go?"

Yussef shrugged, fresh out of ideas.

"Staight ahead is our only option. I doubt we could double back and get around them. Who knows how many are chasing us."

"Did you see who was shooting at us?" Ibrahim asked, already moving again. "Were they soldiers? How many were there?"

Yussef kept moving, too, splattering blood after each deep breath as he answered. "I didn't see them, but they must be soldiers from Ft. Wilson. They must be tracking us up and down the river to find us so quickly after with left the river bank."

Yussef stopped for a moment, bending over, resting his hands on his knees. His lungs burned. Blood dripped steadily from his chin as it trickled down from the wound in his cheek.

"They will eventually surround us or trap us in a canyon. Our only hope is to get back on the river or at least follow it. A road must cross it sooner or later. If we're lucky, we can stop a car and get away. We'll never out run them on foot," Yussef assessed, shaking his head.

They reached the water and started across without trepidation this time, despite their inability to swim. The water, only waist high, still swept them off their feet, sending them tumbling downstream for five hundred yards before Yussef, in the lead, brushed against a root wad, frantically grasping it with one hand. For an instant, he could not see Ibrahim and his heart sank. Just then, his shaven head broke the surface of the roiling water directly in front of him. Yussef, by letting the strong pull of the current stretch him out horizontally, still clinging to the roots with both hands, just touched Ibrahim with the tip of his shoe. Flaying wildly, Ibrahim, with one good hand, latched on to his pant leg and clawed his way up next to Yussef.

Ibrahim coughed violently as they made their way along the downed tree to a ledge of rock. Tugging on Ibrahim's tattered shirt collar, Yussef drug him part way onto the rock and then rolled him over all the way up out of the water. Ibrahim's coughing stopped shortly as he groaned in pain from the weight of his body pressing his exposed humerus into the unforgiving rock.

"Come on, Ibrahim. We must keep moving," Yussef demanded with grim determination.

"No, I...," Ibrahim started before a proxysmal coughing bout stole his breath.

Yussef lifted him to his knees, trying to get Ibrahim on his feet, but Ibrahim waved him off.

"Go on without me," he huffed, his eyes fixated on the rock below him, realizing his fate. "I am finished. I can't go on. They may not know there were two of us. I doubt they saw me back at the clearing. I was already past the ridgeline of the hill when they started shooting."

Ibrahim remained quiet for a minute, panting to catch his breath between coughs.

"Here, take your shirt and mine, too. I will tell them I am alone when they catch up. That will give you time to build a lead and perhaps get away."

Yussef watched as Ibrahim tried in vain to remove Yussef's shirt-turned-sling with one good hand, a hand whose fingers were stiff from the frigid water. Yussef, hands akimbo, turned, pacing a few steps, eyebrows furrowed as he tried to think.

"Yussef!" Ibrahim shouted after him, as if Yussef was already far away, "before you go, I want to say…"

Yussef cut him off in mid-sentence, shaking his head, "I will not leave you behind. We are in this together until the end, whatever it might be."

"No," Ibrahim coughed, "go on without me. I'm slowing you down. You have much more to live for than I do."

Yussef laughed loudly at this comment.

"Everything I own is right here," he explained, waving his hands across his body as he staggered over the uneven rocks back toward Ibrahim. "You are the only friend I have left in the world."

"You've known me for less than a week," Ibrahim countered.

Yussef sat down beside Ibrahim before he spoke, "We are of the same lineage, Ibrahim; both deserted long ago by relatives that cared not for us; given over to a religion that had but one use for us; to exploit us in our innocence."

"Come on, I will not leave this spot without you. Two heads are better than one, even if yours is waterlogged. Together we will find a way out of here. I promise. I'm sure there is a road close ahead."

A wide smile emerged on Ibrahim's damp face, shining like a harvest moon unveiled from a cloudy sky. As Yussef started to get up, Ibrahim grasped his hand to stop him.

"Yussef, I woke during the night, thinking for a long time about all that has happened since I left Ciudad del Estrellas with Jamal and the others," he explained, pausing to search Yussef's eyes. "Did you stop the bomb..., the big one, from going off?"

Yussef averted his gaze before answering, slowly nodding, "Yes, Ibrahim. I could not go through with killing so many people. Some might have been my friends. Jamal was probably right about their military..., about their government, but there were children..., a school. His fight is one I no longer wish to be a part of. There must be a better way. I'm sorry if I ruined your chance at martyrdom and to avenge your father's death."

Yussef wanted to continue but Ibrahim interrupted, putting his good hand on Yussef's bare shoulder.

"It was the right thing to do, Yussef," his dark eyes once again fixed on Yussef's.

Yussef, contemplating their fate, thought Ibrahim possessed wisdom beyond his years. He wished for Ibrahim a future unchained from his religious past, hoping there was indeed a way out for both of them.

A spray of limestone pellets stung their faces as a bullet glanced off the rock ledge inches above them. Yussef and Ibrahim ducked around the edge of the rock wall, scurrying along the cliff like two wild hares being chased by a bobcat, jumping from rock to rock, oblivious to the dangers of falling into the water below, for no wild animal was after them now.

They passed several small caves, hesitating before each one, but both knew that hiding wasn't the answer; confident their cunning adversary would sniff them out.

As the grey, limestone bluff ended, the hills began again. After topping the first, they could see ahead that the river made a sharp bend to the right just over two lower hills.

For the hunted pair, the hills, covered with blooming dogwoods and redbud trees, scattered like buckshot among the old growth forest of oak, hickory, and walnut, gave them cover as they sprinted across the peaks.

On the summit of the last hill, above the bend in the Red Oak River, they gazed down the steep incline to the water's edge three hundred feet below. Directly across the river from them was the top of another sheer cliff. Just visible to them through the flowering trees, was a long sandy beach, two hundred yards in length, produced by the rapid speed of the water as it rounded the bend and slowed.

A bright glint at the water's edge caught Yussef's eye as he and Ibrahim began their haphazard descent. He motioned Ibrahim to stop, grabbing hold of him with one hand while reaching out for a sapling with the other to stop their slide.

There on the beach below them were three aluminum canoes, shimmering in the mid-day sun. Laughter—girlish laughter—reached their ears, coming from further along the golden beach. Its source was blocked from their line of sight by rock outcroppings and thick tree trunks.

Yussef searched the forest floor beside he and a panting Ibrahim, finding a stout walking stick that could double as a club if need be. Without a word between them, they let loose the sapling and slid stealthily down the slope on their backsides for a better view.

Still hidden by the trees, they surveyed the scene unveiled before them. A shallow slough of stagnant water, cut off from the main channel of the river, a five-foot high dune of loose gravel, and, beyond that, sixty feet of sandy beach was all that separated Yussef and Ibrahim from the canoes. A pair of paddle handles jutted skyward from two of the canoes. Both sides of all three canoes were adorned with various articles of women's clothing.

They peered over the top of the dune from their concealed position among the trees to glimpse the source of the laughter. Down river from the canoes, splashing about in the water were a half-dozen, naked, young women; along the bank a campfire blazed from within a ring of rocks and camp chairs.

"Do you think you could drag the closest canoe into the water with your good arm?" Yussef whispered to Ibrahim while devising a plan in his head.

Ibrahim nodded, "Yes, I think so. But what are you going to do?"

"I am going to steal the paddles out of the other canoes so they can't follow us. If they come toward us, I will fend them off with this club until you have the canoe in the water."

Ibrahim gave no second thought to the plan, reviewing the instructions from Yussef instead.

"Let's rest a second while I adjust the sling on my arm," he begged. "Then I will be ready."

"Okay, but we mustn't wait long. The gunmen will be upon us. Once were in the canoe, we'll head across the river toward the cliffs. The water will be deepest there, and the women...," Yussef hesitated, a faint memory beginning to stir in him as he pictured Ray's truck with he and the three girl's in it, on the way to the junkyard.

"...The women will have to swim to reach us over there. We will be able to out paddle them, heading down river with the current assisting us. With this club as our only weapon, our best chance is against those swimmers up ahead," Yussef explained, trying to bolster Ibrahim's nerve as well as his own, lifting the club out before him as if it held magical powers.

They both glanced once more in the direction of the naked girls, up to their thighs in the cold water, laughing and splashing about wildly. A vague sense of recognition continued to plague Yussef's exhausted mind, but, just then, Ibrahim, in a strong voice commanded, "Okay, let's go!"

They broke for the canoes at a dead run, black muck splattering them as they crossed the slough, intent on climbing the dune and reaching what lie beyond: a chance at escape and freedom.

Yussef couldn't explain it. His background in physics defied it to be true, but he swore he heard the shots before he felt the bullet's impact as he topped the dune. The force of it knocked his feet out from under him and sent him reeling backwards. He came to rest with his head and back against the dune, facing the river, his legs stretched out in front as if he were resting there, sunning himself, not a care in the world.

Ibrahim was felled beside him where the dune flattened a bit. His feet and legs were splayed out behind him at what seemed impossible angles from Yussef's vantage point. It was as if he'd knelt down on his knees and then bent over backwards. Ibrahim's eyes were closed and below his chin, square in the center of his neck, was a hole not much bigger than a pea. Pink froth began to erupt from it.

Yussef felt a warmth spreading across his own cold, wet pant legs—like a fluffed blanket settling into place.

Time slowed its pace for Yussef. All of his senses seemed distorted, magnified. He clutched at the sand with his hands and felt the grains wedge beneath his fingernails; felt the grittiness of it in his mouth as he clenched and unclenched his teeth.

He could taste the acidity of his stomach as it welled up into his mouth; tasted the dull richness of blood as his tongue poked at the wound in his cheek.

He could smell the dankness of the wet sand; the easy comfort of wood smoke drifting from the campfire; the promise of a sweet breeze as it channeled up the deep river valley past his flaring nostrils.

He heard: the high-pitched cacophony of human shrieks moving closer toward him; heard the soft gurgling wheeze eminating from Ibrahim lying there beside him; a pair of disgruntled crows squatting on a tree branch overhead, complaining bitterly about the disturbance below them; a familiar voice calling his name in disbelief.

He saw the scarlet stain enveloping his pants; the smooth water, becalmed after discharging its energy from the bend of the river into the deep pool beside him; saw the beauty of their nakedness, the erectness of their breasts from contact with the chilled water.

And, gliding across the water's surface like an angel, he saw the anguished face of a raven-haired, young woman as she moved smoothly toward him—his name appearing slowly on her cherry lips, before covering them with her slender fingers.

"Are we in paradise, Yussef?" Ibrahim called out, sounding far away, wavering on the edge of life, his voice altered horribly by his wound.

Yussef turned toward his fellow jihadist. Ibrahim's eyelids fluttered wildly, while the eyeballs themselves flickered about uncontrollably. No other part of him stirred, all four limbs bent at abnormal angles from his body—like a rag doll tossed carelessly into the corner when it was no longer needed.

"Yes, Ibrahim…," Yussef comforted slowly, his face tormented between laughter, tears, and bitterness. Leaning sideways, he patted his new friend's unfeeling leg. "…this is as close as we'll ever be to paradise."

Ibrahim's eyelids stopped their flutter, his eyes became motionless, an innocent smile, like the one Yussef had seen before, was spread across his face.

The laws of physics regained their rightful order as Yussef scanned the horizon before him. His gaze drifted across the river to the towering bluff. Through the centuries, long before the formation of the nation that claimed it, it had given birth to a quintet of moss-covered boulders, cleaved from its surface and strewn about the deep water below. Its face was pockmarked with small caves and crevices that gave refuge. An occasional, nutrient-starved, pine seedling clung to the sheer rock face, its roots searching endlessly, relentlessly, for invisible cracks in which to gain a foothold.

As he struggled to stand, Yussef's eyes reached the top of the cliff. There, against a cloudless, blue sky; in the shadow of trees that gave shelter to its source, he saw a flash of light, and then: darkness.

Rick Elliott

About the author:

Rick Elliott, a retired veterinarian, was born and raised in the flatlands of Central Illinois. He currently lives in the Ozark hills of Missouri with his lovely wife, Janice. The Reluctant Martyr is his first novel.

www.ingramcontent.com/pod-product-compliance
Lightning Source LLC
Chambersburg PA
CBHW051440260626
47162CB00001B/185